THE LONG ROAD HOME

CHRISTOPHER G. NUTTALL

The characters and events portrayed in this book are fictitious. Any similarity to real persons, living or dead, is coincidental and not intended by the author.

Text copyright © Christopher G. Nuttall

All rights reserved.
Printed in the United States of America.

No part of this book may be reproduced, or stored in a retrieval system, or transmitted in any form or by any means, electronic, mechanical, photocopying, recording, or otherwise, without express written permission of the publisher.

ISBN: 1544770790
ISBN 13: 9781544770796

http://www.chrishanger.net
http://chrishanger.wordpress.com/
http://www.facebook.com/ChristopherGNuttall

All Comments Welcome!

Book One: *A Learning Experience*
Book Two: *Hard Lessons*
Book Three: *The Black Sheep*
Book Four: *The Long Road Home*

DEDICATION

To the memory of HMS *Amethyst* and her crew.

A VERY BRIEF RECAP

*I*n the very near future, a handful of military veterans in the USA were abducted by an alien starship. Unluckily for their would-be captors - the Horde, a race of interstellar scavengers - the humans rapidly managed to break free and gain control of the starship. Steve Stuart, a rancher who had been growing more and more disillusioned with the government, saw opportunity - the starship could serve as the base for a new civilisation, the Solar Union.

Despite some small problems with planet-bound governments, the Solarians - as they would eventually be called - started to both recruit settlers for the new state *and* distribute alien-grade technology on Earth. After defeating a series of Horde ships that attempted to recapture their starship and attack Earth, the Solar Union was firmly in place.

This was, of course, unknown to the rest of the galaxy. To them, Earth wasn't even a microstate. This suited the Solarians just fine. Humans could and did travel beyond the solar system - as traders, mercenaries or even simple explorers - but no one wanted to attract the Galactics to Earth. The Solarians were already making improvements to GalTech that could not fail to alarm the major alien powers, particularly the Tokomak.

Fifty years after Contact, the veil of secrecy fell. Humanity's involvement in a series of brushfire wars at the edge of known space could no longer be hidden, nor could elements of advanced technology. In response, the Tokomak dispatched a massive fleet to Sol with the intention of blasting Earth to cinders. Unknown to the Tokomak, the Solar Navy had *just* enough advanced technology to stand off the alien fleet and smash it. The follow-up attacks shattered the Tokomak grip on the nearby sectors, freeing hundreds of planets from their influence. Humanity had suddenly become a major regional power. A number of naval bases were rapidly established, both to extend human influence and protect human trade.

This had unfortunate effects on Earth. The expansion of the Solar Union - and its willingness to insist that anyone who wanted to emigrate *could* emigrate - accidentally accelerated the social decline pervading civilisation. Europe, America and many other countries fell into civil war, something that caused considerable concern in orbit. One faction within the Solar Union wanted to intervene, others - feeling no loyalty to Earth - believed it was better to let Earthers handle their own affairs.

Captain-Commodore Hoshiko Sashimi Stuart - the granddaughter of Steve Stuart - accidentally stepped into a political minefield when she insisted that Earth should be left alone. Her family's political enemies were quick to use it against them. Accordingly, she was placed in command of a cruiser squadron and dispatched to the Martina Sector, where she would be well out of the public eye. However, she rapidly discovered that the Druavroks - a powerful alien race - were bent on a campaign of genocide against their neighbours, including a number of human settlers. Allying herself with other threatened races, Hoshiko led a campaign that broke the Druavroks and laid the groundwork for a human-led federation - a Grand Alliance.

Unfortunately for humanity - and everyone else - the Tokomak had other ideas...

PROLOGUE

*I*n the end, the coup had been almost laughably easy.

The Elders had never considered, not really, that one of their younger subordinates would turn on them. They'd expected Neola to sit in her quarters and wait while they patiently gathered the evidence to convict her of everything from gross incompetence to dereliction of duty and whatever other charges they managed to make stick. They certainly hadn't expected her to start plotting a coup. Neola had known she wasn't the only youngster to resent the dominance of the Elders, but even *she* hadn't realised just how much resentment and dislike there actually was. Organising a coup, once she'd accepted that a coup was actually possible, had been straightforward.

She allowed herself a tight smile as she sat in her office. The Elders had sputtered impotently when she'd marched in and taken over, but they hadn't been able to resist. There had been no need to kill them, so she'd had them all transported to a reasonably comfortable resort on Tokomak itself, well away from any communications networks they could use to rally resistance. Not that she really expected them to try. Half of the Elders had been so shocked she was surprised they hadn't expired on the spot, while the other half had been so unhinged they'd resorted to begging. Letting them live, she was sure, was more mercy than they'd had any right to anticipate.

And, she told herself, firmly, it was more than they deserved.

The Elders were *old*. Even the youngest was a good thousand years or so older than Neola herself. And they were ossified, utterly unable to conceive that anything might be able to threaten their control over the known universe. But a new threat had arisen, a threat that had started the slow collapse of the empire. No one, not even Neola herself, had been able to comprehend that a race that had barely been out in space for fifty years would be able to threaten the Tokomak. And yet, they had...

Neola looked down at the reports, barely seeing the words hovering in front of her. She'd been lucky - very lucky - to survive the Battle of Earth. Her fleet had been shattered, then abandoned by her allies...it was her fault. She'd underestimated the threat. She'd certainly underestimated humanity's technological skill. But then, she'd been raised to believe that the Tokomak were the masters of the universe. If they couldn't do it, it couldn't be done. And yet, the humans had proved them wrong. The vast fleets that had dominated the known universe for thousands of years were little more than scrap metal.

And because we have been humiliated in battle, she thought sourly, *our other allies are deserting us too.*

It shouldn't have surprised her, she told herself. The Tokomak Empire was bitterly resented by the other Galactics, despite the good it had done for the universe. The younger races wanted to strike out on their own, to build their own empires...even though they would plunge the galaxy into war. And the older races remembered the days before the stardrive, the days when they had competed with the Tokomak as equals. They wanted to be equal again, despite the cost. Slowly, piece by piece by piece, the empire was starting to disintegrate.

And we are not used to reacting quickly, she reminded herself. *The humans can advance in leaps and bounds while we are still trying to decide what to do.*

The latest set of intelligence reports terrified her. Humanity on its own wasn't *that* great a threat. If worst came to worst, she could pour hundreds of thousands of starships into Sol until the human race ran out of weapons. She was *sure* they'd run out of missiles before they ran out of targets. But it looked as though the humans were expanding their alliance structure, inviting more and more races to join their *Grand Alliance*. They'd already convinced a number of middle-rank powers to consider joining, as well as fighting a successful war against a genocidal race. Given vast resources as well as their advanced technology, they might be able to put together a significant challenge in less time than she dared to think possible.

And if we expend millions of starships in crushing Sol, she mused, *we will be significantly weakened elsewhere*.

She cursed the Elders, savagely. The Tokomak had always assumed that they could deal with each individual threat at leisure, before it got out of hand. Their control over the gravity points allowed them to move vast fleets from place to place at will. But now...there were threats popping up everywhere, right across the galaxy. Coping with them all would take more time and resources than even *she* possessed. There was no way she could expend the resources necessary to crush Sol without crippling and ultimately destroying the empire itself.

We don't have time to duplicate the human technology, she thought, sourly. *The researchers are still in denial...*

It was a bitter thought. The researchers had *known* they were at the pinnacle of technological achievement. Nothing significantly new had come out of the labs for over five *thousand* years. They hadn't even made many improvements to old technologies! It would take decades - perhaps longer - for the researchers to comprehend that they *didn't* know everything. And she didn't think they *had* the time. They needed to gain access to human technology and they had to do it now.

She reached for her console and started issuing orders. The oldest patronage networks were still in place, at least. It would take time for *them* to start coming apart. And then...

...It was a gamble, she had to admit. It was a gamble she could easily lose. But the alternative was worse. She hadn't launched her coup and made herself Supreme Ruler just to watch the empire collapse into chaos. The Tokomak had to ready themselves for action on an unprecedented scale, if they wanted to continue to dominate the universe. And they had no choice. They had so many enemies that defeat meant extermination. She didn't dare lose.

And if a few pawns were lost along the way, she told herself, it was a small price to pay for ultimate victory.

ONE

You ask us why we need a galactic alliance? Do we need the galaxy? Say, rather, the galaxy needs us! As a haven, as a pole star, as an alternate - and better - way to live. Let us hold out a welcoming hand to aliens! Let us show them the promise of a better life. There is no need to fight. There is enough for everyone in the galaxy.
-Solar Datanet, Political Forum (Grand Alliance Thoughts)

"Well," Admiral Mongo Stuart said. He studied the holographic image with a sceptical eye. "I suppose that's what you get if you allow a bunch of *Star Trek* fans to design a starship."

Captain Elton Yasser smiled. "The *Odyssey's* designers came from Roddenberry Canton," he agreed, dryly. There was no point in trying to deny it. "But they didn't *quite* copy one of the original designs."

"Only because they couldn't make the *Enterprise-D* with our current tech," Admiral Stuart said. "I'm surprised they didn't insist on naming the ship themselves."

"There's already an *Enterprise* in the fleet," Elton said, seriously. "And a *Defiant*. And a *Voyager*."

He shook his head. *Odyssey* was a flattened cylinder, eight hundred metres from bow to stern. Her prow was an arrowhead; her rear dominated by four massive drive nacelles that glowed against the inky darkness of space. The designers *had* wanted something that looked like an unconventional design - rather than the blunt cruisers that made up the mainstay of the Solar Navy - but technological reality had defeated their best efforts. *Odyssey* was cruder, perhaps, than her designers had wanted.

"She's a good ship," he said. "And she bears a honourable name."

"I suppose she does," Admiral Stuart said. "And yet, I cannot help recalling that the original starship was rammed and destroyed."

He sat back in his chair and studied Elton for a long chilling moment. Elton knew what he saw. A brown-haired man, seemingly in his early forties; his face warm and friendly rather than blatantly attractive; someone secure enough in himself not to body-sculpt himself into an inhumanly handsome caricature of a man. The message would be clearly visible, to someone who'd been born in the Solar Union. He couldn't help wondering what Admiral Stuart made of it. Physical imperfections had been far more common on pre-space Earth. Elton had had the standard bodymods, of course, but he'd long since grown out of simple vanity. There was no place for it in the Solar Navy.

Admiral Stuart himself looked little older than Elton. It would have been hard to believe that he was actually in his second century, if Elton hadn't known quite a few others who were actually older. They had always struck him as being oddly disconnected from the world around them, either seeking sensual pleasure or separating themselves from it entirely, but Mongo Stuart didn't look to have fallen prey to either. His eyes were calm, yet tightly focused. The man who had commanded the Solar Navy for the last sixty years - and had served in the wet-navy, before Contact - was still on top of his game.

The Admiral leaned forward, breaking the silence. "I trust there were no significant problems during the shakedown cruise?"

"No, sir," Elton said. He ran a hand through his brown hair. "We spent the first two weeks flying around the Sol System, testing the drives and weapons. There weren't any major problems. A handful of minor ones, all of which were fixed easily. The shipyard crews did a good job. I was expecting many more problems."

"The AI simulations were very precise," Admiral Stuart noted.

"I didn't place much credence in them," Elton admitted. "Reality always trumps theory."

He shrugged. "We took her out to Varner, then headed downwards to Spiral and Cockatoo before returning to Sol. She handled like a dream. I think we impressed the locals, although there were some questions about our ability to fight. They didn't seem too impressed with the design, at first. We couldn't tell them about the interlocking shield generators or the self-regenerating systems."

"No," Admiral Stuart agreed. "She's tough, but she's still not a proper warship."

"No, sir," Elton agreed. *Odyssey* was armed, of course, but she wasn't a battleship. Her weapons array was lighter than the average warship. "She's designed for more than just military operations."

"A jack-of-all-trades is almost always a master of none," Admiral Stuart said. He tapped a switch. The holographic image vanished. "I cannot say that I approve of a starship that is designed for multiple roles."

"With all due respect, sir," Elton said, "we're going to need more than warships as we expand further and further into the galaxy. We're going to need everything from diplomatic envoys to colony and medical support ships...hell, sir, *Odyssey* does have enough firepower to hold the line against anything smaller than a battlecruiser. She could certainly hold out long enough for help to arrive."

"Assuming anyone knew you were in trouble," Admiral Stuart said. "The concept was hotly debated, as you know. There was a strong feeling that we should concentrate on building warships now, while we have the chance. The Tokomak are still out there."

"Yes, sir," Elton said. He'd fought in the Battle of Earth. "Which makes it all the more important that we build up relationships with the other galactic powers. Our technological advantage only goes so far."

Admiral Stuart smiled, coldly. "It has been hotly debated," he agreed. "And, as it happens, it has some bearing on your mission."

Elton straightened as a holographic starchart appeared in front of them. "There is a great deal of debate over precisely *what* will happen, regarding the Grand Alliance," Admiral Stuart told him. "We don't know if we'll end up starting ... starting a United Federation of Planets or an alliance structure more comparable with old NATO than anything more integrated. It may be years before we have an answer. But unfortunately the universe is still moving on."

He pointed a finger at a star cluster, thousands of light years from Earth. "The Kingdom of Harmonious Order," he said. "Galactics, of course. One hundred and seven systems under their direct control, three subject races held in servitude. And long-standing allies of the Tokomak Empire. They lost their independence shortly after the stardrive was invented, like everyone else, but they were treated surprisingly well. The Tokomak honoured them with a great deal of local autonomy, trusting them to keep the remainder of the sector in line. They even built up a large fleet to support their allies."

His face twisted into a smile. "Until recently, I doubt anyone on Harmony itself knew Earth even existed."

"We were nothing more than a microstate by their standards," Elton agreed. He made a mental note to look up the full details, as soon as he was back on his ship. "Have they decided to change their minds about us?"

"Apparently, there was a coup on their homeworld last year," Admiral Stuart said. "A strong party at court, we have been told, resented being dominated by the Tokomak. That party seized power shortly after the Battle of Earth. They haven't exactly declared independence, but they're looking to...redefine...their relationship with their former masters."

Elton studied the starchart for a long moment. "A dangerous game, I would have thought," he said. "The Tokomak could flood their cluster with warships, couldn't they?"

Admiral Stuart sighed. "Yes, they could," he agreed. "Elton, everything we know is nearly nine months out of date. The Harmonies could have been brutally crushed by now. But, at the same time, it's possible that they managed to talk fast enough to keep *some* of their independence. The Tokomak wouldn't *want* to get involved in a war that would upset their other allies."

He smiled, rather thinly. "ONI is divided on the issue," he added. "One faction thinks that the Tokomak will crush the rebels as soon as possible, just to reverse the decline in their fortunes since the Battle of Earth. They *have* to make it clear that they haven't lost the war, even if they have lost a battle. But another faction thinks that the Tokomak will reluctantly accept neutrality, if the Harmonies are prepared to stay out of the fighting."

"I would bet on the former," Elton said. "How many other Galactics will consider bolting if they think they can get away with it?"

"Good question," Admiral Stuart said. "And that's where you and your ship come in."

He adjusted the starchart, zeroing in on Harmony itself. "We've received a message from the new king," he said. "He has requested that we send an envoy to discuss opening up lines of communication, perhaps even membership in any future alliance structure. ONI believes that the Harmonies want to keep their options open, just in case their former masters decide to crush them."

Elton stroked his chin, thoughtfully. "It seems a little odd," he mused. "They're taking one hell of a risk. It might panic the Tokomak into doing something drastic."

"It might also convince them to leave the Harmonies alone," Admiral Stuart said. "The king may hope to use this to get an official recognition of his kingdom's independence. Or he may believe that working with us is the only way to safeguard the future."

He shook his head. "You and your ship will be heading directly to the Kingdom of Harmonious Order," he explained. "Officially, you'll be transporting an envoy with authority to open discussions - everything from trade agreements to a formal alliance - and escorting a handful of freighters crammed with trade goods. *Odyssey* will be flagged as a formal diplomatic ship for the mission, although I don't know how much protection that will give you in these times. The Tokomak may be fanatical rules lawyers, but they will *not* want to see us extending our influence in their direction."

"Yes, sir," Elton said. "And unofficially?"

"Unofficially, you'll be carrying out a tactical survey of the region," Admiral Stuart said, curtly. "We know - really *know* - very little about the sector. Everything we hear is at second or third hand. Much of it is translated repeatedly before it reaches us. In truth, we *know* very little. The merchants will be making their own inroads, of course, but we need more data."

"Just in case we have to fight up there," Elton said.

"Exactly," Admiral Stuart said. "In particular, we want an assessment of the Harmonies themselves. Their fleet is supposed to be large, but outdated. Are they upgrading their fleets? Or are they gambling on numbers? Who crews the ships, how are they trained...everything we might have to take into consideration, if we have to ally with them or fight them. And if they are upgrading, are they interested in buying weapons and technology from us?"

He looked at the starchart for a long moment. "ONI will give you a full briefing, but realistically...don't take anything they tell you for granted."

Elton nodded. It wasn't uncommon for translation errors to creep into the files, even though the Tokomak had done everything in their power to make sure that everyone spoke one of nine standard languages. The average alien was no more or less intelligent than the average human, but aliens tended to think *differently*. ONI might be being misled - accidentally or not - and never know it.

And the time delay means that everything is out of date, he thought, sourly. *The Tokomak might invade the sector tomorrow and we won't know until we slip through the gravity point and emerge in the middle of a war.*

"We'll try and fill in the blanks," he said, slowly. He knew better than to trust ONI completely. Intelligence officers had a tendency to think they were cleverer - or at least more knowledgeable - than they actually were. "I don't know how long we'll have to explore the sector, though."

"I suggest you consult with the ambassador," Admiral Stuart said. "Truthfully...we know so little, Elton, that we have to be very careful. Showing the flag in the wrong place may provoke a war."

"The Harmonies have their own subjects," Elton agreed. He frowned as a thought struck him. "What happens if *they* choose to rebel?"

"That would be a sticky problem," Admiral Stuart said. "Ideally, you wouldn't be involved at all. You *don't* want to get us into a shooting war with the Harmonies as well as the Tokomak."

"No, sir," Elton said.

"The ambassador will have her own briefing," Admiral Stuart said. "She'll have wide latitude, within reason. Ideally, we won't be making anyone any promises until we actually know what's going on, but...events may move out of control. Use your own best judgement and be *careful*."

"Yes, sir," Elton said. "And if the Tokomak themselves show up?"

"*Odyssey* on her own is unlikely to make a difference," Admiral Stuart said. "Retreat at once."

Elton nodded. He had every confidence in his ship's ability to give the Tokomak ships a bloody nose, but sheer numbers could overwhelm them easily. The Solar Navy was all too aware that the Tokomak had literally *millions* of starships. If they ever managed to concentrate them against Sol, Sol was doomed.

And the Harmonies are far too close to Tokomak bases, he reminded himself. *The Tokomak could muster the force necessary to strike them down at any moment.*

"I understand," he said. Retreat didn't sit well with him, but preserving his ship and crew was his first priority. "When do you want us to depart?"

"Two days," Admiral Stuart said. He grimaced. "You'll be passing through Hudson Base, at the far end of the Langlock Chain, but after that you'll be on your own. We won't expect you to report back for over a year."

"*Odyssey* was designed for five-year missions, sir," Elton said. "We can reproduce almost anything we might require in the fabricators."

"A five-year mission," Admiral Stuart repeated. He shook his head in amused disbelief. "Do you think, sometimes, that the cantons take their identities a little too far?"

Elton considered it. "As long as people can move out, if they wish, it doesn't matter," he said. "A canton that manages to make itself unviable won't survive. Roddenberry Canton has its quirks, but it isn't a disaster area."

He smiled at the thought. Roddenberry Canton claimed to operate on the principles of *Star Trek* - and, if he were forced to be honest, it did a better job of following its source material than many of the other eccentric cantons. But then, it hadn't needed to adapt itself to changing reality or rapid depopulation when its citizens had discovered that their ideals didn't quite work in the real world. It wasn't for everyone, something that was true of just about every canton in the Solar Union, but it worked for those who lived there.

"There are worse places to live," Admiral Stuart agreed.

Elton nodded. Admiral Stuart was in his second century, easily old enough to remember when humanity was confined to a single planet. His brother might have founded the Solar Union - and then departed for deep space, leaving his creation to flourish on its own - but neither of them had anticipated just how deeply their work would change society. Old constants, things that Steve and Mongo Stuart had taken for granted, had fallen by the wayside. Elton and his fellows had grown up in a very different universe. He wondered, sometimes, just how the oldsters coped. They just weren't used to rapid change.

And yet, they have seen so much, he thought. He couldn't help feeling an odd flicker of sympathy. *Do they yearn for constants once again?*

But there were none, not in the Solar Union. Space was vast, with near-infinite resources just waiting to be exploited. Food and energy were cheap. There were thousands of cantons, each one offering a different lifestyle. Humans - and aliens, and AIs - were free to choose their own lifestyles, as long as they honoured the founding principles. And they had *flourished*. The wellspring of science, art and entertainment seemed bottomless. No one, not even Steve Stuart, could have envisioned the universe he'd created. The future seemed bright and full of promise.

But there were threats. And those threats had to be fought.

Admiral Stuart snapped off the holographic starchart. "I won't tell you that this will be a simple mission, because it won't be," he said. "But I expect you and your ship to handle it."

"Yes, sir," Elton said. He rose. "We won't let you down."

"Good luck," Admiral Stuart said. His lips quirked. "I'll see you when you return home."

Elton nodded and walked through the hatch, passing through the security fields as he headed down to the teleport station. A handful of messages popped up in front of his eyes as his implants automatically pinged the local processors, ranging from tactical updates to a detailed briefing of everything ONI knew - or believed - about the Harmonies. He reminded himself to study the information later, as he stepped into the teleport station. He'd have to make sure his senior officers went through it too.

Except everything we know might be out of date, he reminded himself, sternly. *Or it might be completely wrong.*

He couldn't help a flicker of excitement. He was going to be taking his ship thousands of light years from Sol, heading further into deep space than any human had gone before. As far as he knew, he and his crew would be the *first* humans to visit the Harmonies, let alone establish diplomatic and trade links that might reshape the galaxy. It would be one hell of a flight, the kind of exploration he'd signed up to do. He couldn't wait to leave.

And if we do manage to make new friends and allies, he thought as the teleport field gripped him, *so much the better.*

TWO

The Solar Union is for humans. Humans. Not aliens, not beings who are not like us and do not think like us. None of the so-called Galactics had the wit to use their technology to build a perfect society. They could have done, but they chose to stagnate instead. We should not dilute our uniqueness by bringing aliens into an alliance with us.
-Solar Datanet, Political Forum (Grand Alliance Thoughts)

Ambassador Rebecca Motherwell gritted her teeth and closed her eyes as the teleport field shimmered into life around her, feeling an unpleasant itching sensation spreading through her body. The engineers might claim that the feeling was harmless, existing only in her imagination, but Rebecca knew better. There were times when she would sooner have all her teeth removed, without anaesthetic, than willingly step into a teleporter. The timeless sensation of having her entire body broken down into a stream of energy - a sensation that seemed to last forever, as if she were permanently suspended in the matter stream - terrified her.

She opened her eyes, a moment later. It was always a shock, somehow, to find herself somewhere else, even though she'd been teleported hundreds of times over the last fifty years. The Galactics - and the Solarians - accepted it as normal, but Rebecca and her fellow Earthers found it harder to tolerate. It was easy, all too easy, to believe that she'd been killed and resurrected every time she'd stepped into a teleporter. Hell, there were people who steadfastly refused to teleport even to save their lives. They saw teleporting as a death sentence in itself.

"Madam Ambassador," a quiet voice said. "Welcome onboard."

Rebecca looked up. A young man was staring at her, his dark eyes clearly worried. Her implants scanned his tanned face and matched it to a file, identifying the speaker as Commander Rupert Biscoe, the starship's executive officer. A stream of data flowed past her eyes, which she hastily banished with a thought. She'd have plenty of time to get to know the senior officers later, once the starship was underway. If nothing else, she needed to practice her conversational and diplomatic skills before reaching Harmony.

"Thank you," she managed.

Biscoe still looked concerned. "I can take you to sickbay, if you wish," he said. "I..."

"No, thank you," Rebecca said. She knew from experience that no doctors were able to help, beyond prescribing the occasional sedative. "I just don't like teleporting, sadly."

She caught sight of her own reflection, peering back at her from the wall-mounted display and sighed. No *wonder* Biscoe was worried. She'd put a great deal of effort into her appearance, trying to strike a balance that made her seem both fair and reasonable. Her dark hair was tied up in a bun, her face more matronly than beautiful...her robe - modelled on the Tokomak dress for galactic ambassadors - drew the eye. And yet, her dark eyes were wide open, almost terrified. She looked like a woman on the run.

"Ah," Biscoe said. "In that case, please allow me to escort you to the captain."

Rebecca nodded, concentrating on calming herself. She knew she hadn't made a good impression. Biscoe hid it well, but Rebecca could tell he wasn't impressed. Most Solarians would have shared his view. They had grown up with teleporters - and countless other pieces of technology that were almost unknown on Earth. It was just part of their lives, something so mundane they didn't understand when outsiders questioned them.

She sighed, inwardly, as she stepped off the teleport pad. The chamber was smaller than she'd expected, probably reserved for the ship's officers and their senior guests. Her staff would already be onboard, waiting for her. No doubt they were unpacking, then preparing themselves for nine months of utter boredom. Rebecca smiled, despite herself, at the thought of wasting so much time. There were files on the Kingdom of Harmonious Order, as well as countless other galactic powers. She intended to spend at least some of the trip reviewing the datafiles and trying to determine just how much could be taken for granted.

The Tokomak might be bastards, but we can trust them to record everything, she thought, as the hatch hissed open. *There's so much in the files, even the galactic databases we bought or stole, that analysing it all is the work of generations.*

Odyssey hummed around her as she followed Biscoe into the main corridor. The gravity and lighting were Earth-normal, even though a number of cantons quietly raised the gravity to promote muscle development. But then, the Solar Navy wouldn't need such games. Their crews had the best bodymods humanity could produce, ranging from superior eyesight and hearing to increased strength, durability and neural linkage. It made her wonder, sometimes, just how many of them could be considered baseline *human* any longer. About the only thing that *couldn't* be improved was intelligence.

Because the sole attempt to breed a super-intelligent human went badly wrong, she reminded herself. *And further experiments were banned.*

Rebecca frowned as she passed a couple of cyborg crewmembers, their implants clearly visible on their faces. Her blood ran cold, even though she *knew* they were harmless. There was something *wrong* about seeing human flesh warped and mutilated by cold metal implants, even though she had the standard neural augmentation and enhancements. At least *her* implants were concealed under her skin. And yet... something was nagging at her mind. It took her several minutes to put her finger on it. She should have seen many more crewmen as they walked up to Officer Country. The starship was surprisingly undermanned.

She glanced at Biscoe. "How many crew are there on this ship?"

"Around five hundred," Biscoe said. "We're due to take on a number of researchers in the next couple of days, everything from astronomers who want to take a look at a handful of particularly interesting stars to cultural researchers who want to open up ties with galactic universities. I believe we even have a couple of students who are hoping to *join* those universities."

Rebecca had to smile. "So you're planning to show the flag everywhere?"

"Of course," Biscoe said. He smiled with genuine enthusiasm. "*Odyssey* was never designed as a warship, Madam Ambassador. She's intended to be the Solar Union in miniature, a multirole starship that showcases precisely what we can do. We can give foreign guests tours that show off without telling them anything that can be used against us. I've even been told that we can recreate our entire society, given time."

Rebecca had to smile. "Really?"

"Of course," Biscoe assured her. "We can set off tomorrow and fly deep into unexplored space for a couple of years, then get to work. Our fabricators are self-replicating. Given a decade or two, we can build up a strikingly formidable industrial base. And we have a complete gene database, allowing us to clone a vast population. It would take us centuries, of course, but it could be done."

"I see," Rebecca said. She smiled. "It makes one wonder why it hasn't already been done."

"It probably has, Madam Ambassador," Biscoe said.

Rebecca nodded in agreement. It hadn't been *that* long since the Battle of Earth. Everyone *knew* the universe wasn't a safe place. She was sure the government would have sent off a whole string of covert colony missions, dispatching them well away from the crumbling galactic civilisation. If Earth was destroyed, if the Solar Union was smashed to rubble, humanity would survive. And one day, the colonies would come back for revenge.

They stopped outside a sealed hatch. "Captain Yasser will see you now," Biscoe said, as the hatch hissed open. "I'll show you to your quarters afterwards."

"Thank you," Rebecca said.

She stepped into the captain's office and looked around, interested. It was smaller than she'd expected, decorated with a handful of paintings from the pre-steam naval era. The captain himself was sitting behind a desk, studying a holographic starchart. She couldn't help noticing, as he rose to greet her, that the starchart didn't show any cluster she recognised. Her implants switched into primary mode, searching for a match. One blinked up, seconds later.

The Karana Sector, she noted. *Seventy light years from Harmony.*

"Madam Ambassador," the captain said. He held out a hand. Rebecca shook it, firmly. "Welcome onboard."

"Thank you, Captain," Rebecca said. "It's a pleasure to be here. *Odyssey* looks to be a fine ship."

The captain smiled. She'd never met a captain who couldn't be flattered by compliments to his ship. "Coffee? Or tea?"

"Coffee would be fine, thank you," Rebecca said.

She had to smile as the captain keyed the food processor. There were people who swore blind that food processors couldn't match natural food, but *she'd* never been able to tell the difference. It hadn't really helped with her teleport phobia. What was to stop someone producing endless duplicates of *her*, each one convinced - and rightly so - that *she* was the *real* Rebecca? She'd been told, time and time again, that it was impossible, but she didn't really believe it. How could she?

The captain looked competent - and, perhaps more importantly, self-assured. His face might have been handsome once, when he'd been younger, but right now he looked as if his jowls were sagging slightly and his brown hair was starting to grey. He hadn't chosen to freeze his appearance then, she noted, let alone have himself turned into a Greek God.

Indeed, she couldn't help noticing that he was a little overweight. But it spoke well of him. It spoke of a man who saw no need to flatter himself.

Maybe not the most imaginative officer in the navy, she thought, recalling the briefing she'd been given along with her credentials. *But a solid, reliable man.*

She took the coffee and sipped it, silently glad of the chance to collect her thoughts. The Solar Navy and the Solar Diplomatic Service were meant to work together, but the former suspected the latter of being too willing to make concessions and the latter suspected the former of being too willing to resort to gunboat diplomacy and naked force. Rebecca had no illusions about the Tokomak - or many of the other Galactics - yet she knew that humanity couldn't hope to fight and win a war against the entire known galaxy. Diplomacy might just weaken the Tokomak enough to dissuade them from fighting.

"Mountain Blend Coffee," she commented, finally. A neutral subject was always a good place to start. Besides, most of the naval officers she'd met had been fanatics about coffee. "Do you know when the baseline records were scanned?"

"I'm afraid not," the captain said. His lips twitched. "I've never tasted the *real* blend."

"There's no real difference," Rebecca admitted. She took another sip. The coffee was strong. "I assume you've read the mission orders?"

"I have," the captain confirmed. "I confess, though, that I am curious as to *your* interpretation of our orders."

Rebecca shrugged. Captain Yasser didn't seem interested in small talk.

"I have orders to try to open diplomatic channels with the Kingdom of Harmonious Order and the other galactic powers in that region of space," she said. "Ideally, I'm to do it without promising more than the Solar Union can reasonably deliver. In the long term, the Solar Union would like a trade agreement and a military alliance; in the short term, my superiors will settle for opening diplomatic channels and getting some limited trade agreements."

She met his eyes. "Does that match *your* understanding?"

"More or less," the captain said. "*My* superiors want a tactical survey too."

Rebecca made a face. "I hope you can do it without making it obvious," she said. "Would *we* tolerate a spy ship buzzing around the solar system?"

"Probably not," the captain said. His lips twitched. "But we couldn't tell if a visiting starship was using her passive sensors to record data."

"True," Rebecca agreed. She was no military expert, but even *she* knew that was why most research and development programs were housed in deep space, well away from any prying eyes. "My staff and I will also distribute trade goods to the local merchants in the hopes of making new friends and allies."

"That might also cause problems," the captain pointed out. "Local merchant combines might feel threatened."

"It's a delicate balancing act," Rebecca said. "But we have to offer them as many incentives as possible to talk to us."

The captain nodded. "We intend to depart in four days, barring unexpected delays," he told her, curtly. "By then, the remainder of the convoy will be assembled and we'll set off for the first leg of the journey. We'll be calling in at a couple of bases along the way, dropping off supplies and equipment. You should have plenty of time to prepare for your mission."

"I hope so," Rebecca said. "I assume we'll also be collecting intelligence updates along the way?"

"Of course," the captain said. "Everything we know is, at best, out of date."

"A major problem," Rebecca agreed.

It had been drummed into her head, time and time again, that she could not ignore the time delay. She could recall a time when a message could cross the entire world in less than a second. Now, with the Solar Union spread out over a hundred light years and humanity's network of friends and allies spread out further still, the time delay was beginning to bite again. Her orders - and the captain's orders - were vague purely because their superiors didn't know enough to issue more specific instructions. There was certainly no way she could send a message home asking for advice. By the time she got a reply, the problem would have moved on.

And that's why we have been granted such wide latitude, she thought, sourly. *And that's why we'll get the blame if things go south.*

It was, she conceded, an advantage that they'd been granted so much authority. The Tokomak rarely granted *their* local commanders anything like as much freedom of action, insisting that all decisions had to be referred to higher authority. But she couldn't help feeling nervous about just how much could go hideously wrong. A mistake could have disastrous consequences when dealing with prickly galactic powers. Even with galactic protocols for diplomatic discussions, laid down by the Tokomak themselves, there was plenty of room for misunderstandings that could lead to catastrophe.

"My staff and I will try to stay out of your way, during the voyage," she said, putting the thought aside for later contemplation. It wasn't something she could do anything about, at least not until someone invented an FTL communicator. "I plan to spend the time studying the files."

"You may have to drag your staffers out of the entertainment suites," the captain said. "We have a civilian-grade full-spectrum holographic entertainment complex."

Rebecca blinked, then nodded. "For the civilian crews?"

"Among others," the captain said. "*Odyssey* is designed for *very* long-duration missions."

"I'll make sure they keep their noses to the grindstone," Rebecca said. She understood the need to relax and blow off steam, but she *also* understood the need to do background research before reaching their destination. Even a minor diplomatic mistake - serving meat to a race composed of vegetarians - could cause embarrassment, if not disaster. "They can have some fun after they're done."

She smiled, then sobered. "I meant to ask," she added. "I checked the supply manifest for the freighters. Apart from the trade goods - and the gifts - you're taking a significant quantity of weapons and other military supplies. Can I ask why?"

The captain looked surprised, just for a second. Rebecca wondered why. Had he not expected her to check the manifests? She'd known ambassadors who wouldn't have bothered, although *she* had just considered it another piece of background research before setting off on her mission. It was important, vitally so, to make certain that none of the vessels were carrying anything that might cause offense. The last thing humanity needed was more enemies.

"Better safe than sorry," the captain said, finally. "We're going to be a *very* long way from the nearest base, Madam Ambassador. In theory, we can fabricate anything we reasonably need; in practice, I'd prefer to have it on hand when we need it."

"As long as the locals don't think we're planning to arm their sworn enemies," Rebecca said, dryly. "That's happened, you know."

"I would be gratified if we went out there, made all the contacts we could possibly want, and then headed home, our holds crammed with trade goods," the captain said. "And I would be delighted if we didn't have to fire a single shot. But it is better to be safe than sorry."

"Of course," Rebecca agreed. She finished her coffee and placed the mug on the desk. "And please call me Rebecca. We're going to be working together quite closely over the next few months."

"Elton," the captain said. He looked vaguely embarrassed. "My mother was a huge fan of Elton John."

Rebecca had to smile. "Compared to some of the more absurd names going in and out of fashion," she said, "I think you got off lightly."

"That's probably true," the captain agreed.

It was, Rebecca knew. A sprinkling of alien names - and *fictional* alien names - had made their way into society, even though they guaranteed that the poor children bearing them had uncomfortable childhoods. Elton Yasser was surprisingly normal, compared to some of the truly absurd names out there. There were some people, she felt, who really shouldn't be parents.

She rose. "Thank you for your time, Elton," she said. "I hope to see more of you after we enter FTL."

"I'm sure you will," the captain said. He rose, too. "And I wish you luck with the files."

"We'll need more than luck," Rebecca said. "We'll need a miracle."

THREE

We are not unique. Let us not believe that there is anything truly special about humanity. We are smart, but so too are many other intelligent races; we are cunning, but so too are many others. Our sole advantage is a questioning mindset that we have managed to keep, despite the best efforts of our pre-space governments. That is not an advantage we can prevent others from copying. It will not last.
-Solar Datanet, Political Forum (Grand Alliance Thoughts)

"I just had word from *Lady Dean*," Biscoe said. "Her captain apologises for the delay, but insists that his engineering crew has finally tracked down the rogue harmonic in her drive systems. *Lady Dean* should be ready to depart on schedule."

"Let us hope so," Elton said. "And *Kenny Rogers?*"

Biscoe looked irked. As XO, it was his job to keep the merchant starships in line. "Her CO told us that he probably won't make the rendezvous," he said. "She's been delayed at Haverford. Thankfully, she was just begging an escort rather than transporting anything vital."

Elton nodded. "We can't delay departure any longer," he said, shortly. "Drop her from the list."

"Aye, Captain," Biscoe said. He glanced down at the datapad in his hand. "Those two are our only problem children. The remaining freighters are all ready to depart on your command."

"Good," Elton said.

He sat back in his command chair and surveyed the bridge. *Odyssey* hadn't been designed as a warship and it showed. Her bridge was warmer and friendlier than any standard warship's command deck, built more to show off the Solar Union's technological prowess than anything else. He'd honestly wondered if someone had copied the design from a luxury liner when he'd first seen the plans. And yet, he had to admit there was something charming about the design. Humanity's starships were finally developing a distinctive style of their own.

The main display hovered in front of him, showing *Odyssey*, the seventeen freighters holding position near the massive starship, and the giant cluster of industrial nodes and fabricators that made up the shipyard. Dozens of other starships and hundreds of floating weapons platforms hovered nearby, constantly sweeping space for signs of trouble. The Solar Union's immense building program was solidly underway, new starships coming off the slips each month. It seemed impossible that anyone could match humanity's output, but he knew better than to take that for granted. If the Tokomak ever took the limiters off their fabricators, they would start out-producing humanity immediately.

But that would mean giving up too much control, he thought, grimly. *They'd upend their entire economic system just to get at us.*

He shook his head in amused disbelief. Humanity hadn't been able to understand the galactic economy, back when they'd first encountered it. The structure just hadn't made sense. It had been years before anyone had realised that the economy had been deliberately hampered, just to keep the younger races from challenging the established order. The Tokomak fabricators were designed to be very limited, ensuring that the Galactics couldn't move to a post-scarcity society. But now...

More and more races know how to hack the systems now, he reminded himself. He hadn't been a fan of Hoshiko Sashimi Stuart's campaign against the Druavroks - it struck him as something that could have easily gone wrong - but he had to admit that it had boosted humanity's credibility right across the galaxy. *The Tokomak won't be able to stuff the genie back in the bottle.*

He shook his head, dismissing the thought. "I assume that all crew have returned to the ship?"

"Yes, Captain," Biscoe said. "And the newcomers are settling in well, I believe."

Elton nodded. *Odyssey* was comfortable. Maybe she wasn't a luxury liner, but she *was* far more comfortable, certainly, than a regular warship. The short-term crews might be separated from their families, yet they had everything they needed during their off-duty hours. Even the regular crew had large quarters. They'd have real problems adapting if they were ever transferred back to the warships.

"Then inform fleet command that we will be departing on schedule," he said, finally. He looked at his tactical officer. "Do we have a security update?"

"Nothing particularly new, Captain," Lieutenant-Commander Steve Callaway said. "There are vague reports of a couple of brushfire wars breaking out, but both of them are at least forty light years off our planned course."

"Still, better to be careful," Elton said. The steady collapse of the established order was unleashing all sorts of demons. Countless grudges had been held in stasis under the Tokomak. Now, their holders were making up for lost time. "They may try to seize one of the gravity points along the way."

He forced himself to relax as time ticked by, a steady stream of updates popping up in front of his eyes. His ship was ready and raring to go, her crew already starting the endless cycle of training simulations to ensure they were ready to cope with any problems. Elton and his senior officers had devised tactical scenarios covering everything from pirate attack to all-out war, although - if they did get caught up in a war - he knew their only realistic option was immediate retreat. *Odyssey* was tougher than she looked, but she wasn't a real warship. It was something he had to bear in mind.

"Captain," Lieutenant Jonathan Williams said. "Fleet HQ has cleared us and the convoy for departure."

Elton smiled. It wasn't the first time he'd taken his ship out into deep space, but it felt special. This time, they were heading well away from Sol. Maybe it wasn't unexplored space - the Tokomak and their allies had charted the entire region thoroughly - but they would still be the first humans to visit. There were certainly no records, as far as he could tell, that suggested otherwise.

"Then power up the drive," he ordered. The dull throbbing echoing through the ship started to grow louder. "Helm, take us out of here."

"Aye, Captain," Lieutenant Marie Howells said. She worked her console for a long moment, her purple fingers dancing over the keys. "Sublight drive engaged; moving out."

"Ready the stardrive," Elton ordered. "Prepare to take us into FTL as soon as we have cleared the outer defence zone."

"Aye, Captain," Marie said.

Elton smiled at her back. He hadn't missed the excitement in her voice. The entire crew was looking forward to leaving Sol. They'd have some *real* stories to tell when they finally made it home.

"The convoy is falling into position," Biscoe said. "They're ready to enter FTL."

"Good," Elton said.

He took one last look at the main display, his eyes moving over the solar system. Earth itself might be a backwater, the civil war draining the planet's resources faster than they could be replenished, but the remainder of the system was studded with icons. Hundreds of settlements on Luna, Mars, and Venus; thousands of settled asteroids, each one a canton; hundreds of thousands of spacecraft and starships moving from world to world or heading out into deep space. Humanity had come a very long way in a very short space of time.

No wonder the Galactics are so scared of us, he thought.

It was a strange thought. The Galactics were not stupid. As far as anyone could tell, most races shared the same basic level of intelligence. And yet, they'd managed to hamper themselves. No, more accurately, the Tokomak had hampered themselves...and everyone else, to boot. Some races had been held back by force, others had never been taught just how their technology worked...it was magic, as far as they were concerned. But humanity had not only unlocked the secrets of alien technology, humanity had figured out ways to improve it too. Who knew what the next thousand years would look like?

"Captain," Marie said. "We are ready to enter FTL."

Elton smiled. "Engage."

He braced himself, instinctively, as the stardrive came online. But there was nothing, beyond a vague sense of discontent that faded with astonishing speed. He'd been on ships where entering FTL had been a profoundly discomforting experience, but the latest drive modifications had solved that problem. He couldn't help wondering if it was truly a good idea. Humanity needed to remember that the universe outside the starship's hull was cold and harsh. *Odyssey*, for all her comfort, was not a civilian ship.

"All systems check out, captain," Marie said. "We are on a direct course for Varner."

"The freighters have followed us into FTL," Biscoe added. "They're holding course."

"Keep an eye on them," Elton ordered. "I want to know if any of them show signs of drive trouble."

"Aye, Captain," Biscoe said.

REBECCA HAD MADE a point of carefully *not* following *Odyssey's* departure through the vessel's sensors, let alone making her way to an observation blister to watch the stars blink out of existence as the starship entered FTL. She wasn't one of the rare handful of people who had to be sedated for FTL travel, but she didn't like being aware - all too aware - that there was nothing outside the giant starship. It was easier to pretend that she was still on an asteroid than try to convince herself that there was nothing *unnatural* about being in FTL.

And yet, she was surprised when the standard alert popped up in front of her eyes, informing her *Odyssey* was now in FTL. She hadn't felt much, if anything. Was the ship *really* travelling away from Sol at an unimaginable speed? She queried the local processor, just to be sure. It confirmed that *Odyssey* was indeed in FTL.

"Impressive," she muttered.

"Yes, Madam Ambassador," Mickey Tyler said. Her aide grinned at her. "*Odyssey* has the latest drive modifications designed to modulate the gravity flux, ensuring a smooth transit in and out of FTL. I read the file and it was very interesting..."

"All right, all right," Rebecca said, tiredly. "Please, spare me the details."

She kept her expression under tight control as her aide looked back at his file, torn between amusement and annoyance. Tyler was good at his job, but he was also an unashamed starship enthusiast, someone capable of rattling off facts, figures and pieces of thoroughly useless information at a moment's notice. She had no idea why he hadn't applied to join the navy, although she imagined that his constant questioning of everything would eventually grate on naval crewmen. She'd had to speak to him quite soundly after he'd begged a visit to the bridge, two days ago. Captain Yasser had not been pleased.

"I wonder why they haven't put the baffles on civilian liners," Rose Smith said. Her other aide was a little older than Mickey, with a rather more cynical view of the universe. "The ship I took from Mars to Tychy groaned every time it dropped in and out of FTL."

"It's a new technology," Tyler said. "I don't think it's available for civilian use yet."

Rebecca cleared her throat. "And seeing that the pair of you are on duty," she added dryly, "have you found anything useful in the files?"

Rose flushed, casting a dark look at Tyler. "I've been going through the diplomatic protocols," she said, carefully. "I'm not sure which ones apply in this situation."

"I see," Rebecca said. She wasn't surprised. She'd expected that to be a problem the moment she read the mission briefing. Thankfully, they had nine months to work out the details before reaching Harmony. "And which ones do you think apply here?"

"I'm not sure," Rose admitted. "On one hand, we are not going as supplicants - as a lower-class race. We shouldn't have to bow and scrape in front of them. But on the other hand, they're not used to dealing with independent races."

"They invited us," Tyler pointed out. "I don't *think* they'd expect us to kowtow."

Rebecca wasn't so sure. Like so much else, the principles of galactic diplomacy had been laid down by the Tokomak. There was no pretence of equality, merely the submission of the weaker party and the gracious acceptance of the stronger party. The Harmonies, if the files could be trusted, were used to bowing the knee to the Tokomak and accepting tribute from everyone else. There were few other races on their level and almost all of them were hundreds of light years away.

And they might be seen as weak, if we didn't bend the knee to them, she mused. *But, at the same time, we cannot allow ourselves to be seen as weak either.*

She glanced at Rose. "Is there any precedent for meetings between equals?"

"Yes, but we'd have to convince them that we *were* equals first," Rose said.

"We bested the Tokomak," Tyler pointed out. "Surely *that* counts for something."

Rebecca sighed, keeping her thoughts to herself. Diplomatic analysts and intelligence officers had studied the text of the original message over and over again, but they hadn't been able to determine if human representatives had been invited to attend a meeting or pre-emptively summoned, as if they were subjects of a vassal power. She'd read dozens of reports, yet none of them had been truly convincing. It was possible the Harmonies themselves didn't know. They might be trying to tread a fine line between humanity and their former masters.

She allowed herself a moment of annoyance. It was possible, one of the more careful analysts had pointed out, that the Harmonies were aiming for plausible deniability. The Tokomak - theoretically - would not be concerned if the Harmonies spoke to humans like masters to slaves. Indeed, they might be *delighted* if the Harmonies treated humans in a manner calculated to cause offense. The message might have been written very carefully indeed, trying to be diplomatic to human eyes and unpleasantly demanding to outside observers. Or it could be a translation glitch. The language had been so flowery that it was quite likely some of the meaning had been lost.

Which is what happens, she thought, *if a message is repeatedly translated time and time again.*

"Compared to the size of their navy," Rose countered, "we didn't even take out a percentage point of a percentage point of their true strength. They might not even have *noticed*."

"They would have done," Tyler insisted. "I..."

Rebecca rubbed her forehead. "Leave the debate for the moment," she said. She had a nasty feeling that the first week at Harmony was going to be spent ironing out the diplomatic groundwork for the talks. Unless, of course, the Harmonies were actually determined to get to the meat of the matter at speed. *That* would make them unique, amongst the older races. "I want you to put together a plan to meet them as equals."

She held up a hand before either of them could object. "It is important that we represent ourselves as a peer power," she added. "And we cannot be seen to bend the knee."

They said nothing, but she knew what they were thinking. Trying to strike a balance between respecting the other power's feelings and conceding far too much was never easy. At what point did respect become submission? It was easy to *say* that the human race should present itself as an equal, but the Harmonies might try to argue that humans *weren't* equal. And they would have a point.

But they did contact us, she reminded herself. *They decided we were worth trying to talk to.*

Her intercom bleeped. She tapped it. "Yes?"

"Madam Ambassador, this is the captain," Captain Yasser said. He sounded calm and composed, as always. "We have entered FTL and are on a direct course to Varner."

"Understood," Rebecca said.

She thought quickly. There was a fairly major human embassy, as well as a naval base, at Varner, if she recalled correctly. She'd have to make sure that they received copies of her game plan, such as it was. *And* see what, if anything, could be gleaned from the local datafiles. The Varner might know something about the Harmonies they hadn't bothered to share with the human race.

"My senior officers and I are also going to be meeting for dinner this evening," the captain added, after a moment. "Would you and some of your staff care to join us?"

Rebecca had to smile. "It would be an excellent chance for us to practice our diplomacy," she said. Neither Rose nor Tyler would enjoy it - diplomatic dinners weren't meant to be enjoyable - but it would be an excellent learning experience. "I look forward to it."

"Very good," the captain said. "See you there."

"I thought diplomatic dinners were outdated, these days," Rose said. She was young enough not to remember the days when the Solar Union had established embassies on Earth. "Does anything get decided at the dinner table?"

Rebecca shrugged. "It helps to build up personal relationships," she said, sardonically. "And while such relationships can be quite dangerous in places, this isn't one of them."

She smiled at their doubtful looks. Ambassadors had been known to lose track of their actual roles, after forging personal relationships with their opposite numbers. Most people liked doing favours for friends, allowing hostile powers to slowly turn the friendship into something exploitive. It was something she'd been cautioned to watch for as she'd worked her way up the ranks. But it wasn't something she expected from a starship's crew. Indeed, a close working relationship between her staff and the captain's officers could only be beneficial.

And besides, it isn't as though we'll be sitting down to eat dinner with the Galactics, she thought, as she reached for the next set of files. The Tokomak had banned diplomatic dinners. For once, she saw their point. One race's idea of good food was another race's idea of deadly poison. *That would probably start a war all on its own.*

FOUR

There is a fine line between providing support and being overbearing, a balancing act that - let us be honest - most of us tend to fall off very quickly. Indeed, I am old enough to remember the days when 'I'm from the government - I'm here to help' was one of the most terrifying things one could hear. It isn't our job to fix the galaxy's problems, any more than it is our job to fix the problems on Earth.
-Solar Datanet, Political Forum (Grand Alliance Thoughts)

Boredom, in all honesty, was the one thing Elton had never expected when he'd first received his orders. He'd served in the military long enough to *know* that boredom was something to be cherished. And yet, as the days turned into weeks and the weeks turned into months, boredom started wearing down his mind. There was nothing to *do* while the ship was in FTL, save for endless drills, simulations and reading files. The droll awareness that he should be *glad* to be bored didn't help.

He haunted the decks, checking and rechecking every system until he knew the ship like the back of his hand. He ran emergency drill after emergency drill, putting the crew through their paces until he reached a point of diminishing returns. And he read his way through everything ONI had been able to scrape up about the Kingdom of Harmonious Order, even though some of it was contradictory. Even eating regular dinners with the ambassador didn't help. By the time the small convoy dropped out of FTL near a dull red star to update their navigational readings, he was starting to turn a blind eye to crewmen overusing the entertainment suites. He was running out of things to keep them occupied.

And we haven't even reached Hudson Base, he thought, morbidly. *They must be going stir crazy, so far from Earth.*

"Captain," Marie said, breaking into his thoughts. "The navigational database is updating now. I believe the original files were somewhat lacking."

"That's odd," Elton said, walking over to her console. "How so?"

"The gravitational fluctuations in this sector don't match the files," Marie said. "I'm starting to think we got an out of date copy."

"It might date all the way back to the Hordesmen," Biscoe suggested. "We haven't done any proper surveys this far from Earth."

"You'd think the locals *would*," Elton said. The Solar Navy had surveyed the Sol Sector thoroughly, tracking each and every last gravitational flux in the region. "I assume this doesn't pose any threat to us?"

"I don't believe so, Captain," Marie said. "Our navigational readings are just ever so slightly skewed. We would probably find ourselves a little off-course if we didn't update the database."

She frowned. "I do wonder why the Hudson Fleet never sent back an update."

Elton shared a look with Biscoe. "They would have, wouldn't they?"

"Yes, sir," Biscoe said. "But they might not have bothered to drop out of FTL *here*."

Elton nodded. *Odyssey* could, in theory, remain in FTL until she reached the next set of gravity points. She'd already passed through a dozen to reach her current location. But the freighters were another story. Their drives needed to be checked and rechecked, while their crews needed a chance to take some R&R on *Odyssey*. It was possible that the Hudson Fleet hadn't bothered to drop out long enough to update their files. He made a mental note to check, once the convoy reached Hudson, then turned to Marie.

"Keep updating the files," he ordered. "And..."

An alarm sounded. "Captain," Callaway snapped. "I'm picking up three starships on attack vector!"

"Red alert," Elton snapped. He spun around and strode back to the command chair. Three red icons were already clearly visible, bearing down on his ship. "Can you get an ID?"

"Nothing solid," Callaway reported. "I think one of them is a heavy cruiser, but the other two can't be anything larger than light cruisers... they're using some complicated ECM to scatter our sensor probes."

"Send a challenge," Elton ordered.

"Aye, Captain," Lieutenant Jonathan Williams said. The communications officer hurried to work. "No response."

Elton winced. By galactic law, any challenge - particularly in neutral space - had to be answered immediately. The only people who wouldn't answer a challenge were people who had bad intentions, either rebels or pirates. It was possible, he supposed, that a legitimate government *might* want to harass human shipping, but they'd have to be out of their minds to try. The Solar Union and its allies were firmly committed to free trade.

But then, we are over a thousand light years from Earth, he thought, sourly. *These guys might not even have heard of us.*

"Target One is heading directly towards us," Callaway reported. "Targets Two and Three are angling towards the freighters."

"Sweep all three of them with tactical sensors," Elton ordered. It was the clearest warning he could give, the interstellar equivalent of a warning shot. "Helm, bring us around."

He thought rapidly, assessing the tactical situation. The heavy cruiser was probably outdated, but there was no way to be sure. The Tokomak hadn't designed their ships to make it easy for the crews to modify their systems, yet a decent engineering team could probably upgrade the drives, sensors and weapons without too many problems. And while *Odyssey* outmassed her opponent, it was quite possible their weapons might be evenly matched. The standard heavy cruiser hull could be *crammed* with firepower...

"They're still coming, Captain," Callaway said.

"Lock weapons on their hull," Elton ordered. He had permission to open fire without warning if he believed his ship and her charges were under threat. "Prepare to engage..."

"Energy spike," Callaway snapped. "They're firing!"

The display blazed with red icons. "Standard missile load," Biscoe said. He sounded relieved. "Nothing new, Captain."

"Return fire," Elton snapped. The enemy ships were launching a second barrage, trying to overwhelm his defences. They were in for a surprise. "Point defence, engage!"

He allowed himself a cold smile as his ship opened fire, phaser bursts lashing out towards the incoming targets with a rapidity that had to horrify her opponents. They didn't even have the latest *Tokomak* missiles, let alone some of humanity's more interesting designs. Elton doubted that even one of their missiles would get close to his shields. They had to be pirates, then. No respectable government would risk an engagement when they were so badly outmatched.

Odyssey quivered as the two smaller enemy ships altered course, swooping in to engage her with energy weapons. Callaway fired back, blasting one of the enemy ships into an expanding cloud of gas and damaging the other one. Elton was morbidly impressed that the pirates managed to keep their ship intact, even though they were bleeding plasma into interplanetary space. But they didn't have a hope of escape, unless their bigger brother managed to evade *Odyssey* or overwhelm her...

"The enemy ship is altering course," Callaway reported. "Captain, she's trying to escape."

Elton didn't blame the enemy CO. He'd thought he was picking on a sheep, but instead he'd caught hold of a lion. *Odyssey's* missiles were fast, fast enough to make interception almost impossible. The enemy ship's shields were already failing. Clearly, the enemy hadn't bothered to power up their stardrive. They'd have escaped already if they'd bothered to take that simple precaution.

Idiots, Elton thought, darkly.

"Take out her drives," he ordered. "I want her intact."

"Aye, Captain," Callaway said.

Odyssey quivered as she unleashed another spread of missiles. The enemy ship fought back desperately, but simply lacked the point defence to stop them. Elton watched, feeling cold, as the missiles slammed into the rear of the enemy ship, destroying her drive section. The heavy cruiser went dark a second later, venting atmosphere and plasma as she spun out of control...

"Captain," Callaway said. "The enemy ship has been disabled."

Elton nodded. He'd half-expected the alien ship to explode. "Dispatch a boarding party," he ordered, curtly. "And ready quarters for any prisoners, if we find them."

"Aye, Captain," Callaway said.

Biscoe spoke, very quietly. "Captain, they could be waiting for us to send over the marines before hitting the self-destruct."

Elton nodded, grimly. Sending the marines was a calculated risk. On one hand, he could ill afford to lose them; on the other, he needed to know who had attacked them and why. Piracy was a growing problem as the Tokomak retreated from the sector, abandoning control to those with the will and power to take it, but the pirates might have been *encouraged* to attack the convoy. The Tokomak had every reason to want to challenge his ship, if they caught wind of the deployment. Hell, the only reason to doubt their involvement was that they would have had to move quickly and they weren't *good* at moving quickly.

"I know the dangers," he said. "But we don't have a choice."

"Aye, Captain," Biscoe said.

LIEUTENANT LEVI DENNIS closed her eyes and accessed the neural link as the marines were launched out of the assault shuttle and blasted directly towards the giant alien ship. It was small, she supposed, compared to some of the other starships she'd seen, but she was smaller than an ant on such a scale. Her combat suit oriented itself automatically as it closed in on the ship, spinning around to present a slightly harder target. If the aliens had chosen to open fire...

Nothing happened. She landed on the alien hull, glancing from side to side as the remainder of the platoon landed on either side of her. Their formation was ragged - she'd seen more ordered formation from kids just entering Boot Camp - but the marines had learnt from bitter experience that a ragged formation was far harder to counter. Her sensors swept the hull quickly, picking up traces of energy from where missiles and phaser fire had bitten into the metal. There were no signs that the enemy crewmen were just biding their time before opening fire.

Which proves nothing, Levi thought, as she started to hurry towards the nearest gash in the hull. *They might know how to hide.*

"Deploy stealth nanoprobes," she ordered. "Platoon One, with me; Platoon Two, go through the upper airlock."

She reached the gash and jumped inside, hastily searching for targets. Nothing moved. The ship looked like a honeycomb, a melted and twisted structure trapped in hard vacuum. Her suit picked up traces of atmosphere - the crew, whoever they were, had breathed something akin to humanity's ideal oxygen mix - but nowhere near enough to support anyone without heavy cybernetic enhancement. She had the full spectrum of marine augmentation and even *she* would have hesitated to try breathing vacuum unless the alternative was certain death.

"The probes are building up a picture of the interior," Sergeant Kath reported. "Intel matches the design..."

Levi nodded as the plans popped up in her HUD. "We'll go straight for the bridge," she said, picking her way down towards the right deck. "Keep spreading the probes through the ship."

She tensed as she pushed her way down the corridor, but nothing jumped out at her. The gravity was completely gone, leaving pieces of debris floating in the air. She kept glancing into side compartments as she moved, more troubled than she cared to admit by the lack of bodies. A standard heavy cruiser, if she recalled correctly, had over a thousand crewmen. She wasn't sure if that was true for alien-designed ships too, but she couldn't imagine the ship being *completely* unmanned.

An AI could operate a ship, she mused, as she forced her way through a jammed hatch. *But the Tokomak refused to create true AIs...*

She stopped, dead, as she saw the bodies. Her mind rebelled, just for a second. It didn't want to believe what it was seeing. Dozens of bodies, utterly inhuman...their mangled remains strikingly unfamiliar. They looked like giant grasshoppers. She shivered as she pushed her way through the bodies, probing on towards the bridge. The aliens were dead, but her imagination kept insisting that they were moving, their giant insectoid eyes following her every move.

"I have a match," Major Rhodan said. "They're Skirats."

"Never heard of them, sir," Kath said.

Levi nodded, curtly. There were more bodies now, drifting helplessly in the vacuum. Some of the aliens had clearly been armed, others seemed unarmed...she wondered, as she forced her way down to the bridge, if they had been slaves or if she was misunderstanding what she was seeing. Aliens weren't human, whatever the cultural relativists insisted. The Skirats might just be utterly beyond human comprehension.

"They're native to this sector," Lieutenant Alleyway said. The intelligence officer sounded fascinated. "They actually have five genders and..."

Rhodan snorted. "Is this actually important? Or relevant?"

"Sir, I've found the bridge hatch," Levi said, quickly. "It looks as though the safety measures failed. The bridge is open to the vacuum. Nanoprobes report no trace of survivors."

She reached out with her armoured hands and pulled the hatch open. It came off, allowing her to glide into the giant compartment. A dozen aliens were seated at consoles, all dead; three more drifted in the air, one carrying something her suit insisted was a heavily-modified plasma rifle. She checked it automatically as she swept the chamber, but found nothing threatening. The entire ship was dead.

"Weird," Kath observed, as he followed her into the bridge. "The safety systems are usually the last things to go."

"Perhaps they skipped basic maintenance," Levi said. She pulled a standard remote access processor from her belt and placed it by the nearest console. It was unlikely the techs would be able to pull anything from the starship's computers without removing the datacores and powering them up somewhere safe, but it was worth a try. "Or perhaps someone sabotaged the ship."

She was more perplexed than she cared to admit, she decided, as they checked the nearest sections. The entire ship was open to vacuum. None of the nanoprobes reported anything beyond faint traces of atmosphere. The aliens would have found it impossible to wear human or Tokomak spacesuits, she thought, but they should have been able to design something that matched their physiology. It wouldn't have been *that* difficult.

"This place reminds me of a horror movie," Rifleman Jones said, over the communications link. "Everyone is dead..."

"And not going to come to life," Levi said, crossly. She'd seen those movies too. She had never really been able to decide if they were meant to be comedies or bloodstained gore-flicks. The marines in those movies had acted more like trigger-happy punks than professional warriors. "Just in case, don't push down on your trigger and lock it in place."

"No, LT," Jones said.

"Got something for you," Corporal Rollins put in, from the bridge. He sounded deeply shocked. "Someone deliberately fucked the emergency lockdown system."

Rhodan coughed. "Are you sure?"

"Yes, sir," Rollins said. "I'm looking at the hatch. Someone deliberately undermined the safety functions - it snapped closed, but it didn't lock. They're normally designed to be hard to open and remain airtight even if unlocked...here, someone buggered the system so it actually started to open again while the ship was venting. I haven't seen anything like this outside very bad movies. They meant to literally kill the entire crew while leaving the ship relatively intact."

"Fucking A," Jones muttered.

Levi sucked in her breath. Sabotage on this sort of scale...it was unthinkable, outside bad movies. She would sooner believe incompetent maintenance work than...she shook her head, dismissing the thought. There would be time to consider it later, back when they were safely back on their mothership.

"Major, the computer cores are completely depowered," she said, curtly. "If there are any surprises left onboard this hulk, we're not going to find them short of a full sweep. There's certainly no reason to believe that anyone is still alive. I would like to remove the cores, then abandon the ship."

There was a long pause. She had a feeling she knew what was going through her superior's head. The heavy cruiser was a valuable prize, even if she *was* literally decades out of date. The Solar Navy would pay a bounty for her. Perhaps not as much as they would pay for a top-of-the-line Tokomak battleship or a ship from a completely unknown alien race, but enough to buy each member of the squad a luxury holiday somewhere hot and sunny. Or a few thousand beers, if they wished. But, on the other hand, the ship was potentially dangerous. Without shields, without any internal force fields, a mere nuke would be enough to shatter the hull and kill the boarding party.

"Do so," Rhodan ordered. "Recover two of the bodies as well."

Levi allowed herself a moment of relief. "Aye, sir," she said. She switched back to the local channel. "Back to work, all of you."

"I'd like to sweep the cabins too," Sergeant Kath said. "One of the crew might have recorded something useful, if they're anything like us."

"True," Levi agreed. The spacers and marines had been cautioned, time and time again, against keeping personal records in places where they could be stolen by enemy forces. But there had been incidents where marines had been reprimanded - or worse - for doing it anyway. It was possible, vaguely possible, that the aliens had done the same thing. "But don't take too long."

"I won't," Kath said. "I feel naked in here."

"You *are* naked in your suit, Sergeant," Rollins put in.

"Just for that, you can help me," Kath said. "The sooner it's done, the sooner we can get out of here."

And hope that we can recover something that tells us what's actually going on, Levi thought, wryly. *No one wants to come back here.*

FIVE

Ideally, no one would require a helping hand - from anyone. And yes, there is something to be said for solving your own problems. But let's face it - not everyone can solve their own problems. Do we not have the moral responsibility to provide help? Indeed, do we not already help those who are oppressed by fallen cantons?
-Solar Datanet, Political Forum (Grand Alliance Thoughts)

Rebecca had never been a racist. Classical racism was almost unknown in the Solar Union, while anti-alien sentiment was very limited. And yet, looking down at the two dead aliens, she couldn't help feeling that they were just *too* alien. Merely looking at their insectoid bodies sent shivers down her spine. She couldn't escape the sense that they were looking back at her, even though they were very definitely dead. The bodies were completely inert.

"Death by vacuum," Doctor Rhonda Carr said, as she studied the live feed from the nanoprobes she'd injected into the first corpse. "There's no trace of any other factor, as far as I can tell."

Captain Yasser looked displeased. "No Trojan Horses? No enemy nanotech?"

"Not unless they've stumbled on something completely new," Rhonda said. She tapped the computer display. "There's no trace of any augmentation or genetic enhancement. I didn't even find any standard nanities in their bloodstreams."

"Odd," the captain mused.

"Maybe not," Rebecca said. "There are quite a few people who dislike the idea of tiny machines in their blood."

"It's a very unusual attitude for a spacer," the captain pointed out. "They'd *need* nanities for protection."

He glanced at Chief Engineer Daniel Wolf. "Did your team pull anything out of the ship records?"

"I can confirm that the ship's life support and safety systems were deliberately buggered," Wolf said. His voice was very grim. Rebecca knew how he felt. Tampering with the life support systems was an automatic death sentence in the Solar Union. "If the ship took a crippling level of damage, the hatches would spring open and the internal force fields would collapse. The entire ship would be vented at terrifying speed. I suspect the crew were deliberately encouraged not to use spacesuits to ensure a clean sweep."

Rebecca shook her head in disbelief. "If they can do that," she asked, "why not just blow up the entire ship?"

"They might have hoped to recover the hulk at a later date," Wolf said. He snorted in droll amusement. "Frankly, it would be cheaper to build a whole new ship than repair her."

"Probably," the captain agreed. "Did you pull anything from the datacores?"

"Very little," Wolf admitted. "The AIs are trying to dissect the cores now, but it looks as though the crew were careful not to write anything down. The automated systems did keep updating the logs, which will let us trace the ship's movements back in time..."

He shrugged. "From an engineering standpoint, I'd say they were pirates," he added. "They didn't have the experience or knowledge to check their ship for unpleasant surprises."

"Keep me updated," the captain ordered. "Madam Ambassador?"

Rebecca looked up. "There's no one to talk to here, is there?"

"I don't think so," the captain said. "The enemy crews are dead."

"True," Rebecca agreed. "How do you intend to proceed?"

"We'll set out again once we've finished scouring their datacores for anything useful," the captain told her. "I don't think there's anything to be gained by trying to hunt their base down, unless we get a solid lead. We'll pass what we've learned on to the local authorities and let them worry about the pirates."

"If they are pirates," Rebecca said. "They might have been something akin to the Hordesmen instead."

"Perhaps," the captain agreed. "They certainly didn't know how to handle their ships."

Rebecca nodded. The Hordesmen hadn't known how to handle their ships either. They hadn't even developed the wheel when they'd been forcibly introduced to galactic society and put to work as mercenaries. They'd obtained starships, eventually, but they'd never understood how their technology actually worked. Their sheer lack of awareness had eventually cost the group that had stumbled across Earth a starship...

...And unleashed humanity upon the universe.

"I'm sure we'll find out," she said, looking back at the unmoving alien form. "What will you do with the bodies?"

"Store them in stasis, for the moment," the captain told her. "I'll have them transferred to Hudson Base when we arrive. At that point..."

He shrugged. "We'll probably launch them into the sun, unless there is some reason to keep them," he added. "That's what most of the Galactics do with their bodies."

Rebecca raised her eyebrows. "You don't want to send the bodies home?"

"It depends," the captain said. "Would they *want* the bodies sent back?"

"I don't know," Rebecca said. "We'll have to check before we do anything."

She smiled, tiredly. Dealing with so many different races was a headache. There were alien civilisations that would demand the bodies returned, if they knew they'd been recovered intact. And there were others that would throw their hands up in horror if the suggestion was made. She dictated a short reminder to her day-log to research this particular race, just in case they were one of the former. There was nothing to be gained by giving them unintended offense. For all she knew, they might make powerful allies.

"We're going to destroy the hulks," the captain said. "There's no point in trying to salvage them. Right now, they're nothing more than a navigational hazard."

Rebecca wasn't surprised. The engineer had practically called the hulks worthless. She doubted there would be much, if any, prize money if the alien ships were somehow transported home. And yet, it still struck her as wasteful. Surely, the hulls could be broken down and recycled into something useful.

We'd still have to ship them home, she told herself. *And that would be a waste of time.*

She met his eyes. "Who do you think they were?"

"So far, all the evidence insists that they were pirates," the captain said. "Luckily, they ran into us instead of someone defenceless."

Rebecca nodded. Years ago, she'd thought it was odd that a towering galactic civilisation still had criminals and pirates. Now, she knew it was yet another factor ripping the multiracial civilisation apart. The Battle of Earth had unleashed shockwaves that had created a growing power vacuum, clearing the way for pirates, rebels and terrorists. Civil wars were already springing up as the Tokomak retreated from power.

And if we don't get the Grand Alliance up and running, she thought morbidly, *no one else will be interested in policing space.*

"Rebels, then," Elton mused.

"We finally cracked the datacores, sir," Lieutenant Jayne Fisher said. She was a cyborg, her left eye replaced with a series of cybernetic implants.

"They're definitely rebels, part of a faction that launched a military coup in the wake of the Battle of Earth. It's hard to be entirely sure - the translations aren't perfect - but it seems that they lost and had to scatter into deep space. Right now, they're raiding shipping in preparation for a return to their homeworld."

Elton stroked his chin. "So they became pirates," he mused. "Do they have a hope of returning home?"

"I don't know, sir," Jayne said. "Their files suggest that their commanders were optimistic, but they would have *claimed* to be optimistic... wouldn't they?"

"Probably," Elton said. He considered the problem for a long moment. "Their homeworld is...where?"

"Five hundred light years from our current location," Jayne said. "According to our files, sir, we have no direct contact with their rulers. They're a fairly small power that has never impinged on us or vice versa."

"And they don't pose a threat," Elton noted. "They're certainly not trying to block our way to Hudson and the Harmonies."

"No, sir," Jayne said. "Everything we found indicates that they were picking on shipping at random. They must have found the convoy a tempting target."

Elton smiled, rather coldly. If *he* were a pirate, *he* would have hesitated to pick a fight with a starship like *Odyssey*. Maybe she wasn't a true warship, but she was still armed. Had the pirates mistaken her for a liner? It wasn't entirely impossible, he had to admit, yet it still required a great deal of incompetence. Or had they merely assumed they could blow *Odyssey* out of space and then snap up the freighters at leisure?

"They won't be troubling anyone any longer," he said.

He shook his head, slowly. It was tempting, very tempting, to alter course and find out exactly what was going on, but it would take *Odyssey* at least a week to reach the alien homeworld. But it would delay their arrival at Harmony. Besides, whatever was going on, it wasn't *his* concern. He'd pass the whole affair over to Captain-Commodore Jenny Longlegs when they reached Hudson Base. If pirates and rebels were threatening the shipping lanes between Sol and Hudson, she'd have to know about it.

And she wouldn't if we ran into trouble and got blown out of space, he mused. *The Solar Navy would never know what had happened to us.*

He cleared his throat. "Do you think there's anything left in the datacores we can use?"

"The AIs are cracking the remaining files now, but their last update suggested that it was nothing of great interest," Jayne said. Her face, what little was visible, reddened. "There's a considerable number of entertainment files, including something we *think* is alien porn..."

"I don't think that's of great interest," Elton said. He didn't want to know what an insectoid race might consider pornographic. "If there's nothing else we can use..."

He paused. "Is there anything on the Harmonies?"

"Nothing apart from the standard navigational and background files," Jayne said. "I think someone must have purged the core when the starship was sold - probably several times, judging by the degradation. They didn't even bother to download the last set of updates from the galactic libraries."

Elton shrugged. Whatever else one could say about the Tokomak, they built their starships to last...and to endure a degree of mistreatment that would have horrified any reasonably competent starship engineer. The ships he'd captured or destroyed had been in space before humanity had mastered steam power, passed down from owner to owner until they'd eventually ended up in rebel hands. There was a story there, he was sure, but it wasn't one he had time to pursue. His mission to the Kingdom of Harmonious Order came first.

"Finish scanning the cores, then put them in stasis," he ordered. "We'll hand them over to Hudson Base when we arrive. They may have a use for them."

"Aye, Captain," Jayne said. She paused. "Do you think we'll be sending a mission there?"

"That's a decision for higher authority," Elton said, reprovingly. Jayne was young, too young. It wasn't a question she could reasonably ask. "I'm sure they'll decide how best to handle the situation."

Jayne nodded, embarrassed. "Thank you, sir."

Elton dismissed her, then turned his attention to the starchart. The alien rebels - whatever the true story actually was - didn't pose an immediate threat. They were quite some distance from Sol, after all. And besides, unless they had gravity-well technology, they were unlikely to be able to intercept other starships moving between Sol and Hudson Base.

And there aren't that many unescorted starships making the run, he mused. *We normally convoy ships this far from Sol.*

His intercom bleeped. "Captain," Biscoe said. "The freighters report that they are ready to depart."

"Very good," Elton said. "Inform them that we will be departing in ten minutes."

"Aye, Captain," Biscoe said.

"And confirm that their navigational computers have been updated with the next planned waypoint," Elton added. "I don't want to lose them somewhere in interstellar space."

"Aye, Captain," Biscoe said.

He sounded irked, Elton noted. He didn't really blame the younger man. Biscoe had served on *Jackie Fisher*, under Captain-Commodore Hoshiko Sashimi Stuart. He'd done well there, Elton knew, but *Odyssey* was a very different ship. And Elton, in truth, was a very different captain. He was, he knew all too well, far fussier than Hoshiko Stuart.

And I'm not going to hare off in search of adventure, he told himself, firmly.

He rose, feeling a flicker of annoyed frustration as he headed for the hatch. He'd hoped to give the merchant crews more time on *Odyssey*, but there was no way to know if the alien rebels had friends lurking somewhere within the barren system. His sensors *should* pick up approaching starships in FTL, yet...there *were* ways to spoof the system. Did the rebels *know* they'd lost three ships? They shouldn't, unless they'd had a fourth ship watching the battle from a safe distance...

We'll be gone before they can muster a response, he thought, stepping onto the bridge. *They may never know who took out their ships.*

"Captain," Biscoe said. He rose, offering Elton the command chair. "The convoy is ready to depart."

"Very good," Elton said. He sat, studying the display for a long moment. There was no sign of enemy ships, save for the two derelicts. The system was apparently empty. Even the sensors watching for starships in FTL were blank. "Tactical?"

Steve Callaway looked up. "Yes, sir?"

"Target the enemy ships," Elton ordered. "Prepare to fire."

"Aye, sir," Callaway said. "Phasers only?"

"Yes," Elton said. There was no point in wasting missiles on defenceless hulks. "Fire on my command."

"Aye, sir," Callaway said.

Elton sighed inwardly. Fleet HQ wouldn't be too happy with him for destroying the hulks, although they'd understand that *Odyssey* couldn't tow the alien ships to Hudson Base. There was nothing to recover, as far as he knew; there was certainly nothing to gain by leaving the ships intact for later recovery. Besides, it would be months - at best - before human ships could arrive to collect the hulks. Who knew what would happen in that time? The rebels might be so desperately short of ships that they'd try to recover and repair the hulks themselves...

They might not have the funding to buy new ships, he mused. *And even if they do, who'll sell them?*

It wasn't a pleasant thought. The last set of intelligence reports he'd read had insisted that all the known galactic powers were building up their navies as quickly as possible. They'd be putting starships that dated back *centuries* into service, arming them with modern weapons in a desperate bid to deter attack. Or, perhaps, to take advantage of the current power vacuum to start attacking their neighbours. The hulks floating near *Odyssey* might have value, even though they'd need to be almost completely repaired...

He shook his head. "Fire."

Odyssey hummed as her phasers lashed out, digging into the enemy hulls. The smaller ship disintegrated rapidly, practically melting under the onslaught; the cruiser held out, as if the dead hulk was struggling for survival. But it was futile. The hulk started to come apart, shattering into a cloud of debris. It was completely beyond recovery.

"Cease fire," Elton ordered. There was no point in hammering the last few pieces of wreckage. "Helm?"

"Yes, sir?"

"Take us into FTL," Elton said.

He leaned back in his command chair as the main displays went blank. If there *was* anyone watching the system, they'd know that *Odyssey* and her charges had vanished. Maybe they wouldn't have realised that the hulks had been destroyed. He doubted it - they'd made no attempt to hide the phaser fire - but it was possible. The rebels might just waste time trying to recover the ruined ships.

Or they might not have noticed at all, he mused. *Who knows when they'll realise that three of their ships are overdue?*

He shook his head, dismissing the thought. There was no point in feeling sorry for the aliens, even though he could understand why exiled outcasts might want to go home. Humanity had no interest in the alien civil war, as far as he could tell. The aliens certainly hadn't made any attempt to muster support. Instead...instead, they'd just attacked the convoy. It didn't matter if they were fighting for a just cause or not, not after they'd engaged his ship. They'd picked a fight and lost.

"We are underway, Captain," Marie said. "We will reach the next waypoint in two months, five days."

"Enough time for dinner, then," Elton said, wryly. He rose, nodding to his XO. "Mr. Biscoe, you have the bridge. I'll be in my office."

"Aye, Captain," Biscoe said. "I have the bridge."

Elton stepped into the office and sat down at his desk, hearing the hatch hiss closed behind him. A string of reports from the tactical and engineering departments were already waiting for him. He skimmed the first two, noting that *Odyssey* had performed well in her first true engagement. The aliens clearly hadn't expected a *real* fight, but still...

That should do wonders for morale, he thought, as he opened the ship's log. He'd have to write an account of the engagement - and of his thinking - while the whole incident was still fresh in his mind. *We encountered a trio of enemy ships and beat them.*

He shook his head, feeling tired. The voyage had barely lasted two months, so far, but the crew were already feeling the strain. Morale would improve, true, yet he knew that wouldn't last. They'd need a week or two of shore leave on Hudson Base - if it could be arranged - before passing through the next set of gravity points to their final destination. And he wasn't sure if he could arrange it.

I had better arrange it, he thought, morbidly. *We're not going to be in any state to impress anyone if we don't get a chance to blow off steam before we reach Harmony.*

SIX

How many problems have been caused by people claiming they had a moral responsibility to help the less fortunate? Colonialism and imperialism were justified by claims that they helped the natives - so, too, were everything from government handouts to social justice bullies demanding that the majority change to suit the minority. I say no - we do not have an obligation to help the less fortunate!
-Solar Datanet, Political Forum (Grand Alliance Thoughts)

Rebecca hadn't *wanted* to spend her time in a VR sim. She'd never really appreciated why people would *want* to plunge themselves into a virtual reality that was played directly into their heads, rather than a holographic simulation or a physical game. But, as the days turned into weeks and the weeks turned into months, she'd found herself spending more and more time lying in a VR tube, her mind inserted into a remarkably-detailed fantasy world based on a wizard school series she vaguely recalled reading in her youth. It was relaxing, she had to admit, yet...

The scene froze, just as the evil wizard prepared to cast a spell. He'd lost in the original series, if she recalled correctly, but the simulation changed and updated as Rebecca - and the other characters - made different moves. She felt an odd moment of disconnect, as if she wasn't quite sure which world was *real*, then her eyes opened. She was lying in a tube, staring up at a white ceiling. Her body felt odd. It wasn't quite *hers*.

It is, she reminded herself, sharply. The player character was a teenage girl, fifty years younger than Rebecca herself. *You're not her.*

She rubbed her forehead as she sat up. There were people who spent all their lives immersed in simulated worlds, as if they couldn't get what they wanted in reality. She'd thought of those people as pathetic, but she thought she understood them now. The fantasy world was far more *magical* than the real world. They didn't have to work to be great, they didn't have to compete against others who might be better...they could just withdraw into fantasy and enjoy themselves.

Her throat felt dry. She coughed.

"Drink this," Tyler said. He held out a glass. Rebecca took it and sipped gratefully. The high-energy drink tasted odd, but she knew it would replenish what she'd lost. "You asked to be alerted when we reached Hudson Base."

Rebecca frowned. They'd reached Hudson Base? "How long was I in the tube?"

"Three days," Tyler said. "I think you lost track of time."

"Oh," Rebecca said.

She checked her implants. Tyler was right. She'd definitely lost track of time. The VR sim had taken place over a day...her head spun as she tried to make sense of the differential between the illusion and reality. Had she really been in the tube for three days? She looked down at herself and sighed. Her body felt grimy. The tube had taken care of her physical needs, but she still needed a shower and a change of clothes.

"We'll be entering orbit in two hours," Tyler said, as he helped her to climb out of the tube and stand on wobbly legs. "The captain has requested that you accompany him to the naval base."

"Nice of him," Rebecca said. She kicked herself, mentally. If she'd realised she'd remain immersed in the simulation for so long she would have set a timer. "Did you bring my robes?"

"And a change of clothes," Tyler said. "I wasn't sure what you'd want to wear."

Rebecca considered it, even though her head still felt hazy. "Diplomatic robes," she said, finally. "We might be meeting non-human representatives."

"As you wish," Tyler said. He gave her a concerned look. "Can you use the facilities without assistance? I can call a nurse..."

"I'm not *that* old," Rebecca said. The nasty part of her mind was tempted to insist that *he* helped her to undress, just to see the look on his face, but she knew she shouldn't torment her aides. Tyler and his fellows had done a very good job, coming up with hundreds of possible scenarios for the coming discussions. "I'll meet the captain in the teleport bay."

"I asked him to arrange a shuttle instead," Tyler said. "I told him that you wanted to see the base from the outside."

"Thank you," Rebecca said, gratefully.

She headed for the washroom and stepped through the door. Her head spun again as she caught sight of her reflection, her face oddly unfamiliar...she groaned in annoyance as she ran her hand through her hair. She'd seen her face - no, *not* her face; the character's face - in the VR sim. She reminded herself, firmly, that she *wasn't* a teenage sorceress-in-training, but a sixty-year-old ambassador to an alien superpower. It wasn't quite the same, somehow.

Despite the odd sense of unreality - the feeling stubbornly refusing to fade - she forced herself to undress and shower, allowing the warm water to run over her body. Her arm throbbed with sympathetic pain where she'd been grabbed, during a fight...she caught herself rubbing it, even as the sensation faded away into nothingness. The dragons, the magic...it hadn't been real. None of it had been real. The knife she'd taken through the chest - she glanced down at her pale skin just to be sure - hadn't been real either.

There should be laws against using VR sims too frequently, she thought, as she turned off the water. Warm air billowed down around her, drying her bare skin. *They're dangerously addictive.*

She pushed the thought aside as she pulled on her robe, tied her hair back into a long ponytail and stepped out of the washroom. The Solar Union hesitated to ban *anything*, particularly something that posed no threat to anyone else. She could go to her canton's council and demand a ban, but she doubted she'd succeed. Too many of the youngsters saw the VR sims as normal...or, for that matter, regarded addiction as a sign of weakness. Those who fell into the VR sims and refused to come out should be left to it, away from everyone else.

A message blinked up in her implant, inviting her to the main shuttlebay at 1524. She sent back a quick reply, then headed out of the VR chamber and back to her quarters. She'd reviewed the files on Hudson Base, of course, but there was just time for a quick refresher and a large cup of coffee. She was going to need it.

And we're not that far from our destination now, she thought, ruefully. *I won't have time to fall back into the VR world.*

An hour later, feeling moderately refreshed, she hurried down to the shuttlebay. Captain Yasser was already there, his face unreadable. Rebecca felt a flicker of guilt, mixed with a grim awareness that she *needed* to avoid the teleporter. She clambered into the shuttle and sat next to him as he ran through the pre-flight checks, then powered up the craft and guided it out into open space. He didn't seem to need a pilot.

She glanced at him. "I didn't know you were a pilot, Elton."

He snorted. "We're taught how to fly shuttles during basic training," he pointed out. "It's one of the standard requirements before you're allowed to graduate and get unleashed on the universe."

Rebecca flushed. "Should I be trying to learn?"

"It's a useful skill to have," the captain said. "There are training courses on the computer, if you're interested. You never know when you might need it."

He moved them forward as Hudson - an Earth-like world, floating against the inky darkness of space - came into view. Rebecca watched, silently noting the sheer number of starships - almost all of them alien - coming and going, dozens blinking in and out of FTL every minute...she shook her head in awe. Hudson was a neutral system, home to billions of aliens from hundreds of different races, yet it throbbed with more activity than Sol. It brought home to her, in a manner she couldn't ignore, just how far humanity had to go.

And how badly we'll be in trouble, she thought, *if the Tokomak ever get their act together to crush us.*

Hudson - the name was a translation - was surrounded by thousands of orbital stations, ranging from giant industrial nodes to floating space habitats and asteroid settlements. She could see hundreds of warships from nearly every major interstellar power, brought together to guarantee the system's safety and protect the thousands of starships that moved in and out of the system every day. It had been a major coup for humanity, she recalled, when the Solar Union had been asked to contribute a battle squadron to the local patrol. The nine cruisers holding position in high orbit, watching over the system, were proof that humanity had definitely arrived on the galactic scene.

"That's Hudson Base," Captain Yasser said. Rebecca peered forward, finally spotting a large structure in high orbit. "They put her together out of prefabricated materials, rather than take the time to convert an asteroid or purchase a base from one of the other naval powers. Put a few noses out of joint, I believe."

Rebecca nodded. The files had said as much. Hudson was neutral, but the local shipping and engineering combines handled much of the construction work. They'd expected the human newcomers to pay for their services, rather than dragging prefabricated components all the way from Earth. But there hadn't been a choice. Too many Galactics were too keen on spying on humanity, hoping to steal some human technology for themselves. She still smiled whenever she recalled the story of the embassy humanity had opened on an unpronounceable world. The first security sweep, carried out after the building had been completed, had uncovered hundreds of bugs. It had been so overdone that some counter-intelligence officers speculated that there had been at least three *different* galactic powers trying to spy on the embassy and its staff.

She peered out the porthole as the shuttle flew closer to the giant structure. It looked like a wheel floating in space, although it wasn't spinning. Two giant freighters were docked to the outer edge, while three cruisers held position nearby, constantly sweeping space for potential threats. Indeed, there was a crudeness about the design that surprised her. She couldn't help thinking of something theoretical from the pre-contact era, when space stations had been little more than pathetic clusters of modules held together by spit and baling wire. It was easy to see why some of the Galactics looked down on humanity, despite the scale of humanity's achievements. They'd all sprung from a single Horde starship that had been captured by sheer luck.

Most of the other stations looked bigger, she noted. The Galactics had always thought big, even though their technology had remained stagnant for years. Their habitats were huge, bigger than the average canton back home; their industrial nodes were bigger still, turning out a constant stream of everything from starship components to colony settlement tools...everything an interstellar civilisation might need. She wondered, as the giant base overshadowed the tiny shuttlecraft, if the locals were trying to unlock their fabricators. The Tokomak would object, of course, but even *they* might think twice about attacking Hudson.

It's a very useful world, she thought, as the shuttle docked. *They'd be declaring war on the entire galaxy.*

"Welcome to Hudson Base," Captain Yasser said. He rose and strode over to the hatch, opening it. "It's been a long trip."

"Next time, I think I'll just climb into a stasis tube," Rebecca said.

She looked out of the porthole as she stood, trying to pick out *Odyssey* among the other points of light in high orbit. It was impossible. For all she knew, she was looking at a star - or an alien starship. *Odyssey* was huge, with plenty of room for her crew and passengers, but...she shook her head, telling herself that she should be grateful. Spending nine months on *Odyssey* had been heaven, compared to nine months - or even three months - on a cramped freighter or courier boat. She rather suspected she would have gone mad after spending even a *week* on a courier boat. No wonder their crews were regarded as weird by the rest of the navy.

Two young women were waiting for them on the far side of the hatch, both wearing blue naval uniforms without rank insignia. Rebecca frowned as they saluted Captain Yasser, trying to remember what that meant. They looked young...no, they *were* young. It was hard to tell, physically - there were too many middle-aged men and women who looked no older than twenty - but there was something about their attitude that told her they were genuinely young. They didn't have the odd *maturity* trapped behind a young face that she'd come to expect from her fellows.

"Welcome to Hudson Base," the leader said. "Please, will you accompany us?"

"Of course," Captain Yasser said, calmly.

Rebecca walked next to him as they made their way through a twisting series of corridors. Hudson Base was immense, yet almost completely empty. Vast chambers were barren, as if the base had been stripped of everything useful; she saw no one as they walked, not even a single crewman. Her implants pinged the local network, picking up the presence of an AI in the system, but it didn't seem disposed to talk to her. It was almost a relief when they walked through a set of interlocking doors and into a much more homey section. Here, she could believe that the base was actually *manned*.

"Commodore," Captain Yasser said.

"Captain," Captain-Commodore Jenny Longlegs said. She was tall and thin, with long dark hair that fell down her back. She had a friendly smile, but Rebecca couldn't help noticing that it didn't quite touch her eyes. "Welcome to Hudson Base. I apologise for the long walk, but we're not normally set up for guests here."

Because most people beam straight into the command section, Rebecca finished.

"You are a *long* way from Sol," Captain Yasser said. "Do you see many other humans?"

"Only traders, save for the occasional convoy escort," Jenny said. "Normally, I spend most of my time on my ship. The base has yet to be expanded into something more long-term."

She waved a hand at the table. "Please, join us for dinner. I've taken the liberty of having food prepared for you."

"Thank you," Rebecca said.

"Victoria and Cathy will bring it in," Jenny said. She nodded to the two girls, who hurried out of the compartment. "They're technically ensigns, but they're unlikely to see service off this base until we can get them to the academy."

Captain Yasser leaned forward. "Local recruits?"

Jenny nodded. "Their father was a trader - apparently, he was born into slavery but somehow managed to work his way up to command of a starship," she said. "One of his distant ancestors was taken from Earth a couple of hundred years or so ago. They inherited his ship after he died, but...it was seized shortly afterwards by the local authorities. I offered them posts on the base, as we were very short of crew."

"Decent of you," Rebecca commented.

"I prefer to think of it as practical," Jenny told her. There was a faint hint of annoyance in her voice. "Besides, I do have orders to protect humans where possible. Giving them a chance to prove themselves is just an extension of that."

She looked up as the hatch opened, again. "The locals do use food processors, just as we do, but there's a roaring trade in vat-grown meats," she explained. "I've discovered that some of the local animals are quite tasty, if cooked properly. We've had a lot of fun experimenting with different spices and cooking methods."

Rebecca sniffed the air as the girls brought a large stew pot over and placed it on the table, removing the lid to reveal a reddish-brown mixture. She felt her mouth watering - the smell was heavenly - and took the bowl she was offered eagerly. Captain Yasser seemed less interested - she wondered, suddenly, if he had something against vat-grown meats - but he took a careful bite of his stew. Rebecca tasted hers, then started to wolf it down with bread and sour cream. The meat tasted like beef, but different. She couldn't put her finger on it.

"You should sell this back home," she said, when she'd satisfied her first hunger pangs. "It's brilliant."

Jenny smiled. "It took months of work to get a tasty recipe," she said. "I knew it wouldn't be poisonous, but..."

Her smile grew wider. "Taste isn't something you can test for," she admitted. "We've all had experiences where something that smelled good turned out to be inedible. My crews have a contest to craft newer and better recipes using local ingredients."

Rebecca raised her eyebrows. "Your crews *cook?*"

"It's something to do," Jenny said. She seemed amused by Rebecca's surprise. "Hudson is an odd posting, Madam Ambassador. We are really doing nothing more than showing the flag. The most excitement we get here are the occasional convoy escort missions, none of which are particularly interesting. There really aren't enough traders out here to make it worthwhile."

"But showing the flag is important," Captain Yasser said.

"True," Jenny agreed. "The Galactics don't take us seriously. We're still a very small power by their standards. We have to make it clear that we can and we will defend ourselves."

She shrugged. "But we'll talk about that after dinner," she added. "Now tell me...what's been happening on Earth?"

Rebecca glanced at Captain Yasser, then sighed. "Civil war," she said. "And no end in sight."

SEVEN

I quite agree that we do not have an obligation to do everything for those less fortunate than ourselves, particularly those who have access to the same opportunities as us. But what about those who don't? Can we justify doing nothing, for example, if a woman is held down by a patriarchal family? She has no hope of escape without outside assistance. Should we not offer that assistance?
-Solar Datanet, Political Forum (Grand Alliance Thoughts)

"I read your mission brief," Jenny said, once the dinner was over. "I wish I was able to offer more help."

Elton raised his eyebrows. "You don't know anything about the Harmonies?"

"Very little," Jenny admitted. "*Something* has happened in their general direction, but *what*? We don't know. I've made a habit of collecting rumours passing through the system, yet...we don't have any solid answers. I'm honestly unsure why they bothered to send a message requesting an envoy. They certainly haven't tried to contact me."

"They might not have seen you as a senior representative," Rebecca pointed out.

"I *am* the local human representative," Jenny said.

Elton nodded in agreement. The senior officer on the spot, assuming there wasn't a dedicated diplomatic representative, had wide-ranging powers to talk to the locals on humanity's behalf. Jenny couldn't have made any binding agreements, naturally, but she could certainly have sounded out any visitors and forwarded their concerns to Earth. *And* she could have opened up communications channels too, if necessary. The Galactics would have understood that, surely. They'd *designed* the interstellar diplomatic protocols.

"I mean...they'd expect an envoy of high status," Rebecca explained. "Someone directly empowered by the Solar Union."

Jenny shrugged. "Realistically, we know very little about the Harmonies," she said. "I have checked with a couple of my contacts, but they all agree that the Harmonies are a riddle wrapped in an enigma. They control much of the interstellar shipping market in their sector, freezing out just about everyone else. I've heard that their control has gotten tighter over the last few years. They're risking the anger of the Tokomak if they keep going."

"They may already be risking their anger," Rebecca observed. "If they threw out a collaborationist regime..."

"Their borders are closed," Jenny said, flatly. "I can't tell you anything about their inner politics, Madam Ambassador. There's certainly nothing I can vouch for."

She shook her head. "I've established friendly relationships with the planetary council and most of the other powers interested in safeguarding this system," she added, "but the Harmonies won't talk to me. We can't push it, either. This system isn't under our direct control."

Elton frowned. "What is the political situation here?"

"Calm before the storm, I would have said," Jenny commented. She shook her head. "There are five gravity points in the system, each one allowing interstellar freighters to take hundreds of light years off their journeys. The Tokomak ensured that the system would remain neutral, allowing everyone to use the gravity points, but that may have changed now. I think it's only a matter of time before one of the galactic superpowers makes a bid for the system. At that point..."

Her lips thinned. "We may have to retreat at once, without a fight," she added. "My squadron cannot make a difference alone, while we don't have the contacts necessary to convince the other powers to fight beside us. The local government doesn't have the firepower to control the gravity points as well as the high orbitals. Getting back home won't be easy."

"They all signed the local agreements," Rebecca protested.

"Ink on paper," Jenny countered. "Well, electronic signatures in a data matrix, but you get the idea. The only thing keeping the superpowers from breaking them is the threat of force. Those gravity points are a licence to print money. And now the Tokomak are in retreat, no longer able to threaten a thumping to anyone who breaks the rules, you can bet your pension that *someone* is going to try to grab them. They'd be able to charge through the nose if they manage to fortify the gravity points."

Elton nodded. The Solar Union had never carried out a gravity point assault, but he'd seen the simulations and watched records from the pre-stardrive days. Gravity point assaults had been hellishly costly, draining the resources of anyone foolhardy or desperate enough to launch them. Traditionally, the attacker needed an advantage of three to one to guarantee success; in space, attacking through a gravity point, it was more like ten to one. The Solar Navy had done what it could to prepare, but everyone agreed it was unlikely to be anything more than a bloody slaughter.

"I assume you have contingency plans," he mused. "Don't the others?"

"Only to evacuate every human on Hudson and beat a hasty retreat," Jenny admitted. Her lips twisted in disgust "Like I said, we can't hold the system."

She met Elton's eyes. "I wish I had something more to offer you," she added. "Are you going to be staying?"

"If you can arrange shore leave, I'd like to rotate my crew through the facilities," Elton said, slowly. "Is that possible?"

"I should be able to book a beachside resort for your personnel," Jenny said. "It won't be ideal, but...Hudson is fairly used to providing entertainment for people from all over the galaxy. I was thinking more about looking up a few smugglers and seeing what they had to say. Even the Harmonies will have cracks in their defences."

"Good thinking," Elton said. He cocked his head. "Will they tell you anything useful?"

"Nothing of great value, I suspect," Jenny said. "But they *might* be able to tell you what's going on behind the scenes."

She shrugged. "I'll see what I can dig up," she added. "There's no guarantee..."

"We can offer payment," Rebecca said. "Or future favours."

"There's a risk in dealing with smugglers," Jenny noted. "And I'd prefer not to owe them any favours."

She closed her eyes for a long moment, then opened them and looked at Elton. "I read your report," she said. "Pirates and rebels...right now, their civil war isn't a matter of great concern to anyone on Hudson. It's too far away to be important."

"I thought as much," Elton said. "In the long term, though..."

"There are a dozen other such wars underway," Jenny told him. "I'll pass on the warning about raiders, but...most of the galactic races already know about the dangers. We may wind up organising more convoy escorts over the next few months."

Rebecca leaned forward. "Has there been any interest in the Grand Alliance out here?"

"Nothing, save for a few snide remarks about minor powers," Jenny said. She smiled, rather humourlessly. "Smashing a Tokomak fleet is impressive, but the vast majority of the civilians don't really believe it happened. Even if it did, they think, it was a very long way away. A flea bite compared to the towering empire that has dominated known space since time out of mind."

She shrugged, expressively. "I've made the sensor records open to all," she added, "but I don't think they're really convincing. There's even a whole string of sites on the datanet dedicated to debunking them. Some of the details we left out for security reasons have been taken to mean that the whole set of records were faked. Others...well, let's just say that we have been accused of having an overactive imagination. I never knew I could imagine fighting in such a battle."

Elton nodded. Jenny had commanded a destroyer during the engagement, if he recalled correctly. She'd won a medal for taking out an enemy heavy cruiser in a point-blank engagement. It wasn't the sort of thing someone could fake easily, although he had to admit that - with enough computer power - *anything* could be faked. The VR sims that had lured a third of the crew into a fantasy world were proof of that.

Rebecca coughed. "They accuse you of lying?"

"Not directly," Jenny said. "But they do come up with some fairly detailed analysis reports that *prove* the battle never happened."

Elton met her eyes. "How many of the local governments believe it was faked?"

"I don't think the governments *do* believe it was faked," Jenny said. She smiled. "For a piece of fakery, there *is* some fairly impressive supporting evidence. But Elton...many of the local powers are not inclined to annoy the Tokomak, if it can be avoided. Even if they don't care about possible retaliation from the Tokomak, they don't want to lower themselves to joining us. We're tiny by their standards. Any contacts between us and them will be quite under the radar until we prove ourselves."

"Again," Elton said.

Jenny nodded. "I'll ask around," she added. "See if they know anything about the Harmonies and their coup. But I'd be surprised if there was anyone willing to talk to us, even unofficially."

"Of course," Elton agreed. "They might not know anything either."

THE BEACH, ELTON decided two days after dinner with Jenny Longlegs, would have been heavenly, if there wasn't something subtly *wrong* with the sunlight. It was just a shade too bright...no, it was something his mind refused to grasp. His skin had already darkened automatically to cope with the sunlight, but his eyes couldn't adapt so easily. And yet, it was a chance to relax and pretend, just for a day or two, that he wasn't the commanding officer of a starship. He could tolerate an alien sun.

A number of his crew were swimming in the green sea or running up and down on the sandy beach, wearing skimpy bathing suits or going completely nude. His eyes followed a topless young officer, tracking her progress as she played nude volleyball with a number of other officers... he told himself, firmly, that he shouldn't be looking at someone who was indisputably junior to him. Others, not hampered by higher rank, were flirting outrageously or heading off into the bulrushes to have some fun. He couldn't help feeling a flicker of amusement, remembering the last time he'd made love on the beach. He'd wound up with sand in delicate places.

He looked up as a shadow fell over him. An alien was standing there, wrapped in a purple cloak that concealed everything but a pair of terrifyingly dark eyes. Elton sat up slowly, holding his hands out and careful not to make any sudden moves. There was no way to know what he was facing, let alone how the alien would react to anything that seemed hostile. It - he - might be nervous around so many humans.

"Greetings," the alien said. The voice was so flat that it *had* to come through a voder. "You are the human commander of *Odyssey*, are you not?"

"Yes," Elton said. The alien was speaking *English*? That was a surprise. Surely, speaking one of the galactic tongues would help them to understand each other. "I am."

"I am a broker in information," the alien whispered. It still spoke in English. "I have been informed that you are interested in the Harmonies. Is that correct?"

"It is," Elton said. One of Jenny's agents must have passed the word to the alien. "Do you have information to sell?"

"Yes," the alien whispered. "Much information has been denied to us. We know, though, that the Harmonies are quite disharmonious. Many factions are competing over which one will drive their future. Do you wish more precise information?"

"Yes," Elton said.

The alien held out a credit chip. Elton blinked in surprise. He hadn't thought to bring a galactic credit chip, not when everything on the beach had been paid for in advance. He'd certainly had no reason to expect an information broker to seek him out, although he had a feeling it had been done to establish the broker's credentials. Finding Elton amidst his crew was not a small achievement when, to aliens, all humans looked somewhat alike.

And speaking in English is a way of showing just how much they know about us, he thought, reluctantly. *And, perhaps, to put us at our ease.*

"I haven't brought my credit chip," he said, after a moment. "But we will pay a reasonable amount for your data."

"Ten thousand local credits," the alien stated. Its voice seemed louder, somehow. "I have a complete file, including everything I know and can source. It includes political outlines, astrographic data and other such materials."

"Give me a summary," Elton challenged.

"Payment," the alien insisted. "I can provide account details instead, at cost."

Elton sighed. Ten thousand credits weren't *much*, in the grand scheme of things, but he had no idea just how far the information broker could be trusted. ONI had openly admitted that it had no sources within the Kingdom of Harmonious Order. There was certainly no way to verify what they were being told. They might discover, after popping through the first pair of gravity points, that they'd been cheated.

And making us pay the transfer fee will add an extra hundred credits to the bill, he thought, sourly. The local authorities took their cut, naturally. *But we can afford it.*

"Give me the details," he said, finally.

The alien rattled off a string of numbers. Elton activated his implants, contacted the ship and ordered the transfer. There was a long pause as the alien waited, utterly motionless, until it received a confirmation that the transfer had gone through. And then a purple hand emerged from its robe, holding a single galactic-issue datachip. Elton took the datachip, trying to match what little he had seen of the information broker to any known race. His implants threw up too many possibilities for him to be sure.

"We wish you a long and happy life," the alien stated. It shuffled backwards. Elton wondered, suddenly, if the alien even had *legs*. "And you may contact us if you require more information."

Elton's implants flashed up an alert, a second before a teleport field enveloped the alien and carried it away. His implants tried to track the beam, but the best they could do was locate the orbital platform that had scooped the alien up. No doubt it would materialise there and then be beamed somewhere else. Trying to relay a teleport beam through multiple stations was asking for signal degradation and certain death.

He rose, placed the chip in his pocket and took one last look at the volleyball game. It wasn't much, not compared to a VR simulation, but it was *real*. His crew had needed, desperately, time away from their ship, even if it was just a few hours on an alien world. They were looking better already. Their captain probably looked better too.

Shaking his head, he triggered his implants. A moment later, *Odyssey's* teleporter scooped him up and deposited him on the teleport pad.

"Inform Lieutenant Fisher that I have something for her," he ordered, as he strode back to his cabin to change. It was hard to command respect in a pair of swimming trunks. "I'll meet her in her office."

He changed into his uniform, then hurried down to the tactical compartment. Lieutenant Jayne Fisher had been in the first group to go down to the planet, if he recalled correctly. Her visible skin had darkened like his, while she looked happier than the crewmen who hadn't had a chance to go down to the planet. He passed her the datachip, then sat down on a stool.

"See what you make of this," he said, as she examined the chip. "And make sure there aren't any unpleasant surprises."

"A fairly standard datachip," Jayne mused. She ran it through a set of scans. "No hidden nanotech, as far as I can tell. Room for a few yottabytes of data...not used, it seems. I don't think there's more than a few terabytes on the chip."

Elton shrugged. A lone human could spend his entire life reading eBooks or watching movies on a yottabyte-sized chip, if he wished. He doubted anyone could see everything on the chip before death came for them. The chip was staggeringly overdesigned, but that was practically a feature of Tokomak engineering. They'd wanted to make sure that *everyone* had a copy of everything they might *possibly* need.

"I think we can insert it into a secured reader," Jayne added, thoughtfully. "I'll keep it isolated, of course."

"Please," Elton said. Trying to sneak malware onto someone's computer had been a danger even before First Contact, when humanity had discovered a whole string of nastier technological tricks. "Make sure you scan everything."

Jayne nodded and slotted the chip into a reader, then attached it to a remote AI system. The files would be suspended, then dissected and analysed, section by section. If there was any danger, it would be discovered before it could pose a threat. Unless it was something completely new...

"Files scanned," Jayne said, finally. She cocked her head as she read the results, her implants blinking furiously. "Three hundred terabytes of data. No self-adjusting or autonomous programs detected. It's raw data, sir; text, imagery and video files. It appears to be harmless."

"Directly harmless," Elton corrected her, absently. "It proves nothing."

He closed his eyes for a long moment. They were three weeks from Harmony, although they would enter the Kingdom of Harmonious Order much sooner. Time enough, perhaps, to analyse the files...if, of course, they could be trusted. He'd have to ask Jenny about the information broker too. An information broker needed a reputation for honesty, but a desperate one might gamble that humanity wouldn't be in any position to take revenge.

And a piece of false information might just get us killed, he thought. *But we don't have anything else to go on.*

"Have the files copied, then studied," he ordered. "I want the ambassador and her staff to study them too."

"Yes, sir," Jayne said.

EIGHT

So tell me...when do we stop?
Yes, we can offer assistance. Perhaps even we should offer assistance. But when do we stop? Do we help someone who is unwilling to take the opportunities, when offered, or unwilling to summon the nerve to make a clean break from their past? We do not rule their lives, do we? At what point do we say 'enough'?
-Solar Datanet, Political Forum (Grand Alliance Thoughts)

"I cannot vouch for the broker," Jenny said. Her holographic image looked pensive. "I believe him to be honest, but I cannot guarantee it."

Elton nodded. "The data we can match up *does*," he agreed. "But that's only the astrographic data. We cannot verify any of the *political* data."

He sat back in his chair. Two days of careful analysis, while the crew enjoyed their shore leave, had given them new insight into the Kingdom of Harmonious Order...if, of course, it could be trusted. The data packet made it clear that the Harmonies were a *very* ordered society, more caste-ridden than pre-space India, something that made him wonder how they'd ever managed to have a coup in the first place. But then, divine right hadn't stopped countless European kings from being overthrown, murdered or simply rendered powerless by their political opponents. The Harmonies might be more human than they cared to admit.

"I'll be keeping an eye on the situation," Jenny informed him. "My squadron will be at your disposal if you need it."

"If you can afford to leave Hudson," Elton mused. "Can you?"

Jenny shrugged. "Hudson isn't a human world," she said. "Realistically, we're just a large picket out to show the flag. I'm not saying there won't be a price to pay if we go haring off into the unknown, but...better to come to your assistance than leave you to die."

Elton had to smile. The Solar Navy had determined, long ago, that no one would be left behind, even if it meant prolonging the war. Jenny *would* come to his assistance if he ran into trouble, he was sure. But the difficulty would be informing her that he *was* in trouble. The Harmonies - and four other races - controlled the shipping lines between Harmony and Hudson Base. He'd have problems hiring a courier boat if the local powers didn't want to get involved.

Which is why we need to work on those FTL drones, he thought. *But so far the techs haven't produced a viable model.*

He pushed the thought aside. There was no point in wishing for something he didn't have.

"I'll send messages up the chain as long as I can," he said, instead. "Send messages back to me, if you can."

"Of course," Jenny said.

She smiled, rather wanly. "I hope you and your crew enjoyed your shore leave here," she said. "The facilities aren't much."

"I think it will have done wonders for morale," Elton said, truthfully. "Thank you for everything, Jenny."

Jenny raised one hand in salute. "Good luck to you," she said. "Hopefully, we'll see you when you come back."

Her image vanished. Elton leaned back, taking a moment to centre himself. *He* hadn't had much shore leave, beyond a few hours lying on a beach. Nor had his analysis staff. There'd been too much to do. He made a mental note to approve their use of a VR chamber later, if they wanted it. There was no way it could match *genuine* shore leave, no matter what program they ran, but it was better than nothing.

The door chime bleeped. "Captain," Biscoe said, as he entered. "The last stragglers have returned to the ship."

"Very good," Elton said. He nodded to the nearest chair, inviting his XO to sit. "Any issues I should know about?"

"Something pinged the teleport biological hazard filters," Biscoe informed him. "Thankfully, further checks revealed that Ensign Khan had purchased an alien artefact that triggered a couple of alarms. We checked it repeatedly, then bunged it into stasis. It should be harmless, but the import board may want to have a look at it."

Elton frowned. "What *was* it?"

"Local artwork, apparently," Biscoe said. "An insect-like creature, posed and frozen in synthetic plastic. A fly caught in amber, to all intents and purposes. I've had a long chat with Ensign Khan about purchasing alien artefacts without prior approval. It *could* have been dangerous."

"True," Elton agreed. Cross-species infections were vanishingly rare, but almost always lethal when they did occur. The Tokomak had handled two disease outbreaks, according to the files, that had spread over a dozen races, killing millions in their wake. It was why the teleporters were programmed to scan - automatically - for potential dangers. "Did the check reveal anything interesting?"

"Nothing," Biscoe said. "It *should* be harmless."

"Leave it in stasis, for now," Elton said. "He can have it back when we get home."

He shook his head in wry amusement. This was the first time - probably - that Ensign Khan and his fellows had ever set foot on an alien world. He didn't blame the ensign for wanting to take home a souvenir, something his family would never have seen before. Hell, they *were* a very long way from Sol. No one was going to be visiting Hudson for a family vacation when it took eight months just to *get* there. The artefact would be worth more - much more - back in the Solar Union.

If they ever agreed to sell it, he mused. *They'd find it more interesting to keep it.*

He shrugged. "Any other issues?"

"A dozen or so new relationships that I know about, probably a few more that I don't," Biscoe said. "I don't *think* any of them will cause problems, but..."

Elton nodded, grimly. The Solar Union took a relaxed attitude to sex - anything that happened between consenting adults in private was fine - but there were limits. Naval regulations strictly forbade relationships between officers and crew of different ranks, even when people were confined to their ships for months or years. He might turn a blind eye to slips during shore leave - it wasn't as if there was a large human population on Hudson - but not to anything that caused disciplinary problems while the ship was underway.

"Keep an eye on it," he said. "I assume we can depart on schedule?"

"Aye, Captain," Biscoe said. "We've handed a couple of freighters over to Hudson Base - they'll be escorted to their final destination. The others will be staying with us."

Elton glanced at his terminal, then rose. "We'll leave as planned," he said, as he led the way to the hatch. "It won't be long now."

"And then we can do some *real* work," Biscoe said. He shook his head. "This wasn't what I expected after getting the transfer."

"You knew it would be a long and boring voyage when you read the mission orders," Elton reminded him. "Would you prefer boredom intermingled with moments of screaming terror?"

"It does have its moments, Captain," Biscoe said. He chuckled. "Mainly moments of screaming terror, but..."

Elton laughed. "You could be on one of the first starships," he said, as he took the command chair. "They weren't even *designed* for human occupation."

He felt his smile grow wider as he keyed his console, bringing up the ship's status report. Humanity's first interstellar starships - begged, borrowed or stolen - had never been designed for humans, even when the original designers had shared humanity's life support requirements. The lighting had been wrong, the gravity had been weird...even the corridors had been warped and twisted to human eyes, oddly out of proportion. He still shivered when he remembered the days he'd spent on an alien-designed starship, back during officer training. The designers had been humanoid, they'd evolved on a planet very similar to Earth...and yet, there had been something subtly *wrong* about the whole ship.

"Yes, Captain," Biscoe said. He took his own seat. "The ship is ready to depart."

Elton nodded as he worked his way through the reports, then switched his attention to the near-space orbital display. It was hard to be sure, but it looked as though the number of starships moving in and out of the system had actually increased. Hudson's gravity points accounted for a lot of it, he suspected, yet...he checked the records, looking back over the last few days. It *did* look as though the numbers had gone up in the last few days.

It could be a random surge, he thought, slowly. *Or it could be caused by problems further towards the core.*

He pushed the thought aside. His intelligence staff had done their best to draw information out of the alien systems, but - apart from a couple of intelligence brokers - they hadn't been able to make many contacts. ONI's office on Hudson was small, too small. Elton understood the reasoning - Hudson was thousands of light years from Earth - but it was still annoying. He'd have preferred something that told him what he should expect, over the next few weeks.

But they're aliens, he reminded himself. *Predicting their next moves might be impossible.*

"Lieutenant Williams," he said. "Inform the local authorities that we are ready to depart."

"Aye, Captain," Williams said.

Elton forced himself to relax, even though he couldn't help feeling a tremor of excitement. They'd been in transit for months, but now the *real* mission was about to begin. He hoped the ambassador and her staff hadn't wasted the last few months. They were about to discover, too, just how good their preparation work had been.

"The freighters have checked in," Biscoe reported. "They're ready to depart too."

"Good," Elton said. He would have had sharp words for any merchant skipper who *hadn't* been ready to depart. "Remind them to stay in formation."

"Captain," Williams said. "We have been cleared to depart orbit and proceed through the gravity point. They've sent us a transfer schedule."

"Very good," Elton said. He took a breath, taking one last look at the crowded high orbitals. It was an impressive sight, staggering even to one who'd seen the Solar Union. "Helm, take us out of here."

"Aye, Captain," Marie said.

A low rumble echoed through *Odyssey* as she slowly powered her way out of orbit, followed by the freighters. Elton had to admit, reluctantly, that the merchant starships were doing a good job of remaining in formation, insofar as they *had* a formation. The Tokomak had laid down rules for formation flying too, but humanity - and nearly every other race - had a habit of ignoring them. Whatever the original reason for the rules, and he couldn't imagine a largely unimaginative race coming up with them, they'd long since turned into bureaucratic excess. The odds of accidentally ramming another starship were low, very low. But then, he had to admit that a single accident, no matter how unlikely, would be disastrous.

And hundreds of starships pass through this system every day, he mused. *The odds of a collision might be low at any given point, but they probably mount up over the years...*

"Signal from the locals, sir," Williams said. "They're asking us to step down a couple of places in the line. Apparently, there's a priority ship going through."

Elton exchanged a glance with Biscoe. It wouldn't have been a problem, normally, but *Odyssey* was an acknowledged diplomatic ship. Was it a coincidence or a probe to see how they'd react? The bigger powers of the galaxy were used to pushing the smaller powers around...and humanity, despite the Battle of Earth, was still a very small power indeed.

And there might be a reason for a priority ship needing to take the slot ahead of us, he thought. *They may even be hoping we will object so they can claim the moral high ground.*

He shrugged. "Tell them we don't mind," he said. If it was a genuine emergency, there was nothing to be gained by blocking the priority ship. If it was a probe...it wasn't worth wasting energy and diplomatic capital to repel. "But inform them that we have to go through the gravity point in formation."

"Aye, Captain," Williams said.

The gravity point was invisible, at least to the naked eye. Elton had flown through several, during a brief stint on a courier boat. He *knew* there was nothing to see. And yet, *Odyssey's* gravimetric sensors could easily pick out the tight knot of twisted space directly ahead of them. Starship after starship moved up to the gravity point and vanished, others flickering into existence on the far side of the knot. The locals were timing it well, Elton noted. No starship remained within the point long enough to risk a collision.

"It must have been very different, back before the stardrive," Biscoe said, softly. "Spacers would have been *dependent* on the gravity points."

Elton nodded. Humanity hadn't dug up *many* records from that time - the Tokomak had destroyed or classified most of them - but ONI had uncovered enough to confirm that interstellar travel and war had been *very* different. The Tokomak and the other older races had expanded along chains of gravity points, often balked by local powers that dug in and held their gravity point against all comers. Engagements had often boiled down to the attacker trying to shove enough firepower through the gravity point to overcome the defenders before they were wiped out. The sheer slaughter had to have made World War One look tame. No one, not even the Tokomak, had been able to establish a *real* empire until the stardrive had been invented, allowing the gravity points to be bypassed. It had been the end of an era and the dawn of a whole new universe.

And we should be grateful, he thought, as the gravity point came closer and closer. *Sol doesn't have a gravity point, as far as we know.*

"We're in the line, Captain," Marie reported. "I'm powering up the gravity pulse generator now."

"Take us through as soon as you can," Elton ordered. Ahead of them, two alien freighters blinked out of existence in quick succession. "Mr. XO?"

"The freighters are ready," Biscoe said.

"Taking us in now," Marie said. "Jumping...now!"

Elton braced himself as the universe went dark, just for a second. The scientists swore blind that there was no sensation, that there *shouldn't* be any sensation...but everyone, human and alien, reported feeling something similar when they jumped through a gravity point. He looked up at the display as it blanked, then hastily rebooted, picking out a small cluster of space stations and industrial nodes a safe distance from the gravity point. There were starships heading in all directions, some dropping into FTL as they set course for their next destination. Others were heading straight for the next gravity point.

He studied the display as *Odyssey* pulled away from the gravity point, the first freighter materialising directly behind her. The system was useless, on the face of it. There were two rocky planets orbiting a dull red star, both too cold to be successfully terraformed. He was surprised that one or both of them hadn't been blown up to provide raw materials. But the system's *true* value lay in the gravity points. There were three of them, each one allowing starships to take weeks or months off their journeys. The Tokomak had considered the system important...

And they were right, Elton told himself. *The system might be useless in and of itself, but it does allow them to move their forces from place to place with terrifying speed.*

"Helm, set course for the next gravity point," he ordered. "Mr. XO, make sure the freighters stay with us."

"Aye, Captain," Marie said.

"Local command wishes us to remain sublight, Captain," Williams added. "No stardrive between gravity points."

"Bureaucratic excess," Elton said. "Humour them."

"Aye, Captain," Marie said. "ETA Gravity Point Two five hours from now."

Elton rose. "Mr. XO, you have the bridge," he said. "Alert me if anything changes."

He returned to his cabin for a quick nap, knowing that it was unlikely there would be any problems for the next few hours. The Harmonies Chain - the line of gravity points leading all the way to Harmony - was supposed to be relatively safe. There were no pirates, if the information broker was to be believed. The local powers ran patrols through the chain regularly, escorting clusters of freighters whenever they had the opportunity. *Odyssey* was unlikely to be molested in transit.

We really need to survey the Sol Sector for more gravity points, he mused, as he took off his boots and lay down on the bed. The Tokomak *had* surveyed the sector, centuries before humans had mastered fire, but there were officers in the Solar Navy who believed they hadn't done a thorough job. *It would be nice to have gravity points we could use...*

The intercom chimed, waking him. His implants insisted he'd slept for five hours, but he didn't believe them. It felt as though he'd barely closed his eyes. He rubbed his forehead, ordering his implants to flush his system. He'd pay for the fake alertness later, he knew from grim experience, but he had no choice.

"Report," he ordered.

"Captain, we just passed through the second gravity point," Biscoe said. He sounded worried. "I think you should see this."

Elton swore, silently, as he sat up and grabbed for his boots. Biscoe had more tactical experience than anyone else on *Odyssey*. He wouldn't be concerned unless there was a very good reason to *be* concerned. The ship wasn't taking incoming fire - thankfully - but there were plenty of other possibilities...

"I'm on my way," he said. "Hold the fort until I arrive."

"Aye, Captain," Biscoe said.

NINE

We stop when they don't need us any longer.
   Yes, there is the prospect of winding up running a person's life for them. Of wiping their nose and cleaning their arse and generally saving them from the consequences of their own stupidity. And yes, history is replete with idiots who have done just that - to their ultimate cost. But does past foolishness insist that we do nothing? Just because something ended badly, in the past, doesn't mean that history will repeat itself.
-Solar Datanet, Political Forum (Grand Alliance Thoughts)

Rebecca hated to admit ignorance.

It was dangerous, if one was a diplomat. She knew from bitter experience that an opponent who believed she was ignorant was an opponent who might try to take advantage of her. At best, he might assume that he could convince her to believe *his* version of events. But she knew it was better, most of the time, not to try to negotiate without knowing what was actually going on. It almost always led to embarrassing mistakes, if not outright career suicide and diplomatic disaster.

She studied the display for a long moment, wishing she actually understood it, then looked up at the captain. "What am I looking at?"

Captain Yasser frowned. "We popped through the gravity point thirty minutes ago," he said, pointing to an icon on the display. "What we saw" - his finger moved to another point - "was a small collection of fortresses, being assembled near the gravity point."

Rebecca blinked. "They're *fortifying* the gravity point?"

"It looks that way, Madam Ambassador," Captain Yasser said. "Five Class-VI heavy orbital weapons platforms, each one as heavily armed as a battleship. That's enough firepower to hold the gravity point against anything smaller than the First Fleet."

"I..." Rebecca shook her head in disbelief. "Captain, that's against galactic custom and law!"

The captain smiled, rather sardonically. "Tell *them* that," he said. "It was the Tokomak that enforced the laws, Madam Ambassador. Now...the Harmonies seem to believe that they have a right to start fortifying the gravity points in their sector."

Rebecca forced herself to think. "It's the Harmonies who are doing it?" She asked. "I mean...they're definitely the ones building the fortresses?"

"They're broadcasting the right ID," Captain Yasser said. "And realistically, we *are* within space they control. I imagine there would have been *some* reaction if their presence hadn't been approved."

"Probably," Rebecca agreed. The Harmonies were proud, according to the files. They wouldn't allow just *anyone* to move into their sector. "Do they pose a threat to us?"

Captain Yasser glanced at his tactical officer, who looked worried. "They made no attempt to impede our transit, Madam Ambassador," he said. "Technologically, they may not be any more advanced than the ships we thrashed during the Battle of Earth. But if they'd wanted to prevent us from passing through the gravity point, they could have done so. It won't take them long to move into position to blast *anyone* using the point. Even now..."

He keyed a command into the console. "As you can see," he said, indicating a red sphere surrounding the five icons, "they have the ability to fire missiles into the gravity point from their current position. Even one of *our* ships would have trouble realising that they were under attack, let alone raising shields and activating point defence, before it was too late.

If they moved closer, nothing would survive. A stream of unwary ships might be destroyed, one by one, until the defenders ran out of missiles."

Rebecca frowned. "So they could stop us from getting through the gravity point."

"Yes, Madam Ambassador," the tactical officer said. "And we believe that there are other such constructions under way at the other gravity points within the system."

"I see," Rebecca said, slowly. "Did they say *anything* to us?"

"Nothing," the captain said. "We're not even sure if the fortresses are online yet or not."

Rebecca looked back at the display. "There's no way to be sure?"

"They're not broadcasting active sensor scans," the captain said. "But that doesn't prove anything, not really. They could have their missiles and energy weapons locked on us using passive sensors alone. There's no way to tell if they're armed and ready to fire or not."

He dismissed the tactical officer with a nod, relaxing slightly as the younger man left the compartment. "Madam Ambassador...Rebecca... this isn't a good thing."

"I know," Rebecca said. "If they're willing to break galactic law, captain, what *else* are they prepared to break?"

"Good question," the captain said.

He tapped a switch. The starchart zeroed out, showing a cluster of stars surrounding Harmony itself. It looked odd, somehow, as if the kingdom had grown out in random directions. But it had, she recalled. The Harmonies had been spacefaring well before Persia had invaded Greece, intent on bringing the Greek cities to heel. They'd built their kingdom by moving through the gravity points, not by using the stardrive. It hadn't been until they'd copied the stardrive - at a price - that they'd started to occupy the stars closer to their homeworld. They'd been inaccessible without a working FTL drive.

"If they wanted to block an immediate thrust from the Tokomak, they'd need to fortify the gravity points here, here and here," he said, tapping three stars near Harmony. "They *have* alienated their former masters, even without fortifying the gravity points; they may not have a choice, given the firepower disparity. But fortifying the points in our direction, at best, will start an arms race amongst the major powers, as well as pushing the others to start fortifying their own gravity points. I don't like it."

Rebecca cocked her head. "You don't *know* they're planning hostilities against anyone."

"No," the captain agreed. "But if I happened to have physical control of a cluster of gravity points - economically important gravity points - I'd start thinking about charging tolls too. I could probably even use my economic stranglehold to force the other galactic powers to support me. There's no logical reason to have the gravity points out here fortified unless they *did* intend to exploit them."

"I see, I think," Rebecca mused. "Might they not be worried about the Tokomak trying to bypass the first set of fortifications?"

"They'd still need to concentrate on defending the shortest route to their homeworld," the captain said. He shook his head. "I don't like this, Rebecca. I have the uneasy feeling we're caught in a trap."

"But you don't *need* the gravity points to escape," Rebecca pointed out. "*Odyssey* does have a stardrive, doesn't she?"

The captain looked irked. "Of course," he said. "But how long do you think it would take us to get home if we couldn't use the gravity points?"

"Years," Rebecca said.

"Assuming a straight-line course, without being intercepted, we'd need at least seventy-one years to get home," the captain said. "It would take us at least twenty years to reach Hudson Base."

Rebecca considered it for a long moment. "Do you have any *proof* we're in a trap?"

"No," the captain admitted. "But my gut is telling me that something isn't right."

"Galactic order is breaking down," Rebecca agreed. "That makes our mission all the more important, Elton. If we can mediate between the different Galactics in this sector..."

"If," the captain said.

Rebecca met his eyes. "If we had to force our way back through the gravity point," she said, "could we do it?"

"No," the captain said, bluntly. "*Odyssey* doesn't have the firepower to take on five fortresses, even with the advantage of surprise. Those things are built to soak up a great deal of damage. We'd need more starships to assist us, at the very least."

He looked back at her, evenly. "And if we had to pop through a gravity point and discover ourselves under attack...well, it would be disastrous. We wouldn't have time to raise shields before we were overwhelmed."

Rebecca leaned back in her chair. "But you don't *know* we'll be attacked," she protested. "Do you?"

"No," the captain agreed. "I have no reason to believe that the Harmonies are doing anything apart from securing their borders. But as the starship commander, it is my duty to make you aware of the military realities. And those realities say that the Harmonies have gathered the firepower to make transit through the gravity points a very uncomfortable experience."

A very suicidal experience, Rebecca translated, silently.

She studied the display for a long moment, feeling cold. She'd never felt truly vulnerable, even when she'd negotiated with rogue governments on Earth. The Solar Union had been watching her, maintaining a teleport lock at all times. Hell, even the maddest government had known better than to alienate the Solar Union. Fanatics grew a great deal less fanatical when their leaders discovered they could be targeted and killed - ruthlessly - if they threatened the Solar Union. But here...she was on a lone starship - she didn't count the freighters - in the midst of a giant alien realm. It was quite possible that no one would ever know what had happened to them, if they ran into trouble. She couldn't help feeling naked.

And yet, there was no real reason to panic.

The Harmonies, one of the major galactic powers, had contacted humanity, asking for diplomatic discussions. Turning back now, when they were so close to Harmony itself, would be a major insult. At the very least, it would be harder to request another meeting when the first one had never even taken place. She knew the risks, she thought, but she also knew the potential advantages. Even opening up a singular line of communication - with the prospect of an upgrade later on - was worth the risks. And, she had to admit, it wouldn't do her career any harm either. No one else had negotiated with the major galactic powers as an equal.

"They asked us to send an envoy," she said. She looked up at him. "We have to carry on, I think."

The captain looked displeased. She understood, better than she cared to admit. She was the ambassador, but the buck stopped with him. Captain Yasser was solely responsible for the lives of a thousand officers and crew, ambassadorial staffers and merchant spacers. He could lose everything, if he made a single mistake. And yet, his superiors wouldn't be pleased if he turned tail and ran. She didn't blame him for his concerns, but they had to press on.

"They could have agreed to meet us somewhere neutral," the captain said, finally. "Why did they ask us to their homeworld?"

"Galactic custom," Rebecca said. "They're the ones who issued the invitation, so they're the ones who have to host the talks. And besides... we *want* to see their homeworld."

"True," the captain agreed. He strode over to the food processor. "Coffee?"

"Please," Rebecca said. She took the mug he offered her gratefully. "Captain, we cannot allow this opportunity to slip by."

"I hope you're right," the captain said. He sat, facing her. She couldn't help thinking that he looked older, somehow. His face hadn't changed, as far as she could tell. It was something in the way he held himself. "But things are changing, Rebecca."

"That's been true ever since the Battle of Earth," Rebecca said.

She took another sip of her coffee. "We upset the entire galaxy when we crushed a Tokomak fleet," she added, quietly. "We showed them that the Tokomak can be beaten. Captain...this is an opportunity for us to take a place amongst the oldest and most powerful races known to exist.

No, it's more than that. This is a chance to take a hand in reshaping the galaxy itself."

"At a price," the captain said.

"We cannot stand alone, Elton" Rebecca reminded him. "Not against the Galactics. I saw the same simulations you did. We could destroy a thousand starships for every one of ours and still lose. We need allies. We need people who can help us break up and destroy any countermeasures before Sol is crushed. And if that means taking a risk..."

She sighed. "I understand your concerns, Elton," she added. "And I appreciate the risk we're running. But I don't see any other choice."

"Neither do I," the captain said. "It just makes me wonder..."

His eyes slid back to the starchart. "It just makes me wonder, Rebecca, just what *they're* thinking," he mused. "Surely they have to know they're provoking their fellows."

"They may think that they have to block all the paths to their homeworld," Rebecca offered, after a moment. "They have enemies. What if one of those enemies decides to side with the Tokomak against them? The Tokomak could offer the galaxy, literally, to anyone who sided with them."

"At the cost of remaining in eternal submission," the captain pointed out. "But yes, you're right. The Harmonies might not be attacked by the Tokomak alone."

He traced out a chain of gravity points on the chart. "I'd prefer to send one of the freighters back to Hudson Base," he said. "Captain-Commodore Longlegs needs to know about this...I'm surprised she didn't already know. The entire galaxy would be talking about someone fortifying a chain of gravity points. But we need all of the freighters with us."

"You could hire a courier boat," Rebecca offered.

"I'd be concerned about the crew trying to unlock the diplomatic cache," the captain said. "I would happily bet you a thousand credits that the Tokomak designed the system to be unlocked, with the right codes. Even if we give them an encrypted datachip...I wouldn't care to gamble on it being impossible to crack."

"And to think that all the files swear blind that courier boats are never molested," Rebecca said, dryly. "I feel *so* betrayed."

The captain smiled for the first time in far too long. "Everything is changing, just as you said," he reminded her. "And old certainties are falling everywhere."

Rebecca nodded as she looked back at the fortress icons. The Tokomak had insisted on keeping the gravity points completely demilitarised, a measure that came with a nasty sting in the tail. *They* were the ones moving forces around, weren't they? They didn't want anyone trying to impede their fleets as they tightened their grip on their empire. Free trade was the excuse, but the underlying motive was far more sinister...

"I wonder," she mused. "Is this the first sign of a general revolt against the Tokomak?"

"It could be," the captain agreed. "But they're right next door, as far as the Tokomak are concerned. They'll be rushing to get their defences into place before they get hit."

Rebecca frowned. "How would *you* do it? I mean, if you were in their place?"

"I'd try to build up my fleets as quickly as possible," the captain said. "If I could, without being detected. Maybe start converting civilian starships to warships. It would be an uphill slog, though. Rebecca...the Tokomak are supposed to be able to fight and win wars against all of the other major powers at once."

"Supposed to," Rebecca said. "Is that true?"

The captain shrugged. "It depends on the assumptions you feed into the simulations," he said, quietly. "The Tokomak have the raw numbers, in theory. They have a vast stockpile of warships, missiles and other supplies...they also have a cluster of naval bases in position to squash any uprising fairly quickly. They also have interior lines, allowing them to shift forces from place to place faster than any of their enemies. But, at the same time...

"We know their officers are old, that none of them have seen a real war...well, save for whoever survived the Battle of Earth. We also know that their weapons are outdated, although their first set of opponents may be no more advanced. Really, we don't know how many of their reserve warships are functional. Do they even have the crews to refurbish and operate them? And now...some of the Galactics are fortifying their gravity points. The Tokomak might lose the early engagements, dispelling their aura of invincibility. Who knows what will happen then?"

Rebecca tried to imagine such carnage, but drew a blank. It was just numbers, billions upon billions of lives that were truly nothing more than just statistics. They would have had lives of their own, reasons to live, but she couldn't grasp them. It was far beyond her comprehension. She would like to think that the elder races would have enough wisdom to refrain from pointless slaughter, yet nothing she'd seen in her career had convinced her that the older galactic powers were particularly *wise*. Their unchanging universe was changing...

...And their grip on power was beginning to snap. *Human* powers had rarely reacted well to the loss of power, when they'd been aware that their rivals were slowly catching up. War had never been uncommon, wars aimed at preventing disaster...they'd rarely succeeded, even when they'd been superficially victorious. The cost of war had been catastrophic, bringing down the victors along with the vanquished.

The captain shrugged. "It's possible they'll accept whatever losses they have to accept, just to punch through the gravity points and take the high orbitals," he added. "They do have the resources to swallow those losses, if they wish. Like you said, they can trade a thousand for one and still come out ahead. It's also possible that they'll swallow their pride and come to an agreement with their former subordinates. We just don't know."

"That's another reason to be out here," Rebecca said. "We need to fill in some of those blanks."

"True," the captain agreed. "I just hope they're not planning to bar our escape."

"Me too," Rebecca said. "Me too."

TEN

People who do not learn from history always repeat it. And people who do learn from history have to watch, helplessly, as others repeat it. There's no way to avoid making a greater and greater commitment to 'help' without being accused of being heartless, if not worse. In the end, we wind up helping so many people that we beggar ourselves.

I am not heartless. But I believe we should put ourselves first.

-Solar Datanet, Political Forum (Grand Alliance Thoughts)

"There are another five fortresses holding position near the gravity point," Lieutenant-Commander Steve Callaway reported. "And I'm picking up hints of cloaked ships nearby."

Elton scowled. They'd passed two more gravity points, since stumbling across the first set of fortresses, one of which had been heavily defended. The other hadn't been defended, as far as his sensors had been able to tell, but there *had* been hints that dozens of starships had made their way through the system...going where? He'd expected to encounter more freighters, yet there had been almost none. He hated to admit it, but his instincts were telling him that something was deeply wrong.

"Keep us on course," he ordered, coolly. "Tactical assessment?"

"I'm picking up low-level sensor scans and shield generator pulses," Callaway said, after a moment. "I'd say these fortresses were active, if stepped down."

"They could be brought up to full readiness in seconds, Captain," Biscoe commented. "And they'll already have a passive lock on our hull."

Elton nodded, curtly. "Communications, send a standard greeting," he said. "And inform them that we intend to transit the gravity point."

He scowled as time ticked by, slowly. There didn't *seem* to be anyone in charge of controlling passage through the gravity point, but the fortresses were in perfect position to interdict *Odyssey*. He was all too aware that trying to double back would merely bring them up against another set of fortresses. Unless, of course, they headed out into interstellar space and dropped into FTL. He didn't want to take his ship close to that much firepower without permission to proceed.

"Picking up a response," Williams informed him. "Captain, they have cleared us to pass through the gravity point."

Elton knew he should be reassured. Free passage through gravity points *was* a hallmark of interstellar civilisation. It was a relief that *that* hadn't changed. And yet...and yet...the mere presence of the fortresses was ominous. It suggested that the Kingdom of Harmonious Order expected trouble. They might expect to be going to war with their neighbours.

Or they might already be at war with their neighbours, he thought, sourly. *It isn't as if we'd know anything about it until we saw the fighting.*

"Gravity point transit in seventeen minutes," Marie reported. "Gravity jump generator powering up now."

Elton scowled, feeling cold ice congealing in his chest. He'd never seen a gravity point so...so *inactive*. The fortresses were maintaining their silent watch, but nothing was coming in or going out of the gravity point. Perhaps it made sense, hundreds of thousands of light years from galactic civilisation, yet here...there should have been dozens, if not hundreds, of freighters transiting the gravity point. It looked, very much, as though their way had been deliberately cleared.

He watched the fortresses, half-expecting them to bring up their weapons as soon as *Odyssey* was within effective range. His ship was already too close, although he could swing around and avoid their fire long enough to escape. But the fortresses did nothing, even when the starship entered sprint-mode range. They seemed sullen, yet silent. He would almost sooner have been fired upon.

"Transit in one minute," Marie said. "Captain...?"

"Take us through," Elton said. He forced his voice to stay calm. The crew were well-trained, but they'd be shaken - badly shaken - if their commander sounded nervous. "Mr. XO, order the freighters to follow us one by one."

"Aye, Captain," Biscoe said.

Elton forced himself to relax as the last few seconds ticked away. He'd considered trying to take two or more of the freighters through the gravity point in the first jump, but that would have been unacceptably risky. In theory, the odds of interpenetration were low if the ships jumped together; in practice, there was just too great a risk of being slammed together and destroyed. The Harmonies would probably see it as an assault, too. They'd certainly be concerned about three starships exploding as they crossed the gravity point...

"Jumping...now," Marie said.

The universe sneezed. Everything went grey, just for an instant...

...And then the tactical console started to chime an alert.

"Targeting sensors," Callaway snapped. "They've locked on to us!"

Elton tensed. "Raise shields," he snapped. The display was covered in washes of red light, focusing on his ship. They didn't even have a solid lock on whoever was targeting them. "Stand by point defence!"

There was a long chilling pause. "No incoming missiles," Callaway said. Seven new icons - all fortresses - blinked up on the display. "I say again, no incoming missiles!"

"Move us forward," Elton ordered, sharply. The first freighter would be jumping through the gravity point at any moment. "Communications, send a greeting and ask for permission to fly to Harmony."

There was a long pause. "They're hailing us, Captain," Williams said. "Standard galactic communications protocol, galactic two."

Elton nodded, slowly. "Put them through."

He leaned forward, feeling a shiver of excitement, as the Harmony appeared in the display. He - or she - was humanoid, with green skin... what little he could see of it. The alien wore a silver robe that concealed everything, apart from his face. Even his hands were covered by silver gloves. The eyes were dark pools that were utterly inhuman...

"Greetings," the alien said. His voice was surprisingly human. Elton couldn't help wondering if he was using a voder, although most Galactics would rarely deign to use one in front of someone they considered an inferior. "I welcome you to our system."

"I thank you," Elton replied, in the same language. The Solar Union insisted that all naval officers had to have a working knowledge of at least two different galactic tongues, even though there had been complaints that it was a form of subtle imperialism. "We are pleased to finally lay eyes on your world."

He kept his amusement to himself. He'd been carefully briefed on what to say - and what not to say - over the last few weeks. The Galactics had a protocol, after all, and woe betide the person who didn't follow it. They might not be able to actually *see* Harmony - the world was well out of sensor range - but it didn't matter. All that mattered was ensuring that the first contact went smoothly.

"We are pleased," the alien said. "My speaker must now speak to *your* speaker."

The ambassador, Elton thought. The Harmonies, if the files were accurate, insisted on talks being conducted between people of equal rank. His counterpart, he assumed, would be a starship commander. In some ways, it was a concession; in others, it was annoying. *And she's been waiting for this for months.*

"My speaker will speak to yours," he said. He keyed his console, allowing Rebecca to join the conversation. "She will open communications."

The alien bowed and vanished. Elton frowned at the empty space where his image had been for a long moment, then moved his eyes to the tactical display. The Harmonies were *still* targeting his ship, even though they'd opened communications; the remainder of the freighters were spreading out, unsure what to do. Elton nodded to Biscoe - he'd have to comfort the merchant skippers - and then returned his attention to the display. The Harmonies might not be shooting, but it didn't make him feel any better. They were pointing enough firepower at him to vaporise *Odyssey* within seconds...

He looked at Callaway. "Tactical analysis?"

"Most of their tech is Tokomak-level, as we expected," Callaway said. "But some of their ECM generators are stronger than anything we've seen from the Tokomak. They've actually wrapped their fortresses in enough ECM to make targeting difficult."

Elton frowned. "You can compensate for it?"

"Yes, at close range," Callaway said. "At longer range, the fortress's exact location will be a little fuzzy. I wouldn't expect Tokomak-grade missiles to be able to lock onto the fortress without a direct link to a sensor probe."

"Noted," Elton said. He studied the blurred icons on the display, thoughtfully. "And beyond?"

"I *think* there are some cloaked ships nearby, but it's impossible to be sure," Callaway admitted. "Captain, they're jamming our sensors alarmingly well. I honestly can't swear to anything outside close-in sensor range."

"And we're really far too close to their missile batteries," Biscoe added.

Elton nodded. There were three fortresses within sprint-mode missile range, all capable of overwhelming *Odyssey's* defences and blowing her away if they fired in unison. He didn't think they had a hope of escape, unless they managed to jump back through the gravity point...where there were five more fortresses waiting for them.

He looked down at the timer, feeling cold. The Galactics, he'd been told, could take years arguing over the shape of the conference table before discussing the agenda. He wasn't sure he believed it, but as the minutes went on and on...he forced himself to relax, hoping that Rebecca wasn't about to start a diplomatic incident. He'd told her, often enough, just how dangerous it was to jump through a fortified gravity point...

"Tactical," he said. "Can you see the other gravity points? Are they fortified?"

"No, sir," Callaway said. "I can pick up the points themselves, but I can't detect any fortresses or minefields at this distance."

Elton's console bleeped. "Captain," Rebecca said. "I need to talk to you. Please can we meet in your office."

"Ah," Elton said. Technically, a captain wasn't meant to leave the bridge in a dangerous situation. It wouldn't look good on the post-mission report. But then, on the other hand, he couldn't recall any starship that had jumped right into such a dangerous spot before. "I'll meet you in my office in two minutes."

He rose. "Commander Biscoe, you have the bridge," he said. "Alert me the moment *anything* changes."

"Aye, sir," Biscoe said.

Elton took one last look at the display. The sensors were finally starting to compensate for the cloud of ECM, telling him things he hadn't wanted to know about their potential opponents. If their tactical sensors were a mark of their firepower, the Harmonies had crammed more missile tubes into their fortresses than the Tokomak had ever done. And, beyond them, there were very definite hints of minefields and cloaked starships. There was no way to avoid the simple fact that they were in deep trouble.

And this was meant to be a diplomatic mission, he thought, as he headed for the hatch. *I don't want to have to tangle with those defences in wartime.*

"Absolutely out of the question!"

Rebecca sighed, inwardly. She'd expected the response. It didn't make it any easier to bear.

"It's a reasonable request," she said, calmly. She'd talked to rogue warlords and alien governors. She could talk to a single starship commander. "They want you to deactivate and dismantle your weapons array while you're in their system."

The captain took a long breath. "There is no way that I will render this ship defenceless," he said, curtly. "Quite apart from the simple fact that regulations forbid it, I have no way to know what will happen in the future. We don't know what's actually going *on* in this system."

Rebecca rubbed her forehead. Talking to the alien had given her a throbbing headache. He hadn't used one word when twenty would do *and* he'd seemed to take a perverse delight in alternatively being accommodating and demanding. One of her staffers had wondered, on their private channel, if he was being pushed and pulled by two competing factions on Harmony, but there had been no way to know for sure. The Harmonies themselves seemed to be of two minds about the whole affair.

"It's a reasonable request," she repeated. "Would *you* want an armed alien starship orbiting Stuart Asteroid?"

"I would be happy to hold diplomatic discussions well away from anywhere *vital*," the captain countered. "I *certainly* wouldn't invite a starship to come all this way and *then* demand that it disarm itself."

He took a breath. "And I would *also* understand why some people would be concerned about the galactic situation," he added. "We don't know what's going on! Or did they tell you what's going on?"

"Nothing," Rebecca said. She looked down at the deck, wishing her implants would hurry up and fix the headache. "They just talked about security considerations. But we wouldn't be having any substantive discussions here anyway."

"Security considerations," the captain repeated.

"Yes," Rebecca said. She wished she'd been able to learn more, but the alien diplomat had spoken hundreds of words and said nothing. "They have to be a *little* worried about having an armed starship orbiting their homeworld."

"If their homeworld is as heavily defended as this gravity point," the captain said, "they'll have enough firepower to reduce us to atoms."

He calmed himself with a visible effort. "I can safeguard the weapons, of course," he added. "I can certainly make sure that they're not fired without authorisation. However, I cannot deactivate them, let alone dismantle them. It would render us vulnerable when we don't know what's *really* going on."

"Captain..."

"That's not something I can compromise on," the captain said, firmly.

"This might be a precondition for the talks," Rebecca said. She fought down the urge to yawn. She understood his point, but she understood *theirs* too. Seeing things from both sides of the table was the mark of a good ambassador. "Captain..."

The captain scowled. "And how many concessions are you prepared to make?" He asked, bluntly. "For all you know, this is a test to see how far you'll go to talk with them. This might be the first set of unreasonable demands. What next? Will they want to search the ship?"

"They do want to inspect it..."

"No," the captain said, flatly.

Rebecca pulled herself upright and glared at him. "It is a principle of galactic law that ships can be searched, when docked at a foreign port," she pointed out. Technically, the Solar Union had never signed the interstellar treaties, but it had usually honoured them. "And not one we can avoid."

"That only applies if the ship is a freighter *and* suspected of smuggling," the captain countered, stiffly. "As a diplomatic ship, which we are, we should be immune to search."

He looked back at her, evenly. "We have technological secrets," he reminded her. "The Galactics will want to know how we beat the Tokomak, if they have any sense at all. They *need* to copy our weapons, sooner rather than later. There is no way we can allow them to search this ship."

Rebecca scowled. He was right. They'd both be in deep shit when - if - they got home.

She rubbed her head, again. She had a nasty feeling he was right about the test, too. The Harmonies had good reason to believe - correctly - that humanity was eager to come to terms with them. And yet, they wouldn't see humanity as a peer power. Pushing and prodding at her, testing her willingness to make concessions...it might well be intended to weaken her bargaining position.

But if there is a war going on, she thought grimly, *they might have reason to be worried about us too.*

"Offer a compromise," the captain said. He leaned forward. "We'll give them a tour."

Rebecca blinked. "A tour?"

"A sanitised tour," the captain said. He sounded oddly amused. "We can show them around the ship, but never show them anything truly sensitive. They'd know they were being snowballed, yet they wouldn't be able to complain."

"You gave me a tour, as I recall," Rebecca said. Her eyes narrowed. She was in no mood for jokes. "How much did you hide from me?"

"Almost everything," the captain said. "We certainly didn't open compartments for you to take a look inside."

Rebecca made a mental note to discuss that later, although - she had to admit - there was no reason why they *should* have shown her everything. She held a high security clearance, but she doubted she had any reason to look at the starship's innermost workings. There was no need for her to know.

"I'll discuss it with them," she said, tiredly. Her headache was still pounding inside her skull. "And I hope you're right."

"I hope you're right, too," the captain said. He sounded pensive. "I'm feeling rather naked out here."

— —

"Captain," Williams said, an hour later. "They've sent us permission to cross the defences and enter the system. And they've given us a preset flight path."

"Forward it to the helm," Elton ordered. He glanced at the console. The ambassador had obviously managed to convince the Harmonies to drop at least one of their demands. *That* was a relief. He knew he couldn't disarm the ship, but he also knew he was in no state to press matters. "Marie?"

"It's a straight-line course to Harmony, Captain," Marie reported. "They're not trying to be fancy."

"Good," Elton said. The fortresses were still targeting *Odyssey*. A reminder of their power or something more sinister? He couldn't escape the feeling they'd flown into a war zone, if it wasn't a trap. Just what *was* going on? Hopefully, they'd be able to get some answers soon. "Take us out, standard cruising speed."

"Aye, Captain," Marie said.

Elton keyed his console. "Major Rhodan, report to the bridge immediately," he ordered. "We have a tour to plan."

ELEVEN

That is something of my point. We are putting ourselves first. We cannot hope to defeat a towering galactic civilisation without help. Heart - or heartlessness - does not come into the equation. The cold equations of military reality demand that we find allies who can help us defeat our enemies. Even if they do nothing more than soak up enemy missiles, they will be helping us.

We are putting ourselves first.
-Solar Datanet, Political Forum (Grand Alliance Thoughts)

Harmony was an old system. It teemed with life.

Elton was torn between awe and an odd kind of concern as *Odyssey* glided further into the alien system. All seven rocky planets seemed to be heavily populated, while giant structures hung over the three gas giants, and thousands of starships and interplanetary spacecraft made their way from world to world. The asteroid belt buzzed with life, so densely populated that he couldn't help thinking that the Harmonies were literally running out of living space. There were even a handful of habitats orbiting the sun, so close to the photosphere that he wondered just how they managed to remain intact. They had to have some pretty intensive shielding just to make themselves liveable.

The system was pulsing with energy signatures, each one marking the presence of a mining station or an industrial node. It was impossible to be sure, of course, but even the most conservative estimates from the analysis deck suggested an industrial potential that matched or even exceeded the combined industrial base of every star for a hundred light years around Sol. The sheer *potential* of the system was enough to strike him dumb, even if their fabricators *hadn't* been unlocked. He couldn't help thinking that it was no wonder that the Harmonies had convinced the Tokomak to allow them some degree of autonomy. They had enough industrial potential to give even the masters of the universe a run for their money.

His sense of trouble grew worse as more and more details flowed into the master display. It looked as though all of the gravity points were heavily defended, while the planets themselves were armed to the teeth. Harmony itself was surrounded by over forty orbital fortresses, bristling with weapons. And yet, there were some odd gaps in the defences...he puzzled over it for a long moment before realising that the fortresses had been towed to the gravity points and emplaced there.

A neat way of circumventing the ban on fortifying the gravity points, he thought, mentally saluting the Harmonies. It showed a degree of imagination he'd thought the older races had long since lost. *And they have enough firepower surrounding their homeworld, even without the missing fortresses, to give any attacker a very hard time indeed.*

"They must have felt threatened by *someone*, sir," Biscoe pointed out. "They've got enough firepower in orbit to ward off the entire navy."

"It looks that way," Elton agreed. The analysts had yet to calculate how much the defences had actually cost, but he doubted they'd been cheap. Even *Sol* didn't have such a powerful network of fixed defences. The Solar Union was more interested in funding starships than fortresses. "A bargaining chip against the Tokomak?"

"Or a make-work program for their industrial base," Callaway offered. "They might have needed to keep the system in shape."

Elton was inclined to agree. The Harmonies had a vast population - and a captive market - but there had to be limits. Their industrial base looked larger than they needed. And yet, he doubted that anyone was actually complaining. The industrial nodes seemed to be working at full capacity, churning out everything from fixed defences and mines to freighters and warships. Given just how badly the Tokomak grip on power had been weakened, the Harmonies might be trying to break free... or to engage in a little imperialism of their own.

They have quite a few potential targets within range, he thought, grimly. *And all of those targets are probably arming to the teeth too.*

Williams looked up. "Captain, they've selected an orbital slot for us," he said. "And they want to send an inspection party as soon as we enter orbit."

Elton kept his face expressionless. They'd made preparations, ensuring that most of the advanced technology would be permanently out of sight, but it still galled him to allow the locals to inspect his ship. Maybe it was a tour, yet still...he shook his head in cold annoyance. Rebecca was right - he would have wanted to inspect any starship taking up position near Stuart Asteroid - but if *he'd* been organising a diplomatic meeting, *he* would have arranged to hold it somewhere neutral. It wasn't as if there weren't plenty of potential meeting places in the interstellar void between Earth and AlphaCent!

"Send back a confirmation," he ordered, finally. "Helm?"

"I have the slot," Marie said. An icon appeared on the display, marking out a position in low orbit. "Captain?"

"Mr. Williams," Elton said. "Order the freighters to follow us in."

"Aye, Captain," Williams said.

Elton took a long breath. "Helm," he said. "Take us in."

He forced himself to relax as Harmony appeared in the display, a blue-green sphere dotted with grey marks. They were *cities*, apparently. Cities so large that they could be picked out with the naked eye. Even the smallest within view had to be utterly immense. It made him wonder just how the Harmonies managed to live in...in harmony. Humans would go insane if they were forced to live in such close confines. The murder rate in Earth's giant cities had been going through the roof even before the civil war had broken out.

Harmony's orbital space was crammed with giant structures, ranging from immense industrial nodes to immense orbital habitat complexes. None of them appeared to be converted asteroids, as far as he could tell. They'd all been built from scratch. Countless starships and shuttlecraft moved in and out of orbit, the former remaining sublight until they were a *long* way from the planet. It didn't look as though starships were *allowed* to drop into FTL until they were well clear of Harmony, although it struck him as pointless. Maybe it was a security measure...

A new icon blinked into life as the sensor readings were matched against the files from the information broker. "That's one of the Imperial Palaces," Callaway said. "It's currently the sole domicile of the Crown Princess. No one else is listed as living there."

"Noted," Elton said, dryly. "Keep us on course."

He shook his head in disbelief. The Imperial Palace was immense, a giant structure easily two hundred miles from one end to the other. He'd known there were some immensely rich men in the Solar Union who owned their own asteroids - one man had claimed his own moon - but none of them were quite so determined to show off their wealth. It wasn't considered polite, in the Solar Union. And yet, no one doubted that they'd earned their money. A Crown Princess, the heir to a ruling family that had controlled an entire cluster for longer than humans had known how to make fire...how could she have earned her place? She would never have had to compete for it...

"Entering orbital slot," Marie reported. "Taking up position, now."

Elton rose. "Invite our guests to join us," he said, heavily. "Mr. XO, you have the bridge."

"Aye, Captain," Biscoe said. "I have the bridge."

IT WAS GENERALLY believed, not least by the marines themselves, that the Solar Union Marine Corps had hired the most sadistic tailors in the galaxy to produce their dress uniforms. They might be stunning, at least to human eyes, but they pinched the wearer in a number of uncomfortable places. Lieutenant Levi Dennis had even heard, back when she'd been fitted for her first dress uniform, that the sadists hadn't bothered to make allowances for either breasts or penises. Given how badly her uniform pinched her, she had no trouble in believing that it was equally unpleasant for her male counterparts.

But she did have to admit that the dress uniform *did* help to keep her awake. She only ever wore it during formal ceremonies, where the vast majority of the marines either stood in line or marched under the podium. Nodding off wouldn't be disastrous - unlike falling asleep when she was meant to be on guard - but it *would* be embarrassing and probably ruin her career beyond repair. Now...

She stood to attention as the teleport field shimmered to life. The pad glowed with light for a long moment, then faded, revealing a trio of aliens. All three of them wore silver outfits that hid everything, save for their faces. A chill ran down her spine as she realised she knew nothing about them, not even their gender. They looked to be completely asexual, as far as she could tell. But then, she knew that meant nothing. As humanoid as the Harmonies appeared to be, there was no guarantee that they mated in any manner a human would recognise. There were races that laid eggs, races that pollinated like flowers, and races dependent on cloning technology to keep up the numbers.

The Captain stepped forward. "Welcome onboard," he said, in perfect Galactic Two. "My crew and I welcome you."

"We thank you," the alien said. His Galactic Two was perfect too. "We welcome you to our homeworld."

Levi listened, keeping her face impassive, as the captain and the alien exchanged a whole series of meaningless compliments. She understood the value of diplomacy, but did they really have to use such flowery terms? She was almost sure that neither of them really *meant* a word they said. She tensed, inwardly, as the three aliens stepped off the pad - they walked stiffly, as if their legs were shorter than they seemed - and strode past the marines. They paid no attention to the marines *or* their dress uniforms.

She almost smiled at the thought. She'd bet ten credits that no one below the captain would be acknowledged by the aliens and won.

A series of alerts blinked up in front of her eyes as she turned to follow the party. The ship's sensors had detected a number of portable scanners, ranging from fairly standard galactic-level tech to a couple of devices that hadn't been seen before. All concealed under the alien clothing, she noted. Nothing dangerous, as far as the sensors could tell, but she knew that meant nothing too. Her dress uniform included a number of badges that could be fitted together into a makeshift weapon, if necessary. Human - and alien - ingenuity could outwit any sensor, given time.

She'd half-expected the aliens to object to the marines shadowing the group, but they showed no sign of concern. It *was* fairly standard to have guests escorted onboard warships, at least under galactic law, yet the Harmonies might have protested on the grounds that they outranked humanity. She wasn't sure if that was a good sign or not. The alien scanners kept pulsing, sweeping the ship for useful data; the ship's counter-surveillance technology kept spoofing their readings, making it impossible for them to learn anything. Their naked eyes shouldn't see anything useful, she'd been assured. But she suspected that meant nothing too.

You have to be careful what you show a potential enemy, her Drill Instructor had warned, back when she'd gone through OCS. *You might see it as something meaningless, but they might draw meaning from it.*

Levi kept that thought to herself as they moved through the ship, starting with the secondary bridge and heading through sickbay before finally reaching the engineering compartment and pausing long enough for the aliens to ask a number of questions. She wasn't surprised when the level of pinging from the alien sensors increased tenfold, or when emergency sensors picked up the presence of alien nanoprobes. They'd started launching bugs into the ship's interior...Hopefully, the onboard security systems would be capable of neutralising them before they could send anything useful back to their masters. God knew that searching the entire ship for devices so tiny they couldn't be seen with the naked eye would be nightmarish.

She triggered her implant. "Better make sure we keep the communications system on lockdown, sir," she subvocalised. The aliens hadn't paid any attention to her or the other two marines, but there was no point in taking chances. "The nanoprobes might try to get into the system and subvert it."

"Understood, LT," Major Rhodan said. He was monitoring the situation through the ship's sensors, while a rapid reaction force was shadowing the alien party as it moved through the ship. "I'll be deploying countermeasures as soon as they leave the compartment."

Levi nodded, feeling another shiver running down her spine. She knew, logically, that the alien nanoprobes *weren't* crawling over and through her skin, let alone preparing to dissolve the entire ship like a sugar cube. But it was hard to escape the sensation of *danger*, of *violation*, that the mere existence of alien nanoprobes caused. She knew, better than most civilians, just how badly galactic technology could be abused, if it fell into the wrong hands. And trying to introduce them into a starship without permission was, technically, a hostile act.

The aliens showed no sign of awareness that their move had been detected. Instead, after studying the engineering compartment for a long moment, they insisted on returning to the teleport bay. Levi followed them, silently wondering how the captain managed to keep control of himself. No one, not even her very first Drill Instructor, had ever talked to *her* in a manner that suggested she was *nothing* to him. The Harmonies clearly regarded humanity as a *very* young race. Humans were children, as far as they were concerned.

Her lips quirked at the thought. Young or not, humanity had beaten the Tokomak themselves in open battle. Even the oldest Galactics couldn't ignore *that*.

And our technology isn't stagnant, unlike theirs, she thought. *Give us a hundred years and we'll have enough firepower to vaporise their entire navy overnight.*

She didn't relax as the aliens took their places on the teleport pad, ready to be beamed back down to the planet. If they wanted to introduce any more uninvited guests, they'd never have a better chance. And yet... and yet...she tensed, despite herself, as the aliens shimmered and vanished, fading out of existence. The scans were clear, but she wasn't reassured. It was possible - all too possible - that they might have missed something.

"Teleport complete, sir," the operator said.

"Very good," the captain said.

Levi resisted the urge to sag, somehow. Sweat was prickling down her back. She'd been in more engagements than she cared to think about, but none of them had felt quite so *dangerous*. The Galactics had plenty of rules for smoothing out disagreements between alien races - particularly as one race's smile could be another race's scowl - yet the Harmonies might well have been looking for an excuse to cause trouble. She'd seen enough dangerous places, back on Earth, to understand how bullies thought. They might pretend to be civilised, but only as long as it suited them.

"I've got teams already in engineering," Major Rhodan said, "but start running a security sweep anyway. I want every last atom of this ship searched."

"Yes, sir," Levi said.

She shook herself, then led the way to the hatch. The aliens were gone, but duty called. She had been the one who'd followed them...it was possible, just possible, that she would have a better idea where to look for any microscopic surprises. Unless, of course, the aliens had managed to sneak something in that the scanners had missed. A cloud of subversion nanities could do a *lot* of damage if they had time to start reproducing themselves.

We'd notice them before they became a threat, she told herself. *Wouldn't we?*

"THEY INTRODUCED TWO hundred tiny little spies," Major Rhodan said. The Marine CO was also the starship's security chief. "We *think* we caught them all."

Elton studied the datapad for a long moment, glancing at Rebecca before turning his attention back to Rhodan. "You *think* you caught them all?"

"The nanoprobes we discovered were all standard GalTech, sir," Major Rhodan said. "They were little more advanced than the nanoprobes we used ourselves in Afghanistan and the Middle East, back when we were fighting Islamists. If they were *all* on the same technological level, sir, we caught them all. But if some of them were more advanced..."

"They might have escaped detection," Elton finished. A powered-down nanoprobe would be very hard to spot. One programmed to remain hidden for hours - or days - might remain unnoticed until it was too late. "What were they designed to *do*?"

"Spy," Major Rhodan said. "They weren't dissemblers, sir; they were just programmed to spy and broadcast data. I don't see how they expected them to remain undetected indefinitely. Even if we missed them being released, we'd have picked up the signals when they started to phone home."

"It could have been a test," Rebecca said. "They might have wanted to see if we detected them."

"Putting spies on the ship is not a friendly act," Elton said, bluntly.

"I can lodge an official protest," Rebecca said. She leaned forward. "And, as you know, I have to go down to the planet. I can raise the issue with the locals."

"That would also tell them that we found the bugs," Rhodan pointed out. "And we'd lose any advantage that knowledge gave us."

"I think they'd assume the worst," Rebecca said. "We *do* have equal or superior technology to them."

"It makes no sense," Elton said. "But then, *nothing* about this makes sense."

He shook his head. "Be careful," he warned. "We *still* don't know what's really going on here."

TWELVE

Except this comes with a price. Alliance with a single alien race - just one - brings with it obligations. We might be dragged into a war we didn't want, a war fought on terms we didn't choose. How many of our ancestors were killed in wars that didn't concern their homelands, but had to be fought because of alliances?

I understand the value of having allies. But I also understand the dangers of having them, too.
-Solar Datanet, Political Forum (Grand Alliance Thoughts)

Rebecca wasn't sure, as the shuttle flew through the forcefield and out into open space, if she should be relieved or concerned that she was being escorted by a platoon of marines. They didn't wear powered combat armour, they didn't carry weapons so heavy she couldn't lift them without enhancement of her own, but they still looked terrifyingly intimidating. And yet, she knew the marines couldn't guarantee her safety if all hell broke loose. The Harmonies had *Odyssey* and her crew massively outgunned.

Except there is no reason to fear trouble, she told herself, firmly. *They're merely following conventional galactic protocol.*

She forced herself to relax, somehow. She'd studied galactic protocol extensively, but this was the first time she'd actually had to *follow* it.

Humanity's other allies were all younger races, young enough to overlook just how new humanity was on the galactic scene. Most of them had begged, borrowed or stolen their technology from their elders and betters too. But now...now she was talking to a race so old that they predated human civilisation by thousands of years. It was too much to ask, perhaps, that they treated humanity as equals.

The Chinese refused to deal with the Westerners as equals too, she recalled. The contacts between Imperial China and the West had been studied extensively, as part of her training, but Imperial China - at its mandarin-run worst - had been far less stiff-necked than many of the Galactics. *And eventually the Chinese broke under the strain of discovering they weren't the masters of the known world.*

She pushed the thought aside as the shuttle dropped through the planet's atmosphere, jerking gently as it struck patches of turbulence. Harmony was an old world, old and rich. The giant orbital towers - reaching up into low orbit - were an engineering feat beyond anything humanity had attempted, although the Solar Union had no *need* of orbital towers. And yet, Harmony was also incredibly overpopulated. It was impossible to be sure, of course, but the analysts on *Odyssey* believed that there were at least twenty *billion* inhabitants from a number of different races on the surface. Twenty *billion*! Earth, at its height, had never had more than eight billion souls...and *that* had been before Contact. Now, the Solar Union's population was expanding rapidly, but it had an entire universe to fill.

They could be moving thousands of people off-world every day, she thought, grimly. *They certainly have the tech for it.*

The shuttle rocked again, heading down towards Harmony City. The city slowly came into view, glittering under the sunlight. Rebecca had studied the orbital imagery on *Odyssey*, but they hadn't done the city justice. Giant floating buildings, held in the air by powerful antigravity fields; immense skyscrapers, each one over two kilometres high; dozens of smaller conical buildings, resting within green parks and forests. And yet, as she used her implants to peer through the shuttle's sensor array, it was clear that the wealthy parts of the city were surrounded by a sea of poverty. She'd seen poverty on Earth, but this was far - far - worse. Most of the immense city was strikingly poor.

"They're warning us to give the Imperial Palace a wide berth," the pilot said. "I'm swinging around to avoid it."

Rebecca nodded, not trusting herself to speak. This Imperial Palace was huge, far larger than any palace she'd seen on Earth. It looked as though someone had merged the White House with Buckingham Palace and Edinburgh Castle, then covered the resulting monstrosity in statues of famous heroes from the past. Even if the building was an administrative complex as well as the monarch's residence, she thought, it was still far too large. She would have been hopelessly embarrassed if she'd had to live there.

"The building is surrounded with a military-grade forcefield," one of the marines commented, grimly. "There's enough firepower surrounding it to deter a starship."

Rebecca frowned as she studied the complex and the surrounding buildings. It *did* look like a fortress, hidden away behind layer and layer of defences. There was no attempt to *hide* the defences either, no attempt to convince the local population that their masters felt secure in their power. She felt her eyes narrow as the shuttle dropped lower, heading directly for the embassy building. Imperial City didn't feel very safe.

"I've located the landing pad," the pilot said. "They've mustered a welcoming committee."

"Understood," Rebecca said. She glanced at Tyler. "Are you ready?"

"Yes, Madam Ambassador," Tyler said.

Rebecca nodded. As the Solar Union's designated representative, she couldn't talk to anyone below the king or *his* designated representative. Tyler, her aide, would have to handle the discussions with the welcoming committee, making sure the embassy met their requirements while parrying any attempts to speak directly to Rebecca. It would be a loss of face for her if she *did* speak to someone below her, even if it was about a minor matter. There were times when she thought that the Tokomak had devised interstellar codes of diplomatic conduct to provide a substitute for war. Certainly, a single mistake could have dire consequences.

"Take us down," she told the pilot.

The embassy came into view. It was small, compared to the palace, but easily large enough for a small army of humans. Rebecca wondered, dryly, just how many aides they thought she'd brought. Her entire staff - all thirty of them - would rattle around the immense building like peas in a pod. She made a mental note to remind them, when they arrived, to be careful what they said and did. If the Harmonies were willing to try to plant nanotech spies on *Odyssey*, they wouldn't hesitate to bug the embassy itself. The staff were probably spies too.

"The welcoming committee is waiting," the pilot said. The shuttle dropped down and landed neatly on the pad. "Good luck, Madam Ambassador."

"Thanks," Rebecca said. "We're going to need it."

HARMONY SMELLED, LEVI decided, as she and the rest of the marines formed a honour guard for the ambassador's staff. There was no stench of burning hydrocarbons in the air - she remembered that all too well from Earth - but there was the indefinable stench of too many unwashed bodies in too close proximity. Judging by what she'd seen as the shuttle passed over the city, they were right on the edge of the security zone. To the north, wealth beyond her ability to comprehend; to the south, poverty on a scale she understood all too well. It was very *human*.

Without even the chance to head to orbit to start a new life, she thought. She'd served in one of the migrant camps, protecting refugees from their former countrymen while the civil war raged around them. A number had joined the Solar Union, she recalled; some had made new lives for themselves, others had run afoul of the law and ended their days in a penal colony. *The people here are trapped.*

It made no sense to her. The Harmonies were wealthy enough to give *everyone* a decent lifestyle, weren't they? The Solar Union certainly ensured that everyone was fed, housed and dressed, despite a few old-timers muttering dark things about welfare queens. Hell, they could have shipped vast numbers of people to new colony worlds on the edge of explored space. But instead, they preferred to keep their people trapped in poverty. Was it really so important, she asked herself, that they stayed in power?

The wind shifted, blowing the stench over the walls. She hastily triggered her implants, dampening her olfactory senses. It probably *was* that important, if their rulers thought like humans. She'd seen too many tiny states, run by warlords, where keeping the population under control was more important than making their lives better. At least the warlords had known better than to mess with the Solar Union. Here...there was no one, not even the Tokomak, trying to give the poor a shot at a better life.

She forced herself to listen as the embassy staff abased themselves in front of the ambassador's aide. Levi had never heard such grovelling in her life. The leader was literally kissing the ground in front of the aide, while his staff were prostrating themselves as if they didn't dare *look* at their new masters. She supposed she should be glad they weren't human, if their promises of eternal service and servitude were even remotely accurate. The ambassador's staff would probably wind up taking advantage of them. She didn't want to think that some of the marines would do the same.

"Remember to be careful what you say," she subvocalised, as the greeting ceremony finally came to an end. "The embassy is probably bugged *thoroughly*."

She triggered her sensors as she walked through the door, sweeping the entrance hall for unwanted surprises. The hall was huge, large enough to take the entire company of marines and still have room for another platoon or two. It was decorated in a style that reminded her of Ancient Rome, complete with wall carvings of scenes from the past. And yet...her sensors picked up a dozen bugs, all tied into the building's datanet. It was possible - more than possible - that the computers and video systems were also designed to pick up and record conversations. Safeguarding the entire building was going to be a pain in the ass.

And probably impossible, she thought, as she led the way down a corridor. The proportions were all wrong, as if the building had been designed for someone taller and thinner. *There's no way we can rip out the entire datanet.*

"See what the techs make of the system," she ordered, shortly. "But warn them to be careful what they say."

The irony, she discovered as they moved from room to room, was that the Harmonies *had* made an effort to be welcoming. Each bedroom was perfectly designed for humans, while the food processors were loaded with thousands of different recipes for human-specific foodstuffs. *That was more consideration than she'd been led to expect.* She'd served in places where the marines had had to eat alien rations or rely on their nanities to turn alien food into something edible. She still smiled at the memory of trying to coax a fifth-hand food processor into churning out something she could actually eat without fighting her gag reflex.

And yet, the building *was* seeded with so many bugs that privacy was going to be practically non-existent.

"They're not insisting on anal probes, sir," she said, after completing the sweep. "But I seriously doubt we can secure even one or two rooms in this shithole without tearing up and replacing the walls."

"And half the datanet," Lieutenant Roaches added. "Sir, I haven't seen a less secure datanet since I was on Earth. The whole system is designed to record and monitor everything the users *do* on it. It's hardwired."

"I see," Rhodan said. "The Ambassador is going to *love* that."

Levi nodded. She'd grown used to a complete lack of privacy at Boot Camp - the marines had practically lived in each other's pockets - but the ambassador and her staff had presumably grown used to private cabins. Maybe they knew better than to open their mouths when they didn't *know* the room was secure, yet...she doubted they'd be comfortable stripping down when they *knew* they were under surveillance.

But then, the Harmonies are unlikely to be interested in human bodies, she mused. *They'll be more interested in what we're actually doing here.*

The thought made her smile, rather coldly. Interracial relationships - relationships between members of different alien races - were one of the few universal taboos, harshly punished when they were discovered. The Solar Union had never banned them, but most people believed there was no need to bother. Genuine interracial relationships were astonishingly rare. The Harmonies were unlikely to take any prurient interest in human bodies.

She put the thought aside for later consideration. "I don't think this building can be held for very long either," she added. "A single platoon of marines, without armour, couldn't hold the walls if they were attacked. I can and I will devise contingency plans, but..."

"Do the best you can," Rhodan said. She could sense his frustration. He should have been down on the ground with her, but he was also needed on *Odyssey*. "And make sure the ambassador is aware of the problem."

"Aye, sir," Levi said.

She smiled. "I'll also alert her staff," she added. "But I'm fairly sure they have nothing to fear."

"Unless they say the wrong thing at the wrong time," Rhodan said. "Make sure they know to use their implants to talk, if they want to discuss sensitive matters. The encryption codes should be impossible to crack."

Levi nodded. "Yes, sir."

IT WAS A truism, Rebecca knew, that each world had its own smell. She'd certainly learned that over her career, although she'd *also* learned that the smell tended to vary from place to place. Planets might be tiny on an interstellar scale, but they were utterly immense on a *human* scale. And yet, the stench in the air on Harmony was truly revolting. She had the feeling she'd want to throw up, if her implants weren't working to dampen her reaction to the stench. The stench was so strong that it was almost a tangible presence, hanging on the air.

She didn't want to look south, but she forced herself to stand on the balcony and look over the wall. The buildings looked broken down, more by lack of maintenance - she thought - than open war. Stagnant puddles of water lay everywhere, some glittering oddly under the fading light. Hundreds of aliens from a dozen different races moved listlessly around, some sitting down as if they no longer had the urge to carry on. Rebecca couldn't help thinking that they looked pathetic, when judged against the planet's achievements. She only had to turn her head a little to see one of the immense floating structures...

It said much about the Harmonies, she thought, that they tolerated so much poverty. Earth, for all its flaws, was a more civilised place. The Harmonies were a wealthy society - a *strikingly* wealthy society. She'd seen the towering civilisation they'd built. And yet, it was rooted in poverty on a truly horrific scale. She had no way to be sure just how many people lived in the city, but...surely, *something* could be done. Her heart bled for the children growing up in poverty, trying to find enough food to last them a day...surely, something could be done.

They're aliens, she reminded herself. *They don't think like us.*

She turned and walked inside, uneasily aware of the hundreds of bugs watching her. The marines had warned her that there was no way most of the bugs could be removed, not given the way they'd been installed. It was odd, frighteningly odd. Surely, the Harmonies didn't spy on *everyone* who visited their world. Or perhaps they did...GalTech could be abused easily, as she knew all too well. Given a couple of AIs and a complete absence of scruples, the Harmonies could spy on their entire population.

The doors closed behind her. It was a relief to take a breath and taste clean air.

It was a good embassy, she had to admit. She'd been in worse. The Harmonies were at least *trying* to make them comfortable. But the level of surveillance was far beyond a joke. She needed to lodge an official complaint, even though she knew it might make it harder to discuss any matters of substance. And yet, she was starting to doubt that they *would* be discussing anything important. The Harmonies seemed to be of two minds about everything.

She stepped into her office and nodded to Tyler. "Implants only," she subvocalised, using her implants to open up a channel. She'd had a lot of practice over the last few hours. "I assume they didn't get back to us?"

"They did," Tyler said. "We're to be given tours of the city over the next two days, while the Imperial Court considers our gifts and composes a response. So far, there has been no request for any high-level discussions."

Rebecca nodded, impatiently. On one hand, it *was* in line with galactic protocol. On the other, she rather thought the Harmonies couldn't afford to take it slowly. But if they were having faction trouble...

"I'm sure we'll enjoy the tours," she subvocalised. She would have, if she hadn't had the feeling that someone was playing games. "If nothing else, it'll give us a chance to get a feel for the city."

"And a chance to prepare an elaborate speech for the king," Tyler added. "You'll be officially presenting him with his gifts in a few days."

"Joy," Rebecca said. She understood why the king's staff wanted to inspect the gifts first, but she still found it annoying. "Did they have any response to the manifest?"

"No," Tyler said. He cocked his head. "They may find our eagerness a sign of weakness."

"And not lodging protests about the bugs is also a sign of weakness," Rebecca said, crossly. "What *are* they playing at?"

She sighed. "Better get a good night's sleep," she said. She couldn't keep the sarcasm from her voice. "Tomorrow will be a very busy day."

THIRTEEN

These alien races would also have obligations to us. They would be committing themselves to standing beside us and fighting to defend the Grand Alliance from its enemies. The blunt truth is that we need them and they need us. I understand the concern about diluting what we are - about warping our system to meet their demands - but we are locked in a war for survival. The Tokomak and their allies will not *see us as anything other than deadly threats.*

Our mere existence is a spanner in their works...
-Solar Datanet, Political Forum (Grand Alliance Thoughts)

"Captain," Major Rhodan said. "You're not going to like this."

Elton scowled. "I haven't liked anything since the day we popped through the gravity point," he said, darkly. They'd been in orbit for a week, during which time the discussions on the planet's surface had gone nowhere. Rebecca and her staff had been given the tour, but it hadn't escaped her notice that they hadn't even started talking about the shape of the conference table yet. "Hit me."

The marine grinned, then sobered. "This society is a panopticon society," he said. "The locals are *always* under surveillance. Big Brother has *nothing* on it."

Elton leaned forward. "Are you sure?"

"We've been picking up billions - literally - of datastreams from within Imperial City alone," Rhodan said. "I don't think that there's a single adult who hasn't been tagged with a nanotech spy, if they don't have a tracking implant. Everyone is monitored, sir. A couple of AIs would be more than capable of watching everyone on the surface, all the fucking time."

"...Shit," Elton said.

"It's like jail, only worse," Rhodan said. "This level of surveillance is staggering, sir. I don't think anyone dares ask questions, let alone step out of line. Anyone who does is probably snatched up before they can cause trouble and shipped off somewhere. I think the government is in complete control."

Elton swallowed, hard. He'd always been aware of just how easily technology could be perverted. The implants he used in his daily work could be adapted to enslave him, the starship's internal monitoring system could be ordered to spy on the crew...he'd watched the records from the Taliban's last stand. They'd been so utterly outmatched that none of the fundamentalist assholes had even managed to get a shot off before they'd been wiped out to the last man. He wouldn't waste time feeling sorry for them...

...But he knew, all too well, that such technology could easily be turned against its users.

He looked up. "If this is a high-surveillance state," he mused, "how did they manage to have a coup?"

"Good question," Rhodan said. "If the watchers were mere humans, I would have said that they simply got unlucky. God knows that monitoring umpteen billion humans would be beyond any purely human agency. But with a few AIs scanning every word for possible threats...I don't know *how* a coup could be organised. Perhaps it was just an act of desperation."

"Perhaps," Elton said. He was no expert, but he was fairly sure that coup plotters had to do some pretty intense plotting to make sure the coup wasn't followed by an immediate civil war. Getting everyone to go along with the plotters wouldn't be easy, particularly not if the military wasn't secured in a hurry. "Are they still trying to slip bugs onto the ships?"

"All of the freighters were given their own collection of bugs," Rhodan confirmed. "I think we can be fairly sure that this is a fairly regular thing."

"And no one has the nerve to complain," Elton finished. "They *are* a powerful race, aren't they?"

He leaned back in his chair. "What do you make of it?"

Rhodan looked back at him, evenly. "My honest opinion is that this society is going to explode, sooner rather than later," he said. "We may be wrong - so far, we have very little access to their datanet - but it looks as though the planet is rigidly stratified. The poor have nothing, not even the vaguest prospect of rising out of their poverty. There's no escape hatch, as far as we can tell; no political parties promising to make everything better. I think there will be riots on the streets soon enough."

Elton rubbed his forehead. "But you don't *know*."

"No, sir," Rhodan said. "If this was a human world, I'd be telling you to pull the ambassador and her staff out before the shit hits the fan. But this *isn't* a human world. There's no way to know what will set them off."

"I know," Elton said. "Let's hope they're less sensitive than the Tosh."

He scowled at the memory of a lesson, back in the academy. The Tosh had seen nothing wrong with having sex, whenever and wherever they wanted. They had none of humanity's elaborate taboos against public sex, none of humanity's concerns about monogamy and adultery...it wasn't uncommon for visitors to their homeworld to be startled by the sight of two or more Tosh fucking like scaly rabbits. But, for them, eating in public was utterly forbidden. A human visitor had nearly set off a riot by opening a Twinkie and eating it in plain view.

"Let us hope so," Rhodan agreed. "Right now, the embassy is almost impossible to defend, with or without live weapons."

Elton made a face. Firing on someone - anyone - who tried to get over the wall was the sort of thing that would trigger a diplomatic incident, regardless of the provocation. And yet, the alternative was leaving his personnel to be lynched. Rebecca was the ambassador, but *he* was the one in charge. He would have to decide between opening fire, and accepting the prospect of a major crisis, or leaving his people to die. The buck stopped with him.

And we can't even guarantee teleporting them out, he thought, grimly. *There are so many force fields around the complex that getting them up might be impossible.*

"I know," he said, finally. "Tell the guards to watch themselves."

Rhodan met his eyes. "They'd prefer clear guidance on what to do, *sir*."

Elton looked back at him, silently acknowledging the point. It was tempting to use weasel words, to do everything in his power to ensure that the blame landed on the marines - *not* on the man who was supposed to be in charge. His career would be destroyed if a major crisis occurred on his watch, whatever else happened. And *not* giving the marines precise instructions would only make matters worse.

"They are to use lethal force if the wall is breached," he said. "And take whatever steps they believe to be necessary to protect the ambassadorial staff for as long as possible."

"Yes, sir," Rhodan said.

"I don't like this, sir," Biscoe said, an hour later. "This system is mobilising for war."

Elton nodded, studying the live feed from a dozen stealthed drones. Deploying them within the system was an unfriendly act, but after the Harmonies had attempted to bug his ship he wasn't feeling particularly concerned about appearing unfriendly. All three of the gravity points were already heavily fortified, yet the Harmonies were doubling or tripling the defences. He wouldn't have wanted to try to punch through with the entire Solar Navy behind him. The planets weren't much better. There was so much firepower gathered to protect them that even the Tokomak would pause before challenging them.

"We've been tracking hundreds of warships moving in and out of the system," Biscoe added, grimly. "All from the Harmonies, as far as we can tell. They're actually cloaking and decloaking, seemingly at random. I'd say they were trying to confuse any onlookers."

"They've certainly confused us," Callaway added. "Captain, we've picked up enough starships to suggest that they've massed their entire fleet here."

"That's not too likely," Biscoe said. "They'd be leaving the rest of their space undefended."

"But we don't know which of our sensor contacts are real ships and which are nothing more than ECM drones," Callaway said. "They're definitely preparing for war. There's a *lot* of encrypted communications being sent, communications we haven't yet managed to crack. I think trouble is brewing."

"It certainly looks that way," Elton agreed, dryly. "Do you have an updated tactical survey?"

"They're a formidable naval power," Biscoe said. He adjusted the display. Each of the rocky worlds were surrounded by a large halo of tactical icons. "I'd go so far as to say they were fortifying their planets to allow their fleet to be deployed elsewhere."

"On conquest missions," Elton said.

"Probably," Biscoe agreed. He activated the starchart. "We don't know what they're thinking, but if they strike this way" - his finger traced out a pair of gravity point chains - "they could probably safeguard their positions against the Tokomak. It would be an effective declaration of war, I suspect, yet it *would* give them some defence in depth. Given enough time to fortify the new gravity points, they could bleed the Tokomak white."

He adjusted the starchart, pointing to a handful of other worlds. "Alternatively, they could secure these systems instead. That would allow them to block seven more gravity points, letting them counter any Tokomak move to outflank their defences by using alternate routes to get a fleet into striking distance. It would also let them levy a shipping charge on every freighter passing through the sector."

"The other powers would object," Elton pointed out.

"They'd also have problems trying to muster the force to retake the systems," Callaway said, enthusiastically. "Captain, I modelled out the entire war. It depends on the underlying assumptions, but if the Harmonies manage to fortify the gravity points...well, I'd say they had an excellent chance of hanging on to their gains. The only wild card would be Tokomak intervention."

"They're already running that risk," Elton said. *That* was well understood. The Harmonies had broken so many laws that, ten years ago, Tokomak intervention would have been a certainty. "It's quite awkward."

"They'll also lose if they sit back and wait for the Tokomak to drop a hammer on them," Biscoe said. "Going on the offensive is their only real hope for success."

"Maybe," Elton said. He couldn't fault their logic - it made perfect sense - but he felt that something was missing. "Are they launching invasion fleets now?"

"We haven't tracked any large fleets leaving the system," Callaway said. "But if they wanted to hit here and here" - he tapped a couple of stars on the chart - "they'd be hurrying their fleets through the gravity points, not sending them out in FTL."

Elton nodded, slowly. The Harmonies were doing everything in their power to conceal the full scale of their mobilisation, yet...something just kept nagging at his mind. It hovered, taunting him. He knew he was missing something, but what? Callaway might well be right, he admitted. The kingdom's entire fleet could be jumping through the nearest gravity point, one by one...and his ship wouldn't have a hope of tracking them. They were too far to monitor ships moving at sublight speeds. And yet...

"Try and slip a drone or two closer to each of the gravity points," he said. That wasn't the answer. He was sure it wasn't the answer. "See if you can track the forces coming in and out of the system."

"Aye, sir," Callaway said.

He hesitated. "It won't be easy, sir," he warned. "They have a *lot* of active sensors scanning space near the gravity point, including some we've never seen before. I don't think we can get a drone too close without being detected."

And they won't find it hard to guess who launched it, Elton thought, grimly. *It isn't as if there will be a long line of suspects.*

"Do the best you can," he said. "But try to avoid detection if possible."

Elton looked back at the main display. *Odyssey* had a solid lock on everything orbiting Harmony itself, as far as he could tell. It was unusual for cloaked ships to lurk so close to a planet, although he had to admit it was possible. And yet, beyond the high orbitals...the enemy ships were cloaking and uncloaking, seemingly at random. What on Earth were they doing?

They want to keep any watchers in doubt as to where their ships actually are, he mused, thoughtfully. *But they're doing it in a manner that cannot fail to convince any watchers that they're trying to hide something. Why?*

"Commander," he said, slowly. "Why would you want your opponent to *know* you're trying to fool him?"

Biscoe considered it. "To force him to watch you carefully," he said, after a moment. "Or to convince him that you're doing something when you're not. He might waste a lot of time because you jerked his chain. And if he comes up with an answer, he'll be too pleased to question it."

That, Elton conceded, was a good answer. But he didn't think it was the right one.

He shook his head in annoyance. Nothing about the entire situation made sense. The Harmonies had invited humanity to send a diplomatic mission, yet they were now dragging their feet on opening discussions. The Harmonies were fortifying every gravity point in their sector, something they knew would worry the other Galactics, yet they weren't even *trying* to defuse the tensions it would cause. The Harmonies had enough wealth and power to create a paradise, yet they seemed to prefer to keep their people in bondage...

It made no sense. It just made no sense. *Nothing* about it made sense.

He looked up at Biscoe. "Is there no civilian chatter we can intercept? No live-streaming? No television or radio?"

"Not as far as we can tell," Biscoe said. "The entire system is silent."

"We haven't even seen any independent freighters entering or leaving the system," Callaway added. "Not one, unless you count our hulls. I suspect the locals have a cartel system in place. Cargos fly through this system in their ships or they don't fly at all."

Elton nodded. It was technically illegal, at least under galactic law, but who was going to argue with the Harmonies? No one, with the possible exception of the Tokomak, had enough firepower to bring them to heel. They could make whatever demands they wanted, now they controlled the gravity points, and the other powers would have to listen to them - or find a way to force them to comply. There was no hope of comparing notes with an independent freighter. Or, for that matter, of a bidding war that might knock shipping prices down.

And it is frustrating too, he thought, sarcastically. The more he looked at the Harmony System, the less he liked it. *A surveillance state that would make Big Brother wet his pants, a complete lack of free chatter on the datanet...a probable lack of free enterprise too...This system is starting to look better and better every day.*

He looked back at the near-space display. It was impossible to avoid noticing the giant fortresses, well within missile range of their position. *Odyssey* would be in deep trouble if the fortresses opened fire, although only a complete lunatic would fire antimatter warheads anywhere near a populated planet. Not that they were the sole concerns, either. There were a whole string of heavily-armed planetary defence centres on the surface, their heavy weapons no doubt zeroed in on his ship. The tactical scans had told him things he didn't want to know about their weapons and defences.

Wonderful, he thought, as he rose. *This system is definitely starting to look like a trap.*

"Mr. XO, return to the bridge," he ordered, shortly. "Inform me if anything changes."

"Aye, Captain," Biscoe said.

"Mr. Callaway, simulate options for leaving orbit without their permission," Elton added, as his XO left. "See if you can find a way to get us and the freighters out of here."

"Aye, sir," Callaway said. He looked concerned. "Captain, do you think we'll have to blast our way out of here?"

"I hope not," Elton said.

He watched the younger man leave the compartment, then poured himself a mug of coffee and drank it, knowing it wouldn't be enough to stave off the tiredness. He wanted - he needed - something to happen, yet...yet he knew, all too well, that he'd regret it when it did. Perhaps the Galactics were merely trying to take it slowly, as their own protocols insisted. They'd devised the rules after hundreds of years of experience in interstellar diplomacy. But he couldn't help feeling as though something was about to go spectacularly wrong.

And to think we're too far from Hudson Base, let alone Earth, he reminded himself. *We're alone out here.*

It wasn't a pleasant thought. He'd thought he'd known what it meant, back when the mission had been planned, but now...now he was alone, thousands of light years from any potential backup. The buck had always stopped with him, yet now...there was no one he could ask for orders, no one who could take the burden off his shoulders. His instincts were telling him to withdraw the embassy and set off home, even though his career would be ripped apart when he returned home. And yet...

We can't leave orbit without their permission, he thought. *And will they give it to us?*

He cursed, wishing he could somehow lose the unease that pervaded his soul. There were too many things about the whole situation that didn't quite make sense, even for aliens. And yet, he couldn't leave. It would be a major diplomatic incident, at the very least. All he could do was wait and see what happened...

...And try, somehow, to escape the sense that the hammer was ready to fall.

FOURTEEN

That does, of course, raise another point. Can we, in whatever state, hope to beat the massed might of the Galactics? Would it be in our interests to delay the final confrontation until our tech reaches a point where we can crush them like bugs?

Founding a Grand Alliance might merely provoke them to move against us faster.
-Solar Datanet, Political Forum (Grand Alliance Thoughts)

"The crowds are getting bigger," Tyler muttered, as the aircar made its way back to the embassy. "And noisier."

Rebecca nodded. The embassy was surrounded by crowds; some holding up placards marked in a dozen different languages, some just watching and waiting for *something* to happen. It looked about as spontaneous as a pro-government rally in a rogue state, where all the protesters were paid and everything from pre-printed placards to flags for burning were handed out by the organisers. Quite why any of the rogue governments believed the protests influenced opinion in the Solar Union was beyond her...

She shook her head. The gathering crowds could *not* have materialised without someone in the planetary government either authorising them or simply turning a blind eye. And she'd seen enough evidence of just how determined the government was to retain control that she refused to believe that the crowds *weren't* authorised. The Kingdom of Harmonious Order was so repressive that even the Soviet Union looked a model of freedom, compared to the alien society. There was no way the general population could organise a protest march without being squashed ruthlessly. If there was an underground movement, according to her staff, it was buried deep below the surface.

Which makes sense, she thought, as the aircar flew over the walls and dropped down to the landing pad. *They have no way of finding allies without being detected and arrested.*

It wasn't a pleasant thought, she had to admit. Back home, the datanet was almost completely unregulated. Anyone could say anything on a datanet forum without fear of arrest, although it was also true that hardly anyone was given credence unless they attached their name to their posts. She could organise a political movement, for better or worse, in the comfort of her sitting room. But here...the datanet was so rigorously monitored that anyone who sent an encrypted message - or even a message that looked a little suspicious - could expect to have to answer some very uncomfortable questions. The government's control pervaded everything.

She climbed out of the aircar and walked through the main door. Her implants blinked up a series of alerts as the sterilising field flickered to life, sweeping over her body before vanishing again. The marine on the far side of the security field beckoned her through, then pointed to his portable terminal. Rebecca's body was covered in red flecks of light.

"Over thirty bugs today," the marine said, cheerfully. His name was John, Rebecca remembered. He was friendly, but also very professional. "And twenty-seven on Mr. Tyler."

"I must be getting more important," Tyler said, amused. His light tone couldn't conceal his concern. "Did you promote me when I wasn't looking?"

"Your new title is Assistant Paperwork Filer," Rebecca said. "It comes with a pay cut and extra hours."

Her skin itched. She knew she was imagining it, but it still itched. She needed a shower and a good night's sleep. "Did you get all of the bugs?"

"As far as I can tell," John said. He tapped his terminal, meaningfully. "There's no trace of anything left, but they *might* have managed to power down a bug or two before you walked through the field."

"The security sweeps will pick it up," Rebecca said. She glanced at Tyler. "I'll see you tomorrow."

"Of course, Madam Ambassador," Tyler said.

He nodded to her, then hurried down the corridor. Rebecca followed him at a more sedate pace, silently composing her report. There wasn't much to say. They'd been given a tour of yet another industrial complex, followed by a pair of museums showcasing the kingdom's achievements before the Tokomak had invented the stardrive and turned galactic society on its head. She would have enjoyed the latter, she thought, if they hadn't been such obvious propaganda pieces. Entire swathes of history had been glossed over to promote the kingdom's preferred narrative.

And we saw too many poor people struggling to survive, she thought. The sense of pure hopelessness had been overpowering. Even the worst places on Earth hadn't been *quite* so bad. *This place has been stripped of all hope for far too long.*

She walked into her suite, checked the processor for any new messages from *Odyssey*, then undressed and stepped into the shower. The water ran down her skin, making her feel better even though she knew that - too - was her imagination. If a nanotech bug had managed to remain attached to her, despite the security sweep, it wouldn't be dislodged by a tidal wave of water. Rebecca shivered at the thought, despite the warmth. *She* could leave at any moment and go back home, while the locals were trapped. They would spend the rest of their days in a giant prison camp, their every word and deed monitored 24/7. It was utterly maddening.

Her implants threw up another message. Tyler was trying to call her. "Yes?"

"Madam Ambassador, we just received a message from the local diplomatic service," Tyler said. "The king wishes to see you. Immediately."

Rebecca blinked in surprise. She hadn't expected to meet the king personally, only his representatives. The endless dance of galactic diplomacy certainly didn't allow ambassadors to meet planetary rulers, even ceremonially. Everything she'd seen had led her to believe that the Harmonies would sooner have surrendered unconditionally than break the rules of galactic diplomacy. If nothing else, representatives could be quietly overridden if they conceded too much. Meeting the king in person...

Her mouth was suddenly dry. "Inform the diplomats that we will attend him as soon as possible," she said, swallowing hard. What *were* they playing at? Normally, a meeting between high-ranking representatives would be choreographed a week in advance. And a meeting with the king himself was unprecedented. "And then have the aircar put on alert, with a marine escort..."

"They are requesting a *quiet* meeting," Tyler said. "They've already cleared you and one aide through the security zone."

Rebecca gritted her teeth as she stepped out of the shower and reached for a towel. "I see," she said. A *covert* meeting made *some* sense, perhaps. "They don't want any inconvenient witnesses?"

"Or escorts," Tyler said.

They might want to take me prisoner, Rebecca mused. She dismissed the thought as quickly as it had come. If the Harmonies wanted to capture or kill the diplomatic mission, they didn't have to resort to trickery. They were trapped on the surface, while their starship was trapped in low orbit. *They could blow Odyssey away in seconds if they wished.*

She finished drying herself, then donned her robe. "Inform Captain Yasser that we will be accepting their invitation," she said. She had no idea what was going on, but she knew they needed to find out. "And then ready the aircar for immediate departure."

"Of course, Ambassador," Tyler said.

Rebecca took a moment to centre herself, then checked her appearance in the mirror. The Harmonies were stiff-necked enough to use any flaw in her appearance against her, if they wanted to end the talks. But then, the talks hadn't even started yet! She drew on her implants for a long moment, using them to flush the last of the tiredness out of her body. She'd pay for it later, she was sure, but there was no choice. She *needed* to be alert when she faced the king.

A new set of messages popped up in her implants as she strode back towards the main door, each one warning of potential disaster. She didn't blame the marines - or her staff - for being concerned, but they *had* to accept the invitation. Perhaps something had happened in orbit...she checked the latest set of reports from the orbiting starship, seeing nothing that might explain the sudden change in policy. Maybe something had happened further down the gravity point chain. She hoped, as she clambered into the aircar, that the Tokomak hadn't begun an offensive. The Harmonies had fortified the gravity points, but the Tokomak could push through if they were willing to soak up the casualties. *They* could afford to trade a thousand starships for one and still come out ahead.

As Captain Yasser keeps reminding me, she thought, wryly. *But could anyone hope to soak up such losses indefinitely?*

She forced herself to relax as the aircar rose into the air - guided by the automated air traffic control system - and headed north, towards the Imperial Palace. There was little protocol for meeting the king, save for a handful of guidelines for meetings between different heads of state. None of them were particularly helpful. She was neither going as an equal - she was a mere representative - nor was she going to pay homage to her superior. She'd just have to wing it and hope she avoided any catastrophic mistakes. It would have been exciting, she thought, if the meeting hadn't promised to be dangerous.

The aircar passed through a dozen layers of security before dropping down and landing neatly on an isolated landing pad. A team of security officers waved a dozen sensors over their bodies, before - reluctantly - allowing them to proceed through the nearest door. They were silent, but her implants picked up dozens of encrypted burst transmissions...clearly, they were at least as heavily augmented as herself. A lone alien wearing a long silver robe and the insignia of a senior diplomatic official met her on the far side, his face expressionless. And yet, there was something about the way he moved that suggested he was agitated.

Of course he is, she thought, feeling an odd flicker of sympathy. *All the normal rules of diplomatic discourse have gone out the airlock.*

She tried hard not to look around *too* obviously as they were led through a dizzying series of doors and corridors. The Imperial Palace was strikingly barren, lacking the paintings, sculptures or trophies that decorated the other buildings she'd seen. She puzzled over it for a long moment, finally deciding that the king didn't *need* to showcase his power. Merely controlling the Imperial Palace - and the administrative centre below it - was enough to make it clear he was in charge.

"Your aide will wait here," the alien said, as they stopped outside a pair of solid metal doors. It was the first thing he'd said to her. "You will enter alone."

Rebecca hesitated, then nodded. Her implants were reporting an increasing number of jamming fields, but not enough to keep her from recording the entire meeting. Tyler and the rest of her staff would have plenty of time to study the meeting...assuming, of course, she returned alive. She shot Tyler a reassuring look as the doors opened, then turned and stepped into a blindingly white room. The doors slammed closed behind her a second later.

"Greetings," a flat voice said. "I bid you welcome."

She peered forward, silently grateful that her eyes were adapting to the light. The chamber was white, completely white. A lone alien, dressed in a long white robe, stood in the exact centre. His head - his uncovered head - was surprisingly human-like, although it looked a little out of proportion. He wore no crown, no badge of rank...and yet, there was an air of authority surrounding them.

"Your Majesty," she managed. "I thank you for the invitation."

The king bowed his head, then gestured. Rebecca's implants flashed up an alert, reporting the presence of a teleport field, a moment before two chairs shimmered into existence. The king motioned for her to take one, then took the other for himself. Rebecca sat, feeling a little nervous. There was no protocol for this at all.

"These are hard times for the galaxy," the king said, when they were seated. "Your race has destroyed a great many old certainties."

"Yes, Your Majesty," Rebecca managed, carefully. It was impossible to read the king's emotions. "We had no choice."

"You could have submitted," the king said. "But your race is uniquely disruptive."

It would be nice to believe that, Rebecca knew. The idea that there was something unique about humanity, something that made humans special...But there wasn't, not really. The Galactics might have trapped themselves in a socio-political *cul-de-sac*, but they weren't really any more or less intelligent - or disruptive - than humanity. Given time - and the incentive to adapt to a whole new universe - they'd start pushing the limits just as much as the Solar Union.

"Submission would mean death, Your Majesty," Rebecca said, finally. She had to say *something*. "Either the destruction of our entire race or the death of everything that makes us what we are."

"You have changed much," the king said. He didn't respond to her comment, making her wonder if he was running down a long script. "Your technology has advanced alarmingly."

"We saw potentials in GalTech that others missed," Rebecca said. "Other races could do the same."

But, in all honesty, she wondered if that was actually true. If humanity *did* have an advantage, it lay in imagination. The Solar Union had drawn on the unpaid and largely unacknowledged imaginations of countless science-fiction writers. But who among the Galactics would have believed that the gravity trap had been envisaged nearly thirty years before Contact? None of *them* had encouraged writers to push the limits of the acceptable.

"Perhaps," the king mused.

Rebecca studied him for a long moment, wondering if she dared ask him directly what was going on. What was the *point*? They'd summoned a human diplomatic mission...was there something they wanted? Or...or what? Surely, no one would go to so much trouble just to waste time. They were already beyond the limits of diplomacy...

"We would not have believed that one race could cause so much disruption," the king added, slowly. "Nor that you could come so far so fast."

"The Tokomak did, Your Majesty," Rebecca said.

She'd hoped to see a reaction, *any* reaction. But there was none.

"We have been informed that you are building an alliance of other junior races," the king said, instead. "You are sharing your technology with them."

"Some of it, Your Majesty," Rebecca said. She'd been warned it was unlikely that anything humanity had invented would remain exclusive for long. Knowing something was possible was half the battle. It was one of the reasons the Solar Union was putting so much work into research and development. "We are hoping to stand up to the Tokomak when they return to our sector."

The king's head moved, very slightly. A reaction...but a reaction to *what*?

"We require access to your technology," the king stated, bluntly. "You will give it to us."

Rebecca - somehow - managed to keep her face impassive. There was no way the Solar Union would just *give* their technology to anyone, even though there was a very good chance that a number of Galactics were already experimenting with their own versions. The king seemed to believe humanity would hand it over on demand...did he really believe that or was he pushing her, trying to see how far she would go?

"Our technology is only traded to our allies, Your Majesty," she said, carefully. She had very little leeway at all. The analysts had speculated that the Harmonies would want human technology - they were badly outnumbered by the Tokomak and knew it - but there was no way her superiors would sign off on any technological transfers without a signed agreement and some proof it would actually be upheld. "Are you interesting in allying with us?"

The king said nothing. Rebecca wondered what he was thinking. His face was almost completely unmoving - and even if she could have picked out an expression on his alien face, she knew it could easily be misleading. But what *was* he thinking? Did he expect the Solar Union to fall over itself to just *give* him the technology? Or was he playing hardball so he could make a show of granting concessions later? There was no way to know.

"We do not ally ourselves with anyone," the king said, finally. "We have no equals."

"The universe has changed, Your Majesty," Rebecca pointed out. She deliberately echoed the king's words. "Old certainties are falling everywhere."

"That is true," the king agreed. "But it is *also* true that we rule an immense sphere, while you control a handful of stars a long way from the centre of galactic power. Your race and mine are not equals. Our assistance comes at a price."

"Our technology," Rebecca said.

She leaned forward. "Your Majesty, it will take the Tokomak Navy two weeks to reach your space and invade," she added. "It would take them *nine months* to reach us. Your proximity to the centre of galactic power is a liability."

The king showed no visible reaction, but she had the oddest sense he was laughing at her, as if she'd said something funny. But what? The Harmonies had no reason to dismiss the Tokomak so lightly. They'd rebelled against a galactic order that had existed for thousands of years. They needed humanity's assistance more than humanity needed theirs... didn't they?

"A new universe is taking shape, Your Majesty," she said. "Your old status means nothing to the new order. You can no longer look down on the younger races."

The king still looked impassive. "Then we will talk," he said. "And see what we can decide."

Somehow, Rebecca was not reassured.

FIFTEEN

The problem here, of course, is that we might not be able to delay them long enough to put together an unbeatable advantage. Let us be honest - we have no monopoly on wild imagination, let alone researchers and engineers who can turn absurd concepts into practical technologies. The longer we wait to safeguard our position, the greater the chance the hammer will come slamming down.
-Solar Datanet, Political Forum (Grand Alliance Thoughts)

"They're stalling," Rebecca said. "Captain, I'm sure of it."

She sat back in her chair, feeling tired. She'd met the king five times in a row, a honour that was almost unique by galactic standards, yet...yet their discussions had gone nowhere. The king was intelligent - of that she was sure - and yet, he'd managed to talk for days without saying anything beyond mindless platitudes and demands he knew as well as she did would never be met. She had the odd feeling that he was waiting for something, but what?

Captain Yasser's image seemed to loom closer. "Do you believe it's worth continuing the talks?"

Rebecca scowled, wishing she had a drink. Or something stronger. "That's the question, Elton," she said. "*Is* it worth continuing the talks?"

On Earth, the answer would be obvious. The Solar Union eschewed meaningless diplomatic babble with as much enthusiasm as it dismissed academic mumbo-jumbo. It would be obvious that anyone stalling wasn't serious, particularly given the Solar Union's penchant for treaties written in plain English. But here...the king and his court might prefer to follow the achingly slow galactic procedures, rather than move quickly. The Galactics had been known to take years to write treaties that were longer than some doorstopper manuscripts. She had a private theory that hardly anyone, including the heads of state, actually bothered to read the damn things. It would certainly explain a great deal about galactic society.

"You're the diplomat," the captain said. He shot her a mischievous grin that made him look younger. "Did they even agree to allow our freighters to attempt to trade their goods?"

"Not yet," Rebecca said. "Captain...I don't know if we can push it."

And that, she knew, was the crux of the problem. Humanity *needed* allies. Having a race as powerful and respected as the Harmonies on their side would be very helpful. But, at the same time, they could hardly afford to humour the Harmonies indefinitely, let alone grant them major concessions as a prelude to more formal talks. The Grand Alliance would be dead in the water if one race was treated as superior to the others. She couldn't help wondering if that was exactly what the Harmonies had in mind.

But that would require more subtlety than they've shown us so far, she thought. *And more awareness of the younger races...*

"Perhaps you should just ask them what they want," Elton said, breaking into her thoughts. "Cut right through the diplomacy and *ask* them."

Rebecca considered it for a long moment. "It would be a diplomatic nightmare," she pointed out, finally. "Just asking..."

The captain snorted, rudely. "Rebecca, I cannot help but wonder if we're being conned," he said. "What are they *doing*?"

"I've had the same feeling," Rebecca agreed. "But I don't see the *point*."

She looked down at her fingers, wishing she could take a nap. Or perhaps go back to the ship for a few hours. There was nothing to *do* in the embassy, save for studying files and reading reports from the intelligence staff. She'd be happy just to take a rest somewhere she didn't have to worry about being watched. The marines were *still* turning up bugs all over the giant building. And yet...

She'd studied psychology during her training. Her instructors had told her, more than once, that people could be conned easily, *without* the sort of blatant lies that were instantly noticeable. And while there were some people who were prepared to admit that they had been deceived, others would often throw good money after bad because they didn't want to stand up and *admit* that they had been tricked. There came a time, they'd said, when the mark's mind grasped what had happened to him.

"They want to *believe*," her instructor had said. "That's the key to a successful con. A person who wants to believe will overlook *anything*, as long as they have their eyes firmly fixed on the future. And a good con man will ensure that the mark keeps his eyes on that future as long as possible."

And if we are being conned, she mused, *what's the payoff? What do they want?*

She cleared her throat. "I'll give it a week," she said. "And if they don't get to the point by then, I'll insist on shutting down the talks and see what happens."

"A week," the captain commented.

"That's fast by galactic standards," Rebecca countered. "It might convince them to actually put their cards on the table. I..."

She broke off as an alert flashed up in front of her eyes. "Captain, I think we have a situation," she said. "It's not good."

"The crowds are pushing closer," Rifleman John Stewart warned. "And the chanting is growing louder too."

Levi nodded, grimly. The crowds might be composed of aliens, but they had the same sense of barely-restrained violence she recalled from Earth. She could feel their eyes following her, following every human within the complex...hatred mingled with bitter frustration throbbing on the air. It must be nightmarish, utterly nightmarish, to grow up in a world where every last word was monitored, where there was no hope at all for freedom...the crowd was angry, yet helpless.

And someone encouraged them to come here, she thought. *And no one is driving them away.*

She studied the wall for a long moment. The marines had checked the material and discovered that it was composed of a composite substance that could stand up to anything below a shaped plasma charge, but somehow she didn't find it very reassuring. There was no way to be *sure* the crowd wasn't carrying any weapons, either stolen from military bases or handed out by whoever had organised the protest. She'd rigged up portable forcefields to provide additional security, yet she had no illusions. They wouldn't hold out indefinitely.

John Stewart was right, she decided. The chanting was definitely growing louder, an xenophobic rant that was blurring into a single solid tone that slammed into her ears. Her implants unhelpfully provided a translation, warning her that the protesters intended to tear her limb from limb and then eat her mangled remains. She reached for her rifle and touched it, cursing the Rules of Engagement under her breath. On Earth, they'd be allowed to move the protesters away from the building if the local authorities refused to oblige; here, they had to grin and bear it. Thankfully, the embassy was largely soundproofed.

The explosion came without warning. Levi spun around, just in time to see a large section of the wall crumble inwards. Dozens of protesters were badly injured, their bodies falling to the ground, but the remainder started to push forward, into the embassy. Someone was shouting orders through a megaphone, whipping up hatred as the crowd surged forward. Levi drew her rifle and searched for the shouter, hoping he could be taken out before matters got any worse. But she couldn't find him.

She keyed her throatmike. "Security alert," she snapped. "Get the staff into the shelter!"

She gritted her teeth as the howling protesters slammed into the security field and sparks started to fly. It was designed to shock everyone who touched it with their bare skin. Levi couldn't help feeling a flicker of sympathy, even though she was sure the protesters definitely intended to tear her limb from limb. She'd been shocked herself, during training, and it hadn't been pleasant. The protesters at the front were being forced against the field by the others, unable to escape the jangling...

"LT," Stewart called. "The field is starting to fail!"

Levi cursed under her breath. They'd gone through a hundred contingency plans, but all of them depended on help arriving from the local authorities. A distress call would have gone out automatically, if the authorities weren't already monitoring the situation, yet she had a feeling help wasn't going to arrive. The protest was hardly spontaneous. She rather doubted the riot was any more so.

"Send a distress signal to the ship, then start pulling back to the interior defence lines," she ordered, grimly. It meant giving up the embassy grounds and some of the outer rooms, but she didn't have the manpower to defend them. "Make sure you get the ambassadorial staff into the panic room."

"Aye, LT," Stewart snapped.

The field crackled loudly, then snapped out of existence. A hundred protesters fell to the ground, twitching helplessly. Extensive contact with the security field would probably cause permanent nerve damage, if they lived long enough to care. Their comrades trampled over them as they rushed the building, hurling stones and bottles towards the marines on the rooftop. Levi hoped the doors would hold, but she had a feeling they wouldn't. Someone had gone to a lot of trouble to set up the protest.

And if we open fire, she thought as the marines opened the hatch and dropped through to the highest floor, *we risk starting one hell of a diplomatic incident.*

New alerts flashed up in front of her eyes. The crowd had smashed the main doors and was now heading in all directions. Other alerts followed, warning of microscopic bugs shadowing the protesters as they started to tear the building apart. Levi hadn't really *doubted* that the protest was being organised, but it was nice to have confirmation. She just wished she had a set of armoured combat suits too. No protester could break a combat suit without heavy weapons...

And we don't have anything beyond BDUs, she reminded herself. The entire building shook, violently. It sounded as though the protesters *did* have some weapons after all. *We're dead.*

"Get them out of there," Elton snapped.

"We can't, sir," Lieutenant Rogers said. "There's too much jamming in the air! We can't teleport them out or they'll wind up with their heads coming out of their asses!"

Elton glared at him. The live feed from the embassy was flicking in and out of existence, but he could see enough to tell that all hell was breaking loose. It was only a matter of time before the crowds found Rebecca and her staff. And then...he had no doubt that the entire staff would be brutally murdered. He had no idea what was going on - or who was behind the protest - but he couldn't let the ambassador be murdered...

He keyed his console. "Major Rhodan, can you get armoured troops down there?"

"Not in time," Rhodan said. The marine sounded grim. "I have two platoons suiting up now, but getting them down in time will be impossible, even if the local defences don't try to stop us..."

Shit, Elton thought. The orbital defences were coming online, their sensors already sweeping space for potential threats. They weren't locked on *Odyssey*, but they hardly *needed* to target her directly to blow her out of space. His ship was orbiting far too close to enough firepower to deter the First Fleet! *What on Earth are they playing at?*

He turned to Williams. "Any response?"

"None, sir," Williams said. "There's no response from any of the local channels."

A new icon popped up in front of Elton's eyes. Lieutenant Jayne Fisher wanted to talk to him.

"What?"

"I've been analysing the live feed, sir," Jayne said. She didn't sound bothered by his tone. "I think they're trying to con us."

Elton resisted the urge to hit the console as hard as he could. "Explain."

"My first thought was that someone had launched a coup, with us caught in the middle," Jayne said. "However, further analysis has picked up no trace of military movements, fighting or even additional communications bursts. There's certainly no *reason* for their failure to respond to our hails. I believe that they are trying to create a *perception* of chaos, rather than actual chaos."

"Oh, *goody*," Elton snapped. "And..."

"Captain," Williams said. "I've had an idea. We might be able to get them out."

"One moment," Elton told Jayne. "You think it would work?"

"I think so," Williams said. "But we'd have to fly a shuttle through their airspace."

Elton considered it, wishing - not for the first time - that there was someone higher up who could make the final call. Launching a shuttle into a planet's atmosphere without permission was a hostile act...and he was aware, all too aware, of just how much firepower was orbiting Harmony. And yet, the Harmonies had either organised the riot or were doing nothing to stop it. Either one was a hostile act in and of itself. Earth might be on the verge of war...

"Launch the shuttle on remote control," he ordered. There was no point in risking more lives. "And pray it gets there in time."

"Aye, Captain," Williams said.

"ARE WE GOING to die?"

Rebecca had no idea who'd spoken, nor did she care. "Shut up," she ordered, sharply. "Use your implants to calm yourself and *wait*."

She took a deep breath, trying to keep *herself* calm. She'd been in tight spots before, back on Earth, but she'd always known that she could be teleported out in a moment. Very few warlords would risk trying to take her hostage - or kill her - when they knew the retaliation would be crushing. But here...*Odyssey* might not be able to yank them out before the protesters fought their way into the panic room. In theory, it should keep them safe indefinitely; in practice, she doubted it would hold the protesters out for long.

"They're mad," the girl said. "I..."

"I told you to shut up," Rebecca snapped. She heard the girl gulp and felt a flicker of guilt, which she ruthlessly shoved into the back of her mind. There was no time to be nice to anyone. "So *shut up*!"

She forced herself to *think*. If she'd offended the king...he would have expelled the diplomats, perhaps sending them back with a demand for *new* diplomats or a declaration of war. *None* of the Galactics would tolerate a power attacking or killing ambassadors, no matter where they came from. And it was unlikely that they'd believe the whole protest had been spontaneous. They'd prefer to use the whole event to embarrass the Harmonies...

They're insane, she thought. The Harmonies *had* to have gone mad. They didn't benefit from any of this, did they? *What are they doing?*

"LT, THE SHIP's sending in help," John said, as Levi led the marines down a corridor. New icons flared up in front of her eyes. "We have to be ready to teleport out."

"Great," Rifleman Wahid said. He'd got the briefing too. "If this goes wrong, the doc will be removing your head from my ass afterwards."

"Maybe they'll just force you to take a course of laxatives," Stewart jeered.

"Or perhaps some of your cooking," Wahid jeered back. "It put half the squad out of commission last time."

Levi cleared her throat, meaningfully. "Don't worry about it," she told him. "It's much more likely that you'll just dissolve into your constituent atoms."

She ran around the corner and stopped, dead. A stream of protesters were charging right at her, screaming and howling...the ones at the rear, as always, pushing the ones at the front forward. She unhooked a stun grenade from her belt and hurled it into the crowd, using her implants to send the detonation command a second later. Blue light flared, sending the first protesters falling to the floor. But the remainder just kept coming...

"About face," Levi said. She wanted to open fire. But she knew what would happen if they fired plasma rifles into the crowd. The aliens would be butchered, mercilessly. They'd have all the excuse they needed for a diplomatic incident. "Fall back."

She searched her mind, desperately, for options. But there were none. Their only real hope was to join the ambassador's staff in the panic room, yet she doubted it would last for more than a few seconds. She tossed two more grenades behind her as she ran, hoping it would slow the crowd down for a while. Perhaps shoving their former comrades out of the way would restore sanity to the rest of them...

Of course not, she thought, as the howling grew louder. *A crowd is only half as smart as the stupidest person in it.*

"They're not going to open the doors for us," Wahid said. They'd outrun the crowd, but they were all too aware that that wouldn't last. "I don't think they could close them in time."

Levi nodded. She understood. The ambassador's staff could not open the doors. It would just get everyone killed quicker. "We make a stand just outside the doors," she said. There was no alternative. She'd just have to pray the ship came through with a rescue before it was too late. "Get ready."

She cursed, again. They were about to die, hundreds of thousands of light years from home. Hell, hundreds of *aliens* were about to die, just because their leaders wanted a diplomatic incident. Or whatever...she still had no idea what was actually going on. She braced herself as they reached the locked doors, then took up position. Her platoon fell into place beside her, ready to fire.

"Take aim," she ordered, as the crowd came into view. Some hesitated, she thought, but the remainder pushed them on. "Fire!"

SIXTEEN

And yet the mere act of safeguarding our position may provoke attack.
Look, I see your point. But two hundred years of freedom and isolation, during which we can build up an impregnable position and an unbeatable technological lead, is worth almost anything. A Grand Alliance, on the other hand, will invite attack. The Tokomak and their allies/subordinates will see it as a threat and rightly so. They didn't take us seriously, fifty years ago, because we were a microstate in their eyes. Will that be true of the Grand Alliance?
-Solar Datanet, Political Forum (Grand Alliance Thoughts)

"The shuttle is on the way, Captain," Williams said.

Elton nodded, trying to look calm and composed. He'd been taught to take decisive action, if a crisis exploded while he was in the hot seat, but he'd never been prepared for a situation where he didn't have the slightest idea what was actually going on. He *knew* the embassy was under attack, he *knew* the local government was probably aiding and abetting the attack, yet...why? There was no data. No one was answering his calls. The only thing he could do was try to withdraw the ambassador and the rest of the embassy staff before it was too late, if he could.

And yet, sending a shuttle into their atmosphere without permission is an act of war, he thought, grimly. *Is that what they want? To provoke an act of war?*

His gaze slipped to the tactical display. *Odyssey's* shields were up, ready to protect her; *Odyssey's* weapons were charged, ready to return fire. And yet, he had no illusions about their ability to survive if the orbital weapons platforms opened fire. The freighters had even less hope than his ship. They'd be vaporised within microseconds. He contemplated, briefly, evacuating them before deciding it was pointless. The entire convoy was at risk.

"Mr. Callaway," he said. "Has *anything* transited the gravity points?"

"Not since the last update, sir," Callaway said. "But we are picking up signs that cloaked ships are moving closer to the planet."

As if they needed them, Elton thought.

"Keep me updated," he ordered. "Mr. Biscoe?"

"All decks are ready, Captain," Biscoe said.

Elton nodded, curtly. There was nothing they could do, but wait - and hope that the shuttle got into position before it was too late. The entire planetary defence grid was slowly coming online, PDFs powering up their heavy weapons and force shields as they swept low orbit for targets. Elton had to admit, reluctantly, that the Harmonies *definitely* hadn't skimped on their defences. Picking them apart, if he had to engage the planet, would be costly as hell.

We probably couldn't do a lot of damage to the planet before they blew us into atoms, he thought, grimly. *Not unless we set out to slaughter the population...*

"Captain," Williams said. "They just sent us a message, text-only. We are ordered to withdraw the shuttle at once."

Biscoe coughed. "They didn't even add an *or else?*"

"I think that was implied," Elton said. He forced himself to think. The shuttle wasn't trying to hide. It was barely even shielded. He had no doubt the defenders could blow the tiny craft out of the air in seconds. But...the shuttle was also expendable. "Keep the shuttle on its present course."

"Aye, Captain," Williams said. "Time to target - two minutes, forty seconds."

Elton glanced at Biscoe. "Begin evacuation as soon as the datalink is established," he ordered. "And don't stop for anything."

"Aye, Captain," Biscoe said.

Was that a hint of respect in his voice? Elton wasn't sure. Hoshiko Sashimi Stuart would probably have blasted her way out by now, although Elton rather suspected that even the famed maverick would have hesitated when confronted by so much firepower. His best-case estimates suggested that *Odyssey* would last around five minutes, if she didn't have to worry about covering the freighters. He had a nasty feeling that that was ludicrously optimistic.

"They're repeating the demand," Williams warned.

"Keep the shuttle on course," Elton ordered.

And pray, he added, silently.

LEVI HAD SEEN horror. She'd seen good men and women injured or killed on a dozen battlefields, she'd seen civilians - caught up in war - brutally abused or raped by enemy soldiers; she'd even helped recover and bury bodies after countless engagements with various enemy forces. But she'd never watched dozens - perhaps hundreds - of bodies being ripped to shreds by plasma fire. The alien protesters never stood a chance.

She gritted her teeth, silently grateful for her nose protectors as the plasma bolts burned through their bodies. The stench was horrifying. They didn't wear combat armour, they didn't even wear basic protections...nothing that could stop the superhot plasma tearing through their bodies like machine gun fire. The shock alone would kill dozens, she thought, even if they hadn't been critically wounded. For once, the ones at the rear were just as vulnerable as the ones at the front. There just weren't enough bodies between them and the plasma fire.

"Dear God," Wahid breathed.

Levi swallowed, hard, as time itself seemed to slow down. Hundreds, perhaps thousands, of protesters had forced their way into the building, but - just for a second - things had slowed down. The protesters had stopped trying to force their way into the panic room, although she was uneasily aware that they were hacking away at the rest of the building. It was shaking so alarmingly that she was starting to wonder if they were tearing down the supporting walls...

A low *thump* echoed through the build. Pieces of plaster - and something- started to drop from the ceiling.

"We can't stay here," she snapped. The panic room was *meant* to be safe, but she wasn't prepared to gamble on it. They had to get the staff out before the entire place collapsed around their ears. "Stewart, you and your squad secure the corridor; Wahid and I will get the staff out and on their way."

"Gotcha," Stewart said. "Weapons free?"

Levi shuddered, inwardly. "Weapons free."

She kept her face expressionless as she sent a message to the ambassador, hoping the older woman could open the door without trouble. The civilians were probably panicking. No doubt they'd trusted Galactic Law to protect them. They'd be shocked beyond measure when they saw the burned and broken bodies...she shook her head, in annoyance. There would be an inquest, at the very least, when they got home...*if* they got home. She had no illusions about just how long they'd last if they failed to get back to the ship. The crowds would hunt the humans down and kill them.

The door clicked open. "Get out," she snapped. The ambassadorial staff were cowering, as if they were reluctant to leave their safe space. She didn't blame them, but it wouldn't remain safe very long. "Follow me if you want to live!"

"Very droll, LT," Wahid whispered.

Levi barely heard him as she shepherded the last of the staffers out of the panic room, then set the terminals to self-destruct. Everything they'd collected would be backed up on the ship, she hoped. In any case, she didn't have time to carry it out. They'd have to make sure that everything they couldn't take with them was destroyed too. She didn't *think* the staff had brought anything *really* advanced down to the surface, but it was better to be sure. A lone eReader, crammed with textbooks or even fiction, would give the aliens all kinds of insights into humanity. God alone knew what would flower from *that*.

"I've established a direct link to a low-orbit drone," Stewart said. "There are more protesters on the way, but the rear of the embassy is clear for the moment."

"Understood," Levi said. The protest - and the riot - had been planned. She was sure of that, if nothing else. But...leaving the rear open was sheer carelessness. Unless, of course, the planners had deliberately left the way open to lure her and her charges into the open air. "The shuttle?"

"Still a minute out," Stewart said.

Levi nodded. "Start moving the evacuees towards the rear," she ordered. She couldn't see any other way out. Either the shuttle got into position or they were run down and brutally slaughtered. "Now."

"Aye, LT," Stewart said.

REBECCA CHOKED. THE air stank of burning flesh, of horrors beyond her imagination. She'd thought she'd seen violence - in a VR sim, if nothing else - but this was *real*. The embassy had changed, warped overnight into a hellish nightmare. She had to fight to breathe as she stumbled down the corridor, choking on the smoke in the air. There was no way she could look at the bodies on the ground.

"They've set fire to the building," someone shouted. "Fire!"

"Stay in line," the marine thundered. "Don't panic!"

I'm trying, Rebecca thought.

She bent over, vaguely remembering that smoke rose towards the ceiling. It was getting warmer...or was it her imagination? In truth, she wasn't sure if she was imagining the heat or not. The shouts and screaming echoing down the corridor chilled her to the bone. Her implants kept flashing up incomprehensible alerts, messages she couldn't read. She wanted to contact the ship and demand immediate evacuation, but she'd been locked out of the main communications network. Desperately, she hoped that wasn't a sign that the communications network itself was gone.

The ship acts as the exchange hub, she reminded herself. The briefing had made it clear that they couldn't rely on the local datanet for secure messages. *They'd have told us if she was gone, wouldn't they?*

The building shook, so violently that she lost her footing and fell. A strong hand caught her arm, a second before she would have hit the floor. She looked up to see a grim-faced marine, staring down at her. Rebecca nodded her thanks as she regained her footing, then started to stumble onwards down the corridor. It seemed never-ending, as if they had died and gone to hell. There was no escape...

Another quiver ran through the building, followed by another. She fought down the urge to whimper as they hurried down the stairs, then stopped as she heard gunshots somewhere ahead of them. The marines hissed at them to keep moving, pushing them onwards past a pair of alien bodies. Rebecca glanced at one of them, then had to swallow hard to keep from throwing up. The plasma burst had burned a hole right through his chest, leaving a black-edged hole...she hoped, suddenly, that it had proved fatal. She doubted any regenerator kit could save someone after they'd been hit so badly.

She tasted fresh air as the marines kicked down the door leading to the rear garden. She'd admired it, once upon a time, even though it was as thoroughly bugged as the rest of the complex. The understated elegance had been quite relaxing, while she'd been waiting for more substantive talks to take place. Had it really only been two weeks ago? She felt as if she'd been trapped in hell for years.

"They're coming around the side," a voice snapped. "Move into the garden!"

Rebecca turned her head to look at the embassy. Smoke was billowing out of a dozen windows, flames dancing in and out of visibility...she'd disliked the building, but she still hated to watch it burn. The alien staff had insisted that it was older than Jesus, literally. She had no reason to doubt them. And yet...she sucked in a breath as a mob of howling fanatics appeared at the side, running towards the fleeing humans. The marines opened fire a second later, blowing them apart...

A hand caught her shoulder. "Move," a marine snapped. "They'll catch you if you stay still."

Somehow, Rebecca forced herself to keep moving.

STUPID CIVILIANS, LEVI thought, as she blasted down two more aliens. *Why can't they just do as they're told?*

She pushed the thought out of her head and concentrated on keeping the evacuees moving away from the burning embassy. The orbital drone was sending a constant series of updates, warning her that thousands upon *thousands* of protesters were heading straight towards her, even though hundreds - perhaps more - had already been killed. Didn't they *know* the ROE were no longer in effect? Did they *want* to die?

Maybe they just know they'll be shot for treason if they don't charge us, she thought, remembering a deployment in the former Middle East. The poor bastards she'd fought there had feared their commanders more than the marines. They'd been certain they'd be shot in the back if they failed to keep moving. *And they're probably right. There's no privacy here at all.*

A drone - not one of hers - floated over the remaining wall, sensors probing the garden. She blasted it out of the air automatically, hoping she hadn't just caused another diplomatic incident. At this rate, her court martial was going to bog down in arguments over just *which* capital charge was going to head the bill. God alone knew how it was going to end up - she didn't *think* she'd done anything a board could question, but there was always some REMF who thought he knew better than the woman on the spot...

Not that it matters, she thought, checking her implants one last time. *If they don't get us out of here in the next couple of minutes, we're as doomed as the dodo.*

LIEUTENANT GEORGE BONE had been fascinated by teleportation from the day he'd first entered GalTech University and started studying alien and alien-derived technology. The teleport was a remarkable invention, even though it had odd limitations that had never been truly understood, let alone circumvented. Jokes about teleportation duplicates aside, no one had actually managed to *make* a duplicate...almost as if, a number of scientists had noted, there was something about a living being that was beyond duplication. A number of them had even embraced religion because of it.

His fingers flew over the console as he tried to establish a matter stream, followed by a teleport lock. The Tokomak had designed the teleport systems carefully, building so many safeguards into their teleporters that some humans had remarked that it was a surprise they actually managed to teleport *anyone*. Humanity had kept most of the safeguards, after discovering just how much could actually go wrong. A shift in the matter stream would kill anyone unlucky enough to be teleporting at the time.

And we have to establish a link through the shuttle, he thought, sourly. *The craft has to boost the signal.*

He gritted his teeth, cursing as a series of alerts popped up, each one warning of imminent disaster. The Harmonies hadn't set up a teleport jammer, thankfully, but there were so many stray signals in their city that they barely needed to bother. George compensated for each of them, silently grateful for the RIs backing him up. They lacked the finesse of a full AI - unless one of them had grown into sentience and was keeping it quiet - but they could keep the signal intact. He just hoped they could hold it in place long enough.

The intercom bleeped. "Mr. Bone," the XO said. He sounded as if he was frantic and trying to hide it. "Do you have a lock?"

"I think so, sir," George said. "I don't think we're going to get anything better, not with all the haze down there."

"Then bring them up," the XO ordered. "Now."

"Aye, sir," George said.

He ran his hand down the panel, authorising the teleport. It wasn't going to be easy. Too many people were running around, probably firing weapons. They'd been warned to stand still and take their fingers off the triggers, but...he knew better than to think that was possible. The folks on the ground were in deep shit.

"Teleport locks established," he said. They weren't perfect, but he didn't think there was any way to harden them. "Teleporting now..."

A low hum echoed through the cargo teleporter as it came to life. It was taking longer than normal...he'd expected that, he reminded himself. Using a shuttle as a relay station would add seconds to the teleport. He'd just have to hope the integrity of the matter stream remained intact. If it didn't....

Twenty-five people shimmered into view. George cursed under his breath, checking and rechecking his equipment. He'd had thirty-one locks, hadn't he? Two more materialised a second later, followed by a third...three people were missing. Their matter streams had desynchronised during teleport. They were gone.

He swallowed, hard. "Commander," he said. "I have twenty-eight people here. The remaining three didn't make it."

There was a long pause. "Understood," the XO said, finally. "Put quarantine procedures into place. Marines are on their way."

George nodded. There would be time to mourn later.

"Aye, sir."

THREE DEAD, ELTON thought. He knew he should be counting his blessings, but he still felt wretched. *Three dead...*

"Captain," Williams said. "They just blew the shuttle out of the air."

"Noted," Elton said. "Tactical?"

"No change," Callaway said. He nodded towards the hulking icons, orbiting menacingly over the planet. "It's like they're ignoring us."

"They know where we are," Biscoe said, harshly. "They could hit us at any moment."

"Get the ambassador and her staff through security screening as quickly as possible," Elton said. There was no way to know if the aliens had taken the opportunity to plant more nanotech on the evacuees. The teleport crews hadn't had time to run a proper scan. "And see if they have any insights they can offer."

He took a long look at the tactical display, one thought echoing through his head.

What now?

SEVENTEEN

The fact remains that they no longer see us as a microstate. We are not an isolated single-system power that somehow lucked its way into first-rank GalTech, not any longer. We are a technologically-advanced race that bested the unquestioned masters of the known universe. They are hardly going to leave us alone for another two hundred years. I know they're slow and steady, not given to rash action, but if they have any idea of the scale of the threat we represent - ideologically as well as technologically - they'll act sooner rather than later.
-Solar Datanet, Political Forum (Grand Alliance Thoughts)

She felt...she felt unclean.

Rebecca stood in the shower, silently welcoming the water as it washed her bare skin. She'd nearly been killed...no, she'd nearly been lynched by a mob. *That* hadn't happened for over sixty years, not when local governments had *known* there would be retribution. Now...she closed her eyes and forced her head under the water, trying to blot out the smell of burned flesh. It clung to her, a grim reminder that she had failed. There would be...what?

War, perhaps, she thought. *But why?*

She forced herself to open her eyes, even though part of her wanted to retreat into a VR sim and leave the whole affair to someone else. There was *no one* else. She'd accepted the mission, when it had been offered to her. She couldn't back out now when the closest possible replacement was weeks away, if not months. And yet...she'd clearly failed as a diplomat. What had she done wrong? Had she made a mistake by agreeing to talk to the king? Or had she been set up to fail? Perhaps the Harmonies had been more interested in looking for a provocation than anything else.

They haven't fired on the ship, she told herself, firmly. *And that means... what?*

She stepped out of the shower and grabbed a towel, hastily drying herself off. She'd washed herself thoroughly, yet she could still smell burned flesh...she gritted her teeth, telling herself that she was imagining it. The evacuees had gone through a full security sweep before they'd been allowed out of the teleport bay, their clothes removed and probably fed into a matter recycler. She should be clean, yet...yet it was impossible to believe that she *was* clean. Her hands were shaking helplessly.

"I made it out," she muttered, studying her right hand. It was trembling. "We escaped before we could be killed."

Her body didn't seem to care. It *knew* she'd barely escaped certain death. She'd played countless VR sims where she'd been captured, tortured or killed, but she'd always known - back then - that she could just disconnect if it got too intense. Or pop back to the last checkpoint, if she was killed. The real world wasn't nearly so obliging. She'd come very close to dying outright, despite the marines and her augmentation. And that would have been the end. The e-personality recording she'd made before departure wasn't *her* and never would be.

She stumbled to the bench and sat down, hard. Her entire body was trembling. Her implants flashed up a set of options, offering everything from hormonal readjustments to direct neural simulations, but she ignored them. She couldn't hide from the world. She couldn't hide from what had nearly been done to her. She thought she understood, now, why so many recent immigrants always looked as if they were constantly glancing back, as if they expected someone to stick a knife in their backs. They'd understood the realities of the universe far better than herself.

She'd left Earth before the descent into civil war - and a hellish multi-sided blood swarm - had truly begun.

"Fuck," she muttered.

Her body was still trembling. She gritted her teeth, then asserted control. The trembling seemed to subside, just for a moment. Forcing herself to stand, she reached for a robe and pulled it over her body. It smelt fresh, as if it had just come out of the fabricator. And yet...her stomach heaved as she scented burned flesh, again. She told herself, savagely, that she was imagining it...

...But it didn't seem to work.

She walked through the hatch and out into her stateroom. It was surprisingly large, she'd thought. The last starship she'd spent any time on had been tiny, so small that her stateroom barely had enough room to swing a cat. And yet, right now it seemed too large and empty to suit her. She didn't want to be alone. She wanted someone to hold her as she slept, just to remind her that she was still alive. But there was no one.

Shaking her head, dismissing the thought, she sat down at her desk and checked the local processor. *Odyssey* was still in orbit over Harmony, waiting for something - anything - to happen. Rebecca wasn't sure why something *hadn't* happened. The Harmonies were clearly up to something, but what? A counter-coup? Or...or perhaps their society had finally started to break down. But...

Nothing is happening on the surface, as far as we can tell, she thought, as she studied the analyst reports. *If their society was breaking down, surely we would be seeing something.*

She looked at the timer. It was 1700. Really? It felt like days - perhaps weeks - had passed since her last meeting with the king. Had it really been less than an hour since she'd been teleported out of the burning embassy? She felt as if she'd grown older overnight, as if her body had somehow shifted to match her chronological age. And yet...some of the older people she knew, the ones who had been in their nineties before Contact and rejuvenation, had been oddly detached from the world. She couldn't help wondering if it would be better to be more like them...

"Idiot," she told herself, sharply. "You don't have time!"

Bringing up her personal files, she started to go through them. Her body craved sleep, but she didn't have the time. The captain would want to see her soon enough, if the shit didn't hit the fan - again - in the next few hours. By then...if there was an answer in the files, she wanted to find it. The captain would want answers and, in truth, so did she.

Because they have a plan, she thought. *And if we don't figure it out before it's too late, it might be the end of us.*

"YOU'RE CLEAN," LIEUTENANT Jansen said. He waved one last scanner over Levi's naked body, then stepped back. "They did manage to attach a couple of bugs to you, but I think we got them all."

"Hah," Levi said. "And what if you're wrong?"

"Then we're fucked," Jansen said. "But then, we're probably fucked anyway."

Levi nodded as she took the new uniform and started to get dressed. She was used to taking sonic showers, even though she could probably convince Major Rhodan to give her and the rest of the platoon an extra water ration, but they didn't have the time. And yet...she had no illusions. Ten marines wouldn't make a difference if the massive orbital fortifications surrounding Harmony opened fire. *Odyssey* and her crew would be dead before they knew they were under attack.

"The civilians aren't bearing up well," Jansen said. "I think half of them are going to want to go into the stasis tubes before the end of the day."

"Cowards," Wahid commented.

"They haven't been stress-tested," Levi pointed out. "How many of them went through Boot Camp?"

She smiled, grimly, at the thought. Her Drill Instructors had told her that the only easy day at Boot Camp was yesterday, but she hadn't believed them until she'd actually started training in earnest. A quarter of the new recruits had quit within the first day, when they'd discovered that their implants were deactivated or denied access to the datanet. Others had decided the military wasn't for them when they realised it wasn't like a VR sim. You couldn't dial the pain and suffering down in real life.

Well, you can, she thought. *But that doesn't help recruits build character.*

"Be nice," she said. She glanced at Stewart. "Take the rest of the platoon to Marine Country, then get orders from staff. I'll report to the Major."

"Ouch," Stewart said. "Good luck."

Levi resisted the urge to make a rude gesture as she left the compartment. Her new uniform itched, even though it was designed for combat wear rather than ceremonial functions. She just hadn't had the time to break it in, not yet. But then, her old uniform had been broken down to its component atoms just to make sure it wasn't carrying a powered-down bug. The sheer level of surveillance on Harmony was enough to turn the most trusting man in the universe into a twitchy neurotic shell of a man.

And the level of surveillance in Boot Camp has been known to wear recruits down too, she reminded herself. *They just hate being monitored all the time.*

"Lieutenant," Major Rhodan said. They exchanged salutes as she stepped into the compartment. The marines were preparing counter-boarding deployments, although she had a nasty feeling that they would be next to useless. "I'm glad you made it."

"Thank you, sir," Levi said. She didn't know Rhodan that well. They'd served together for the past ten months, but she'd never served with him in combat. It was impossible to get the measure of a man until the bullets started flying. "Do we have any idea why they went mad?"

"No," Rhodan said. He gave her a humourless smile. "I was hoping that you had some insight."

"It was a pre-planned riot," Levi said. "And it was about as spontaneous as early-morning drill."

Rhodan nodded, curtly. "They just knocked down the wall?"

"Blasted it down," Levi said. "And then they forced their way into the embassy."

She wondered, as she outlined everything that had happened, if Major Rhodan was looking for a scapegoat. *Someone* would have to take the blame and she'd been the marine on the spot. It wasn't *common* for senior officers to try to escape responsibility, but this was a little more serious than a pack of marines getting drunk or a squad heading in the wrong direction because someone had trusted a lieutenant with a map. She told herself, firmly, that she'd done nothing wrong. She tried not to consider the possibility that it wouldn't matter.

"I believe we did the best we could, under the circumstances," she finished. "We certainly could not have engaged the crowd with lethal weapons as long as there was a way to get out."

"I agree," Rhodan said. "And I will make that clear in my report."

Assuming we see home again, Levi thought. Marines were used to being a long way from home, but Harmony was nine months from Earth... assuming unchallenged passage through the gravity points. *It won't be easy.*

"Thank you, sir," she said, instead.

Rhodan met her eyes. "Is your squad up to going back on duty now?"

"Of course, sir," Levi said. "Where do you want us?"

Her lips twitched in droll amusement. Marines couldn't stop just because they wanted a break. The real world was rarely so obliging. She'd certainly never heard of an enemy force that put the brakes on because their quarry needed a rest. The constant marching - and shifting of the goalposts - at Boot Camp had seen off a few hundred more recruits. But the ones who had passed stopped for nothing.

"Draw combat armour from the stocks, then join the Rapid Reaction Force," Rhodan ordered, shortly. "If they try to board us, I want the RRF to move out to back up the local defenders and drive the boarding parties back to their shuttlecraft."

Levi kept her expression under tight control. *Odyssey's* crew would be armed, of course. They'd all had basic weapons training in the academy and constant refresher courses over the last few months. But she had no illusions about their ability to do more than slow any enemy intrusion down for a few minutes. The Harmonies wouldn't send unprepared or unarmoured troopers to board an alien starship.

"Yes, sir," she said. She had the nasty feeling it would prove useless, but she kept that thought to herself. "We'll get right on it."

"No rest for the wicked," Major Rhodan agreed. He sounded frustrated. "Maybe next time we can wrangle a deployment to Chicago."

"*Semper Fi*," Levi said.

"THEY'RE TRYING TO wear us down, Captain," Biscoe commented.

"It's working," Elton said. It had been an hour since he'd yanked the ambassador and her party out of the embassy gardens, an hour since the shuttlecraft had been picked off by the ground-based defences...an hour, during which nothing had happened. He'd expected to be challenged, he'd expected to be fired upon...but the Harmonies had said nothing. "How long can we keep the crew at full alert?"

He rubbed his forehead, tiredly. He'd had to send the alpha crews to catch some rest - the beta crews had taken over - but he couldn't take some rest himself. Even stepping into his office was a risk, if the Harmonies decided to open fire. Not being on the bridge in the middle of a war zone was a court martial offence...

His lips twitched. Under the circumstances, he would happily have faced a kangaroo court if it meant that he'd managed to get his ship and crew home.

"Not long, sir," Biscoe said. "No military crew can remain on full alert indefinitely."

Elton nodded, irritated. *That* was conventional wisdom. And it was true. The wear and tear on the crew - as well as his ship's defences - would grind them down, eventually. The longer the stalemate continued, the greater the advantage to the other side. *They* didn't have to worry about keeping all their weapons and defences at full alert. Elton didn't have to look at the display to know that a number of fortresses had stepped down their weapons and sensors...why not? It wasn't as if they were *needed* to reduce *Odyssey* to free-floating atoms.

"Make sure the alpha crew gets enough rest," he ordered, although he knew it would be difficult. Being trapped in low orbit, surrounded by enough firepower to vaporise a planet, was enough to keep even the stoutest crewman awake. He might have to order them to run sedative programs through their implants, but they created their own problems. Waking the crew in a hurry would be impossible. "And get some rest yourself."

Biscoe frowned. "I submit, Captain, that *you* should get some rest."

Elton glanced, longingly, at the couch. A few hours of sleep were tempting...

"I can't leave the command deck," he said. He looked back at the display. The red icons hadn't moved, but it was hard to escape the sense they were looming closer. "You should go for a rest."

He shook his head in annoyance. There were stimulant programs that would keep him awake, if he wanted to use them. But they tended to have side effects he couldn't afford when he was in the command chair. He'd overused them at the academy and wound up seeing things during an exam. The proctors had been very sarcastic, he recalled...

...And his mind was wandering. That wasn't good.

"I should be on the bridge too," Biscoe said.

"Get some rest," Elton said. He understood how his XO felt, but his presence on the bridge wasn't going to make a difference one way or the other. "That's an order."

Biscoe nodded. "Yes, sir."

Elton watched him go, wondering - not for the first time - what Hoshiko Sashimi Stuart would have done. Tried to leave orbit, daring the fortresses to open fire? Or tried to blast her way out? Or...Elton cursed, under his breath. He didn't know what was going on, something that made it impossible to come up with any plans. The only thing he was sure of, really, was that time was running out.

And that I'm in the hot seat, he thought, numbly. *And to think I wanted starship command.*

He rose and headed for the hatch, stepping onto the bridge. Nothing had changed; his ship still held position in low orbit, watched by enough firepower to deter an entire fleet. He was morbidly surprised the Harmonies hadn't simply opened fire by now, although a miss would send their missiles plunging into Harmony's atmosphere. But then, if they were concerned about accidentally striking their homeworld, all they had to do was summon their own warships to drive *Odyssey* away.

"Captain," Lieutenant Suborn said. He looked young, surprisingly young. Elton told himself, firmly, that he wouldn't have won a coveted promotion if he hadn't been reasonably competent. Besides, looking youthful was fashionable these days. "The freighter crews are getting antsy."

"Tell them to hold position," Elton ordered, stiffly. He understood how the merchants felt, but there was no choice. "They can't go anywhere right now."

"Aye, Captain," Suborn said. "I..."

He broke off as his console bleeped. "Captain, they're hailing us!"

"Put them through," Elton ordered. He leaned forward, eagerly. He had a feeling he wasn't going to like what he was about to hear, but he found it hard to care. Something was happening, at last! "And call Mr. Biscoe back to the bridge."

A low atonal voice echoed through the compartment. "You will surrender your ship or be destroyed," it said. "You have twenty minutes to comply."

Understanding crashed down on Elton as the pieces finally fell into place. *Dear God*, he thought. *That's what this is all about. That's what they were aiming at, all along. They want the ship!*

EIGHTEEN

Does it actually matter?
Yes, we won a victory. BUT...that victory was won through surprise, long enemy supply lines, and advanced technology. The Tokomak were operating right at the limits of their logistics chain. Any halfway competent post-battle analysis would tell them so. I'm sure, once they stop panicking, that they will come up with all sorts of reasons to dismiss the threat we pose. There is no reason to assume that they will immediately decree a final solution and bend their every effort to carrying it out.
-Solar Datanet, Political Forum (Grand Alliance Thoughts)

"They want the ship," Captain Yasser said.

Rebecca sucked in her breath. "Are you *sure*?"

The captain paced the conference room, looking grim. "Yes," he said. "Everything they've done, everything they told us...it was intended to get their hands on our technology. I suspect they wanted to dicker with you, but when you refused to hand over the tech they decided to provoke an incident and just *take* it."

"They'd be breaking galactic norms," Rebecca said, honestly shocked. "Captain..."

"They can tell the Galactics that we killed their people," the captain said, bluntly. "And the other Galactics will accept it, because it's what they will want to believe."

"They may have had this in mind all along," Lieutenant Jayne Fisher said. "Captain...Madam Ambassador...how do we *know* there was a coup?"

"They told us," Rebecca said. She broke off. "They *told* us."

"Precisely," Jayne said. "We have no independent verification that the Harmonies actually *had* a coup. All we know is what they told us - and they might have lied."

Rebecca swallowed, hard. It was difficult to look Jayne Fisher in the eye - the woman had butchered her face with cybernetic implants - but she forced herself to meet the younger girl's gaze. She couldn't be serious, could she? No one could plan and carry out such a deception and expect it to work...could they?

"If that's true," she started. She caught herself. "Do you have any proof?"

Jayne gazed back, evenly. "We have no independent sources within the kingdom, nothing to tell us what is actually going on," she said. "Given what we've learned about their society, planning and launching a coup without being detected seems impossible. There's no way they just started mass surveillance of everyone unlucky enough to live on their homeworld, Madam Ambassador. Their system has been in place for centuries.

"We know that they have been fortifying the gravity points between Harmony and Hudson," she added, after a moment. "We also know that such actions *should* have brought down the wrath of the Tokomak, but - as far as we know - no hammer has actually descended. Does that mean, for example, that the Tokomak actually *approved* the fortifications? And do we actually *know* that the gravity point chains leading to Tokomak space are actually fortified?"

She looked at the captain. "If I were the Galactics, sir, I'd do everything in my power to get my hands on human-grade technology," she insisted. "And we obligingly sent them a whole starship to capture and take apart to see how it works."

"That would mean war," Rebecca said.

"We're already at war, Madam Ambassador," the captain said, harshly. "A Phony War, perhaps, but a war none the less. If the Harmonies are actually still allied with the Tokomak..."

Rebecca cursed under her breath. *That* made sense, too much sense. In hindsight...perhaps they should have suspected they were being played. It *had* been a con trick - and, like any other con trick, it had worked because they'd wanted to believe what they were being told.

She looked at the captain. "And they're not going to let us go, are they?"

"I doubt it," the captain said. "They take us and the freighters, then ship *Odyssey* off to somewhere isolated for dismantling while dumping us on an isolated world...if they're feeling merciful. It's a bit more likely that they'll dispose of us in a matter recycler. We didn't manage to send a message back once we entered the fortified zone, so they *might* be able to convince Sol that we vanished somewhere in deep space..."

He shook his head. "We weren't expected back for at least two years," he added. "Even Hudson Base wasn't expecting to see us for less than six months. By the time Sol realises we're gone, everything will have been nicely smoothed over and no one will have the slightest idea what happened to us."

Rebecca closed her eyes in pain. Captain Yasser was right. Sol would never know for sure what had happened to *Odyssey* and her crew. Or, perhaps, the Harmonies would present the Solar Union with a narrative suggesting that *Odyssey* had deserved her fate. Even if the Solar Union refused to believe it, the other Galactics would take it as an excuse to do nothing. And waging war this far from Sol would be impossible. The Harmonies might get away with it.

She opened her eyes, forcing herself to remain calm. "Can we get out of the trap?"

"We'll have to find out," the captain said. He sounded grim - grim and determined. "We're not going to surrender *Odyssey* to them."

Of course not, Rebecca thought. The standard POW conventions, laid down by the Tokomak, probably didn't apply in this case. She had no doubt that the Harmonies would do everything in their power to ensure that no one ever found out what they'd done. *Better to risk everything on a single throw of the dice than to surrender meekly.*

"Good luck, then," she said. "Good luck to us all."

The captain's lips twitched into something that might - charitably - have been called a smile.

"Thank you," he said, dryly. "We're going to need it."

Rebecca nodded. "Where do you want us?"

"I want you to talk to them," the captain said. "Stall them as long as possible. Dig up every precedent you can remember to delay any attempt to seize the ship. I know...they're not likely to listen to you for long. Just try to keep them talking."

"I'll do my best," Rebecca said. "You do realise" - she swallowed, again - "you do realise they're unlikely to pretend to take me seriously any longer?"

"Do your best," the captain said. "Going by their original ultimatum, there are only five minutes left before they open fire."

"Oh," Rebecca said.

"So talk fast," the captain added.

THERE COULD BE no question, Elton knew as he returned to the bridge, of surrendering his ship to the enemy. Quite apart from the simple fact that his crew would be killed, just to keep them from popping up later, he couldn't let the Galactics get an insight into humanity's technological advantage. Two years of duplication and mass production would prove, once again, that God was on the side of the big guns. Humanity would advance too, but not enough to stave off the massed enemy fleets.

"The ambassador is talking to the enemy," Lieutenant Williams reported. "So far, they appear to be talking back."

Elton nodded. "Let's hope she can string them along for a few hours," he said, although he knew that was unlikely. There were few inconvenient witnesses in the system, something that - in hindsight - ought to have alerted them ahead of time. "Tactical?"

"I've completed the analysis," Callaway said. "But getting us and the freighters out of here is going to be tricky."

"I know," Elton said. "Mr. XO?"

"The freighter crews are ready," Biscoe said. "But they don't know what to do."

"Tell them to stand by," Elton said.

He forced himself to think. Their one advantage was that the orbital fortresses couldn't risk firing antimatter-tipped missiles towards *Odyssey*, if only because they would run the risk of hitting the planet. The warheads probably couldn't crack the forcefields protecting the PDCs, but they'd wreak inconceivable devastation on the rest of the planet. And yet...the moment *Odyssey* moved out of orbit, it was going to be open season. It was probably too much to hope that one fortress would accidentally blast another.

We might make it out, if we deploy all of our technological surprises, he thought. *Odyssey* might not be a cruiser or a battleship, but she did have *some* surprises hidden within her hull. *And yet, where do we go from there?*

He glanced at the live feed from the long-range drones. The system's gravity points were heavily fortified. Even if they managed to jump through without being blown to atoms, they'd materialise within the gunsights of a *second* set of fortresses. An idea nagged at the back of his mind, but refused to solidify into something useful. *Odyssey* would have to head for interstellar space, assuming they managed to get away from the planet. The more he considered it, the more he realised just how badly they were trapped. They'd be running a gauntlet of enemy fortresses, all shooting from point-blank range.

"Captain," Biscoe said. He spoke through his implants, using a private channel. "We could threaten the planet."

It was a mark of Elton's desperation that he found himself considering it for longer than a few seconds. Threatening to commit mass slaughter - if not genocide - would not only get him hauled in front of a court martial, it would get him hurled in front of a firing squad. The Galactics could threaten extermination, if they wished. The Solar Union liked to think it was a little more civilised. And yet, would it work...?

They don't give a damn about their civilians, he thought, numbly. *And everyone who matters on the planet is hidden under a forcefield. The remainder... don't count.*

"No," he said, flatly. "We won't take that step."

"Yes, Captain," Biscoe said.

"I've plotted out several possible paths through the fortresses," Callaway said. "But they all expose us to *some* fire."

"We'll just have to minimise the risk," Elton said. He knew there was no way it could be negated completely. Some of the fortresses were clearly not on alert, but the Harmonies would have plenty of time to flash-wake their systems before *Odyssey* passed within firing range. Unless, of course..."Are they sending ships into low orbit?"

"Not as far as we can tell," Callaway said. "Stealthed probes are revealing nothing."

"It would be risky to try," Biscoe offered.

"We can't stay here indefinitely," Elton said. Right now, it was a stalemate. He couldn't escape and they couldn't capture him. But that would change when - if - the Harmonies decided to abandon their plan to capture *Odyssey* intact. "Sooner or later, they're going to demand we surrender - again."

"And then decide there's no point in prolonging matters any longer," Biscoe finished.

Elton nodded. "Start deploying the drones," he ordered. He glanced at his console. The ambassador was *still* talking to the aliens. "We'll go in twenty minutes, once the drones are in place."

"Aye, Captain," Callaway said.

Rebecca braced herself as the channel opened, wishing - for the first time - that she had more experience negotiating from a position of weakness. She'd dictated to warlords on Earth - knowing that she was backed by more firepower than any of those monstrous assholes could comprehend - and spoken to alien powers as equals. But the Harmonies not only considered themselves superior to a junior race like humanity, they had the firepower to back it up too.

A face appeared in front of her, wrapped in a silver cloak. All she could see was the eyes and hints of green skin.

"You will surrender..."

"I am an ambassador, accredited by my government to treat with ambassadors of equal rank," Rebecca said, casually. "Are you an ambassador?"

The alien hesitated, just long enough to let her know she'd scored a hit. There was no point showing weakness, not when neither she nor the captain had any intention of actually *surrendering* the ship. And if she knew one thing about the Galactics, it was that they thought in terms of masters and slaves. If they could be convinced that *she* was the master...

"I am a representative of my government," the alien managed, finally. "I..."

"I'm afraid I must speak to an ambassador," Rebecca said. She spoke from memory, silently grateful that her instructors had forced her to wade through the material until she didn't need her implants to remember it. "Galactic Diplomatic Protocol, Book Four, Chapter Five, Section Eight, Subsection Twelve. All discussions between diplomatic representatives are to be conducted between equals. I must insist that you find me an ambassador at once."

She leaned back in her chair, making it clear that she was fully prepared to wait. It was unlikely the alien could read her body language, any more than she could read his, but it was better to be safe than sorry. They *might* have a translation and analysis program monitoring the conversation. She'd found that they tended to make entertaining mistakes - which were less entertaining when lives were at stake - yet the Galactics still took them seriously. It helped, she supposed, that they didn't have true AI.

A new face appeared in the display, five minutes later. It wore the same silver robes, bearing a set of diplomatic insignias. Rebecca made a show of examining them while the alien presented his credentials, including a long list of postings she suspected were intended to either impress or intimidate her. It wasted his time, so she made no attempt to stop the recital. If she was lucky, she could waste even *more* time by reciting her credentials right back at him.

"You are ordered to surrender," the alien said, once he had finished his recital. "The interstellar court has sat in judgement and determined that you are responsible for numerous crimes against the Kingdom of Harmonious Order."

They want the ship, Rebecca reminded herself. *They want us to hand her over to them.*

"It has been clearly determined by Galactic Courts that any such hearing is only legitimate if both parties have a chance to present their stories," Rebecca said. "I can cite hundreds of precedents if you wish."

"A message was sent, demanding that you dispatch a representative," the alien countered. "A failure to attend a hearing, when given sufficient notice, is a *de facto* refusal to enter a plea. I can cite hundreds of precedents for that too."

"No such message was sent, let alone acknowledged," Rebecca said. "Absent a formal demand for submissions, any attempt to take possession of our ship is of questionable legality. Furthermore" - she pushed on, trying to force the alien to respond to her - "such hearings have to be carried out by neutral judges. There is no one neutral on this planet."

The alien made a hissing sound. "The courts on this world are renowned for their harmony."

Rebecca wondered, absently, if that was an alien pun. "The court cannot be considered neutral, as it is sited on Harmony and the judges are drawn from the planet's governing body," she said. She'd read enough horror stories about Galactic courts to understand their weaknesses. "In all such cases, the inquest should be shifted to the nearest neutral world."

There was a long pause. "This is not a simple inquest into smuggling," the alien said. It was hard to be sure, but Rebecca thought he was angry. "This is an inquest into the deaths of seven hundred and fifty thousand civilians on our homeworld."

Rebecca blinked. Seven hundred and fifty *thousand*? The marines had estimated that around a thousand Harmonies had been killed, although they'd admitted that there was no way to be sure. Seven hundred and fifty would have been a believable number. Seven hundred and fifty *thousand* was so far beyond believable that no one would believe it. Maybe they'd just jacked the number up to impress the other Galactics. A thousand dead would pass unremarked on many overpopulated worlds.

"We have ultimate jurisdiction in such matters," the alien continued. "You are ordered to surrender your ship now or we will take it by force."

"We fly under a diplomatic flag," Rebecca said. She used her implants to send the captain a message, warning him that they were running out of time. She'd hoped the Harmonies could be stalled for longer, but clearly time was not on their side. "An attempt to seize the ship is prohibited by Galactic Law..."

"Which can be put aside by your refusal to collaborate," the alien said. "Surrender your ship."

Rebecca smiled, rather coldly, as the captain's response blinked up in front of her eyes, informing her that they were ready to go.

"No," she said.

The alien recoiled. "What do you mean, *no?*"

"I mean no," Rebecca said, airily. It felt *good* to throw diplomacy aside, just once. She might be about to die, along with the rest of the crew, but at least they'd go out swinging. A dull vibration ran through the ship as she started to move. "I mean we *won't* surrender. And if you are wise, you will make no attempt to bar our way."

"You cannot escape," the alien said, flatly. She was surprised he didn't say *resistance is futile*. "You will be destroyed."

"We shall see," Rebecca said.

She sent a single command to the cabin's processor. The alien's face vanished. She smiled, then poured herself a drink and sat back in the chair to wait as the noise of the ship's engines grew louder. There were only two options. Either they'd make it out or they'd be dead in the next few minutes. One way or the other, she wouldn't have to pretend to be polite to them any longer.

And maybe if I fall asleep, she told herself, *I might just sleep through all the excitement.*

She shook her head. She knew that wasn't going to happen.

NINETEEN

I cannot believe that anyone would argue that, not seriously. The Tokomak do not lose. The Tokomak DID not lose...until the day they did. This is not a small defeat, even if we didn't take out a percentage point of a percentage point of their mobile firepower. We gave their reputation for invincibility a black eye. There is no way they will allow us to slip back into obscurity. They have to smash us flat before we give others ideas. Even the proof the bastards can be beaten - alone - will cripple their power.
-Solar Datanet, Political Forum (Grand Alliance Thoughts)

"Enemy fortresses are bringing up tactical sensors," Callaway reported. "Captain?"

"Activate drones," Elton ordered. "And then start spoofing their sensors."

"Aye, Captain," Callaway said. "Drones going active...*now*."

Elton nodded, grimly. If they were lucky - if the Harmonies hadn't improved their sensor suites - they should have problems localising *Odyssey* and her charges. But if they were wrong...he pushed the thought out of his head. They'd been committed, even if they hadn't realised it, the moment they passed through the gravity points. All that mattered now was escape.

"Bring up the drive field," he ordered. The enemy sensors were *definitely* having problems locking onto their ships. "And take us out of orbit."

"Aye, Captain," Marie said. "Moving...*now*."

"The freighters are falling in behind us," Biscoe put in. "I've got the drones shadowing them too."

"Tell them to stay close," Elton ordered. "We won't be able to go back for any stragglers."

He took a breath as the enemy sensor sweeps glided closer. "And stand by point defence."

"Aye, Captain," Callaway said.

Elton gripped his chair, bracing himself. The Harmonies knew they'd never be able to take *Odyssey* intact, not now. Their only priority was destroying his ship before they could escape and warn the Solar Union. When would they open fire? It would be safe enough in a few minutes, when *Odyssey* was no longer between the orbital battlestations and a very vulnerable planet...

"They're launching gunboats, Captain," Callaway snapped. New icons flashed to life on the display. "And I'm picking up starships decloaking in high orbit."

"Understood," Elton said. It was a race now. They'd be in the danger zone within sixty seconds, perhaps less. "Engage the gunboats as soon as they enter range."

He gritted his teeth as the gunboats came closer, their sensors sweeping space for human targets. The enemy CO hadn't made a bad call. An individual gunboat wouldn't be much of a threat, but collectively...if they blasted the drive section, *Odyssey* would be trapped, helplessly dead in space. No doubt someone would whine that he'd fired the first shot, yet...he shrugged. They were well past that stage now.

"Enemy gunboats entering phaser range," Callaway reported.

"Fire at will," Elton ordered.

The first wave of gunboats didn't realise, part of his mind noted, just how effective human phasers had become over the past fifty years.

For better or worse, they were about to find out. Phaser bursts flashed from *Odyssey's* arrays, each one striking a gunboat and vaporising it. The second wave hastily went into a series of evasive manoeuvres, spinning madly through space and dodging bolt after bolt as they tried to get closer to *Odyssey's* hull. Elton's point defence computers, primed to deal with smaller and faster targets, updated their targeting programs and continued to fire. More gunboats vanished from the display before they had a chance to get into firing range.

"The remaining gunboats are entering their attack run," Callaway snapped. "Point defence systems are engaging..."

"Deploy a second flight of drones," Elton ordered. The gunboats had been cut down sharply - he doubted they could do real damage, unless they were armed with antimatter warheads - but they could still help the fortresses to target his ships. "Prepare to take incoming fire..."

"They're angling the gunboats towards the freighters," Biscoe put in. "But the freighters can take care of themselves."

"Not enough," Elton said. He cursed under his breath. The freighters were barely armed with popguns. They might be able to ward off a gunboat, but not a true warship. In hindsight, they shouldn't have brought them. "Can you hit the gunboats?"

"Not unless we reverse course," Callaway said.

Elton cursed, again. He was an officer in the Solar Navy. Defending humanity's trade was one of his duties. But if he reversed course, he risked losing everything...for one ship and her crew. He knew he couldn't take the risk, even though he'd hate himself later.

"Continue on our current course," he ordered.

"*Hilton* has been destroyed with all hands," Biscoe reported. There was no condemnation in his voice. Somehow, that made it worse. "*Frankfurter* has taken damage, but her drives remain intact."

"Understood," Elton said. He'd mourn later, he promised himself. "Keep alert for an opportunity to evacuate *Frankfurter*."

"Aye, Captain," Biscoe said.

Elton heard the doubt in his voice, even though it wasn't expressed. And he was right. It was unlikely, vanishingly unlikely, that they'd have a chance to teleport *Frankfurter's* crew to safety. Even the relatively light bursts of phaser fire they'd exchanged would be enough to disrupt a teleport beam. The crew might be safer on their damaged ship.

The last of the gunboats fell back as *Odyssey* raced onwards, clearly unwilling to push the offensive into the teeth of her fire. Elton wasn't reassured. The gunboats hadn't even managed to scratch his paint, but they *had* forced him to reveal too much about his weapons and defences. He had no doubt that the fortresses were already adjusting their targeting patterns to compensate, now they knew what he could do. A few minor modifications and they'd give him a whole series of black eyes.

And we're entering the danger zone now, he thought, numbly. They can fire at will.

"They're launching missiles," Callaway reported. He sucked in his breath, sharply. "That's overkill..."

"As you were," Elton said, quietly. It *was* overkill. There were so many missiles coming at them, from five different directions, that the display had given up trying to designate each of them with a separate icon. "Are the drones active?"

"Aye, Captain," Callaway said.

"Then spread them out," Elton ordered. "And bring up the full ECM fields now."

He braced himself as the swarm of missiles came closer. It was enough missiles, even if they were nukes rather than antimatter warheads, to smash *Odyssey* to dust. No one would ever find a trace of her remains, if she was struck by over a thousand missiles. And yet...and yet, a number were already being decoyed away, lured towards the ECM drones. He hoped, gripping his seat so hard it hurt, that the fortresses didn't have time to take control of the missiles manually and redirect them. The gunboats might still be close enough to see through the ECM.

"Missiles are entering engagement range," Callaway said.

"Engage with point defence," Elton ordered, shortly.

It was a gamble, but one he had to take. There was no way the *drones* could fire a single phaser bolt, let alone match *Odyssey's* point defence. The moment the point defence opened fire, the fortresses would know *precisely* which image was the real starship. And then...they'd adjust their targeting projections and resume fire.

"I think we decoyed away two-thirds of the missiles," Callaway said, as the icons swerved to follow the drones. "The remainder are being engaged...now."

Elton leaned forward as missiles started to disappear from the display, each one vanishing in a brilliant flash of energy. Antimatter warheads, then. It was a display of overkill unseen since the Tokomak had crushed one particularly annoying race by using antimatter to literally wipe out the entire system, even the gas giants. Perversely, it might just work in their favour. Each missile would - hopefully - take out several more missiles when it died. And, if they were *very* lucky, it would disrupt enemy sensors.

Or maybe not, he thought, as another wave of missiles flickered into existence. The fortresses had resumed fire, pouring missiles towards *Odyssey* at terrifying speed. They'd expend all their missiles at this rate, leaving the planet apparently undefended. *They can still target us even through the haze...*

"Incoming," Callaway snapped.

Elton hit his console. "Brace for impact," he snapped. "All hands, brace for impact..."

The starship shook, violently. Elton held on for dear life, staring at the main display as the shields struggled to cope with the impact. They'd taken the impact without failing, but he knew that wouldn't last. Several more blows like that would be enough to do real damage as they burned out shield generators, leaving the hull bare. And then a single warhead would be enough to vaporise the entire ship.

"The second wave of drones are gone," Callaway said. "Request permission to deploy a third."

"Granted," Elton said. The next wave of missiles was getting closer, even as the tiny convoy altered course to avoid it. "The freighters?"

"No further losses, so far," Biscoe said. "Captain..."

"I know," Elton said. "That won't last."

Odyssey rocked, again. "Direct hit, port shields," Callaway reported. "Shield Generators Three and Four have taken a beating, Shield Generator Five is gone."

"Dispatch a damage control team," Elton ordered.

"Aye, Captain," Biscoe said.

Elton gritted his teeth as another missile slammed into his shields. The enemy had found their range now, throwing hundreds of missiles into the killing zone in hopes of scoring a handful of hits. *Odyssey's* point defence was burning dozens of missiles out of space, while others were being lured away, but the remainder kept boring in towards his ship. A handful even passed within touching distance of his shields before losing their missile locks and plunging on into empty space.

There's going to be one hell of a clean-up bill after this, he thought, numbly. *Luckily, we won't have to pay it.*

"They're dispatching another wave of gunboats," Callaway said. "I..."

"*Billy Butcher* is gone," Biscoe said. He cursed, savagely. "*Frankfurter* has been destroyed too."

Seven left, Elton thought. He felt a bitter stab of guilt, mingled with grief for the freighter crews. They'd travelled tens of thousands of light-years to die. *And every time one dies, it gets easier for the remaining missiles to target us.*

"Target the gunboats with shipkillers and open fire," he snapped. It was a waste, but he saw no alternative. The point defence had too many other targets to take out. "Try and angle some additional drones towards them."

"Aye, Captain," Callaway said.

Elton forced himself to take a step back and consider the situation. *Odyssey* was midway through the planetary defence network, twisting and turning to avoid coming into energy range of any of the orbital battlestations. They were still belching missiles, but with more caution... he wasn't sure if that was a good sign or not. Their tacticians could be busily trying to reprogram their missiles to compensate for humanity's ECM. Elton's lips twitched at the thought. If Jayne Fisher was right, if the Harmonies were still in league with the Tokomak, their masters hadn't bothered to share what they'd learned from the Battle of Earth.

Or they might have thought they had enough massed sensor power to burn through the ECM, he admitted, silently. The enemy wouldn't have been too far wrong, if they'd been challenging a proper warship. *Odyssey* was lousy with ECM projectors in hopes of avoiding a major confrontation. *Given time, they'll learn to compensate properly.*

"Damage control teams have fixed Shield Four," Biscoe reported quietly. The hull quivered again as a nuke struck the shields. Compared to the antimatter warheads and the tempest raging outside, it was barely noticeable. "Shield Five is beyond repair."

And needs to be replaced, Elton finished. *And doing that in the middle of an engagement may be impossible.*

"Tell the teams to do what they can," he ordered. "But right now it might be the least of our problems."

"Understood," Biscoe said.

"Incoming gunboats," Callaway snapped. "They're keeping their distance, right on the edge of point defence range..."

"Stupid," Williams muttered.

Elton took one look at the display and knew that Williams was wrong. "Target the gunboats and take them out," he snapped. The tidal wave of missiles moving up *behind* the gunboats would be taking their targeting data from them. At that range, no ECM known to exist could fool their sensors. *Odyssey* could *not* leave those gunboats intact, even if it risked taking two or three more hits. "Fire!"

"Aye, Captain," Callaway said.

"They're evading," Biscoe commented.

"Launch scatterpack missiles, targeted on the gunboats," Elton ordered. It was another waste - and the beancounters would probably demand his hide when they got home - but cheaper than losing the entire ship. "Drive them back!"

"Aye, Captain," Callaway said.

Elton held himself calm as a dozen gunboats vanished from the display, followed by a cloud of missiles. Thankfully, the enemy were *still* hurling antimatter warheads at them. But the remainder closed in, even though Marie threw the ship into a dizzying spiral that should have convinced any missile to go seek easier prey. He braced himself as alarms howled through the hull, a moment later before the entire ship rang like a bell...

"Starboard shield down," Biscoe snapped. "Damage to sectors..."

"Dispatch damage-control teams," Elton ordered. A bare hull meant certain death, if the enemy managed to pop a missile through the gap. "Try to keep the exposed hull away from their fire!"

The ship shuddered, again. "Direct hit," Biscoe reported. "Luckily, the prow shield held."

"*Lucia* is gone," Biscoe said. "*Jackdaw* has taken heavy damage..."

Damn it, Elton thought. *Odyssey* wasn't in the best of shapes herself. If he'd been fighting a normal enemy, he would have offered to surrender. But the Harmonies couldn't afford word getting out. Even if they did manage to convince the other Galactics that *they* were the injured party, it still wouldn't look good. Elton knew, all too well, that his crew were doomed unless they made their escape soon. *We're in deep shit.*

He forced himself to concentrate as they flew into a quiet patch of space. The enemy seemed to be regrouping, secure in the knowledge that *Odyssey* had to run another gauntlet before breaking out into interplanetary space. A second network of orbital battlestations waited for them, their sensors already locking onto the hull. It wouldn't be long before the gunboats came creeping back, ready to guide the missiles to their target...

"They've adjusted Shield Nine," Biscoe reported. "We have full shields again, but not for long."

Elton nodded. Shield generators had their limits. The more space they had to cover, the weaker the shields would be. Perversely, incoming missiles couldn't be used to drive wedges between the different generators, but there was enough firepower heading towards them that it hardly mattered. They were doomed if they stayed where they were.

"Alter course," he ordered. "Take us straight towards Target Nine."

"Aye, Captain," Marie said.

"Mr. Callaway, deploy the next set of drones," Elton added. "And bring them online on my mark."

"Aye, Captain," Callaway said.

Elton leaned back in his chair as the next set of antimatter missiles flashed into existence on the display. The Harmonies had to be raging, given how much firepower they'd expended in the last seven minutes. He had a feeling that, whatever happened, there were going to be a few shakeups in orbit. The Harmonies had practically shot themselves dry trying to take out a single cruiser.

Although they did score a few nasty hits, his thoughts added. *And one or two more will be the end of us.*

"Drones deployed, Captain," Callaway said. He paused. "I'm picking up more starships decloaking near the planet."

"Someone must be feeling antsy," Biscoe commented.

Elton shrugged. "Stand by to bring the drones online," he ordered. "Stand by..."

The moment came. "Now!"

He leaned forward as the drones came online. The enemy saw - *had* to see, if the plan had any chance of working - a dozen starships, each one an exact copy of *Odyssey*. And they were all ramping up their drives, charging madly at the nearest battlestations. The Tokomak had designed the fortresses to soak up damage, but none of them could stand up to an 800-metre-long starship moving at even a tiny percentage of the speed of light. Just for a few seconds, they'd panic; each fortress would be thrown back on its own defences...

"Launch Hammers," he ordered. Technically, he was breaking regulations by deploying them so close to an enemy sensor network, but...under the circumstances, it was just another charge for his court-martial. "And take us in after them."

"Aye, Captain," Callaway said.

Elton prayed, silently, as the missiles roared away from *Odyssey*, straight towards Target Nine. The giant battlestation was *right* in their path, perfectly positioned to engage them with its energy weapons as they passed. But...did the Harmonies *know* about Hammers? The Tokomak had seen them in action, back during the Battle of Earth...had they told the Harmonies? A secret weapon that could smash through their battleships as if they were made of paper...

And one that could be countered, if they knew what they were facing, he thought. *Now...*

"They're trying to engage with point defence," Callaway said. There was an undertone of cold delight in his voice. "Useless."

Elton nodded. They were - literally - firing into a black hole. They wouldn't stop the Hammers like that...

The first Hammer slammed into the fortress's shields, punched through and smashed into the hull. The second followed, a moment later. Elton braced himself - the fortresses *were* designed to soak up a *lot* of damage - then pretended not to hear the cheers that echoed around the bridge as the fortress exploded. The two Hammers died a moment later, caught in the blast. Target Nine had been vaporised.

He let out a breath. "Take us through," he ordered. "And ramp up the drives as much as you can."

"Aye, Captain," Marie said.

TWENTY

So what?
Losing so many ships has to have hurt, even though - as you say - the total losses are a very tiny percentage of their overall numbers. You can bet anything you care to put forward that they will be pushing that interpretation as hard as they can. They'll want their allies to believe that the Battle of Earth was nothing more than a stubbed toe. A panicky reaction will only undermine that narrative.
The fact that none of this will be actually true will not bother them.
-Solar Datanet, Political Forum (Grand Alliance Thoughts)

"I always wanted to fly through a fireball," Biscoe commented.

"Remain focused," Elton ordered. The fortress had been largely vaporised, but chunks of debris and clouds of space dust still posed a threat. "Tactical?"

"Enemy ships are moving to block our escape," Callaway said. "The fortresses are resuming fire."

Elton nodded, glumly, as the nearest fortress icons belched clouds of missiles towards *Odyssey*. His ship was fast, one of the fastest starships in known space, but she couldn't outrun Galactic-grade missiles. The Harmonies had clearly decided they could fire freely, now that there was no real danger of hitting the planet. He had to admit that they might well be right.

"Deploy drones to protect the freighters," he ordered, shortly. Logically, the decloaking warships wouldn't be providing the fortresses with updated targeting information. Galactic tactical manuals warned of the dangers of trying anything so complicated outside a simulation chamber. But it was impossible to be sure. The Harmonies had to be getting desperate. "Helm?"

"We can drop into FTL now," Marie reported. "But they *might* have a gravity well generator."

"The freighters can't," Biscoe added. "We need to get further from the planet."

"Understood," Elton said. Charging the enemy ships was insane, but he didn't see any other way to escape. Remaining within the planet's gravity shadow would lead to certain destruction. Given just how badly matters had moved out of control, he had no doubt the Harmonies would do everything in their power to destroy his ship. "Helm, take us directly towards them."

"Aye, sir," Marie said.

Elton forced himself to think clearly as *Odyssey* picked up speed. There was no time to evacuate the remaining freighters...in hindsight, he should have evacuated the entire convoy as soon as the embassy was attacked. If he'd yanked out the crews and destroyed the freighters, his ship could be in FTL by now. A mistake, one of many. He promised himself, silently, that he'd mourn the dead as soon as his ship was safe.

And we don't know if they have gravity well technology, he reminded himself. *We might drop into FTL only to be dragged back out a microsecond later.*

He glanced at the live feed from the analysis deck, but saw nothing useful. It was frustrating as hell. The analysts were telling him countless details about the enemy defences, yet they couldn't answer any of the questions he *needed* answering. He bit down on his annoyance as he scanned the flagged messages, trying to determine if there were any hints.

In theory, a standard stardrive could be turned into a gravity well generator, if the engineers knew what they were doing. In practice...

We don't know if they were told what happened during the Battle of Earth, he thought. *They certainly weren't prepared for Hammers.*

"Captain," Callaway said. "The fortresses are continuing to fire."

"The drones are making hash of their targeting," Biscoe said. "I'd hate to see the bill for this little skirmish."

"It could cost us our lives," Elton said. The first wave of missiles were entering *Odyssey's* point defence zone, hundreds getting burned out of space every second. But there were always more...the Harmonies probably wanted to overwhelm his defences. If they managed to keep up such a colossal weight of fire, and theoretically they could, they might just succeed. "I..."

The ship rocked, sharply. "Two direct hits, rear shield quadrant," Biscoe reported. "The shield held, barely."

"Order the damage control teams to work on additional generators," Elton said. Under the circumstances, keeping the ship reasonably intact was their top priority. "And warn engineering to be ready to repair the drive."

"Aye, Captain," Biscoe said.

Callaway cursed. "Enemy starships on attack vector," he snapped. A stream of red icons were advancing towards *Odyssey*. "Captain?"

"Engage at will," Elton said. He sucked in his breath as the icons grew closer. "Helm, prepare to take evasive action."

"Aye, Captain," Marie said.

Elton gritted his teeth as the enemy starships - they looked like destroyers - opened fire, their missiles roaring towards *Odyssey* as they closed to energy weapons range. Callaway returned fire, scoring five direct hits in quick succession. One destroyer exploded, another rolled to one side streaming plasma...the remainder kept coming, their energy weapons lashing out at *Odyssey*. Marie altered course sharply, dodging one destroyer that had threatened to come far too close to the hull. Elton would have been surprised, normally, if the Galactics had resorted to kamikaze tactics, but they were definitely desperate. The destroyer was blown out of space a second later, before it could alter course and try again.

"They're holding the heavier ships in reserve," Biscoe said.

"We'll enter their firing range in two minutes," Callaway added. "They want us to run *another* gauntlet."

Elton nodded, feeling a flicker of contempt. The Harmonies had organised their fleet with all the precision of an armchair admiral. Their formation was perfect, utterly perfect. He doubted a single ship was even a few metres out of place. And yet, if they'd piled all of their ships into the engagement, they would have won by now. *Odyssey* was going to take a beating - more of a beating. But she hadn't lost.

Losing the fortress must have shocked them, he reminded himself. *Two missiles took out a fortress that was designed to take one hell of a pounding.*

He forced himself to remain calm. He couldn't afford to feel contemptuous, not when *Odyssey* was still in terrible danger. There was still enough firepower ahead of him to destroy his ship, if they weren't lucky. And while it was painfully obvious that the enemy commanders hadn't seen real action in their lifetimes, it didn't mean that they hadn't run countless simulations over the last few decades.

Just because they haven't seen action in centuries doesn't mean they're useless, he told himself, as more icons flickered to life on the display. *There's certainly nothing wrong with their missiles.*

"They're spreading out," Callaway reported. "Captain?"

Trying to make it harder for us to dodge, Elton thought. *They should have done that earlier.*

"Take us right through their formation," he ordered. "Mr. Biscoe?"

"The freighters are on our tail," Biscoe said. "Two of them have taken heavy damage, but their drives are still functional."

Elton nodded. "Punch it!"

Odyssey picked up speed as she hurled herself into the teeth of the enemy formation, weapons blazing. The enemy returned fire, great battleships launching wave after wave of missiles towards the human ships.

Elton couldn't help noticing that the shipboard missiles were actually *less* effective than the fortress-launched missiles, although there were enough of them that it probably wouldn't matter. Thankfully, the fortresses had slowed their rate of fire dramatically. *Odyssey* was still in range, but her decoy drones were soaking up all the missiles from the fortresses. They just couldn't get a solid lock on her hull.

"Recommend engaging with Hammers," Biscoe said.

Elton hesitated. *Odyssey* didn't *have* many Hammers. The bureaucrats had been reluctant to issue *any* to his ship, pointing out that *Odyssey* wasn't an actual warship. Even for the Solar Union, Hammers were expensive. And yet...*Odyssey* herself was *far* more expensive. It would be cheaper to replace a few dozen Hammers than the entire ship.

"Fire," he ordered. "And rig the other missiles to provide cover."

"Aye, Captain," Callaway said. "Hammers launching...*now*."

Elton watched as his ship plunged into the teeth of enemy fire. Someone on the other side had been thinking, he noted. They'd activated all of their ECM systems, trying to disrupt or break *Odyssey's* missile locks. False sensor images grew and multiplied...they didn't last long, no more than a few seconds as *Odyssey's* sensors burned through the ECM, but they made it harder to score hits. Elton would have sold his soul for an arsenal ship...

And as long as I'm wishing, I'd like the entire Solar Navy, he thought, sardonically.

An enemy battleship, a five-kilometre-long engine of mass destruction, disintegrated into a ball of expanding plasma as a Hammer punched through its shields and into its hull. The Hammer itself was caught in the blast and destroyed, even though it *should* have been able to escape and find a second target. Two more enemy battleships were wiped out, moments before the remainder started firing their missiles to sweep the remaining Hammers out of space. Elton scowled, even though it kept the battleships from pouring their missiles towards *Odyssey*. It proved that someone on the other side was thinking too clearly.

He looked at Williams. "Can you locate the command ship?"

"I think so, Captain," Williams said. A series of lines appeared on the display, centred on a blinking red icon. "The ship that appears to be issuing orders is *that* one."

That proves nothing, Elton thought. The Galactics did normally fly in strict formation, with orders passed down from a central command ship, but any smart commander would know better than to broadcast his presence so obviously. *And yet, if that is where the signals are going, we might just fuck up their command network if we took it out...*

"Tactical, target that ship," he ordered. "Fire!"

"Aye, Captain," Callaway said. "Firing...now!"

Odyssey shook, again. "Four direct hits, forward shields," Biscoe reported. "Shield Two is down; Shield Seven is destabilising!"

"Rotate shield generators to compensate," Elton snapped. If Shield One failed too, there would be a gaping hole in his defences. The Harmonies would have an excellent chance to slip a missile through the gap and vaporise his ship. "Get teams on it!"

"Engineering reports that it will take at least ten minutes to recycle Shield Seven," Biscoe said. "They're requesting permission to reformulate the shield matrix!"

"Tell them they have five minutes," Elton snapped back. Another shudder ran through the ship as an enemy destroyer pounded *Odyssey* with phaser fire. Callaway blasted her, a second later, but the damage had been done. "Hurry!"

He gritted his teeth. The enemy had had a fright, but they *knew* they were running out of time. They were bringing their battleships closer, slinging hundreds of missiles...even using half of them to take out the human missiles wasn't helping, not at such close range. The only thing forcing them to stay back were the Hammers and he didn't have enough of them to make a difference.

"The enemy flagship has been hit," Callaway reported. "But she's still in the fight."

"Keep firing," Elton ordered, sharply. His ship rang like a bell. Red icons flashed up, once again. "Mr. XO?"

"They got a nuke through the shield gap," Biscoe reported. "The hull took most of the blow, but we've lost a dozen phaser arrays and a couple of missile tubes."

"Point defence has been reduced by thirty percent," Callaway added. "Captain, they're adjusting their fire to take advantage of it."

Crap," Elton thought. "Keep rotating the ship," he ordered. "And keep hammering anything that you can hit!"

"Aye, Captain," Callaway said. *Odyssey* jerked, again. "I..."

The enemy flagship vanished. "Enemy target destroyed," Callaway said. "They've lost their main command and control network."

Elton nodded, grimly. It would take the enemy time - he had no idea how long - to adjust their datanet to compensate for the loss of the command ship. A human formation could do it in seconds, if necessary. But there were so many ships - and so many missiles - that it barely made any difference. The enemy could keep pounding his hull with or without the central command network.

Unless they're unwilling to do anything without orders, he thought. *And they won't be able to get orders until they work out who's in charge.*

He pushed the thought out of his head. It was insanely optimistic.

Odyssey rocked. "Two direct hits," Biscoe said. "The hull in sector three is threatening to disintegrate."

"Evacuate that section, seal all hatches," Elton snapped. Sector three wasn't *important*, not compared to the stardrive or the bridge, but a gash in the hull would present the enemy with an irresistible target. And, in the long term, it would weaken the hull's overall integrity. If the hull started to collapse, they were doomed. "Get those shields back up!"

"They're working on it," Biscoe said. "Captain, I..."

"The enemy command network has rebooted," Williams reported. "Captain, they're scattering their signals. I can't determine which ship is the new flagship."

Which they should have been doing all along, Elton thought. *We might be able to pick out the new commander, but it will be slow going.*

"Concentrate on jamming their signals as much as possible," he ordered. One advantage of *Odyssey* being alone, save for the six remaining freighters, was that he didn't have to worry about damaging his own tactical net. "If you do locate the new command ship, pass it to tactical."

"Aye, sir," Williams said.

"Got the shields back up," Biscoe reported. A low tremble ran through the ship, followed by a thunderclap. "Just in time too."

"Pass my compliments to the engineering and damage control staff," Elton said.

He took a long breath as *Odyssey* raged towards the edge of the gravity shadow. They *had* to cross the line for the freighters to escape, but the enemy knew it too. The Harmonies had thrown all decorum out the airlock. They were firing so madly that there was a valid chance that their missiles might target their own ships.

Just a few minutes more, he thought, numbly. The damage was mounting up, but...but they still had a chance. *Just keep going a few minutes more...*

"*Baker's Dozen* has been destroyed," Biscoe said. "*Innocently Insensitive* has taken significant damage. Her captain fears she will be unable to jump into FTL."

Elton cursed under his breath. There was no hope of stopping long enough to teleport the freighter's crew, not when there were so many waves of electromagnetic distortion washing through space. He briefly considered dispatching a shuttle, but even that ran an immense risk... there was nothing he could do. In a normal engagement, lifepods would be left alone for later recovery; now, he had no doubt that the lifepods would be vaporised along with the rest of the convoy.

"She's altering course," Biscoe added. "Captain...she's on a direct course for an enemy ship!"

She's going to ram, Elton thought. There was nothing he could do, not to save the freighter or her crew. All he could do was hope that her death would count for something. *Shit*.

The enemy ship realised the danger, a moment too late. *Innocently Insensitive* was already too close to the enemy ship by the time it opened fire. The freighter staggered under the impact, but kept coming. A moment later, the freighter rammed the battleship and both starships vanished in a colossal explosion.

"They're gone," Biscoe said.

"Keep us on course," Elton ordered.

"We'll be leaving the gravity shadow in thirty seconds," Marie reported.

"Take us into FTL as soon as the freighters are gone," Elton said. "Mr. XO, order the freighters to head to the RV point as planned."

"Aye, sir," Biscoe said.

The enemy kept firing, closing the range as *Odyssey* shot past their remaining ships and dived for open space. Elton allowed himself a moment of pride in his ship and her crew, then braced himself as a final salvo of missiles snapped at their heels. Two slammed home, one striking the shields hard enough to convince one of the remaining shield generators to give up the ghost. But it was already too late.

"The four remaining freighters are jumping into FTL," Biscoe reported.

"Deploy jamming drones," Elton snapped. It wasn't *too* likely they could disrupt the enemy's gravimetric sensors, at least long enough to matter, but it was worth trying. The researchers had been talking about creating a disruptor that would foul up any gravimetric sensor within range, yet so far the concept hadn't become reality. "Are we clear?"

"Yes, sir," Biscoe said. "All four freighters are gone."

On the display, the enemy ships were turning in a desperate bid to run *Odyssey* down. Elton smirked, despite himself. Anything fast enough to *catch* his ship was going to wish it hadn't, even though *Odyssey* had taken one hell of a beating. The Harmonies had given it their best shot and failed. They'd need to rethink their tactics before they came after *Odyssey* again.

"Then take us out of here," he ordered, shortly. It wouldn't be long before the Harmonies decided to try to track *Odyssey* down. They didn't have a choice. "*Now!*"

"Aye, sir," Marie said. "Drive engaging...now!"

Elton braced himself. *Odyssey* had taken damage, a *lot* of damage. The drives were still intact, according to the engineers, but...if they were wrong, they might have fought a running battle for nothing. If they were wrong...

The display blanked. "FTL engaged," Marie said. The relief in her voice was unmistakable. "We're on a direct course to the first waypoint, best possible speed."

"Very good," Elton said. Even if the enemy *did* have gravity well technology, they'd have to be precognitive to put it in his path. "Mr. XO, stand the ship down from red alert."

"Aye, sir," Biscoe said.

Elton sighed. "And now the hard work begins," he added. "We're still a very long way from home."

TWENTY-ONE

And yet, we don't really think ill of a man who jumps up and down, shouting and cursing because he's stubbed his toe.

Yes, it can be funny to watch. We might even think he was overacting in the hope of some sympathy from any watching eyes. But we wouldn't think there was anything odd about it, would we? The Tokomak would have the same advantage. Yes, they've been embarrassed; yes, they've stubbed their (metaphorical) toe...yes, they are justified in sending a large fleet to squash us.

We cannot avoid this war. All we can do is fight it on favourable terms.

-Solar Datanet, Political Forum (Grand Alliance Thoughts)

It wasn't common, even in the Solar Union, for starships to drop out of FTL in the interstellar wastelands between stars. There was nothing there, save for the occasional rogue planet and deep-space colony ship that had long-since been forgotten by the race that had launched it. Indeed, most races did their best to pretend that the interstellar void didn't exist, as if not thinking about it would make it go away. They knew, even if they didn't want to admit it, that losing stardrive between stars meant almost certain death. Very few starships would last long enough to limp to the nearest star at sublight speeds.

Elton floated in the inky darkness of space, studying his ship. *Odyssey's* white hull was scorched and pitted, the scars showing where enemy weapons had found their mark. Dozens of engineers - and hundreds of other crewmen with engineering training - were swarming over the ship, patching up cracks in the hull, replacing destroyed or damaged components and doing everything in their power to rig the ship for a further engagement. Beyond them, invisible in the darkness, the four remaining freighters were steadily being unloaded. Three of them, thankfully, had been crammed with supplies for his ships.

A shame we managed to unload most of the trade goods, he thought, tersely. *We might have had a use for them if we'd kept them.*

He cursed under his breath as the next set of reports flashed up in front of his eyes. Three men - all from the ambassador's staff - dead on Harmony. Nineteen more killed on *Odyssey*; fifty-seven killed on the destroyed freighters. And over ninety crewmen wounded, some so badly that they'd been placed in stasis until they could be taken home. The battle had been won, but victory had come with a very high price.

And we may not even get home, he reminded himself. *We're a very long way from home.*

Elton looked up, his eyes seeking Harmony's star. It was nothing more than a pinpoint of light, burning constantly against the inky darkness of space. There was certainly nothing to distinguish it from the other stars he could see. And yet...civilians didn't understand, not really, just how vast the distances between stars truly were. *Odyssey* could move at speeds beyond human comprehension, but even *she* would need years to get home without using the gravity points.

He sighed, tiredly, as he triggered the suit's gas jets and steered his way back to the nearest airlock. He'd always enjoyed going EVA, when he'd been at the academy, but there was no time to enjoy it now. Instead... the airlock opened, allowing him to glide inside and land neatly on the deck. The gravity field asserted itself as he stepped through the force-field, removing his helmet as soon as he could breathe freely. His ship seemed to be quieter than usual, even though the faint humming was still omnipresent. But then, they *had* stepped down the drives to allow the engineering crew to work on them.

Elton keyed his wristcom. "Mr. XO," he said, as he removed the rest of the suit and hung it on the rack. "Status report?"

"Gravimetric sensors are reporting a number of contacts moving through FTL," Biscoe said, grimly. "So far, none of them seem to have a precise lock on our location."

They'd be on top of us if they knew where we were, Elton thought. *Our course change must have thrown them off badly.*

He smiled, rather coldly. One advantage to hiding in interstellar space was that it was vanishingly unlikely that anyone would just *stumble* across their location. It was possible - he'd certainly feared the possibility - that the Harmonies would have a more extensive deep space tracking network than they'd suspected, but so far no one had tracked them down. As far as he knew, the enemy didn't have even a *hint* of where they were. Even a *best*-case scenario would force the Harmonies to search over twelve square *light-years* for *Odyssey*.

"And the repairs?"

"Mr. Wolf believes we will be back to eighty percent readiness by the end of the day," Biscoe said. "By then, exhaustion will probably be snapping at our heels."

"If they haven't found us by then, they probably won't until we light up the drive again," Elton said. He strode out of the compartment and walked up towards the bridge. "I suspect they have a number of ships lurking in interplanetary space, just waiting for us to show ourselves."

"They're not going to find it an easy task," Biscoe pointed out. "Even if they do get a lock on us, they're going to have to drop back into FTL just to give chase."

Elton shrugged. The Harmonies might have insurmountable problems finding *Odyssey*, as long as she remained in interstellar space, but they wouldn't have to worry about their secret getting out. *Odyssey* had to break through to another galactic power - or sneak back to Hudson Base - if the crew wanted to tell the known universe just what had *really* happened over Harmony. And they knew it, too. He'd bet half his salary that the Harmonies were already taking precautions to bar *Odyssey's* escape.

And we made it out of space they controlled completely, he thought, as he stepped through the hatch and onto the bridge. *They're going to be nervous about facing us again.*

He took his command chair and studied the updates. Most of the shield generators had already been repaired or replaced, although some of the former had been listed as unreliable by the engineers. Elton would have preferred to replace them all, but the four remaining freighters simply hadn't carried enough spares. One of their resupply ships had been vaporised back on Harmony. Given two or three days, *Odyssey* would be as ready as she would ever be, without a shipyard. And then...

And then we have to find our way home, Elton said. He pulled up a starchart and studied it, grimly. *That isn't going to be easy.*

DIPLOMATS, REBECCA HAD been told years ago, weren't meant to *die*. They were asked to leave the host country, they were declared *persona non grata* and forbidden to return...but they weren't mean to die. The Solar Union had made it clear, more than once, that any attack on its diplomatic missions and personnel would be severely punished. She'd read about societies that had done nothing, save from meaningless protests, when their diplomats were lynched by angry mobs, but the Solar Union had never been that weak. It said something about the success of the policy that no Solar diplomat had been killed on Earth, *ever*.

She knelt in front of the burning candles, positioned neatly in the memorial chamber, feeling a sharp pang of pain mingled with bitter guilt. Daniel Newcomb had been a friend, someone she'd asked to accompany her on the mission. They'd even been lovers, once upon a time; she remembered, as the candle flickered in front of her, long evenings spent making love when they'd been attached to the embassy on Varner. That affair had long since ended, but she'd still felt a certain level of affection for him. And now he was dead...there wasn't even a body to take home.

I'm sorry, she thought, grimly.

David Arthur had been a stranger when she'd boarded *Odyssey*. An experienced middle-aged man in the diplomatic service, their paths had never crossed...but she'd gotten to know him as *Odyssey* made her stately way from Earth to Harmony. He'd been in a group marriage, back home; he'd talked about the nine kids he and his fellows had brought into the world, nine kids who had five mummies and five daddies. And yet...now he was dead. She didn't know *what* she was going to say to his remaining partners. They'd known they'd be separated for months, perhaps years...

She shook her head. David Arthur had deserved better. They'd *all* deserved better.

Her gaze moved to the third and final candle. At twenty-five, Melanie Fusco had been the baby of the mission. It was unusual for anyone under forty to be assigned to a deep-space diplomatic mission, but Melanie had clearly impressed her superiors. She'd actually spent seven of her formative years on an alien world, growing up surrounded by more aliens than anyone else on *Odyssey*. Her insights into how the Galactics thought had been considered invaluable. And, realistically, she was hardly a child...

She wasn't a child, Rebecca told herself. Melanie had been four years over the age of majority. To call her a child...Rebecca knew she shouldn't think of Melanie as a child. *And yet, she died on the mission.*

Rebecca closed her eyes for a long moment, silently mourning the dead. It was hard to remain focused...she wanted to lash out, she wanted to scream and shout at the nearest target. But there was no one who could be blamed. The teleport crews had done the best they could, she knew; the captain had made the right call, yanking them out of the embassy before the mob killed them all. The people who had triggered off the riot - and then forced *Odyssey* to run a deadly gauntlet - were back on Harmony. It was unlikely they would ever be brought to justice.

"I'm sorry," she muttered. "It was my failure."

She silently reviewed everything she'd seen and heard - everything she'd done - since the mission had begun, nearly a year ago. There had been no clues that the coup had been faked, no clues that the Harmonies had set out to lure a starship into a trap...no doubt they *would* have cooperated for a while, if they'd thought humanity *would* obligingly provide them with their technology. She hadn't seen anything wrong - nor had anyone else - and yet, that didn't absolve her of her failures. She'd failed in her mission.

They never intended to take the talks seriously, she thought, numbly. *They just wanted to trap a starship.*

The thought *hurt*. She *knew* she wasn't to blame, not really. No one had realised that the original message was nothing more than bait in a trap. And yet, she didn't believe it. She had been brought up to believe that great powers might compete, but they didn't wage war. They certainly didn't do things that would inevitably *provoke* war, when the truth managed to break free. And yet...

Daniel Newcomb had been a friend and a former lover. He hadn't deserved to die. David Arthur would probably have earned an ambassadorship of his own within the next decade, unless he blotted his copybook spectacularly. He hadn't deserved to die. And Melanie Fusco...she'd been young and enthusiastic, her joy in her career undaunted by the real world. She had even had a string of lovers amongst the crew...she'd enjoyed life, enjoyed a freedom Rebecca wished she'd had in her youth. Melanie hadn't deserved to die either. *None* of them had deserved to die.

She shuddered. Death in a teleport stream...

Maybe it wasn't the worst way to go. She'd seen worse. But still... there were stories, horror stories, of teleport accidents where the victim forever haunted the matter stream. She'd seen a dozen movies where someone entered a teleporter, only to be possessed or forced to share a body or...most of the movies were clearly fiction, yet they lingered in her mind. Perhaps they, rather than her age, accounted for her teleportation phobia.

"I'm sorry," Rebecca said, addressing the candles. They flickered as she spoke. "I wish I'd seen something sooner. I wish I'd urged the captain to turn back the moment we realised they were fortifying the gravity points. I wish...I wish I hadn't dragged you along on this madcap adventure. I wish..."

She rose, feeling her knees ache. She wanted to believe in life after death, in a place where the good went to eternal happiness after they died, but she was too much a realist to place her faith in God. The Christianity of her parents and the odd melange of faiths that existed within the Solar Union offered no answers, not to her. If there was a God, how could He allow suffering? How could he allow people to suffer when there was *no hope of escape?* It almost made her want to believe that e-personalities were *real* personalities, that some shred of her friends would remain alive...

...And yet, she didn't believe it.

You accept AIs as intelligent beings in their own right, her thoughts mocked her, as she turned and walked out of the chamber. The candles would be left to burn until the formal ceremony, whereupon they would be snuffed out for good. *Why is it so hard to accept an e-personality?*

Because it doesn't feel right, she answered herself, numbly. She'd read all the reports, even spoken to a couple, but had never been able to convince herself that an e-personality was actually real. *The e-personality is, at best, the shell of a mind.*

She headed back to her quarters, moving aside as crewmen hurried pallets of supplies through the giant ship. They'd spent the last day working on repairs, even drafting half of Rebecca's staff into helping them. She didn't begrudge Captain Yasser calling on her staffers - she just wished there was something she could do herself. But there was nothing. She could barely program her portable terminal, let alone fix the food processors, adjust a VR sim or repair a drive module while under enemy fire. It looked so easy in the simulations, but...

Apparently it's a little harder in the real world, she thought. Two crewmen were kneeling in front of an open hatch, doing...*something*. She peered into the hatch and saw a confusing mass of blinking circuits. It meant nothing to her. For all she knew, they were just trying to *look* busy when the Senior Chief was nearby. *Nothing is simple in real life.*

She nodded to the crewmen, then walked past them and through the hatch into her suite. The lights came on as she entered, revealing that several items she'd left lying on her desk had been tossed around the compartment and dumped on the floor during the battle. She smiled - all the sims showed consoles exploding, as if the designers hid explosive packs underneath just to detonate at the right moment - and started to pick them up. It wasn't much, but it wasn't as if anyone else was going to do it for her. Personal servants were very rare in the Solar Union.

Unless you happen to be an admiral or staggeringly wealthy, she thought. An admiral having a personal assistant would be understood; a wealthy man hiring servants would be seen as tasteless conspicuous consumption. *But a mere diplomat isn't important enough to have a steward.*

The display lit up as she approached, showing a series of icons and status reports that were beyond her comprehension. She tried to parse a couple of them out, then gave up. The only thing that made any sense was a note that - so far - the Harmonies didn't seem to have tracked them down. Rebecca hoped - prayed - that they'd remain unmolested until they finished repairing the ship. *Odyssey* had done a lot of damage during the breakout, but she doubted their luck would last indefinitely. The Harmonies would be more determined to hunt them down than ever before.

She glanced at the bed, wishing - suddenly - that she'd started a relationship with someone on the ship. Her body wanted someone to hold her, after the battle; someone to celebrate their escape, someone to reassure her that she was still alive. Male or female, she wasn't fussy...no one would care, as long as her lover wasn't someone who reported to her. But even if she had, her lover would probably be repairing the ship. She didn't want to think about the captain's likely reaction if she asked permission for her lover to join her in bed. She'd probably be safer standing next to an antimatter containment centre during a power outage.

The thought made her smile, humourlessly, as she pulled up a string of files. She'd made sure to download everything on the Harmony Sector, even though most of the information was significantly out of date. And everything the information broker had given them had proved accurate, just...just incomplete. In hindsight, that should have tipped them off that *something* wasn't right. But then...

No, she told herself, firmly. *There's no point in second-guessing ourselves now.*

She started to work. It was unlikely she'd find something the analysts had missed, but she might just be able to see things from a civilian point of view. The military mindset wasn't stupid, yet she'd often noted it could be limited. Perhaps there were other things that should be taken into consideration. Perhaps, even, she could find them. And then...

And if we don't find a way home, she thought, *we could spend the rest of our lives in this wretched sector.*

TWENTY-TWO

Assuming that that is actually true - that we must fight the war - how do we fight it on favourable terms? The only advantage we have lies with our technology. In everything else, from raw population numbers to fleet sizes and military bases, we are grossly outmatched by the Tokomak and the other Galactics.

How, then, does adding a number of other races to our defence commitments work in our favour? Does it not, instead, spread our forces out, allowing the enemy a chance to defeat the dispersed units one by one?
-Solar Datanet, Political Forum (Grand Alliance Thoughts)

*I*t was a relief, Elton decided, to head back to the conference room after the brief funeral service. He knew it was important to mark the passing of the dead, but they'd barely had time to do more than say a few words. He'd have to write letters to each and every one of the families, after they returned home...he sighed, knowing it wasn't going to be easy. He'd done his best to learn the names of each and every crewman under his command, without using his implants to cheat, but he just didn't know enough about the dead to write a proper letter.

And it won't matter at all, he told himself, *if we don't get home.*

He took his seat and motioned for his senior staff to take their places, while a young ensign handed out coffee. Ambassador Motherwell - *Rebecca,* he reminded himself - had asked to join them and he'd agreed, although reluctantly. It wasn't that he disliked Rebecca - he'd found himself rather fond of her - but he was fairly sure they were beyond diplomacy after everything that had happened. The Harmonies were no longer interested in talking.

"Mr. Wolf," he said, once everyone had a cup of coffee. "Our current status?"

"Acceptable, under the circumstances," Wolf said. The Chief Engineer didn't sound happy, but *that* was no surprise. "We've repaired as much of the damage as possible, Captain, and replaced what we can't fix. The hull is as solid as its going to be, I think. I believe we cannot go any further without a shipyard and some specialist help."

"Understood," Elton said. "Mr. Callaway?"

"I've transhipped all the remaining missiles and other supplies from the freighter," Callaway said. "We have enough firepower to give the enemy a bloody nose, if they find us. The freighter herself is empty now. I think we may want to consider abandoning her."

"That'll go down well with her commander," Biscoe commented.

"She took some damage, sir," Callaway said. "Frankly, the freighters are liabilities. We could have evaded their ships altogether if we hadn't had to take care of the freighters."

"We'll table that for the moment," Elton said. He had no compunctions about abandoning the freighters, if necessary, but he was reluctant to make any final decisions as long as he didn't have to. "Mr. Biscoe?"

"Morale is good, under the circumstances," Biscoe said. He smiled, rather thinly. "I don't think the gravity of our situation has sunk in, yet."

Elton nodded. "And our situation is...?"

Callaway tapped a switch. A holographic starchart, centred on *Odyssey*, snapped into existence above the table. "We have been tracking a number of battle squadrons leaving Harmony," he said, as newer icons flickered into life. "As you can see, they dropped out of FTL at the marked locations, allowing them to extend their gravimetric sensors. When we go FTL, they'll know it."

Rebecca leaned forward. "How do you know those ships are still there?"

"We'd see them leaving," Callaway said. His voice was carefully toneless. "The interlocking spheres on the display show their likely sensor range from their current positions. At least three battle squadrons will see us when we go."

"And then give chase," Elton said. "We're not going to be able to evade them indefinitely."

"No, sir," Callaway said. "We can play cat and mouse for quite some time, according to the simulations, but they'll run us down eventually."

"And as long as we remain hidden in interstellar space," Elton mused, "they win anyway."

"Yes, sir," Callaway said.

"In theory, we could set out for home at once," Elton added. "But that would take years. It would take months, at least, to reach a gravity point they didn't control, by which time they would probably be ahead of us. We have to find out what is actually going on *and*, somehow, get into the gravity point chain without being detected."

Biscoe looked doubtful. "We *might* be able to get one of the freighters through the chain," he offered. "But they'd recognise *Odyssey* on sight."

"Yes, they will," Elton said. He met his XO's eyes. "This isn't something we can blast our way out of, I think. We have to use cunning."

Rebecca coughed. "Captain...there *are* other galactic powers," she said. "We could head to Refax or even Keevan. Both of them are known rivals to the Harmonies. Even if they refused to help us, they'd get the word out."

"We don't know if they can be trusted," Major Rhodan said. "Madam Ambassador, we did everything right when we reached Harmony. We handled matters in line with protocol that was laid down long before humans learned how to write. And they still turned on us. They granted safe conduct and renounced it, they threw aside their strongest traditions, just to get their hands on this ship. We cannot risk putting ourselves in their hands."

"True," Elton agreed. "We have to be careful."

He took control of the starchart. "They control most of the worlds in this sector," he said, thoughtfully. "They definitely control most of the gravity points. However, there are some worlds they don't control - Kami, for one. It's a major shipping nexus, but isolated enough to escape their domination."

Biscoe frowned. "You think we can go there?"

"I think it's our best chance to find out what's *really* going on," Elton said. "And it will also let us offload someone who can find passage back to Hudson Base. It should give us a second chance to get the word out."

"Risky," Biscoe said.

"Risk is our business," Elton said. He grinned. "And now we've recited clichés at each other, I have a cunning plan."

He looked at Wolf. "We'll abandon the damaged freighter here, rigged with an antimatter warhead," he said. "The remaining ships will accompany us to one of the shipping lanes, where they'll take us in tow. Hopefully, that will throw them off the scent for a while and give us a chance to make contacts on Kami."

"Even if it doesn't," Callaway said, "they'll need more than a single battle squadron to overwhelm Kami."

"They just need to scare the inhabitants," Biscoe pointed out.

Elton nodded in agreement. The files had made it clear that Kami was a disunited world, a mélange of colonies and settlements from a hundred different races that barely paid any heed to the planetary government. It *was* advanced, but it would never be a galactic power. No wonder, he'd thought while he was skimming the files, that smugglers regarded it as a key base. The inhabitants paid as little attention to galactic laws as possible.

"I also want to see if we can obtain a new ship," he said. "Madam Ambassador, I want you and your staff to go through the manifests on the remaining freighters and put together a list of things we can sell. We're going to need galactic credits."

"We do have some credits," Rebecca said. "How many more do you need?"

"Enough to purchase a bulk freighter," Elton said. "And perhaps more, if we can."

"We'll do our best, Captain," Rebecca said.

Elton nodded. "I don't doubt it," he said. "Mr. XO, find someone with experience on alien worlds, someone who can be sent off on detached duty. Two, perhaps - if necessary. Make sure its volunteers only."

"Aye, Captain," Biscoe said. "Do you think they can get back to Hudson Base?"

"We can, but hope," Elton said. He looked at the display, silently calculating the time it would take for the Harmonies to jump them. "That's the trouble with cunning plans. They have a tendency to go wrong."

— —

"MAJOR," LEVI SAID, as she stepped into his office. "You wanted to see me, sir?"

"I did," Major Rhodan said. He motioned for Levi to take a seat. "A little bird told me that you have experience on alien worlds - and not just as a marine on active deployment."

Levi frowned as she sat down. "My father was the descendent of a couple of abductees," she said, feeling a flicker of distaste for the term. Her great-great-grandfather might have been kidnapped from Earth back before humans had started experimenting with steam ships, but her father and *his* father had grown up amongst the Galactics. And yet, they were *still* called abductees. "He joined a trading ship after Contact and spent a couple of decades playing tour guide before marrying my mother. I practically grew up on their ship."

Rhodan lifted an eyebrow. "Why did you decide to join the Marine Corps?"

"I wanted a challenge," Levi said. She shrugged. "A couple of the traders I met along the way were retired marines. They told me a great many tall tales about service in the corps."

"Very good," Rhodan said. He leaned forward, resting his elbows on the desk. "I have a mission. It needs someone who can operate on an alien world. Are you interested?"

"*Semper Fi*, sir," Levi said. Rhodan wouldn't have considered her unless he'd thought she could handle it. "But I'd be happier if you told me what the mission actually *was*."

"The ship is *en route* to Kami," Rhodan said. He held up a hand before Levi could start querying her implants. "You can look up the details later, if you wish. For the moment, all you need to know is that someone - two people, if we can spare a second - will be detached from the ship with orders to buy passage back to Hudson Base. Ideally, we'd want you to get there as quickly as possible."

Levi considered it for a long moment. "I assume you don't want me to raise eyebrows?"

"Correct," Rhodan said. "Speed *and* stealth, LT."

"Then I'd have to book passage on a freighter," Levi mused. "Ideally, I'd need to find one heading somewhere else, then switch ships at their destination. Booking a courier boat would be quicker, but it would probably attract attention."

"Particularly as you would be cooped up with someone non-human for weeks on end," Rhodan said. He made a face. "I won't presume to give you precise instructions, LT. You will have to do what seems best to you, at the time. And if you get caught...you *cannot* afford to have anything connecting you to *Odyssey* on your person."

Levi nodded, stiffly. It *was* possible that there were humans on Kami already, either the descendants of other abductees or traders from Earth. But if *she* was hunting for *Odyssey*, she'd take a sharp look at *any* humans who showed up on the radar. She'd need to be very careful if she passed through a gravity point on a smuggler ship. The crew would have no motive to hide her.

"I'll see to it, sir," she said. She'd feel odd, going down to the planet in civilian clothes, but she'd get over it. "Do you have another candidate lined up?"

"Not as yet," Rhodan said.

Levi nodded, trying to remember if any of her squadmates had any useful experience. They'd all served on alien worlds, but...she didn't *think* any of them had served as anything other than marines. They didn't know how to comport themselves, they didn't know how to find anything, they certainly didn't know how to avoid attracting attention. Hell, they didn't know how to find someone who could set them up with fake ID cards. Kami might not ask too many questions, but she doubted the Harmonies would be so obliging.

"I'll review the files tonight," she promised. Perhaps she'd be lumbered with a starship crewman...at least, he'd know what he was doing. "I won't let you down."

Rhodan looked relieved. It struck her, suddenly, that there *weren't* many candidates, even on *Odyssey*. There just weren't that many humans with her background. And to think there had been times when she'd considered it a liability. The recruiter had made it clear that there would be certain aspects of the marine corps - intelligence, in particular - that would be forever closed to her. She didn't really blame him, either. The Galactics had no compunctions about using forced implantation to control slaves.

She shivered. Extensive checks had revealed nothing. Hell, she'd never had any reason to think she *might* have been implanted. She'd certainly never been born and bred to be a cyborg soldier. But there was still the quiet lingering doubt in her mind...

"You're on detached duty, as of this moment," Rhodan said. "You're excused all duties here - I want you to spend the next week preparing for the mission. If we find a second volunteer, you'll be working with him. You can draw whatever you need from stores - just remember, if you waste all the credits, the beancounters will want your head."

"As long as it's attached to the rest of me," Levi said, lightly. "The platoon?"

"Will be fine in Stewart's hands," Rhodan assured her. "Will you need to sleep apart too?"

"I don't get antsy when I sleep alone," Levi said, crossly. Some marines *did*, for reasons she'd never been able to understand. Growing up on a starship - and then going through Boot Camp - had taught her to value what little privacy she had. "I assume I'm still on the reserve list, if the starship gets boarded?"

"If the starship gets boarded," Rhodan said dryly, "we're all in deep shit."

He rose. "Good luck, LT," he said. "And God Bless."

Levi returned his salute. "You make it sound like I'm leaving now," she said. She didn't really blame him, though. The Major had to start planning for the day she left the marines and headed off on her own. He'd no longer be able to call on her. "But thanks anyway."

—

"You know, I always expect to see stars flashing past," Rebecca said, as she stood under her stateroom porthole. "Not..."

She waved a hand towards the darkness. It was dark in FTL, so dark that there were people who refused to look outside the ship or go EVA on the hull. *Odyssey* seemed to be all alone, even though there were three freighters following the cruiser and - no doubt - hundreds of alien warships in hot pursuit. There was something about the darkness that captured her eyes and drew her forward...

"We are in a twist in the fabric of space and time," Captain Yasser said. His voice was very composed. "Light vanishes somewhere within the FTL field."

Rebecca nodded, blanking the porthole. "We're taking a risk," she said, as she turned to face him. "Do you think we're doing the right thing?"

The captain looked back at her, evenly. "Do you see any other option?"

"...No," Rebecca admitted. She'd thought about it ever since they'd fled Harmony, but nothing had come to mind. "There's no way to escape destruction, is there? Not if we go back to Harmony."

"They can't let us go home," the captain agreed. He looked tired and grim, as if the burden of his role was wearing him down. "I don't think they can even risk keeping us as prisoners."

Rebecca shook her head, sourly. She'd spent *years* learning the rules of galactic diplomacy, a dance so complicated that few humans cared to master the steps. And yet, all the rules had changed. The Harmonies had broken the rules, just to gain a tactical advantage; now, they had to break *more* rules just to cover up their original crime. All her work had been for nothing.

"I feel useless," she admitted. She nodded towards her desk. "I couldn't even find someone to *negotiate* with on Kami. Hundreds of enclaves, countless asteroid habitats...each with their own governments! The planetary government is a joke! It makes the UN look like a masterpiece of international cooperation."

"That actually suits us," the captain pointed out, mildly. "A strong government might bow the knee to the Harmonies."

"They might bow the knee anyway, when the Harmonies drop a battle squadron into the system to demand submission," Rebecca said. Kami was heavily defended, but the system was disunited and the Harmonies were vastly more powerful. "We *were* thinking they planned to go on a rampage, weren't we?"

She started to pace. "I feel *useless!*"

"You did everything you could," the captain said. "What happened... none of it was your fault."

"I wish I felt that way," Rebecca said. "Captain...my staff and I didn't pick up any sign that something was wrong."

"Neither did mine," the captain said. "Rebecca...there's no point in fretting over it. Right now, we have to figure out how best to escape before they catch up with us."

Rebecca looked back at the porthole. "They can't yank us out of FTL, can they?"

"We don't know," the captain said. "We could yank a ship out, if we wanted. Them? I'm not so sure. The Tokomak saw gravity well generators in action...they should have passed on a warning, but it looks as though they didn't bother."

He smiled, humourlessly. "And if I'm wrong," he added, "I'd prefer not to find out the hard way."

"Me neither," Rebecca said. "But that doesn't stop me feeling useless."

"Cheer up," the captain assured her. "There will be something for you to do soon."

TWENTY-THREE

The simplest answer to your question is that a defence in depth, one that allows us to trade space for time while delaying the enemy, will offer us the greatest chance of systematically defeating enemy probes and defeating enemy fleets. Right now, we have one system - Sol - which absolutely MUST be defended. We lose Sol...game over. And while the Tokomak would pay dearly if they attacked Sol again, they have the firepower to win the battle.

The more systems we control, the more allies we have, the greater the challenge we present to the enemy.
-Solar Datanet, Political Forum (Grand Alliance Thoughts)

"Approaching the shipping lane, sir," Marie said.

Elton nodded. If they were lucky, they *should* have enough time to drop out of FTL and hook *Odyssey* to the freighters before the enemy warships caught up with them. The enemy might be snapping at their heels, but they'd have some problems getting a *precise* lock on *Odyssey* before it was too late. Thankfully, the Harmonies didn't seem to have invented anything completely new.

If they figure out how to track starships in FTL while they're in FTL themselves, he thought, *we may be in some trouble.*

"Take us out of FTL," he ordered. "Mr. Biscoe?"

"I'll get the freighters hooked up," Biscoe said. "Their drives are already synchronised."

"Make sure the gravity waves are overlapping perfectly," Elton reminded him. "If they don't overlap, this is going to prove worse than useless."

Odyssey shivered as she dropped out of FTL, the display lighting up as the ship's passive sensors scanned for possible threats. Elton *knew* the odds were astronomically against the enemy deducing their destination and preparing an ambush, but he couldn't help tensing before the display finished updating. There were no ships - or anything else - within detection range.

"Picking up three enemy battle squadrons in FTL," Callaway reported. "They're heading in our direction, but they won't have seen us drop out of FTL."

"Good," Elton said. There were enough enemy ships to allow half of them to remain in FTL, getting into position, while the remainder monitored *Odyssey's* course and speed. His worst-case estimate insisted that the Harmonies would be on top of them in less than two hours. "And the shipping lane?"

"Very busy," Callaway said, as a stream of blue icons appeared on the display. "We should merge with the flow."

"Have the freighters secured to the hull," Elton ordered. "Tactical?"

"Weapons and defences are fully charged," Callaway said. "If they catch us, sir, we'll give them a bloody nose."

Elton pushed his doubts aside as he waited, patiently, for the engineers to finish connecting the freighters to *Odyssey*. It was a simple trick. *Odyssey's* FTL signature was quite distinctive, allowing the enemy to track her in FTL, but the freighters were very similar to thousands of other designs used by just about every interstellar power. *Their* drive signatures were practically identical to every other mid-sized freighter in the galaxy. If *Odyssey* and her crew were lucky, the Harmonies wouldn't figure out what they'd done until *Odyssey* was already at Kami.

He forced himself to relax as the gravimetric sensors kept updating. The shipping lane wasn't really a lane, not in the sense a canal was a shipping lane, but there were still hundreds of starships passing through the same general region of space, the least-time course between Kami and Cereus. It felt odd to look at the display and compare the emptiness of realspace to the starships in FTL. He was an experienced spacer, yet even he flinched at the thought of a collision between two ships...

Which is impossible, he thought, dryly. *FTL drives don't work that way.*

"Two of the enemy battle squadrons just dropped out of FTL," Callaway reported. "A third just jumped back *into* FTL."

"Telling the first squadron where we are," Elton said. He was fairly sure the watchers had a solid lock on *Odyssey's* location. "How long will it take them to link up?"

"Seventeen minutes, I think," Callaway said. "Force Two is a little further away from Force Three."

"That won't stop Force One from informing Force Two," Elton said. "Watch for them detaching a ship."

He sucked in his breath, resisting the urge to contact Biscoe and tell him to hurry. Having to jump back into FTL ahead of time would be disastrous. And yet, there was no need to panic just yet. He'd spent a lot of time wishing for an FTL communicator, like most spacers, but for once he was grateful that even the Galactics hadn't been able to produce a working model. Force One would have to send a courier boat to Force Two. Thankfully, it was clear the Harmonies hadn't planned a search and destroy operation before *Odyssey* had escaped Harmony. If they had, they would have made sure that they had hundreds of courier boats on station.

His console bleeped. "Captain," Biscoe said. "The freighters are linked up. Drive fields have been resynchronized, crews have returned to their ships. We are ready to go."

Elton glanced at Marie's back. "Helm?"

"I have control of their drives," Marie said. "Gravimetric fields appear intact."

"The enemy shouldn't be able to pick us out from the crowd," Callaway added. "We'll just be another freighter, perhaps a trifle older than the rest."

The Harmonies *would* notice eventually, Elton was sure. They'd go back and study their sensor readings very carefully, once they decided that *Odyssey* wasn't trying to wait them out. At that point, they'd notice a freighter with an oversized drive field and draw the correct conclusions. Trying to evade detection by using one ship to tow another had been old when the Trojan Horse had been pushed to the gates of Troy. But the deception would win them time. He just hoped it would be long enough.

"Take us back into FTL," he ordered. "And set course for Kami."

"Aye, Captain," Marie said. "Interlocking drive field activating... now!"

Odyssey shuddered. For an appalled moment, Elton thought they were under attack. The truth wasn't much better. The drive field, maintained by three stardrives working in combination, wasn't quite stable. Powerful enough to take them into FTL, but not powerful enough to ensure a smooth flight. The only upside, as far as he could tell, was that it provided an excuse for dropping out of FTL in interstellar space.

But they'll know where we arrived, he thought, grimly. *And they won't think a crippled freighter leaving from the same location was a coincidence.*

He cursed under his breath as the display blanked. *We might have less time than we thought.*

"The FTL field has stabilised," Marie reported. "We should be at Kami within two days."

"Understood," Elton said. He looked up as Biscoe stepped onto the bridge. "How are the freighter crews taking it?"

"Not too well," Biscoe said. "But they understand."

Elton nodded. Freighter commanders, even ones with open-ended contacts with the Solar Union, enjoyed a degree of independence few others shared. They wouldn't be remotely comfortable with slaving their ships to *Odyssey*, let alone abandoning them at Kami. Elton would do everything in his power to ensure that the Solar Union paid compensation for the lost ships, but it wouldn't be the same. He was surprised one or more of the merchant skippers hadn't demanded the right to leave the convoy and go his own way.

They're not stupid, he told himself, sternly. *They know what's at stake.*

"You have the bridge," he said, rising. "Be ready to bring us out of FTL in a hurry if the drive field starts to collapse."

"Yes, sir," Biscoe said. "I have the bridge."

— —

KAMI WAS AN odd world, Levi thought, as the shuttle headed towards the planetary ring. Too inhospitable to attract one of the major powers, it had found itself playing host to hundreds of settlements of varying size from all over the galaxy. The ring itself was a teeming mass of disconnected principalities, while the planetside settlements and asteroid habitats jealously guarded their independence. There was a network of planetary defence stations orbiting the planet - and a surprising number of warships and armed freighters - but she doubted Kami had any hope of standing off any of the Galactics. The planetary government might *claim* to rule the system, yet it was clear that it had no real power.

Which works in our favour, she thought. *No one asked questions when we arrived and requested a docking slip.*

She smiled, thinly, as she glanced at the young man sitting next to her. Mickey Tyler had been born in the Solar Union, but - like her - he'd spent a surprising amount of time on alien worlds. His father had been a diplomat who'd held down a number of minor positions in a dozen embassies, the file so bland that Levi was sure it was a cover for something more sinister. She hadn't *needed* to see the embassy on Harmony to know that diplomatic missions were often covers for spies.

"This is your last chance to back out," she said, as the shuttle headed towards the ring. "You can go back to the ship, if you like."

Tyler shook his head. He was clearly nervous - she'd been careful to make it clear to him that *she* was in charge - but he hadn't changed his mind. Even running through a dozen simulations with Levi hadn't changed his mind, although she was forced to admit that their chances of blasting their way out were precisely nil. If they were discovered, and she knew it was quite likely that the Harmonies would be looking for humans, they were dead. Their suicide implants would see to that.

"Just remember, if anyone asks, you're a free trader fallen on hard times," Levi reminded him, dryly. "And don't let them try to hire you."

Tyler gave her a sharp look. "Wouldn't they be suspicious if I didn't at least *listen?*"

Levi shrugged, silently conceding that he had a point. There were probably hundreds of thousands of free traders - merchant crewmen, human and alien - on Kami, all looking for a billet on a starship heading out into deep space. Some of them would be in debt, some of them would probably be arrested if they reached a more civilised world...she shook her head in wry annoyance. Screwing up the mission because they were offered a job would be embarrassing.

She activated her implants, contacting the ring's datanet. It was a shambles, a nightmarish network of processors and servers that refused to work together. She'd seen the internet on Earth, but this was worse - far worse. Warnings blinked up in front of her eyes, alerting her to malware and processor viruses lurking within seemingly innocuous messages blasting out from a dozen different servers. She'd never seen anything quite so dangerous outside isolated worlds like Kami. Thankfully, her implants couldn't be overwritten and subverted by any malware known to exist.

"I think I have a possible contact," she said, as she brought up a set of listings. "A couple of traders...they'll help fence the crap we brought."

The XO turned to look at her. "Are you sure?"

"They'll screw us like we're a two-bit whore," Levi said, frankly. She ignored the shocked look Tyler gave her. She'd heard worse during Boot Camp. "I doubt we'll get even a fifth of what the trade goods are actually worth. But the money will be up front and untraceable."

And we don't have time to dicker, she added, silently. *We need to complete the first part of the mission before the enemy fleet arrives.*

The shuttle docked, the airlock mating effortlessly with its counterpart. Levi checked her weapons, then hurried out of the hatch as it opened. She'd expected a standard security sweep, but there was nothing beyond a stern notice warning that shuttles would be seized and confiscated if the docking fees were not paid. There were no lists of forbidden merchandise, no warning notices about customs duties...she rather suspected that the only security checks would be done on the surface, if they went down to one of the enclaves. She had no intention of leaving the ring until they found a suitable freighter.

"This place is impressive," Biscoe said. "Why don't *we* have one of them."

"They're also pretty big targets," Levi pointed out. "I'm surprised the planetary governments managed to cooperate long enough to build *this* ring."

She downloaded a map from the nearest processor, then pointed down the corridor. "Let's go," she said. "Time is not on our side."

The ring *was* impressive, she had to admit. It encircled the entire planet, providing more living space, storage chambers and docking ports than Kami could possibly use. Large sections had been colonised by transient workers, producing a dozen subgroups that were effectively enclaves in their own right. There were no laws, she noted; a dozen adverts popped up in front of her, offering everything from slaves to interspecies brothels. And everyone within view was clearly armed. The richer ones were surrounded by augmented guards.

An armed society is a polite society, she thought. *No one dares start anything because everyone else will start something too.*

The fence was a plant-like alien, shifting backwards and forwards as if he was being pushed around by the wind. Levi tried to figure out how he saw - or even if he saw at all - while the XO tried to bargain, struggling to get the best possible price from the strange creature. It wasn't easy to communicate, either. The voder seemed to stutter more than once, as if it couldn't provide a proper translation. Levi just hoped that, for once, galactic society actually lived up to its billing.

"Twenty-two thousand credits," the XO said, finally. "Is that enough?"

Levi shrugged. She'd been checking the starship listings. "It should be enough," she said, grimly. "We don't have time to argue."

The fence seemed delighted to advance them a promissory note as soon as they'd made arrangements to begin transfer. Levi rather suspected that the fence thought that their goods were stolen, but it hardly mattered. She drew up a handful of listings and forwarded them to the XO, then waited while he studied them.

"This one should do," he said, finally. "It's a fairly standard bulk freighter, at fifteen thousand credits."

"Yes, sir," Levi said. She led the way down the corridor, carefully giving a trio of spider-like aliens plenty of room. They weren't notably unfriendly, according to her implants, but she firmly believed that spiders shouldn't be quite *that* large. "You'll have to be *very* careful with the dealer."

The starship dealer turned out to be a tall humanoid alien with fishlike scales and big, oversized eyes. Levi had the impression that he - she assumed the alien was a male - wasn't exactly comfortable in the ring, although it wasn't as though it would be hard to adapt a small section to suit his race. Perhaps he was just trying to be accommodating to his alien customers. And yet, the more he spoke, the more she thought of a used aircar dealer. He seemed convinced that the universe would end if they didn't buy this particular freighter.

"Only fifteen thousand," he insisted, as they teleported to the freighter and examined it in cynical detail. "And five careful owners."

Right, Levi thought. The bulk freighter was immense. Her drives and control systems seemed to be in good shape, but her crew sections needed a thorough clean before they were suitable for human habitation. *And how many careless owners?*

"I can offer ten thousand," the XO said, as they stood on the cramped bridge. "And eleven thousand if you throw in a couple of ID codes, too."

The dealer produced a hissing sound. "*Eleven* thousand?"

"This freighter is too big for an independent merchant," the XO pointed out. "She's just too expensive to run when you can't fill the hold.

The only people who'd be interested in buying a ship this size are governments and big corporations and neither one would be interested in buying from you. I don't think you'll get a better offer."

"I have two open offers for thirteen thousand," the dealer insisted.

"Then take them," the XO said. "Teleport us back to the ring and we'll go somewhere else."

The dealer gave them a nasty look. He had remarkably sharp teeth. "Twelve thousand," he said. "I'll throw in the ID codes *and* a free service."

"The codes have to be verified," the XO said. "And we need the ship now."

"You can fly the ship out of here as soon as you pay," the dealer said. Levi wasn't surprised that he didn't bother to mention the other offers again. The bulk freighter would be so hard to sell that any reasonable dealer would have sold it at once, if someone had offered thirteen thousand. Commander Biscoe hadn't been fooled by the bluff. "You can have it now, if you want."

"The money will be transferred within the hour," the XO said. "We thank you."

The dealer said nothing. Levi rather suspected that meant he was relieved to have finally sold the ship.

"We'll get a crew over here now, then take her out of here," the XO said. "I..."

His wristcom bleeped. "Mr. Biscoe, we've picked up a large enemy force heading towards Kami," the captain said. "I suggest you expedite matters."

"Understood," the XO said. "We'll move as quickly as we can."

Levi was already checking the listings online. Finding a smuggler - and an ID forger - was surprisingly easy. But then, no one was interested in actually hunting them down. Kami had no laws, after all. The only question was how much they'd charge to do the work.

"You have seven hours," the captain warned. His voice was grim. "And then they'll be on top of us."

"Yes, sir," the XO said.

TWENTY-FOUR

Is this actually true?

The majority of worlds that have applied to join the Grand Alliance are not significant industrial powers, even with their industrial fabricators unlocked. They are about as useful as the Channel Islands in World War Two - nice to have, perhaps, but hardly important targets. The Tokomak are unlikely to waste time and starships capturing Rugad or Fiddle when neither world offers anything of value.

Why should we expect the Tokomak to leave Sol alone when it is the most important target in the galaxy?

-Solar Datanet, Political Forum (Grand Alliance Thoughts)

"Captain," Callaway said. "Force Two has now reappeared. It will enter the Kami System in nine hours."

"Noted," Elton said. "And Force One?"

"Still on course," Callaway said. "She'll be on top of us in less than an hour."

Elton nodded in grim understanding. The analysts hadn't had time to carry out a proper tactical survey, but they'd concluded that Kami lacked the unified defence network necessary to stand off even a single battle squadron. He couldn't help feeling that the locals evidently agreed. Hundreds of starships were already undocking from the ring and heading out into deep space, even though - technically - Kami was a neutral world. But then, a battle fleet heading towards *any* world was bad news.

At least we'll have plenty of cover when we run, he thought.

He glanced at Williams. "Did you get an update from the engineers?"

"They think the bulk freighter is in - barely - acceptable condition," he said. "She's a real fixer-upper. She won't last forever without some proper work, but she'll do for now."

"Good," Elton said. "Order them to take the freighter to the RV point, then have the other freighters moved to the second RV point."

"Aye, sir," Williams said.

Elton took one final look at the display, then resumed his pacing. The Harmonies were bearing down on them, yet...yet they couldn't leave until they picked up the supplies and ID codes they needed. There was too great a chance of being caught as they made their way through the enemy lines without them. He wished, just for a moment, that they could recruit help, but it was unlikely that any of the Galactics would stick their neck out for a lone human starship. Sol was a tiny star thousands of light years away, while the Harmonies were practically next door.

If we're lucky, maybe they'll breach the planet's neutrality in a way no one can ignore, he thought, grimly. *That might give them something else to worry about.*

— —

"People are starting to panic," Tyler said.

Levi nodded in grim agreement. Hundreds of ships were hastily jacking up their prices, demanding that customers pay two or three times over the odds just to get a seat on a ship leaving the system. Everyone knew, now, that the Harmonies had sent a battle squadron to Kami, even though they didn't know why. There was a lot of outraged shouting on the datanet, with theories ranging from a full-scale invasion to a search and destroy mission. The latter was surprisingly close to the truth, but - so far - no one seemed to have any theory on just *what* the Harmonies were looking for. The smart money seemed to be on a pirate who'd raided their shipping.

She looked up as the XO came out of the forger's office, clutching a pair of datachips. The codes *should* get them through the gravity points, as long as the Harmonies didn't have a reason to start taking a very careful look at the ship. He looked grim, unsurprisingly. The forger would have jacked up his prices too. Levi had no doubt that *he* was also bidding for a seat on a starship too.

"They should be sufficient," the XO said. He passed her the credit chip. "Are you ready to find a place to hide?"

Levi nodded, wordlessly. She'd considered bidding for a slot on a departing ship now, but the prices were skyrocketing. Someone was more likely to remember a pair of humans if they paid a vast price without complaint. Besides, there was no way to know where they'd be going. She'd prefer a freighter with a guaranteed destination.

As long as they don't occupy the ring, she thought, numbly. *We might have to cosplay as Klingons just to escape notice.*

"Good luck," the XO said. "And try not to get caught."

"Thank you, sir," Tyler said. Levi could tell he was nervous, although she wasn't sure if it was because he'd be alone with her or because they'd be trapped on the ring. "We'll do our best."

"We will, sir," Levi said. "Get the ship home."

She watched him turn and hurry back to the airlock, dodging a pair of aliens trying to purchase tickets off the ring. The datanet was filling up with demands, offers and counter-offers as more and more people started to panic. An alert warned that the space elevators between the ring and the planet's surface were crammed - no matter how many people wanted off, the elevators couldn't move any faster. Another alert reminded everyone that teleportation within the ring was strictly restricted.

"I have a place to go," she said, catching Tyler's arm. The transient flophouse wouldn't be very pleasant - she'd been in a couple during her childhood - but it was rated suitable for humans. No one would be interested in asking questions, she thought. Even if the Harmonies *did* board the ring, most of the residents would tell them nothing. "Come on."

Tyler nodded, his face pale. Levi forced down her annoyance as he followed her down the corridor, hurrying past a pair of crowded airlocks. Hundreds of armed guards, some wearing planetary militia uniforms, were taking up position, ready to prevent the locals from storming the airlocks. They weren't human - she'd only found a handful of humans on the datanet - but she had no trouble telling that they were nervous too. It wouldn't be long until there was a nasty incident and people got hurt.

Barely twenty minutes left, she thought, as they found a transit tube and hurried down it. *And then...*

She winced as she heard the sound of shooting behind her. *That* hadn't taken long.

"Keep moving," she hissed. "We do *not* want to get stunned - or killed."

They reached the flophouse ten minutes later. A couple of armed guards - and a single manager - eyed them with open suspicion until she showed them one of her credit chips, then greeted her as though she was a honoured guest. They'd gouge every last credit from her they could, she knew from bitter experience, but they wouldn't actually try to rob her. Even so, she was careful not to show them *all* her money. The transients who used flophouses regularly might not be so willing to uphold the rules.

"Hey," a voice called, as they entered the common room. Levi looked up to see a middle-aged human, leaning against the bulkhead as he watched the viewer. He spoke Galactic One with a strong accent. His hand trembled as he spoke. "What are *you* in for?"

"We just got kicked off the *Pallas*," Levi lied. It wasn't the best cover story she'd ever had, but it had the advantage of being impossible to disprove. No one bothered to keep track of starships entering or leaving Kami. "The bastard of a captain couldn't make book unless he shed a few crewmen."

"Poor you," the human said. He winked at her. "You looking for work?"

"A new billet, as soon as possible," Levi said. She knew what sort of work *he* had in mind. "But right now we need to keep our heads down."

"Of course," the human agreed.

Tyler coughed. "What are *you* in for?"

"Been here a while," the human said. He reached up, as if he wanted to touch his forehead, then stopped himself. "Got kicked off my ship too. Do some work down at the promenade for people...you know how it is. Need to find another ship..."

An addict, Levi thought. She'd seen the signs before. *You kept stimulating your pleasure nerves until you lost touch with the outside world.*

She felt a stab of pity, mixed with contempt. There was no way an addict could be trusted, not completely. He'd do anything for his next pleasure jolt. She didn't blame his former CO for kicking him off the ship. He was so far out of it that he didn't seem to have noticed the emergency situation.

"We'd better get to our room," Levi said, glancing sharply at Tyler. "We can start looking for our next billet after we get some sleep."

And after the Harmonies have departed, she added, silently. *If they ever do.*

"THE BULK FREIGHTER has departed, Captain," Callaway said. "The enemy fleet is entering the system."

"Take us away from the planet, best possible speed," Elton ordered. They'd messed up the timing. He'd hoped to have *Odyssey* towed out of the system again, but there just hadn't been time to rig the freighters a second time. "And prepare to go into stealth mode."

We could do with a cloak, he added, in the privacy of his own head. If he ever got back home, he was going to say a great many sharp things to the designer who'd thought *Odyssey* didn't need a cloaking device. There was optimism and then there was pointless idealism, the latter actively dangerous. *We could slip away without being detected...*

The display lit up. "Force One has dropped out of FTL," Callaway reported. "They're scanning the system now."

"Keep us moving," Elton said. *Odyssey* was distinctive enough that he'd be astonished if they made it away without being detected. But they might get lucky. "Stand by all weapons."

"Aye, Captain," Callaway said.

"They're broadcasting a message to the entire system," Williams said. "Captain, they're ordering the entire system to stand down."

"That's not going to go down well," Callaway said. "The local defences are already scrambling."

Elton nodded, curtly. Kami might not be able to stand off the battle squadron, but they could make it pay...

"Force One is bringing up its weapons and tactical sensors," Callaway reported. He paused as the display washed with red light. "They found us!"

Damn, Elton thought.

"Increase speed," he ordered, sharply. On the display, the main body of the enemy fleet was turning to face them. "Weapons?"

"All weapons are ready, sir," Callaway said.

Elton gritted his teeth. They could drop into FTL - and they would - but the enemy would just come after them. Instead...they needed to *lose* the enemy ships. The plan he'd devised *might* work, but...

"Let them come after us," he ordered.

"They're broadcasting a message to the entire system," Williams said. "They're not being very complimentary about us, Captain."

Elton snorted. "Why am I not surprised?"

"They're promising a major reward to anyone who assists in capturing or destroying us," Williams added. "Should I shoot them a truth bomb?"

"No," Elton said. It *was* tempting to tell the entire system the truth, to inform them just how badly the Harmonies had sinned against galactic law, but it would only provoke the Harmonies to attack Kami. He didn't want that on his conscience. Besides, it would also make it difficult for the away team to sneak back to Hudson Base. "Helm, keep us on our current course."

"Aye, Captain," Marie said.

Elton watched as the situation developed. The Harmonies *had* to be intensely frustrated, even though he doubted they'd ever admit it. Force One had enough battleships to overawe the defenders, but their battleships were the only vessels they had that had a reasonable chance of destroying *Odyssey*. They had to balance their need to keep the planet under control with the need to chase down *Odyssey* before she escaped, again.

But sending all their battleships after us doesn't make them look good, Elton thought. The Harmony warships were gaining, but slowly. *It makes them look weak.*

"They're locking missiles on our hull," Callaway reported. "Captain?"

"Deploy ECM," Elton ordered. Would the Harmonies actually open fire at this range? ECM or no ECM, the odds of scoring enough hits to matter were minimal. "Stand by point defence..."

The display sparkled with red icons. "The enemy ships have opened fire," Callaway said, in surprise. "They're right at the edge of powered missile range."

"Then we'll try and open it a little," Elton said. He said a silent prayer for Kami. The Harmonies were about to be embarrassed. He hoped - prayed - they didn't take their humiliation out on the helpless world. "Helm, increase speed."

"Aye, Captain," Marie said.

Elton gritted his teeth as the missiles roared closer, icon after icon vanishing from the display as their drives burnt out. The remainder kept coming, the majority grimly refusing to be distracted by the ECM. They'd definitely improved their targeting programs, Elton noted, as the point defence phasers opened fire. Too many of the missiles would have hit their target if they hadn't been burnt out of space.

"The enemy is launching a second salvo," Callaway reported. He paused. "Captain...the odds of them scoring a hit are practically *zero*."

"Watch them anyway," Elton ordered. Either the enemy were trying to swamp *Odyssey* or they had something up their sleeves. "And continue to target any missiles within point defence range."

"Aye, Captain," Callaway said.

"Picking up messages from the planet," Williams said. "The planetary government is ordering the Harmonies to stand down. They're citing chapter and verse from interplanetary treaties..."

"I doubt the Harmonies will pay any attention," Elton said. The planetary government might have been wiser to keep its mouth shut. Force One alone could devastate the system and their reinforcements were already on the way. The Harmonies didn't need to listen. "If they contact us, don't bother to reply."

"Aye, sir," Williams said.

Marie coughed. "Captain, we're approaching Point Loki," she reported. A new icon blinked to life on the display. "We'll be in position in two minutes."

Elton wished, again, for a proper cloak. Stealth mode was sufficient against passive sensors, but the Harmonies were using their active sensors on full power. It was quite possible that they'd burn through stealth mode before it was too late. If he ever got home...

We'll have a war on our hands, he thought, numbly. *And too much else to worry about.*

"Tactical, prepare to deploy ECM decoys," he ordered. On the display, the enemy ships belched a third volley of missiles. Their targeting locks were so imprecise that he doubted half of them were going to come within a million miles of his ship. "Launch on my mark."

"Aye, Captain," Callaway said. "Do you want to engage the enemy?"

"No," Elton said, after a moment. "We cannot risk expending our remaining Hammers."

"Aye, sir," Callaway said.

Elton heard the discontent in his voice, but said nothing. He understood *precisely* what the younger man was feeling. Firing back would have been pointless, yet it would have been satisfying. He dismissed the thought in some annoyance. They'd stripped the freighters bare, just replacing everything they'd expended at Harmony. They couldn't afford to waste missiles just to distract the enemy.

"We'll be at Point Loki in thirty seconds," Marie reported.

Timing is everything, Elton thought. He felt sweat trickling down his back. *Screw this up and we're dead.*

"Deploy ECM," he ordered. "And send the go signal to the *Filial*."

"Aye, Captain," Williams said.

Elton leaned forward. The sudden torrent of ECM would confuse the enemy sensors, just long enough - he hoped - for the *Filial* to jump into FTL. His engineers had worked for hours, modifying her drive so her signature was close to *Odyssey's*. She wasn't an exact match, but combined with the ECM it would be too similar for the Harmonies to ignore...

"Take us into stealth," he ordered. The last flight of enemy missiles had lost their targeting locks completely and gone ballistic. He couldn't help thinking that the alien beancounters were going to go ballistic too. "Now!"

The light dimmed, automatically. On the display, *Filial* raced away in FTL. The enemy ships seemed to hesitate, then jumped into FTL themselves. They'd take up position outside the system, hoping to track *Filial* down. And they would succeed, they'd think...

We loaded the ship with enough antimatter to give them a nasty surprise, Elton thought, as the enemy ships vanished in the distance. They'd missed *Odyssey* completely. *And they won't have a hope of escaping contact.*

"Captain," Callaway said. "The enemy ships have departed."

Elton nodded. "Get us to the remaining freighters, then start towing procedures," he ordered, shortly. The enemy ships would get a nasty surprise, true, but he knew better than to think it would take them all out. They'd know they hadn't found *Odyssey* the moment they set eyes on *Filial*. "We have to get out of here before they realise they've been tricked."

"Aye, sir," Marie said. "ETA twenty minutes, unless you want to drop out of stealth mode."

"No," Elton said. The enemy would figure out what they'd done, sooner or later, but he would prefer to keep them guessing as long as possible. "Keep us stealthy."

"Force Two is still inbound," Callaway reported. "But a number of civilian ships are still fleeing the system."

Elton glanced at the display. If anything, Callaway had *understated* the case. *Thousands* of starships were fleeing in all directions. He hoped, desperately, that Kami would return to normal soon enough. The inhabitants hadn't done anything to deserve punishment. But there was no way to be sure. He'd just have to pray.

"We'll blend in with the crowd," he said, finally. "And once we link up with the bulk freighter, we can start the next part of the plan."

TWENTY-FIVE

And yet, mustering the force necessary to take out Sol will leave them weak elsewhere. Our most pessimistic projections still predict that the Tokomak will literally lose hundreds of thousands of ships attacking Sol, regardless of the outcome. Giving them more targets to test themselves against, before moving on to the hardest target, may convince them to prepare for a long war.

Who knows? It may even encourage them to consider peace.
-Solar Datanet, Political Forum (Grand Alliance Thoughts)

"This bridge is a mess," Biscoe said. "If this ship was assessed by the SUCB, Captain, it would fail."

Elton couldn't disagree. The Solar Union Certification Board would have had a collective fit of the vapours if they looked at the bulk freighter. She was functional, by the strict definition of the word, yet most of her systems really needed to be replaced. Her bridge was not only weirdly-proportioned - a regular problem when dealing with alien ships - but dirty and cramped as well. The SUCB would probably have denied the bulk freighter a licence, preventing her from docking at most Solar Union facilities. And while her commander *could* file an appeal, no Citizen's Jury would ever support him.

"Her main computer has also been replaced with something from another ship," Biscoe added. "The links to the drives are fine, as far as we can tell, but some of her internal communications nodes are crapped out because they're incompatible with the new computer system. I've got the engineers installing some bypasses, yet...frankly, calling this ship a mess is an insult to messes."

"As long as she gets us through the gravity point," Elton said. "Is the hold suitable?"

"We can fit *Odyssey* into the hull," Biscoe said. He smiled, rather thinly. "I don't think *anyone* has ever tried this before."

"I saw it in a movie once," Elton said. "Let's hope the Harmonies didn't see it too."

He smiled at the thought. Human movies - and television series - had been a surprising hit across the Sol Sector, although he didn't *think* they'd spread much further. The Galactics hadn't shown anything like as much imagination as humanity when it came to popular entertainment. They might view *Independence Day I, II and III* as light comedies, rather than serious movies, but they had nothing to match them. Elton had seen a couple of galactic movies, back when he'd been in the academy. They'd been bland and completely forgettable. Maybe it was a translation problem, but he couldn't see how anyone could stand to watch them for more than twenty minutes or so.

"I've got the engineering crew working on struts and explosive bolts," Biscoe said. "We can break free within seconds, if necessary. But..."

He met Elton's eyes. "If they slam a missile into the freighter's hull," he warned, "we might be blown away too."

"I know," Elton said. "There's no way out without taking a serious risk."

The concept had seemed simple enough, when he'd thought of it. Buy a large bulk freighter, one that had no obvious ties to the Solar Union. Put *Odyssey inside* the freighter - the largest freighters in the galaxy could have carried a battleship comfortably - and then fly the freighter through the gravity points. As long as the Harmonies declined to inspect the ship physically, they should have no reason to suspect trouble.

But we don't dare return to Harmony itself, he thought. *We'll have to enter the gravity point chain from another direction.*

And yet, the more he thought about it, the more he realised just how much could go wrong.

Biscoe cleared his throat. "We should be ready to depart in five hours, assuming the engineering crew finish their work on time," he said. "Captain?"

"That should be fine," Elton said. "Are the control links in place?"

"Yes, sir," Biscoe said. "Williams is currently devising a holographic head for any communications. As long as they don't want a face-to-face meeting, sir, we should be fine."

"And if they do, we'll just have to make a run for it," Elton said. He'd simulated possible engagements time and time again. If they were *very* lucky, they might *just* make it through the gravity point before the enemy had a chance to react and open fire. But there would almost certainly be defenders on the far side too. "And then it will be *your* turn to think of something clever."

"Of course, sir," Biscoe said. He shrugged. "At that point, sir, we might want to consider heading for another set of Galactics."

Elton shook his head. There was no way to know who could be trusted - and who they didn't dare touch with a barge pole. If they were completely barred from Hudson Base...he wasn't sure *what* he'd do. Perhaps they'd have to obtain another freighter and try to sneak through the gravity points, leaving *Odyssey* behind. He couldn't think of anything else.

"Inform me as soon as you're ready to start moving *Odyssey* into the freighter," he said. It should work, theoretically, but he'd never heard of it being done outside bad simulations and worse movies. "I'll be in my quarters."

"Aye, Captain," Biscoe said.

Elton teleported back to *Odyssey*, then walked slowly to his quarters. They had made a clean break, he thought. The Harmonies hadn't passed within half a light year of their position, as far as they could tell. But that didn't necessarily mean anything. The Harmonies knew as well as he did that *Odyssey* needed to pass through the gravity points if she wanted to go home. He would be surprised if they weren't rushing to fortify every gravity point within their sector.

If they hadn't started already, he thought, remembering the fortresses they'd seen on their way to Harmony. *Who knows just what they're doing with the other Galactics?*

He opened the hatch to his quarters, then sat down on the sofa. His doubts were mocking him, reminding him - again - of just how little he knew. There was no way he could show his concerns on the bridge, not in front of the crew. And yet...what *was* going on? Was humanity doomed to war with *all* the major powers? Or were the Tokomak hoping to use the Harmonies to do some of the fighting, thus winning time to prepare for the coming offensive?

His intercom bleeped. "Captain," Rebecca's voice said. "Can I join you?"

Elton hesitated. He was surprised the ambassador hadn't summoned him to *her* quarters, although he did have to admit that Rebecca seemed more understanding than some of the other diplomats he'd known. But part of him just wanted to be alone for a while...he shook his head in frustration. Duty called, even if they *were* well beyond diplomacy.

"I'm in my quarters," he said, finally. "You're welcome to visit."

He rose and ordered two coffees from the food processor, placing one of the mugs on the table. Rebecca might want something stronger but, even with implants and nanities to flush alcohol and its effects out of his system, Elton knew better than to risk it. He looked up as the hatch hissed open, allowing the ambassador to step into his cabin. She looked around with considerable interest.

"Captain," she said, seriously. "You have a nice cabin."

"I don't spend enough time here," Elton said. "Someone in the design centre assumed that the captain would have a family with him, people who'd need all the space."

He picked up his coffee and sat down facing her. "And I don't *have* a family, so the space is wasted," he added. "Rats."

Rebecca smiled. "I thought the idea was that getting bigger quarters matched getting a higher rank," she said. "Or was I misinformed?"

"You also get more duties and more things to worry about," Elton said. "And while you *do* get a bigger cabin, you don't get to spend so much time in it."

"Perhaps you would, if you had a family," Rebecca said.

Elton considered it. He understood the reasoning - *Odyssey* and her sisters were intended for long-term missions far from Earth - but he wasn't sure he liked it. Having families - including children - on the ship would just present him with more problems. But then, they *had* run into deadly danger. A ship on a long voyage without running into anything dangerous might be quite a welcoming environment for a family.

"I doubt I'd have the time," he said, finally. "The captain is never truly off-duty."

"And there would be political implications too," Rebecca added. "What happens if the captain is married to one of his officers?"

"It would be awkward," Elton said. The Solar Navy did have a fair number of officers who were married to other officers, but the personnel department worked overtime to keep one partner from being superior to the other partner. It would definitely mess up the ship's internal politics. "And it would cause trouble."

"True," Rebecca agreed. Her lips twitched. "But what if the captain started an affair on the ship, during a very long-term mission?"

Elton leaned forward, unable to hide his annoyance. "Is there a *reason* you wanted to see me, Madam Ambassador?"

Rebecca seemed oddly surprised, although the expression vanished quickly. "I've been reviewing the files," she said. "We might be able to find *some* allies if we head away from Harmony."

"Might," Elton repeated. "Can you promise anything?"

"No," Rebecca said. She met his eyes evenly. "But it's something to bear in mind."

Elton was tempted to order her to leave. He could - he was the master of his ship, at least while she was well away from Sol. Rebecca might be offended - she might even file a complaint when they got home - but she would have to leave. And yet...it struck him, suddenly, that she felt isolated too. She'd been head of her department before they'd had to escape Harmony, a department that was now completely useless...

"It is," he said, feeling a flicker of affection. "What did you find?"

— —

"They're not monitoring the system, as far as we can tell," Tyler said, as they made their way through the network of passageways. "Are they?"

Levi shrugged. "Marines can chew nails and shit iron ka-bars," she said, sarcastically. There *were* bodymods that allowed marines to do just that, if they wanted. "But even the greatest marine in the world couldn't sense an alien starship lurking near the ring."

She resisted the urge, barely, to tell Tyler to shut up. *She'd* been taught patience in Boot Camp, where hiding under cover could eventually lead to the chance to take a shot at a known terrorist shithead. She liked action, but she knew when to wait for the best chance to make her mark. Tyler, on the other hand, didn't have *any* of that training. He wanted to do something now, instead of waiting for four days before leaving the flophouse. She didn't really blame him, but there were limits.

The ring wasn't deserted, but there *were* fewer people in the main thoroughfares. Most of the ships that had fled when the Harmonies had been detected were still gone, although a handful had come creeping back when the Harmonies had abandoned the system. A number were probably still running, Levi thought. Kami played host to smugglers, pirates and terrorists from all over the sector. Quite a few of them had probably suspected that Judgement Day was approaching when the Harmonies had arrived.

Serve the bastards right, she thought, although it was a problem. Fewer starships meant fewer chances of finding a berth. *Maybe one of them would have taken us straight home.*

"Here," Tyler said. His implants pitched a set of listings at her. "All going to Hudson Base."

"And all likely to be searched thoroughly," Levi said. Maybe they *could* dress up as Klingons - there were enough *real* aliens that no one would pay much attention to a fake one - but a blood test would reveal the truth. If *she* was in command of the enemy forces, *she* would make sure that everyone passing through the gravity points was vetted. "They *know* we were here, remember?"

She skimmed through the listings until she found the one she wanted. It would be costly, of course, but they could afford it. And it had some very definite advantages.

"You have to be out of your mind," Tyler said, when she shot him the listening. "Levi..."

Levi smirked. "Trust me," she said. She composed a short message, then sent it into the datanet. "It's the last thing they'll expect."

They saw fewer and fewer people as they made their way towards an isolated section of the ring. Alerts flashed up in front of their eyes, warning them that several sections up ahead had been configured for races that breathed methane, rather than oxygen. She took a mask from a rack and checked it was correctly configured, then passed a second one to Tyler. He had the sense to check it and insist on checking hers before they walked into the viewing room.

She sucked in her breath as they stared at the large window. The chamber was dark, save for a foggy white light on the other side of the window. She couldn't help feeling as though she was in a petting zoo, instead of the VR zoos that could be found everywhere within the Solar Union. And then a...*shape*...smashed against the far side of the window, making Tyler take a step back. Levi almost joined him. The alien was a grotesque mass of tentacles, eyes and things she didn't want to look at too closely. It - she couldn't think of it as either male or female - was completely inhuman.

There was a faint hiss from a hidden speaker. "You wish passage to YAR-873?"

"That is correct," Levi said, dropping into the fussy cadence of Galactic Four. The Tokomak had devised the language for talks with methane-breathers, although it was run through another translator before it was presented to the alien. It was better to speak as simply as possible and hope everything held together. "Two of us, both humans."

The alien seemed to press against the glass. Levi forced herself to look back, even though all her instincts were telling her to run. "My ship is not configured for humans," it said. A low whistle echoed through the speaker. "Do you want to travel in stasis?"

"No," Levi said. It was tempting, but they would be completely helpless. "We want a small module, configured for human life. And we want to remain completely unnoticed as we pass through the gravity points."

"You do not want to be detected," the alien said. It whistled, again. "It can be arranged."

Levi allowed herself a tight smile. Tyler hadn't been too far wrong. No one would willingly travel on a methane-breather's ship unless they were desperate. Even if the Harmonies suspected something, they'd find it hard to *search* the ship. It was far more likely they'd just let them slip past without looking too closely.

"Very good," Levi said. "Once we reach our destination, you will help us to land and then bid farewell."

"If you wish," the alien whistled. "The price will be five thousand credits."

"Five hundred," Levi said. Five *thousand* was so far above the going rate, despite the gross inconvenience of obtaining a life support module, that the alien would suspect something if she agreed. "And we'll pay an extra two hundred for the module."

"One thousand," the alien said. "The module will be left with us."

"Unless we need it," Levi said. "Six hundred, plus the module fee."

They haggled backwards and forwards, finally settling on the price of eight hundred, counting the module. Levi sent the alien the first payment at once, receiving in return detailed instructions for how to find the correct docking bay. It was unlikely the Harmonies would pay any attention to the freighter, but she resolved to be careful travelling there anyway. There weren't many humanoids who also breathed methane.

"Done," she said, to Tyler. "Ready to leave this place?"

"We'll be spending the next week in a cramped module," Tyler muttered. "You sure we can't go into stasis?"

"Not unless we want to be caught," Levi said, practically. "It's too great a risk."

She smiled at him. "Look at it this way. We've picked up plenty of files from the shopping mall. You can read all the way."

Tyler looked unimpressed. "Let's go," he said. "The sooner we leave, the sooner we can arrive."

"Very good," Levi said, dryly. She had a feeling he'd be even *less* enthusiastic when cabin fever began to settle in. She'd known hardened marines that would have hesitated to spend two weeks in a tiny module. She hoped she didn't go stir crazy herself. "Let's go."

She checked the ring's datanet - again - as they made their way down towards the docking bay. There were no updates from any of the planetary governments, but there *was* an increasingly long list of theories about what was actually going on. Some of them were actually quite close to the truth, although none of them mentioned humans. Others were so completely implausible that they sounded to have come from particularly idiotic conspiracy theorists. It was amusing, in a dark sort of way, to know that humans and aliens had quite a few things in common.

"The ship got away," Tyler said. "Where are they going now?"

"I don't know," Levi said. She hadn't been told. There was too great a chance she'd fall into enemy hands. "But let's hope they're safe, out there."

Tyler caught her arm. "And what if they get caught?"

"Then we make sure Hudson Base finds out what happened," Levi said. She slipped the mask into place as they reached an airlock. "And then we will take revenge."

TWENTY-SIX

This is self-delusion.
Everything we know about the Tokomak tells us that their standard response to any challenge is to reach for the biggest hammer they can and throw it at the target. This is what they tried to do during the Battle of Earth, when they sent what they thought would be a large enough hammer to finish the job. We beat that offensive, but that will merely force them to launch another - much larger - offensive.
It is unlikely we can distract them with anything.
-Solar Datanet, Political Forum (Grand Alliance Thoughts)

"She handles poorly," Marie complained. "I've flown freighters that moved with more grace than this...*this*..."

"Steady as she goes," Elton advised, dryly. "The freighter wasn't designed for speed."

He leaned back in his command chair as another low tremor ran through the ship. He'd never heard of one starship nesting inside another, not outside bad movies and theoretical studies that no one had ever expected to have to try in the real world. The freighter barely had enough speed, even when empty, to reach its destination in a reasonable space of time. He had a feeling, although he suspected it would never be confirmed, that the design actually dated all the way back to the pre-stardrive era. It would certainly explain the ship's size and low speed.

"Her stardrive is online," Biscoe confirmed. "She's ready to make the jump into FTL."

And hope to hell the drive doesn't crap out on us halfway there, Elton thought. *We should have offered to take the damn ship for free.*

"Very good," he said. "Have the remaining freighters been emptied and powered down?"

"Yes, sir," Biscoe said. "Their crews are not happy."

"They'll have to live with it," Elton said, tartly. He understood *precisely* how the freighter crews felt, but their ships were just too noticeable. If he'd been in command of the enemy fleet, *he* would make sure to inspect any freighter that matched their description. "We'll be back to pick up their ships later."

"Or we can just pay out compensation," Biscoe said. He smiled, humourlessly. "We'll have to get home first, of course."

Elton nodded. "Helm, take us into FTL," he ordered. "And set course for Night's Dawn."

"Aye, Captain," Marie said. She ran her hand down her console. "FTL...*now*."

Odyssey shivered. Elton braced himself, unsure what to expect. They'd powered down *Odyssey's* stardrive completely, just to ensure that there were no stray gravity pulses that would upset the freighter's drive, but he was uneasily aware that the freighter's drive was *not* in perfect condition. If they'd had more time, they would have looked for a better freighter...if one was to be found. Bulk freighters were rare outside the main shipping lines. They were just too costly to operate.

The ship shook violently, then settled. The display blanked.

"We are in FTL," Marie said. She sounded concerned. "Captain, the drive is going to require careful supervision. I'd like to dedicate an RI to the task."

"See to it," Elton said. No human mind could hope to keep up with the twisting gravimetric surges. An AI would do a better job, but there was no AI on *Odyssey*. "And take us back into realspace if it looks like the drive is going to fail completely."

Biscoe looked pained. "I wonder how the dealer even *found* the ship," he said. "She should have been scrapped long ago."

"We'll probably never know," Elton said. He rather assumed the freighter had passed through dozens of hands before finally reaching Kami. She might be uneconomical for normal shipping, but she *could* help set up and support a new colony. "Mr. Williams, do you have our talking head ready to go?"

"Yes, sir," Williams said. He turned to face Elton. "As far as anyone should know, sir, we're a lone Horde freighter transporting goods from Alpha Trion to Altadena. We're not carrying anything interesting, so they probably shouldn't take *too* close a look at us."

"Let us hope so," Elton said. On one hand, if *he'd* been in charge, *he* would have insisted on searching anything that wanted to pass through the gravity points. But, on the other hand, the Harmonies presumably didn't want to slow interstellar trade down any further than strictly necessary. "Can you respond to any questions they might have?"

"I think so," Williams said. "But if they want to search the ship, sir, we will be in deep shit."

"And we'll have to make a run for it," Elton agreed.

He forced himself to relax as the freighter picked up speed, the hull shaking every time the drive field threatened to flare out of control. None of the Galactics would be particularly surprised to see a bunch of Hordesmen in an outdated freighter, one that seemed to be permanently on the verge of disaster. The Hordes couldn't build their own ships, let alone do proper maintenance on the ones they begged, bought or stole from the more senior races. It was unlikely, he told himself, that any watching eyes would do more than laugh at the primitive race in starships. The Galactics held the Horde in utter contempt.

And that might change, he thought, remembering the Horde colony on Mars. *They're not stupid, merely ignorant. And ignorance can be remedied.*

The hours ticked by slowly, broken only by faint tremors running through the hull. Elton snatched a nap in his office, then brought his log up to date. He knew it was unlikely that they'd be able to make it all the way to Hudson Base without being detected, but *not* filling in his log would have felt too much like giving up. By the time the freighter groaned and wheezed its way into Night's Dawn, he felt as if he was ready for anything.

And if there's one advantage to flying this crappy freighter, he thought as he stepped back into the bridge, *it's that no one will ask too many questions when we drop out of FTL several AUs from the gravity point.*

"Tactical," he ordered. "Deploy stealth drones."

"Aye, Captain," Callaway said. "Drones deploying...*now*."

Elton nodded, feeling the tension rise on the bridge as more and more details popped up on the main display. Night's Dawn was unusual, almost unique. Binary systems were far from unknown, but the secondary star in *this* system was a small black hole. The Galactics had been driving themselves crazy, according to the files, in trying to understand how the black hole had even formed. It simply wasn't *massive* enough, they insisted, to exist. And yet...

"I'm picking up seventeen battleships, holding station near the gravity point," Callaway said, grimly. "I'm also picking up tugs towing fortresses from the inhabited worlds to the gravity point."

"They must not have fortified this system so extensively," Biscoe commented. "They can't put a *complete* lock on shipping moving through *this* part of the sector."

"It would have tipped off their enemies," Elton agreed. The Harmonies might have had a very good excuse for fortifying the gravity points, but the other Galactics would have seen it as a threat. They didn't want the Harmonies to decide, one day, that ships passing through the gravity point needed to pay a toll. "But now they're trying to stop us."

A cold shiver ran down his back as the freighter steadily approached the gravity point. *Odyssey* could outrun the battleships, given a slight head start, but not when she was trapped inside a giant freighter. He had no illusions about what would happen if the Harmonies realised what was going on, yet did nothing until the freighter was far too close to escape. If they were caught at point-blank range...he shook his head, telling himself that it would work. It *had* to work.

"Picking up a message," Williams said. "They're demanding our ID codes and ship logs."

Elton wasn't surprised. Hundreds of starships were entering the system and dropping out of FTL, only to have the battleships ordering them into line while they were inspected. It was easy to see that freighters that matched standard designs were being searched, even though none of them were *identical* to the ships he'd left behind. He wondered, grimly, what would happen if a freighter CO started to power up his stardrive. Would the battleships fire into his hull?

Probably, he thought. *But that might just start a war.*

"Send them the prepared data," he ordered. "And then prepare to trigger the explosive bolts."

He sucked in his breath as they glided towards the gravity points. The analysts had done a good job of putting together a fake set of logs, ones that matched data recovered from captured Horde ships. No one would seriously expect the Hordesmen to match the Galactics for sheer love of bureaucracy and records-keeping. Hell, there was a very good chance they'd done too *good* a job. But it was too late to worry about it now.

If they insist on inspecting us, he thought, *we'll have to blow the hull and run.*

"Picking up a response, Captain," Williams said. "They're allowing us to enter the fast track."

Elton nodded, although he wasn't reassured. The fast track appeared to be composed of courier boats, a handful of warships from several different powers and a number of starships that clearly *weren't Odyssey* or her consorts. They seemed to be going through without more detailed inspections, let alone searches. And yet, he knew they were passing far too close to two enemy battleships. If they'd been caught...

"Order the drones to go dark, then take us into the fast track," he ordered. "And jump us through the gravity point as soon as we can."

He watched the display, numbly, as the gravity point grew closer. The Harmonies were taking one hell of a risk, stopping and searching hundreds of freighters. There was no way the other Galactics wouldn't be pissed. Word would already be spreading, even though the full story would probably remain unknown. His eye tracked a shuttle, escorted by a pair of gunboats as it moved towards a large freighter. The ship was nothing like anything humanity had ever deployed. He wondered, absently, why it had been singled out for special attention.

"Approaching the gravity point now," Marie reported. "Jump in five...four...three..."

The universe sneezed. The display blanked, then hastily started rebooting itself. Five red icons jumped to life, looming over *Odyssey* as a cat might loom over a mouse. Elton took firm control of his emotions as the battlestations scanned his ship, then dismissed her. They didn't even bother to sneer. He felt a surge of pure relief, mixed with an odd kind of icy contempt. The Hordesmen hadn't known how their starships worked, but that hadn't stopped them wreaking havoc on Earth. They shouldn't be treated as jokes.

"Take us to the next gravity point," he ordered, grimly. "Best possible sublight speed."

"We'll be there next year," Biscoe joked. A thin chuckle ran around the ship. "They let us go through without question."

"We're not out of the nebula yet," Elton pointed out, dryly. "Helm?"

"ETA twenty-seven hours in sublight," Marie said. "There's no way to boost our speed without discarding the freighter or jumping into FTL."

"We'll just have to live with it," Elton said. He glanced at Biscoe. "Get some rest, Mr. XO. I'll be on the bridge."

He turned his attention back to the display as *Odyssey* crept further and further into the system. It was heavily populated; one world had given birth to an intelligent race that had found itself subjected by the Harmonies, while four more had been terraformed to provide living space. Hundreds of asteroid settlements orbited the primary star; thousands of starships made their way towards the gravity points or headed out into interstellar space. And yet...

"I'm picking up a lot of chatter," Williams reported. "The locals are not pleased at having martial law declared, it seems."

"I don't blame them," Elton said.

He smiled, rather coldly. In theory, inspecting a ship shouldn't take long; in practice, each inspection could easily take up to an hour, even if the inspectors didn't have any reason to be suspicious. Passing through a gravity point took weeks or months off someone's trip, but the delays would still mount up. A freighter captain could easily lose his ship if he arrived late - or didn't arrive at all - even if it wasn't his fault. He'd certainly have to go to the courts to escape blame, which would take months...if not years. The Harmonies were *not* making themselves popular.

We'll just have to hope they pay an immense price for trying to cut us off, he thought.

"Have the analyst deck scan the communications for anything we can use," he ordered, shortly. It was unlikely that they'd stumble across any genuine revolutionary group - there was no reason to believe that this system wasn't as heavily monitored as Harmony itself - but there was no harm in trying. "And see if you can pick up any news broadcasts."

"Aye, Captain," Williams said.

"They're bringing in more warships," Callaway said. "I'm picking up another battle squadron in FTL, ETA seventeen hours."

"We'll be gone by the time they arrive," Elton said. They were due to cross the gravity point in fifteen hours, unless they were challenged. If that happened...he sighed, inwardly. If that happened, they would have to flee. "Do you have any updates on the gravity point?"

"Seven fortresses, nine warships of various classes," Callaway said. "And probably more, outside sensor range."

Elton nodded. "Keep monitoring the situation," he ordered, stiffly. "And alert me if anything changes."

He took another nap when Biscoe returned to the bridge, then toured his ship, inspecting the different compartments. His crew were bearing up well, although he was grimly aware that they knew the odds of getting home as well as he did. And yet, they hadn't given up. They knew that humanity had survived vast challenges in the past and would survive more in the future. He couldn't help feeling proud of them as he walked slowly back to the bridge. His ship and crew had proved themselves, even though it was possible that no one would ever know what had happened to them.

At least I know, he thought. *And that's all that matters right now.*

"Captain," Biscoe said, as he stepped through the hatch. "We are approaching the gravity point."

Elton nodded and took his seat. The second gravity point looked very much like the first, with lines of starships waiting for inspection before they were allowed to make transit. His sensors were picking up dozens of messages running from ship to ship, mostly from freighter crews bitching about being forced to wait. Elton rather hoped that some of the crews would start a charge at the gravity point, although he knew it would end badly. Fortresses designed to stand off battleships wouldn't have any trouble scything down unarmed freighters.

"Send them our ID and ship logs," he ordered. "And then request permission to jump."

He felt his heart sink as he studied the display. *This* gravity point was clearly better manned, allowing the locals to inspect far more freighters before allowing them to head through the gravity point. Dozens of shuttles were flying around, shadowed by armed gunboats...just in case some of the crews didn't get the message. There was a fast lane, true, but this one seemed restricted to warships and courier boats. He had the nasty feeling that they might have stumbled into a trap.

"Prepare to trigger the explosive bolts," he ordered. They didn't dare get much closer without clear permission to proceed. *Odyssey* was already far too close to a number of enemy warships. And their weapons were presumably already charged and ready to fire. "Mr. XO, withdraw all the crew from the freighter."

"Aye, Captain," Biscoe said. "They're already heading back to *Odyssey*."

Williams looked up. "Captain," he said. His voice was very cold. "They're ordering us to prepare to be boarded."

Elton exchanged a long glance with Biscoe. Had they been spotted, somehow? Or had they merely been unlucky? Or...he wondered, suddenly, if they'd been a little *too* quick to send their ID to the fortresses. The Hordesmen liked to pretend that they didn't have to acknowledge any outside authority. Maybe they hadn't acted like Hordesmen...

He cursed under his breath. There was no way they could fool an inspection party, not for more than a few seconds. He didn't have any Hordesmen on his ship...he didn't know why they'd decided to search *Odyssey*, but it didn't matter. They were trapped, unless they moved now.

"Incoming shuttle," Callaway reported. A new icon appeared on the display, followed by five more. The gunboats were no threat to *Odyssey*, normally, but they'd be a menace as long as the cruiser was trapped within the freighter. "ETA seven minutes. Captain?"

"Trigger the explosive bolts on my command," Elton ordered. The freighter could do one last job for them before its inevitable destruction. "And prepare to transmit a distress signal."

"Aye, Captain," Callaway said.

"The freighter is clear, sir," Biscoe reported. "Mr. Wolf reports that the explosive bolts are ready to detonate."

Elton gritted his teeth. The Galactics would probably believe that the freighter had suffered a catastrophic failure, given how little regard they had for the Hordesmen, but that wouldn't last long. They'd see *Odyssey* as she appeared from the expanding cloud of debris. And then...

"Mr. Williams, prepare to transmit the full account of our adventures," he ordered. The Harmonies would have to keep the message from spreading, whatever it took. It might just keep them from giving chase. "Mr. Callaway...?"

"Yes, Captain?"

Elton took a breath. "Trigger the bolts," he ordered. "And then get us out of here!"

TWENTY-SEVEN

Point of order.
Accusing someone of practicing self-delusion is not helpful. If you believe someone is wrong, point out - calmly and reasonably - why you believe they are wrong. In line with forum guidelines - paragraph two, subsection one - please consider this an official warning. A second offense will result in a kick or a back.
Your friendly moderation staff.
-Solar Datanet, Political Forum (Grand Alliance Thoughts)

Odyssey shook, violently.

"The explosive bolts have triggered," Biscoe reported. "The freighter is coming apart."

"Bring up the drive field," Elton ordered. An outside observer would see an expanding sphere of debris, but it wouldn't take them long to see what lurked *inside* the sphere. "Shove the debris out as hard as you can."

"Aye, Captain," Marie said.

"Enemy warships are activating their sensors," Callaway said. "I think they've noticed us."

"Bring us about, then start transmitting the message," Elton ordered. He considered, briefly, trying to race for the gravity point, but they'd have to run another gauntlet before jumping out of the system. "And prepare to enter FTL."

"Aye, Captain," Williams said. "Transmitting now."

And let's hope that's enough to shatter whatever lies the Harmonies have been telling, Elton thought. A dozen red icons were gliding forward, their sensors sweeping through space towards *Odyssey*. *We might find that we have some allies after all.*

"Enemy warships moving into attack position," Callaway said. "They have a solid lock on our hull."

"Stand by point defence," Elton ordered.

"Picking up an all-ships message," Williams said. "The local system control is ordering all ships to cut their drives or be fired upon."

"They're panicking," Biscoe said.

Elton nodded in grim agreement. The Harmonies should know better than to issue an order that wouldn't be obeyed. Sure, there were plenty of civilian ships that were too close to the warships to escape - they'd do as they were told - but there were hundreds of others that were out of effective range, to say nothing of the neutral warships. *They* would probably be bringing up their stardrives and preparing to flee.

And they'll be taking the message with them, he thought. *The Harmonies have just dropped the ball.*

The display lit up as the enemy warships belched a giant volley of missiles. "Captain," Callaway said. "Incoming missiles."

"I do believe I noticed," Elton said, dryly. "Helm?"

"Four minutes to FTL," Marie said. "Picking up speed now."

"They're also dispatching gunboats," Callaway said. "But there's some confusion about the target."

Elton nodded. He'd been right. Hundreds of civilian ships were scattering, heading in all directions. Hunting them all down would be a bitch of a job, particularly as the Harmonies hadn't even been able to catch *Odyssey* alone. Word would spread, no matter what the Harmonies did. He just hoped they wouldn't be able to weather the coming storm.

"Target them if they come within engagement range," he ordered. The enemy missiles were closing in, rapidly. "But remain focused on the missiles."

"Aye, Captain," Callaway said.

Elton gritted his teeth as the missiles closed into attack range. There was no time to launch decoys, let alone set up ECM fields. They were just too close to the warships for trickery to work. Instead, he watched helplessly as dozens of missiles were burned out of space, leaving dozens more to roar towards his ship. The tactical staff hastily reinforced the rear shields...

Odyssey rocked, violently. "Two direct hits," Callaway reported. "Shields held. The enemy is firing a second salvo."

They should have fired immediately after reloading their tubes, Elton thought. *Did they think they'd impress us...*

...Or are they concerned about looking like idiots in front of hundreds of witnesses?

He dismissed the thought for later consideration. "Damage report?"

"Nothing beyond a few bumps and bruises," Biscoe said. "Shield Seven is showing signs of overloading, but Shield Six and Shield Eight are ready to take up the strain."

"Good," Elton said. "Time to get out of here?"

"Two minutes," Marie said. The display changed to show hundreds of freighters dropping into FTL and fleeing in all directions. "We'll be in good company."

"Take us into FTL as soon as the drive is powered up," Elton ordered. "Do *not* wait for orders."

"Aye, sir," Marie said.

"Enemy missiles closing to engagement range," Callaway said. "Request permission to return fire."

"Denied," Elton said.

He shook his head. He understood why Callaway wanted to return fire, but Elton was all too aware of the practical limitations. *Odyssey* didn't have the firepower to prevail - or even inflict significant damage - unless she used her remaining Hammers. And he didn't have enough of them to waste. Besides, there were too many watching eyes. A display of humanity's weapons technology would kick-start hundreds of research programs into high gear. An arms race so far from Sol might set off a war...

...Or it might leave the Galactics better armed against Sol, when the cold war turned hot again.

"Missiles entering attack range," Callaway said. He cursed under his breath. "Captain, they've improved their targeting programs. The missiles are targeted on weak patches in our shields."

Elton cursed. "All hands, brace for impact," he ordered. "I say again..."

The starship *yawed*, the gravity field flaring madly for a long second. Elton clung to his console and looked up at the display, cursing under his breath as a multitude of red icons flared into existence and stubbornly refused to fade. They'd been hit and hit badly.

"Damage to Drive One," Biscoe reported, grimly. Another series of quivers ran through the ship. "Damage control teams are already on the way."

"Adjusting drive field nodes to compensate," Marie said. "FTL in twenty seconds."

Elton sucked in his breath as the reports streamed into his console. Drive One had taken heavy damage, damage that might not be repairable outside a shipyard. It would slow them down, perhaps significantly. The engineering crews would do their best, but fixing the damage might be beyond them...

"FTL in ten," Marie added.

"They're launching a third salvo," Callaway warned. "Captain, they're deploying warships to block our escape."

"Evasive action," Elton ordered. It probably didn't matter. They didn't realise just how quickly a human-designed stardrive could be powered up. "Their missiles are not going to reach us in time."

"FTL," Marie said.

Odyssey lurched, again, as the drive nodes struggled to compensate for the damage. Elton felt the gravity twist for a second time, then snap back to normal as *Odyssey* dropped into FTL. The display went blank, a second later. He leaned back in his chair, trying to keep the relief off his face. *That* had been far too close for comfort.

And we're going to have to find another way through the next set of gravity points, he thought, numbly. He hadn't had time to come up with any contingency plans. *They'll be searching every last ship after this.*

"Tactical, project a location where we can make repairs in reasonable safety," he ordered, slowly. "Helm, takes us there as fast as you can."

"Aye, sir," Callaway said. "Why is there never a really good nebula around to hide in when you need it?"

Elton snorted. "Mr. Biscoe?"

"Engineering is working on Drive One now," Biscoe said. "They don't have a proper report yet."

"Let me know when they do," Elton said.

He brought up a starchart and studied it thoughtfully, turning options over and over in his head. The Harmonies couldn't have *expected* to run into *Odyssey* in their system, not like that. In hindsight, they'd probably decided to search all the ships and managed to snag *Odyssey* through sheer luck. If *he* was lucky, that meant they hadn't had time to plan a search operation, let alone launch it before *Odyssey* dropped back out of FTL. But that meant that they now had a rough idea of where *Odyssey* was.

His lips twitched. *Somewhere within twenty cubed light years*, he thought. *They've sure got us now!*

It wasn't as reassuring as it seemed. They'd jumped through one gravity point, presumably escaping whatever forces were still combing space near Kami, but now the Harmonies knew where to look for them again. It wouldn't be long before they summoned reinforcements *and* started to bar all the remaining gravity points. *Odyssey* was still trapped, merely trapped in a different section of space. They had to get further away before it was too late.

"Captain," Marie said. "We are slowing to sublight now."

"Prepare to return to FTL," Elton ordered. "Tactical, scan for incoming enemy ships."

"Aye, sir," Callaway said.

Elton closed his eyes for a long moment. They *should* be out of sensor range...but the Harmonies had plenty of practice in deploying their ships to extend their range and track fugitives down. *Odyssey* had been damaged, too. They had plenty of incentive to try to get a fix on her position before it was too late.

Odyssey quivered as she returned to realspace. Elton hoped that was a good sign.

"Scan complete," Callaway said. "The enemy ships are fanning out. They don't appear to have a solid lock on us."

"That won't last," Elton said. He rose. "Mr. Biscoe, you have the bridge. Keep monitoring the situation. If they come after us, I want you to take us out of here."

"Aye, sir," Biscoe said. "I have the bridge."

— —

REBECCA WISHED, JUST for a moment, that she understood the icons and text boxes hovering around the holographic image of *Odyssey's* rear drive nacelles. Her implants attempted to provide some technobabble translations, but the more she looked at them, the more confused she became. She just didn't have the background to understand them.

She looked at the captain, feeling cold. Captain Yasser looked haggard, as if he was reaching the limits of his endurance. He hid it well, but Rebecca knew him well enough to tell that he was at the end of the line. She didn't blame him, either. His ship had been badly hurt, while they were still trapped an unimaginable distance from home. She knew he loved his ship.

"Tell me," she said, more to get him to talk than anything else. "How bad is it?"

"We won't know until we find out if we can repair Drive One," the captain said. He picked up his coffee and took a long sip. "If we can, we should be able to hold the ship together long enough to get home. If not...we may be in some trouble. We'll be too slow to escape."

He looked down at the deck, his eyes haunted. "We planned for the ship to serve as the nucleus of a colony, if there was no other choice," he added. "But in this region of space, we'd be found and slaughtered within a year."

Rebecca nodded in agreement. "So...what do we do?"

"Good question," Captain Yasser said. He glanced up at her. "Right now, I don't have the slightest idea."

The despondency in his voice worried her more than she cared to admit. She'd seen him in tough situations before, but this...if he'd started to give up hope, what hope *was* there? She tried to think of something to say, yet nothing came to mind. He needed a distraction, something that would pull his mind away from the looming disaster. Who knew? Perhaps it would help him think of something else.

She leaned forward. "Talk me through it," she said, evenly. "What are our options?"

He looked back at her. "Do you think that will help?"

"It might," Rebecca told him. "Talking about a problem often helps to solve it."

The captain smiled, rather wanly. "I thought that was discredited years ago."

"A lot of psychology was discredited," Rebecca agreed. She'd studied the field as part of her diplomatic training, although her instructors had cautioned her that aliens operated on different rules. "But I think the Solar Union made a deliberate choice to step away from psychology rather than discredit it."

"I'm not surprised," the captain said, sardonically. "It's astonishing just how many people were pronounced cured when they ran out of money to pay the shrinks."

"That's something of an exaggeration," Rebecca said. "The *real* problem was that psychology was being used as an excuse for everything."

"And no one was supervising the psychologists," Captain Yasser agreed. "They had power without responsibility or accountability and that always goes sour."

Rebecca smiled. She'd distracted him. All she had to do was keep him talking.

"It depends," she said. "Humans are often guided by factors they don't understand."

The captain shrugged. "That might be true," he said. "But when someone claims that they have an *excuse*, because of something subjective that cannot be proven, it stinks. And when someone claims that someone *else* must be restricted, because of something that only makes sense to so-called professionals…well, it's one step from there to locking up people because you don't like their race, religion or eye colour."

He nodded to the display. "I can prove the FTL drive works by building one and testing it," he said. "Can you say the same for psychologists?"

"It is an imprecise science," Rebecca said.

"It isn't a science," Yasser said. "Any more than *economics* is a science. You can't fine-tune a person's brain any more than you can plan a free economy."

His intercom bleeped. "Yes?"

"Captain, this is Wolf," a voice said. "We should be able to complete repairs on Drive One within forty-eight hours, if you give us the go-ahead now."

Rebecca saw the captain's face darken. "Can we go FTL while the work is underway?"

"Yes, but we'd have to stop working during the drive surge," Wolf said. "The radiation sleet would be enough to kill anyone in a suit."

"Then start work now," the captain said. "Inform me the minute the work is completed."

He closed the connection and looked up at Rebecca. "Forty-eight hours," he said. "And then…"

She saw him smile. He suddenly looked a great deal younger. "You were distracting me, weren't you?"

"Just a little," Rebecca confessed. She allowed herself a smile. "If I'd been younger, I might have kissed you instead."

Captain Yasser laughed. "I assure you it would have worked," he said. "For a while, perhaps."

Rebecca had to smile too. They were both older than they looked. And, despite all evidence to the contrary, they were too mature to allow sex to blind them to reality for long. The loves and lusts of their teenage years had long since faded into the background, save for short affairs that both sides knew would burn themselves out with no hard feelings. She wouldn't have minded taking the captain to bed, she had to admit. He would be a better lover than any young man. But he had too many other things to worry about.

"I hope you thought of something," she said. "There was a movie when the scientist comes up with a brilliant plan while being sucked..."

The captain shook his head. "That won't be necessary," he said. "I think I've had an idea."

"Oh, what a pity," Rebecca teased. "I was quite looking forward to it."

"We'll have to wait until the repairs are completed," the captain said. "But afterwards...we might just have a way out after all."

— —

"NEXT TIME, I want to book passage on a ten-star liner," Tyler said. "And get a stateroom with a complete VR simulator package."

Levi was tempted to agree. The module on the alien ship wasn't any larger than an ensign's quarters on *Odyssey*. It certainly hadn't been designed for two adults. The aliens had done a better job than she'd expected - it wasn't the first time they'd smuggled oxygen-breathers around the sector - but it was still cramped, smelly and thoroughly unpleasant.

"Maybe later," she said. She had no idea what they'd find when they reached their destination. "We might be stuck on another smuggler ship."

"As long as there's more room to pace," Tyler insisted. "I've been in *jails* that were more roomy than this."

Levi lifted her eyebrows. "Why did you go to jail?"

"I was meant to interview a despot who'd been snatched as punishment for crimes against the Solar Union," Tyler said. "The bastard never stopped complaining about the food."

"I guess he never saw Boot Camp," Levi said.

"No," Tyler said. "I saw the recordings from his regime. He would have underage children raped, just to make their parents suffer. He ordered mass castrations of male prisoners, then allowed his female prisoners to be raped and impregnated by the guards. He had some kind of belief that a woman had no say in her child's genes - his captive women would give birth to the next generation of *his* people. He even had a harem of brain-burned beauties..."

He shook his head. "People suffered on the outside while he pleasured himself," he added, stiffly. "And we let him live...and he had the nerve to complain about the food."

"How nice," Levi said. She leaned back on the makeshift bed. "Just relax, really. I'm sure we'll be there soon enough."

"I think we'll die of boredom first," Tyler said. He looked around the tiny chamber. "I spy, with my little eye..."

"Oh, shut up," Levi said. "I can knock you out, if you like."

For a moment, she thought Tyler actually considered it. "No thanks," he said, finally. "It would just give me a headache."

"Your babbling is giving *me* a headache," Levi snapped. She forced herself to calm down with an effort. He wasn't trained for this. Neither was she, not really. "We'll be there soon, I think. And then we can pace somewhere else."

"I hope so," Tyler said. "Right now, I just want to scream."

"Me too," Levi admitted. "But I'm not going to. I'm just going to wait."

She picked up the datapad. He was right. It *was* boring. The constant uncertainty about their safety only made it worse. But there was no other way through the blockade...

...And if they didn't make it back to Hudson Base, no one would ever know what had happened to them.

TWENTY-EIGHT

I beg the forgiveness of the magnificent God-Admin for my intemperate post. I shall flagellate myself immediately with a rusty chainsaw.
(And that was sarcasm, in case anyone missed it.)
But the fact remains that we cannot allow ourselves to believe that this is anything other than a fight to the death. The Tokomak cannot allow us to exist. Even if we weren't committed to waging war against them - and I believe that a peace with honour would suit us perfectly - our nature is a challenge to their authority. They will not see us as equals, but as a disruptive force questioning their social order. Even if we make no more technological advances, we still pose an ideological threat.
They must destroy us. They have no choice.
-Solar Datanet, Political Forum (Grand Alliance Thoughts)

Elton couldn't help smiling as he strode into the conference room. The knowledge that some of his crew - the younger ones, certainly - would think that he and the ambassador had been having passionate sex in his cabin was amusing, even though nothing of the sort had actually happened. But then, the young thought *everything* was about it. They needed to grow older before they realised that companionship and respect were just as important.

He took his seat and waited for the rest of the senior crew to join him. *Odyssey* had lurked in interstellar space for nearly three days, first carrying out the repairs and then stress-testing the repairs as much as possible. Elton had no illusions about how long the repairs would hold up, if they had to go straight into another battle, but it would suffice for the moment. He accepted a cup of coffee from one of the ensigns, then leaned forward as the hatch hissed closed. It was time to discuss their next move.

"So far, they have shown remarkably little activity in our direction," he said, tapping the display to bring up the starchart. "However, it is quite likely that they have deployed scouts to watch for us and rally the troops."

"We spotted several ships dropping out of FTL at the edge of sensor range," Callaway offered. "They'll probably spot us when we leave."

"True," Elton agreed. "This gives us a problem. We need to work our way closer to Hudson Base, but they have probably slammed the door behind us tightly. Getting through will be difficult."

"Impossible," Biscoe corrected. "Throwing ourselves into the teeth of enemy defences will result in our destruction."

Elton nodded. "I've been looking at the starcharts of the sector," he said, after a moment. He took control of the projector and oriented the display on Celadon. "This system is of particular interest. You'll note that it is technically neutral, so the enemy won't have had any emplaced fortresses in place to support their blockade. Furthermore, the gravity point chain starting there *doesn't* double round to link up with any other gravity chain until Karma, *here*."

He pointed to the blinking star. "We actually passed through Karma on our way to Harmony," he said. "I have no doubt that they're actually rushing reinforcements in our general direction even as we speak, but Celadon is right on the edge of a gravity point chain and - I think - would have had a pretty low priority before we sneaked into the *last* gravity point."

"Putting warships in *that* system would be an act of war," Rebecca added, calmly.

"They don't seem to care," Biscoe muttered.

Elton shot him a warning look. "They probably *shouldn't* have been able to get many ships up to Celadon," he said. "Jumping through the gravity point gives us the best chance of cutting a few hundred light years off the journey."

"We *might* run into a fleet of warships heading in the other direction," Callaway pointed out, slowly. "And they *might* have managed to fortify the Celesta gravity points. Celesta is only a small colony, but she *is* in a vital position."

"We'll be going through the gravity point at speed," Elton said. He held up a hand. "I understand the dangers, but we have no choice. Staying where we are is not an option."

Biscoe cleared his throat. "Captain, we *could* wait and see if the last engagement embroils the Harmonies in war," he said. "We *are* fairly certain they shot hell out of a number of innocent freighters."

"It would take time for the other powers to mobilise, sir," Callaway pointed out. "Even if they declared war at once, we'd have to wait at least nine months for major fleet operations."

"Unless they started preparing for war months ago," Biscoe countered. "They *can't* have missed some of the fortification efforts."

"We don't know enough to be sure, one way or the other," Elton said, cutting off the debate. "I don't think we can rely on anyone to help us until we return to Hudson Base."

He took control of the display again. "We'll set course to Celadon immediately," he said, firmly. "As there's no way we can pretend to be a helpless freighter *this* time, we'll fake a catastrophic drive failure instead" - he tapped a location several AUs from the gravity point - "*here*. They know they hurt us. Hopefully, they'll believe it and be lured out of position."

"If there *are* any warships there," Callaway said. "They may have a couple of watchdogs on *this* side of the gravity point and the whole fleet on the *other* side."

Elton nodded. "We'll just have to be careful," he said, shortly. "If they do come after us, we'll slip away under stealth mode and punch our way through the gravity point. Any questions?"

There were none.

"Good," he said. "Ms. Howells, set course immediately for Celadon," he ordered. "Mr. Wolf, prepare to emit a drive flare as we crash out of FTL."

"Aye, Captain," Marie said.

"I'll get right on it," Wolf said. He sobered. "Although, with all due respect, if we place too much stress on the drive nodes we won't *have* to fake a flare."

"I have every faith in you," Elton assured him. "Mr. Biscoe, Mr. Callaway; run a series of simulations, based on the different possible scenarios we might encounter. See if you can stack the odds in our favour as much as possible."

"Aye, Captain," Biscoe said.

Elton resisted - barely - the urge to ask if Hoshiko Sashimi Stuart would have come up with something better. But then, she'd commanded a full battle squadron instead of a single damaged starship. *She* could probably have forced her way through a gravity point and made any surviving defenders regret ever having heard of the human race.

"Dismissed," he said, quietly.

"It sounds chancy," Rebecca said, once they were alone. "Can we make it?"

"I don't have any better ideas," Elton said. "The only other options are setting course for the nearest Great Power and throwing ourselves on their mercy or heading straight for Hudson Base in FTL. Either one puts us out of commission for far too long."

"I see," Rebecca said.

Elton rather doubted it. The Harmonies had launched a full-scale war, to all intents and purposes. They'd ignored galactic protocols designed to *prevent* war and embroiled themselves with both humanity and a number of other galactic powers. The implications couldn't be ignored indefinitely. If *he'd* found himself in such a mess, with a good third of the galaxy out for his blood, he might have tried to discuss peace...or doubled down by attacking Hudson Base. Smashing Commodore Longlegs and her squadron would buy them time before the reprisals arrived.

It would piss off the rest of the galaxy still further, he conceded, but right now the Harmonies didn't have much to lose.

But their offensive could be already on the way, he thought coldly, as *Odyssey* slid back into FTL. This time, thankfully, the transition felt normal. *We have no way to know.*

"I'm fed up of not knowing," he added, reluctantly. "We really need to learn what is going on."

"I agree," Rebecca said. "Now how do you plan to do *that?*"

"Good question," Elton said. He rose. "I'll try to think of something."

Rebecca nodded. "How long do you have until you're needed on the bridge?"

"We'll be in transit for at least thirty hours," Elton said. "Why?"

"Come to bed," Rebecca said. "It'll do you good."

Elton hesitated. Sexual relationships led to emotional relationships... they were both mature enough to understand that the relationship wouldn't last, but still...He could spend a few hours in a VR sim, if he wished, enjoying sexual congress in every manner known to man and a few that had only been considered theoretically possible, before the technology had reached the point necessary to support them. And yet...

It wouldn't be real, he thought.

He'd grown tired of the sims very quickly, just like most of his fellows. They just weren't *real*. Indeed, they were nothing more than a form of masturbation. Those who chose to fall into them were held in contempt. And why not? They'd given up all hopes of a normal life for an illusion.

Rebecca rose and held out a hand. "You have time," she said. "And you need it."

"Thank you," Elton said. He took her hand, feeling - oddly - like a blushing schoolboy. He should be more mature, damn it! "Coming?"

She smiled.

"BETTER GET YOUR clothes on," Levi said, as the module began to shake. "We're here."

Tyler gave her a tired smile. "You sure we don't have time for one more round?"

Levi rolled her eyes. Having sex was just another way to pass the time. She hated to admit it, but she'd been as bored and cranky as him after five days in the module. Tyler wasn't her usual type - she preferred men with more muscles - yet they were alone. Besides, he hadn't done too badly. She had the feeling he'd be seeking out more bodymods to improve his stamina in the years to come.

"No, we don't," she said. She reached for her panties and pulled them on, followed by her trousers and shirt. "Get dressed, now."

The module shook again. She linked into the local datanet and discovered that they were being unloaded and pushed into a small warehouse. A couple of aliens - oxygen-breathers - were nearby, probably supervising the work. A moment later, a loud *bang* echoed through the module and the hatch sprang open. She tensed, one hand reaching for her pistol, as a grey-skinned alien peered into the module. It was naked, as far as she could tell, but there was no sign of any genitals. Its dark eyes were almost hypnotic.

"You are welcome," it said, in a reedy voice. It held out a portable terminal. "Payment?"

Levi reached for her credit chip and pressed it against the terminal. It bleeped, accepting the payment. The grey alien would forward two-thirds of it to the smugglers, she knew, keeping the rest for itself. She stepped out of the module, taking a long breath. The air was hot and dry, so dry that it made her throat itch, but it smelled better than the module. Tyler followed her, doing up his shirt. The scene almost made her smile.

"Proceed through the airlocks, then do not come back," the alien said, jabbing a finger at the hatch. "Farewell."

"Polite," Tyler muttered, as they stepped through the hatch. "What now?"

Levi said nothing. She was too busy scanning the local datanet for useful listings. The asteroid was independent, with dozens of freighters arriving and departing every day, but there was very little to tell her where the freighters were actually *going*. She checked the datanet for other humans, finding none. Humans didn't even seem to be included in the catalogue. She shrugged, then located a Pan-Gal Hotel. They might not have any rooms suitable for human occupation, but they'd make one up for enough money.

"This way," she said. "Let's go."

The asteroid was immense, she discovered, as they made their way down the central core and into the lifts. Its original owners had mined it hollow, then spun the rock to produce a gravity field. She'd seen quite a few low-tech asteroid settlements that used similar principles, but they were quite rare outside the Solar Union. She kept checking the listings as she walked, coming to the grim conclusion that they were going to have to hire a facilitator to assist them. The bastard would probably drain their finances in short order.

"Here we are," she said, as they reached the Pan-Gal Hotel. "Let's see what they have for us."

Once she'd shown them her credit card - and humanity's requirements - the hotel staff could not be more accommodating. Their room was comfortable, the bath and shower were perfect...she wondered, as she checked the room for bugs, if they'd had it designed a long time ago for human visitors. But then, humans weren't *that* unique. They'd probably just swapped out a few of the furnishings and removed anything that humans couldn't use.

"I need a shower," Tyler said. "Do you want to join me?"

"Go first," Levi said, absently. She sat on the bed, probing through the listings for starship departures. "I'll take a shower later."

The listings didn't get any better, no matter how she looked at them. Reluctantly, she sent a message to the hotel staff, requesting the name and contact details for a facilitator who could be trusted. It wasn't a request she wanted to make, but the Pan-Gal chain was renowned for its discretion. She stripped off and joined Tyler in the shower, rolling her eyes when she saw the immense chamber. It was easily large enough to hold an elephant. Perhaps the Pan-Gal hadn't made as many changes as she'd thought.

"This is heaven," Tyler said. He reached out and pulled her under the water. "Don't you think?"

Levi laughed. "Now you know why marines get so much enjoyment from the simple pleasures," she said. "We don't have *any* of them while on deployment."

She scrubbed herself clean, feeling - not for the first time - that she was removing layers of grime before leaving the shower. A message had already popped up in the hotel's inbox, offering her the services of the hotel's facilitator. Levi wasn't sure she trusted the hotel, but they were short of options. She shot back a request for a starship heading to Hudson, then changed into a new set of clothes. They'd have to buy more if they remained on the asteroid for more than a few days.

Tyler stuck his head out of the shower. "Any news?"

"I hired a facilitator," Levi said. Another message popped up in front of her. "Let's see..."

She sucked in her breath as she skimmed the options. Five starships were going to Hudson itself, two more were heading to Wahiawa, a star only five light years from Hudson. The latter offered more discretion, although none of them were perfect. They'd have to make it clear to the ship's captain that they had to remain undetected. Hiding someone on a starship wasn't hard, even if it was designed for oxygen-breathers, but she had no doubt that the Harmonies knew how to search carefully...

If they know they have to look, she mused, thoughtfully. There wasn't much *news* on the datanet, but there *was* a string of complaints about starships being delayed, denied transit or searched thoroughly before they were allowed to proceed. *Our ship wouldn't stand out amongst the crowd, would it?*

"We'll go to Hudson Base," she said, finally. There was a ship that promised to get them there within two weeks, assuming the gravity points were open. "We might just have to hide when we pass through the gravity points."

"I hope you're right," Tyler said. "Is there any news?"

"Nothing of great value," Levi said.

She thanked the facilitator, then opened up a channel to the starship's commander and started negotiations. The alien life support requirements were close enough to humanity's to avoid accidentally poisoning themselves, although she suspected they wouldn't find the alien foodstuffs to their taste. She made a mental note to get some ration packs before they left, just to ensure they had something tasty to eat. Even cheap slop from a food processor would be better than alien food.

"We have a compartment," she said, when she was finished. "We're leaving in two days."

"Great," Tyler said, tiredly. "What do we do until then?"

Levi nodded to the bed. "Get some rest, then spend some time exploring the asteroid and gathering news," she said. There would be an information broker somewhere on the asteroid or she'd been born on Earth. They'd find him and, hopefully, get some more up to date information. "We'll be back in closed quarters soon."

"Joy," Tyler said. He didn't sound pleased. She didn't really blame him. Even the most human-like alien race wasn't *human*. "Why don't we ever travel on ships crewed by naked green-skinned alien space babes?"

"Because such babes only exist in adolescent fantasies," Levi said. She stuck out her tongue, rather childishly. "And you're old enough to know they're not real."

"I've seen women with green skin," Tyler objected. "They're everywhere on Orion Asteroid."

Levi sighed. She was as committed to the principles of the Solar Union as any other marine or naval officer, but there were times when she thought some of the independent cantons went a little too far in trying to claim their own identities. Nudist colonies, religious colonies, colonies based on political theories that rarely lasted in the real world...It didn't matter, she told herself firmly. She didn't have to live on Orion, nor did anyone else who wanted to leave. Perhaps it was better to keep all the crazies on one asteroid. It certainly made for simplified management.

She pointed to the bed. "Sleep," she ordered. "You'll be moaning about the next cabin soon enough."

TWENTY-NINE

Your sarcasm is duly noted and reported to the Sarcasm Inquisition, who will see your rusty chainsaw and raise you a Papa Angel Torture Machine thingy.

That said, I take your point about the war being inevitable. But we remain a small power, with a single point failure source. Sol cannot be lost, as you have stated yourself. And that means we need allies, allies who can be turned into military powers...given time. Our own forces should be used to stiffen their posture and reinforce them when necessary.

Or do you have other objections to founding an alliance?
-Solar Datanet, Political Forum (Grand Alliance Thoughts)

"We're approaching the waypoint, Captain," Marie said. Elton nodded, curtly. The drive had held up better than he'd dared hope. Wolf and his team had done a superb job. But dropping out of FTL so violently risked turning their fake emergency into a *real* emergency...he shook his head in annoyance, dismissing the thought before it could be spoken again. They *had* to get through the gravity point before it was too late.

He glanced at Biscoe. "Mr. XO?"

"Drive flare programming engaged," Biscoe reported. "We're ready to drop out on your command."

"Helm, punch us out at the waypoint," Elton ordered. He keyed his console. "All hands, brace for crash transition. I say again, all hands brace for crash transition."

"Waypoint in three...two...one..."

Odyssey shuddered, then shook so violently that - just for a moment - he honestly thought they'd struck an asteroid. A loud *bang* echoed through the ship. Elton could have sworn he heard the hull *squeal* in protest at the rough handling as the starship dropped out of FTL. The hum of the drives grew louder, just long enough to make his ears hurt, then faded back into the background. He rubbed his ears, trying to banish the uncomfortable sensation, as he leaned forward. Red lights were flashing up on the display.

"Status?"

"We took about forty *years* off the primary drive nodes," Biscoe reported. He looked up from his console. "But it *looks* as though the damage isn't serious."

Elton nodded. He'd give himself a moment to be relieved later. "And the flare?"

"Should have looked like an utter disaster," Callaway said. "They'll know we crashed out of FTL."

"Take us into stealth," Elton ordered, shortly. "Helm, sneak us towards the gravity point."

"Aye, Captain," Marie said.

Elton leaned forward, studying the display as data started to flow into the ship's sensors. Celadon hadn't been considered very important before the stardrive and - even now - it hadn't attracted much investment from the Galactics. Gravimetric sensors picked up a handful of starships flying through the system, almost all of them heading towards or away from the gravity point. The lone inhabited planet wasn't as important, economically speaking, as the gravity point itself. It was practically a backwater.

But then, if there had been two or more gravity points in this system, they would have been dragged into the galactic mainstream, he thought. *The inhabitants wouldn't be given a choice.*

"Launch a probe towards the gravity point," he ordered. "See what you can detect."

"Aye, Captain," Callaway said.

"They *will* have seen our arrival," Biscoe said. "Unless they're blind."

Or not there at all, Elton thought. He dismissed the thought instantly. The lone gravity point *was* on one end of a chain that eventually led to Hudson Base. He had no doubt the Harmonies would attempt to reinforce the defences - would have already started to reinforce the defences, even before they'd stumbled across *Odyssey* in the last system. *They'll have a squadron - at least - covering the point.*

"We'll see them when we get closer," he said. "If, of course, they're fooled."

The Harmonies *should* be fooled, he told himself firmly. *Odyssey* was a pretty distinctive starship, even before the Harmonies had declared her Public Enemy Number One. The defenders would know, he was sure, that they were about to encounter their quarry. But...what would they do? Logically, they *should* try to take advantage of the drive failure to run *Odyssey* down before she managed to make repairs...

But what if they think we actually blew ourselves up, he thought. *Or if they don't have enough ships to detach a squadron to catch us?*

He dismissed that thought, too, as the minutes slowly ticked by. The enemy *would* know, he was sure. And they *couldn't* let the opportunity slip past, could they? The chance to catch a crippled starship could *not* be ignored...he told himself, sharply, that he was fretting over nothing. He'd have to think of something else if he couldn't get through the gravity point and into the next system...

"Captain," Callaway said. "I'm picking up an enemy squadron, heading directly for the waypoint. They're trying to be sneaky."

Elton carefully hid his relief. "Can you get a ship count?"

"Two battleships, seven cruisers," Callaway said. "Plus one ship of unknown configuration, purpose unknown. I'd say it was a freighter if it wasn't in the middle of a battle squadron."

"It could be a gunboat carrier," Biscoe pointed out.

"Perhaps, sir," Callaway said. "But they can't be *that* short of hulls."

Elton considered it for a moment - freighters couldn't be turned into warships, nor could they stand in the line of battle - and then dismissed it. They'd find out what the Harmonies were planning sooner or later, he was sure. For the moment, all that mattered was that a sizable percentage of the enemy force was off on a wild goose chase. They'd be too far out of position to intervene when *Odyssey* showed herself.

"Keep monitoring them," he ordered. "And warn me if they try to drop into FTL."

"Aye, Captain," Callaway said.

"We'll be within passive sensor range of the gravity point in twenty minutes," Marie added, shortly. "I can pick up speed."

"Not yet," Elton said. The urge to race down the rabbit hole was almost overpowering, but he had no idea what was waiting for them. "Tactical?"

"I'm picking up at least one transit station," Callaway reported. "And some unsecured chatter, but no starships as yet."

Elton nodded. The Harmonies would have stepped down their drives and sensors to avoid detection...assuming, of course, that they were there at all. He leaned back in his command chair, forcing himself to relax as the enemy fleet swept past and headed for the waypoint. It would take them at least thirty minutes to realise they'd been tricked, at which point - he hoped - it would be too late...

"Picking up four ships, two destroyers and two ships of unknown configuration," Callaway said, as new icons flashed into existence on the display. "The latter look like freighters, but they appear to have military-grade drives. They *could* be designed to keep up with a fleet train."

"Confirming that the Harmonies do have imperialistic ambitions," Biscoe said. "I thought that military-grade freighters were technically forbidden."

Elton shrugged. It was true, *technically*. The Tokomak had banned fleet trains, save for themselves. Practically speaking, there was nothing to stop any imperialistically-minded power from either converting civilian freighters for military purposes or simply constructing a basic freighter design with military drives. Or, for that matter, just using the freighters without bothering with a refit. The Tokomak bureaucrats clearly hadn't understood the realities of interstellar shipping. No doubt they hadn't bothered to consult their own military before issuing the edict.

His lips quirked. "We'll report them to the Tokomak on the way out," he said, dryly. The Tokomak bureaucracy was large enough to take the complaint seriously, no matter what was actually going on. Who knew? Perhaps it *would* cause trouble for the Harmonies. "Does the station have any defensive potential?"

"Not as far as I can tell," Callaway said. "She looks like a fairly standard traffic control station - there aren't any free-floating warehouses or R&R facilities. I think there are a couple of weapons platforms in close orbit, but not enough to threaten us."

"This system is nothing more than a waypoint," Biscoe said. "The destroyers are the real threat."

"No," Elton said. "What's lurking on the other side is the *real* threat."

He took a moment to contemplate the tactical situation as *Odyssey* inched closer to the gravity point. The enemy destroyers were no match for his ship, but if one of them managed to jump through the gravity point and scream a warning before *Odyssey* could jump...he scowled, bitterly. They'd be blown apart at point-blank range. Both enemy destroyers had to be taken out before they had a chance to react. And then there were the two unknown ships...if they were merely freighters, they were harmless, but if they were modified warships...

"Target the destroyers," he ordered. "Keep updating the passive locks as we move closer to the gravity point. If they get a sniff of us, blow them away."

"Aye, Captain," Callaway said. "Weapons locked and set to automatic firing mode."

"Confirmed," Biscoe said. "Automatic firing sequence confirmed."

Elton sucked in his breath as they glided into firing range. They needed to be close, very close, before opening fire. He could throw enough missiles to overwhelm their defences in seconds, but they still had the option of popping through the gravity point. And yet...they were in one of the very few regions of interplanetary space where a head-on collision was actually probable. His instincts were urging him to pick up speed and get out of the danger zone before it was too late...

They'll see us soon, he told himself, grimly. *And then they'll start running.*

Two more freighters flickered into existence on the display, barely pausing long enough to exchange messages with the station before they brought up their stardrives and vanished into FTL. The station didn't seem to make any effort to search them, something that bothered Elton more than he cared to admit. Either the station's crew wasn't inclined to search ships popping through from the wrong side or they were confident that the defenders on the far side had already done the work. If *that* was the case, it suggested worrying things about the forces waiting for him.

We need a recon drone that can be popped through a gravity point, he thought. *But so far none of the researchers have managed to miniaturise a gravity pulse generator so we can pop a gunboat though, let alone a drone.*

"Entering medium range now," Marie reported.

"Hang tight," Elton ordered.

He braced himself. The enemy *would* spot them soon. He had no doubt of it. *Odyssey's* stealth mode was inferior to a proper cloaking device. Even if they *had* had a cloak, they couldn't have crept to point-blank range without being detected. The gravity point was playing merry hell with his sensors, but the enemy had had plenty of time to adjust their systems to compensate...

An alarm sounded. "They saw us," Callaway snapped. *Odyssey* rumbled as she unleashed her first broadside. "Missiles away, Captain! I say again..."

"I heard," Elton said. "Raise shields. Ramp up the drive!"

"Aye, Captain," Callaway said.

"Enemy ships are raising shields," Biscoe reported. "One of them is heading towards the point!"

Damn, Elton thought. *They must have been on alert, even if they weren't putting wear and tear on their shield generators.*

He cursed under his breath. He'd miscalculated. The enemy knew that *Odyssey* was in the system, even if they believed her to be seven AUs from the gravity point. They'd put their ships on alert. And that miscalculation might have cost them everything, unless...the missiles reached their targets and slammed into their shields, smashing them down. A moment later, both destroyers were blown into dust.

"Targets destroyed," Callaway reported.

"Helm, take us through the gravity point," Elton said. There was no point in wasting time destroying either the station or the two freighters. They'd just soak up missiles he knew he'd need on the far side. "Tactical, reset the weapons. Prepare to engage any nearby enemy battleships or fortresses with Hammers."

"Aye, sir," Marie said. "This is going to be a rough transition."

"We can handle it," Elton assured her. Celesta *wasn't* that important a system, but he was fairly sure the Harmonies would have done their best to fortify her. They couldn't risk popping through the gravity point at zero velocity. "Stand by to transit..."

"Captain," Callaway snapped. "I'm picking up targeting emissions from the freighters!"

Impossible, Elton thought. *They have to be mad to pick a fight with a warship.*

He turned his attention to the display. The enemy freighters had raised shields - military-grade shields - and were manoeuvring into attack position. And *that* suggested they weren't insane after all. What were they *doing*?

"Target them, standard warheads," Elton ordered. *Odyssey* was still picking up speed. A few more minutes and they'd be through the gravity point and into the next system. "Mr. Williams, order them to back off."

"No response, Captain," Williams said. "They didn't even bother to tell us to surrender."

"I think we're way past that now," Biscoe said. "We wouldn't let them have the ship, even if we surrendered the crew."

"Missile separation," Callaway snapped. "*Multiple* missile separation!"

Elton felt his eyes go wide as he saw the new wave of icons on the display. A freighter couldn't carry so many missiles, could it? A battleship couldn't fire so many missiles in a single salvo. And yet...he pushed his disbelief aside. The freighters had been configured to carry missiles, adding to the firepower defending the gravity point. Dismissing them as harmless had been a terrible mistake.

"Bring up point defence, prepare to engage," he ordered. "Mr. Biscoe?"

"Analysis indicates that they're single-shot weapons," Biscoe said. "Someone crammed the hulls full of missile pods...they can't reload."

"I hope you're right," Elton snapped. He silently saluted the enemy commanders. They'd taken full advantage of his blunder. And it *had* been a blunder. "Helm?"

"We'll be through the gravity point in one minute," Marie said.

"Configuring warheads to swat enemy missiles," Callaway said. "Firing...now!"

Elton nodded, suppressing his annoyance. If they made it through the point, they'd just wasted a ton of missiles...it was no consolation that the enemy had done the same thing. He didn't even have time to blow the freighters away. Destroying them, now they'd shot themselves dry, would have been nothing more than pointless spite. But...

"They're too bunched up to be effective," Callaway reported. "I'm taking out hundreds of them."

"There are hundreds more," Elton said. He clenched his fist. After everything they'd done, he was damned if they were losing to a pair of crappy makeshift warships based on freighter hulls and crewed by amateurs. "Deploy drones."

"Gravity point in thirty seconds," Marie said.

The weapons fire shouldn't have any effect on the gravity point, Elton told himself. He'd scanned the records during the long flight to Harmony. *The*

Tokomak threw thousands of warships through one gravity point, back during the wars...the gravity point didn't even twitch.

He shook his head. The Tokomak believed that gravity points were natural outgrowths of the gravity field that held the galaxy - and the universe - together. Some parts of space, they'd reasoned, were weaker than others, linking two regions of space together and allowing starships to hop hundreds of light years in an eyeblink. Elton didn't pretend to understand the math, but everyone agreed there was no way to disrupt a gravity point. And yet...*finding* a way might be very interesting indeed.

"Point defence going active, sir," Callaway said. "Missile impact in fifteen seconds."

"Get some more *push* out of the engines," Elton said. A *real* warship would have been able to overstress the drives, if only for a few minutes. Right now, it would have made the difference between life and death. "Divert power to shields and drives."

"Aye, Captain," Biscoe said.

"Captain, the enemy ships are reversing course and dropping into FTL," Callaway added. "I think they've realised they were played."

"It doesn't matter," Elton said. His ship was shaking as Marie overpowered the drives. He was grimly aware that they were trapped, if anything went wrong. Losing the drives completely would spell utter disaster. "They can't interfere now."

"Gravity point in five seconds," Marie said.

"Hammers pre-programmed to engage," Callaway added. "Firing sequences ready to go."

Elton tapped his console. "All hands, brace for rough transit," he snapped. He hoped the crew remembered what to do. It wasn't a drill they practiced very often. In hindsight, it was another oversight. "Brace for rough..."

The universe sneezed, violently. Elton doubled over, feeling as though he'd been punched in the gut. A faint haze hovered at the edge of his vision as he retched uncontrollably, swallowing hard to keep from throwing up on the deck. His head ached...just for a second, he honestly believed that someone had stabbed a knife deep into his brain. He sniffed, recoiling as he scented vomit. Someone behind him hadn't managed to keep their lunch. He carefully didn't look around to see who'd vomited. Normally, they'd be relieved at once, but there was no reason to assume that the beta crew was in any better state. His head *still* felt like broken glass...

"Transit complete, Captain," Marie said. Her face was pale. She sounded badly shaken, her hands trembling as she worked her console. Beside her, Callaway looked exhausted, as if he'd just run a race. "The drive is cycling down now."

"Launch drones," Elton ordered. His voice threatened to tremble too. "Tactical?"

"I'm picking up two enemy fortresses and a squadron of smaller ships," Callaway reported, grimly. New icons flared up on the display. "Hammers are engaging...now!"

Elton nodded. "Helm, get us out of here," he ordered. They were in no state for an engagement. "Best possible speed!"

"Aye, sir," Marie said.

THIRTY

I believe I have made my objections quite clear.

I'm sure you're about to accuse me of being racist against aliens, even though - let us face it - the vast majority of the Galactics view us as children, upstarts or prey. They think of us as something akin to 'uppity niggers.' Yes, I used that word and it fits, because the contemptuous mindset that allows someone to dismiss someone from a lesser race - as they saw it - is exactly the same attitude the Galactics use to dismiss us.

Be honest. Even our allies think of us as the new kids on the block.

-Solar Datanet, Political Forum (Grand Alliance Thoughts)

"Impact in ten seconds," Callaway said.

Elton nodded, stiffly, as he fought to remain calm. His stomach felt queasy, as if he'd eaten something rotten. His implants couldn't do anything about the sensation, either. It wasn't a *real* sensation. Reports were flooding in from all over the ship, informing him that one in ten crewmen were no longer in a fit state to carry out their duties. There was a *reason* why starships always crept through the gravity points after all, rather than charging through like a bat out of hell.

The enemy, at least, had been completely surprised by *Odyssey's* arrival on their side of the gravity point. Elton watched, grimly, as the fortresses struggled to bring their shields and weapons up, even though it was far too late. They should have kept everything at standby, he noted, as the Hammers slammed into the fortresses and destroyed them. It would have given the Harmonies their best possible chance at smashing *Odyssey* before she made her escape.

"Targets destroyed," Callaway reported. "The enemy starships are bringing up their shields and weapons now."

"Engage all targets within range, but hold back the remaining Hammers," Elton ordered, shortly. The Harmonies didn't have enough firepower to keep him from escaping the gravity point. "Helm, get us away from the gravity point!"

"Aye, sir," Marie ordered.

Elton watched as the enemy ships opened fire. Their fire was sporadic, as if they weren't quite sure of their target. The drones were probably confusing them, if they hadn't been shocked - badly - by the loss of the fortresses. They'd been absolute masters of the Celesta System for so long that *Odyssey's* arrival was pretty much an outside context problem. He felt a flicker of contempt, even though he knew he should be glad. The Harmonies had *known* they might be called upon to fight at any moment.

"They're scattering," Callaway said. "I think we killed their CO."

"They'll pick another one soon," Biscoe said. He cursed, softly. "Captain, long-range sensors are picking up an enemy fleet coming from Gravity Point Two."

Elton keyed his console, bringing up a starchart. Gravity Point Two wasn't on the direct route to Hudson Base, but it *did* provide a shortcut for enemy forces that might have been diverted towards Kami before being called back. The Harmonies had deduced their likely path, even if they hadn't reacted in time to keep him from jumping into Celesta. They'd know now, he was sure. The alert would already be racing out from Gravity Point Three.

"They can move to block us," he said, coldly. "Or..."

He forced himself to *think*. The alert would already be going out, but - thanks to the speed-of-light delay - it wouldn't have reached the enemy ships. Not *yet*. No alert had come through from Celadon or the defences at Gravity Point Three would have been ready for them. And that meant...there was *just* time to take advantage of the situation, if they were lucky.

"Helm, bring up the stardrive," he ordered. "Take us directly to Gravity Point One."

"Aye, Captain," Marie said.

Elton shared a long look with Biscoe. It was a gamble, one *hell* of a gamble. The enemy commanders would see them the moment they dropped into FTL, unless their sensor operators happened to be asleep at the switch. And there was no way *that* would happen, unless the enemy was overwhelmingly confident. He rather doubted it. *Odyssey* escaping Harmony and then blowing her way out of a number of traps would probably have dented the enemy's pride badly. They wouldn't take her lightly any longer.

"They'll adjust course as soon as they see us," Biscoe muttered.

"I know," Elton said.

He scowled. The records insisted that Gravity Point One was lightly defended, but the records were *years* out of date. He'd be astonished if the gravity point *wasn't* heavily defended. And yet, blasting their way through would cut *years* off their journey. They needed to break through, if it was humanly possible.

And if it isn't, he thought grimly, *we'll at least give them a scare.*

"Take us out two minutes from the gravity point," he ordered, as the display blanked. "And cycle the drive as soon as we arrive."

"Aye, Captain," Marie said.

"Message from sickbay," Biscoe said. "We have over a hundred crewmen who have to go off duty."

"Understood," Elton said. He still felt fragile himself. Two bridge crew had already been replaced. "We won't make a note of it in their personal files."

He smiled at his weak joke. "Make sure the remaining personnel are moved around to cover for any holes," he added. "And put the sufferers to bed."

"Aye, Captain," Biscoe said.

"Leaving FTL in one minute," Marie said.

"All weapons and sensors at full alert," Callaway added.

Elton braced himself as *Odyssey* slipped back out of FTL...and swore. The display lit up like a Christmas tree. Gravity Point One was orbited by four fortresses, two full enemy battle squadrons and a swarm of gunboats. Their weapons were already charged...thankfully, *Odyssey* hadn't tried to drop out of FTL right on top of them. There was no hope of getting through the gravity point in one piece.

"Sir, the enemy fleet is on our tail," Callaway reported. "They're..."

The display lit up, again, as the enemy ships materialised near the gravity point. Elton cursed under his breath. The enemy had jumped into FTL as soon as they'd detected *Odyssey*, then - they'd deduced their destination and hurried to intercept. They hadn't *quite* managed to bring themselves out of FTL in firing position, but they *were* close enough to do real damage if they had a chance.

"Helm, bring us about," Elton ordered, harshly. "Get us out of here!"

"Aye, Captain," Marie said.

"Enemy ships are moving into firing position," Callaway said. "I'm picking up a disturbing number of missile-armed freighters."

"They must have designed them as a stopgap gravity point defence system," Biscoe said, looking down at his console. "They certainly have the firepower to give someone a bloody nose."

"Probably," Elton agreed. He sucked in his breath. "Time to FTL?"

"Two minutes, at best," Marie said. "Engineering would prefer five."

"We'll see," Elton said. "Punch us up as hard as you can."

"Aye, sir," Marie said.

"Enemy ships are opening fire," Callaway said. "Request permission to deploy drones."

"Granted," Elton said.

He couldn't help feeling a flicker of *Déjà Vu* as *Odyssey* retreated from yet another gravity point, struggling to bring her FTL drive up before it was too late. It looked like any one of their previous engagements.

And yet, there were subtle differences. It was growing more and more apparent that the enemy had updated their missile targeting systems to compensate for *Odyssey's* superior ECM. Maybe they were still firing at long range, running the risk of burnout before they reached their target, but the odds of scoring a hit were considerably higher.

"They're not being spoofed so well," Callaway commented. "Drones two through five haven't managed to lure *any* of the missiles out of place."

Elton scowled as the point defence opened fire. He'd assumed the Harmonies wanted the ship intact - or as intact as possible - and he still thought that that had been the original plan. But the Harmonies were learning from their engagements too, testing themselves against a human starship in fairly controlled circumstances. Commodore Longlegs might find herself at an unexpected disadvantage if the Harmonies attacked Hudson Base, if some of her technological tricks were useless. *Odyssey* wasn't a warship, but her defences were very definitely military-grade.

"Missiles closing to attack range," Callaway warned. "Impact in seventeen seconds."

"Brace for impact," Elton ordered.

"Targeting data suggests they're trying to hammer our drives," Biscoe added. "Captain, they *know* we're damaged."

"Yeah," Elton said. "But we won't die easily."

Odyssey rocked as two missiles slammed home, but neither penetrated the shields. "Shields holding," Callaway reported. "The impact may have shook a few things loose."

"FTL in one minute," Marie said. "Captain?"

"Take us into FTL as soon as possible," Elton said. "We may not have a ship left if we hang around for much longer."

"Aye, Captain," Marie said.

The enemy ships opened fire again, pouring out a torrent of missiles. Others jumped forward in FTL, trying to get into firing position to force *Odyssey* to run the gauntlet. Elton wondered, absently, just how many neutral worlds were now aware of what was going on...and what, if anything, they'd do about it. The Harmonies had broken so many interstellar conventions that there *had* to be war. Hadn't they?

"Stardrive engaging...now," Marie said.

The display blanked as *Odyssey* dropped into FTL. Elton allowed himself a moment of pure relief. They'd escaped, barely. *And* they were several hundred light years closer to their destination.

And, on the other hand, half the crew is in no state to do much of anything, he reminded himself. *And we're still a long way from home.*

He rose. "Keep us in FTL, on a rough course for UTU-758, and drop us out once we are outside enemy sensor range," he ordered. There was nothing orbiting UTU-758, as far as he knew, which would probably excite the enemy's paranoia. "Be prepared to move at any moment. They'll be searching for us still."

"Aye, Captain," Marie said.

"Mr. XO, you have the bridge," Elton added. His chest still hurt, a dull throbbing that felt too real to be anything else. "Concentrate on repairing and then cleaning the ship."

"Aye, sir," Biscoe said.

"And we have to figure out what to do next," Elton said. "We're not out of the woods yet."

"This isn't going to make for an interesting chapter in my memoires," Rebecca said, as she stripped off her tunic. "I didn't join the diplomatic service to spend my days cleaning vomit off the decks."

"My old instructors used to say it built character," Captain Yasser said. He sounded happier than the last time Rebecca had seen him, before they'd blasted their way through the gravity point. "Actually, they said that *anything* we didn't like built character. Getting out of bed at stupid o'clock? That built character. Getting our asses kicked at three-dimensional combat simulations? That built character. Facing a burly marine in the combat ring? Believe me, *that* built character."

Rebecca snorted. "What about going off on shore leave with a local beauty?"

"I believe the hangover afterwards was known to build character too," the captain said.

"Hah," Rebecca said. "There are pills for that, aren't there?"

She stepped into the shower, trying not to smell herself. Her body felt sore, but she hadn't disgraced herself by throwing up helplessly. Luckily - or unluckily - she'd been rounded up by one of the crew to help clean the decks. She didn't mind, not really, but after four hours of scrubbing the decks she was all too aware that she smelt terrible. And yet...

I could be one of the unlucky crewmen who ended up in sickbay, she told herself, as she turned on the water. *It could be a great deal worse.*

The warm water ran down her body, splashing over her breasts and down her legs. She looked down, half-expecting to see savage bruises covering her abdomen, but her skin was utterly unmarked. She bent over and touched her leg, unsure what she expected to feel. But there was nothing, just a dull throbbing pain that refused to fade. If it had been quite bad enough for her - and it had - she hated to think what it must have been like for the poor souls in sickbay.

"I ache," she said, sticking her head out of the shower. "Why does that happen?"

"I don't think anyone ever came up with a universally-accepted theory that explains everything," Captain Yasser said. He was lying on his bed, studying a datapad. Rebecca was torn between amusement that he wasn't paying attention to her - let alone joining her in the shower - and wry understanding. The captain had to take care of his ship and crew. Besides, it wasn't as if she was a teenager who needed attention and approval at every moment of her day. "The Tokomak claim that a starship passing through a gravity point actually drops out of the known universe for a nanosecond, accounting for the sensation, and that moving faster only makes the sensation worse. They might be right."

Rebecca nodded as she washed her hair, then turned off the water and dried herself. "We made it through the gravity point," she said, as she walked into the bedroom. The captain barely looked up from his datapad. "You *did* come up with something."

"And now I have to come up with something else," the captain said. He held the datapad out to her. "There are three more possible ways to get to Hudson Base, but they'll have made sure to secure them all by now. We might have jumped a great deal closer to the base, yet...not close enough to matter. They may have driven us too far from the only hope of survival."

Rebecca cocked her head as she sat on the bed. "What about finding another world like Kami?"

"It's a possibility," the captain conceded. "But what do we do once we get there?"

He shook his head. "They were surprised, once, with our little Trojan Horse," he said. "I don't think we'll get away with that a second time. They'll merely insist on inspecting every freighter that tries to pass through the gravity points. We could try to pick up a second freighter and transfer the crew, abandoning *Odyssey*, but even that would be risky. I have no idea what happened to Lieutenant Dennis and your aide."

Rebecca winced. She would have preferred to go herself, rather than send Mickey Tyler into possible danger. But she had to admit he was - on paper - one of the best-prepared people on *Odyssey* to slip onto an alien world. He'd make it to Hudson, she was sure, even if no one else made it there. And then someone, at least, would know what had happened to *Odyssey* and her crew.

"They'll probably blood-check the crews too," she added. "Won't they?"

"If they're paranoid enough," the captain said. He frowned. "That fleet we encountered at Celesta could pose a serious threat to Hudson Base, if they chose to attack instead of continuing to hunt for us. We know that most of the fleet didn't follow us into FTL. I don't like the implications."

"Attacking Hudson Base would embroil most of the galaxy in a war," Rebecca pointed out.

"Perhaps," the captain agreed. "All the simulations concur that any such war will be utterly devastating."

Rebecca nodded. She'd seen some of the simulations herself. If the Tokomak lost their grip on power - which was already weakening - God alone knew how many old grudges would suddenly become important again. Or maybe old grudges wouldn't be necessary. An attack on Hudson Base was an attack on a dozen different powers, even if the Harmonies claimed to be merely fighting a single race. They'd all see it as a *de facto* declaration of war.

"They must assume they can ride out any retribution," she said, finally.

She ran her hand through her long hair, feeling thoroughly useless. She was a diplomat, with proper credentials from Sol and a thorough grounding in interstellar diplomacy. She'd been assured that everyone obeyed the rules, even when they were at daggers drawn for the rest of the time. She even held a degree from a university vetted and approved by the Tokomak themselves...

But the Harmonies had broken the rules and, so far, they'd gotten away with it.

Which goes to prove that the Galactics are very much like us, she thought. *They're neither demons nor angels. Merely...living beings.*

"We shall see," the captain said. "But right now, Rebecca, we have other problems."

His intercom bleeped. "Captain," a voice said. "We have a situation."

Captain Yasser's eyes narrowed. "Mr. Callaway," he said. "This is not the time for Underling's Inability Descriptive Syndrome. What *sort* of situation?"

"We're detecting an enemy warship on a direct course for us," Callaway said. "She's actually on a course for UTU-758, Captain, but she'll pass within a light-day of our position. She may know where we are."

"Then they should have moved sooner," the captain said, slowly. "They wouldn't have given us time to make repairs if they knew where we were, would they?"

A slow smile spread across his face. "A single warship?"

"Yes, Captain," Callaway said. "Judging from her mass readings, I'd say she was a heavy cruiser or a battlecruiser. There aren't any signs that she's stepped down her drives."

"I see," the captain said. "And when will she make her closest approach to us?"

"Two hours, forty minutes," Callaway said. "Your orders, sir?"

"I've just had an idea," the captain said. He smiled. "Alert the crew. Senior officer's meeting, ten minutes from now."

"Aye, Captain," Callaway said.

Rebecca looked at the captain as he jumped off the bed. "An idea, Elton?"

"Yes," Captain Yasser said. "One ship, coming in fat and happy. I think we can give her a very nasty surprise."

THIRTY-ONE

Then it is obviously our job to teach them otherwise. Yes, many of the Galactics - even the younger ones - see us as 'uppity humans.' And they do have a point. It's been a mere seventy years since we first learned how to build FTL drives for ourselves. We would not even have done that, would we, if we hadn't captured an alien ship.

This isn't the time to whine about being the victims of discrimination, regardless of if that is a valid complaint or not. This is the time to prove to them that we do have a place amongst the stars.
-Solar Datanet, Political Forum (Grand Alliance Thoughts)

"She's still heading directly towards us," Callaway reported. "There's no hint she's preparing to drop out of FTL."

Elton nodded, slowly. The Harmonies *couldn't* have an exact lock on *Odyssey's* location or they would have sent a much larger fleet after her. It was much more likely that they'd sent a single warship to UTU-758 in hopes of chasing *Odyssey* back into interstellar space. Elton had no idea precisely *why* the Harmonies weren't focusing on Hudson Base - for all he knew, they *were* focusing on Hudson Base - but the lone ship *did* offer him a chance to actually get some answers.

And get some payback into the bargain, he thought, grimly. *Unless, of course, that lone ship is actually towing several more.*

He looked down at the live feed from the analysis department. The analysts - and the RIs assisting them - *believed* the ship was on her own, but what if they were wrong? Elton had no illusions. The Harmonies had been well aware of how one ship could tow another through FTL long before he'd used the technique himself at Kami. They might easily have decided to take a page out of an ancient tactical manual in hopes of hoisting him on his own petard.

"Activate the gravity trap," he ordered. "Stand by all weapons."

"Aye, Captain," Callaway said. "Gravity trap engaging...now."

Elton leaned forward. The stardrive, even a military-grade system, couldn't be used too close to a gravity well. The Tokomak had actually built all kinds of safeguards into the original designs in hopes of preventing an outright disaster, although Elton rather suspected they'd overdone it. Human designers had very little compunctions about allowing warships to drop into FTL as soon as they cleared high orbit. And the Harmonies...

Either their emergency sensors will pick up the gravity well and crash them out of FTL, he thought, *or they'll run right into the gravity well and get smashed back into realspace.*

"Ten seconds," Callaway said.

"Mr. Wolf reports that the gravity well is putting undue strain on the drive nacelles," Biscoe said. "Engineering may be unable to hold the gravity field in place without shattering the drive nodes completely."

"Tell them to hold the well in place for as long as possible," Elton said. A human ship might *just* be able to smash its way through choppy gravity fields and escape. The Battle of Earth proved that Tokomak ships *couldn't*. But then, they *had* had five years to modify their drive systems to prevent a second defeat. "They're to drop it, though, if the system *is* about to blow."

"Aye, Captain," Biscoe said. "I..."

"Enemy ship is entering the gravity well," Callaway reported. "Feedback building..."

A red icon flashed into existence on the display. "Enemy ship has dropped out of FTL," Callaway added. "Sensors indicate that she's lost two of her three drive nodes..."

"Tactical, take out her shield generators and weapons," Elton ordered. They were alarmingly close to the enemy ship. The crew had had no reason to *expect* that they'd suddenly be yanked out of FTL and crashed back into normal space, but they *might* just be alert enough to find *Odyssey* and open fire. "Communications, hail her and demand surrender."

"Aye, Captain," Williams said.

The enemy ship was a battlecruiser, shaped roughly like a crude arrowhead. Elton smiled, coldly, as phaser bursts crashed into her hull. She looked punch-drunk already, heeling over as her sublight drive field flickered in and out of existence. Her crew had to have been taken by surprise, Elton noted. Callaway was systematically wiping her hull clear of any offensive weaponry, yet they hadn't even managed to muster a response to his demand. Had they killed the captain? He wouldn't have thought it possible, but a power surge in the wrong place might just have triggered off a series of catastrophic internal failures.

"Enemy ship has been disarmed," Callaway said. "Captain?"

"Mr. Williams," Elton ordered. "Raise them again. Tell them that we will treat their crewmembers in line with the standard protocols, if they surrender now. Their computer files are to be left untouched, along with everything else. That ship is to be handed over to us intact."

"Or as close to intact as possible," Callaway said.

Elton shot him a sharp look. "Send the message," he ordered. "And alert me the moment they reply."

He waited, impatiently. Major Rhodan and his marines could board the enemy ship, of course, but he was reluctant to do anything of the sort until he knew what sort of reception they'd receive. A maddened enemy, one reluctant to surrender, might just wait long enough for the marines to arrive and then switch off the antimatter containment chambers. He needed the ship, but he also needed the marines.

And they know their government intended to dispose of us and every other inconvenient witness, he thought, grimly. *They might expect us to do the same to them.*

"Picking up a message," Williams said. "Captain, it's a standard interstellar surrender. They have wounded, apparently."

"Understood," Elton said. Did he dare send the marines? A starship crew that had no reason to expect mercy - and knew perfectly well that there were no witnesses for five *light-years* - might try to lure the marines into a kill zone anyway. And yet...he *needed* the enemy ship and its records. "Inform them that the marines are on the way."

"Aye, sir," Williams said.

Elton tapped his console. "Major Rhodan, you are cleared to board the enemy vessel," he said. The marines had been waiting in their assault shuttles ever since he'd devised the interception plan. "Good luck."

"Thank you, Captain," Rhodan said. Two new icons appeared on the display as the marines undocked. "We'll be back before you know it."

THE ARMOURED COMBAT suit *itched*.

Major Peter Rhodan told himself, firmly, that it was just another case of pre-combat jitters, made worse by the combat suit. His armour was hot and warm and itched every time he donned it, an itch that miraculously vanished as soon as the mission actually began. If there were marines who got the shakes before a drop or others who spent time looking at photographs of their loved ones, why not marines who got an itch?

He shoved the thought out of his head as the assault shuttle closed in on its target. The alien battlecruiser was a solid kilometre long, two hundred metres longer than *Odyssey*...her hull scorched and pitted by multiple phaser hits. His sensors reported that the alien hull was bare of weapons, although he knew better than to take that for granted. A simple railgun would be enough to vaporise the assault shuttle. *Odyssey* would take a terrible revenge, of course, but he and his marines would still be dead.

"Zeroing in on the forward hatch," the pilot called. "One minute to unforced docking."

"Understood," Peter said. He tongued his mouthpiece, widening the channel. He needed to speak to the entire platoon. "Remember, these are POWs; not terrorists, not pirates, not some bug-eyed scum-suckers from some godforsaken rock a billion light years from home. Treat them with respect until they give you a reason to do otherwise."

He cut off a couple of complaints as the shuttle hovered in front of the forward hatch and began docking procedures. The Galactics, in their bureaucratic zeal, had devised rules for each and every possible situation, including unconditional surrender. He'd had those rules hammered into his head during advanced training, but he knew - all too well - that the Harmonies might not honour them. They'd already broken so many rules that they had no reason to expect their opponents to honour them. The Galactics made an exemption for rule-breakers...

...And the marines were uncomfortably exposed.

He checked his weapons as the hatch linked up and hissed open. Air flooded into the depressurised shuttle, bringing with it a series of warnings about atmospheric contaminants and potential damage to the life support. Peter took a moment to compare the readings to the data they'd collected on Harmony, then stepped through the hatch. His skin started to itch, again, as the inner hatch opened. If someone was plotting an ambush, they'd have an easy target.

His suit started to deploy nanoprobes as soon as he stepped through the second hatch, the probes hastily spreading out and heading into the giant ship. The enemy should have had nanoprobes of their own configured to catch and destroy *his* probes, but nothing attempted to impede their progress. Perhaps the aliens *would* honour the surrender after all. He caught himself as three aliens stepped into view, all hatless. It was the first time he'd seen a Harmony without something covering his head.

The three aliens looked...*battered*. He wasn't sure how he got that impression - he'd seen marines take worse damage in mock fights - but it stuck. They moved as if they expected to be struck at any moment, as if they were *scared*. It dawned on him, suddenly, that they probably *were* scared. They'd *known* they were perfectly safe in FTL. Nothing could touch them there...

...Until they'd been yanked out of FTL and smashed into submission.

"Greetings," the lead alien said. He knelt, looking down at the deck. "Under the Galactic Conventions of..."

"You will assemble your crew and prepare to have them transported off the ship," Peter said, cutting them off. He was in charge and he had to act like it. The Galactics could *not* be allowed to think they could weasel their way out of trouble. "You will ensure that they are not carrying weapons nor anything that could reasonably be defined as a weapon. They will not remove anything else from the ship, save for the clothes they're wearing. If you have wounded, they will receive treatment."

The alien didn't look up. "We understand," he said. He looked up, suddenly. "It is my duty to warn you that failure to treat my crew under the Galactic Conventions will result in punishment."

Peter bit down a sarcastic remark about the Harmonies ignoring the Galactic Conventions when it suited them. Coming to think of it, there was no reason to believe that the *Tokomak* intended to honour the Conventions either...and they'd *written* them. Instead, he checked the live feed from the nanoprobes and then peered down at the alien.

"The Conventions will be honoured as long as you and your crew behave themselves," he said, finally. "And I suggest you start by following my orders."

The next stream of updates from the nanoprobes arrived. There were over two *thousand* aliens on the battlecruiser, more than double *Odyssey's* crew. Peter made a mental note to organise life-support modules - there was no way he could risk moving so many prisoners to *Odyssey*, even without their senior officers - and then sent the alien officers onto the shuttlecraft. They, at least, would be separated from their crewmen.

Which wouldn't slow us down, Peter thought. *But it might just keep the Harmonies from doing something stupid.*

"Move the crew into the holds and keep them there," he ordered, as more marines flooded onto the alien ship. "Draw a full manifest from the ship's computer and get a full list of crewmen, then account for every man jack of them."

"Aye, Sir."

Peter nodded as they fanned out through the alien ship. Its designers hadn't made too many changes to the original Tokomak design, although they'd widened the corridors for reasons that escaped him. Most of the Harmonies were inhumanly thin, by human standards. His suit kept picking up traces of damage, including the residue of power surges that had probably wreaked havoc inside the ship. He couldn't help thinking that the interior of the ship looked like something out of a bad movie. The Harmonies had never expected to have to compensate for such a radical crash out of FTL.

He braced himself as he stepped onto the bridge. As per orders, only two officers had been left on the deck, both of whom surrendered at once. Peter sent them to join the others in the shuttle, then studied the alien bridge. It looked like a throne room, with the captain sitting well above the others. He couldn't help thinking that it was more than a little pretentious, even by Galactic standards. But maybe it suited them.

"Captain," he said. "The ship is secure. I'm moving the crew to safe quarters."

And hope to hell they are safe quarters, he added, silently. *We might not recognise an alien weapon until it was shoved into our backs.*

"Very good," Captain Yasser said. "Lieutenant Fisher is on her way over. Clear the way for her."

"Aye, Captain," Peter said.

His earpiece buzzed. "These guys are creepy, sir," Lieutenant George said. "They're just shuffling along like...like electro-druggies."

"They're not used to thinking for themselves," Peter said. "Just keep a close eye on them."

LIEUTENANT JAYNE FISHER sucked in a breath as she materialised on the bridge of the alien battlecruiser. She wasn't scared of the teleporter, unlike some of the old fogies who could remember the days before First Contact, but - as an intelligence expert as well as a cyborg - she knew all too well just what a tiny little flicker in the matter stream could do. Sure, the teleport blocker - standard-issue on just about every starship - had been turned off, but the battlecruiser was not in good shape. It would be no consolation to know the aliens hadn't *intended* to kill her if a stray energy pulse scattered her atoms over the quadrant.

She looked around, hunting for the nearest computer access port. There would be one, she knew. The Harmonies had copied practically everything from the Tokomak, after they'd accepted a position in their empire. She checked her records, worked out where the nearest port had to be and carefully removed one of the chairs to expose it. The port was just as she had expected, perfectly designed to allow access. Bracing herself, she unhooked a cyborg cable from one of her implants and plugged it into the system. There was a moment of utter darkness, then...

...She plunged into a whirlwind of data. Even damaged, even with half its remaining systems powered down, the starship was *still* absorbing data. The *King Hakim XIII* - the ship's identity was easy to pick out amidst the storm - might be old, but she was still a mighty machine. She couldn't help a flicker of admiration for the Tokomak as she started to access the ship's innermost datacores, looking for the classified safe. The Tokomak might be bastards, but they definitely knew how to build starships.

Her smile widened as she pushed further and further into the network. *This* was what she loved. One day, she'd make the jump completely into e-personality and abandon her human body completely. Until then...bursts of data shot at her, everything from fleet movement orders to encryption protocols. She eyed the latter warily - a human computer would have an AI or RI watching for any intrusion - but they remained motionless. It puzzled her, even though the ship *had* been blasted out of FTL and the crew shocked...

Maybe they never considered that they would lose a ship, she thought. *Or maybe they just expected to have the time to destroy the datacores.*

It was a remarkably ordered system, she noted, even by military standards. *Odyssey* - and some of the other ships she'd served on - had little subsections that belonged to various crewmen, ranging from porn to private chat compartments. Finding such subsections and ensuring they didn't pose a danger had been one of her duties. But there...there were no individual subsections at all, not even the standard folders assigned to each crewman. There was almost no individuality at all.

She put it aside for later consideration, then dug deeper. The classified datacore was secure, surprisingly so. Indeed, she was tempted to wonder if it had come from a different designer altogether. She tried to get in, discovered that it was impossible without direct access and carefully pulled out of the network. Her head spun as she slammed back into her body, recoiling instinctively. It always felt as if she was being shoved out of heaven.

A hand fell on her shoulder, steadying her. "Are you all right?"

She looked up to see a marine, his face worried. When had *he* entered the bridge? He hadn't been on it when she'd arrived, had he? She didn't think so, but she lost track of so much time when she interlinked directly with a computer core...

"I think so," she said. She shook her head. There was no point in worrying about it. "I'll need to get direct access to the classified datacore."

"Cool," the marine said. He helped her to her feet. "Where is it?"

Jayne shrugged. "I have no idea," she said. The core could be anywhere within the alien ship. For all she knew, it was under the captain's bed. If the officers didn't know - or refused to tell her - she would have to trace the datalinks herself. "But I'm going to have a lot of fun looking for it."

THIRTY-TWO

Comrade, we have come full circle.
You argue in favour of an alliance. And most of your arguments are good ones. But consider - how can we expect aliens to join the Solar Union? They do not share the mindset of a Solarian! If many Earthers do not share the mindset - if we have to take strong action to remind the Earthers that they are guests in our universe- why should we expect more from aliens?
This is not interspecies racism. This is a simple statement of fact. How can we trust them to play their role?
-Solar Datanet, Political Forum (Grand Alliance Thoughts)

*T*yler snored.

It wasn't something Levi found particularly annoying, in and of itself, but it grated on her after five days on the alien freighter. She shouldn't be that annoyed, she told herself - the barrack room habits of young marines weren't a subject for polite company - yet it still wore at her. But it was preferable, she supposed, to either reading the updated interstellar news, such as it was, or endless discussions that threatened to become arguments.

She leaned back in her chair, rubbing her eyes as cold air blew over her naked body. She wasn't so much physically tired as mentally tired, her mind wanting to sleep even while her body was brimming with energy and wanted to *run*. The freighter *did* have plenty of space for her - and she didn't have to worry about accidentally breathing a poisonous atmosphere - but the ship's captain had told her to stay in the cabin as much as possible. It was better, he said, that the crew had as little contact with them as possible. Levi rather suspected he hadn't told his crewmen just who or what they were carrying, trying to keep as much as possible of the carriage fee for himself. Human smugglers often did the same.

Her implants bleeped up an alert as the freighter dropped out of FTL, then tried to download an updated status report from the local network. There was no response, something that bothered her more than she cared to admit. The freighter was well over three hundred years old, at least, but the computer network had been isolated and carefully secured. Her hacking programs hadn't been able to make any headway, even though they should have been able to slide effortlessly into a civilian-grade network. And while she wasn't a novice, she didn't have the skills necessary to hack the system herself.

And now we don't know where we are, she thought, feeling a dull thrumming running through the freighter. She had a basic astrographic database in her implants, but no way to check it against the sensor readings. Her implants threw up a dozen different suggestions, ranging from their planned destination to an enemy naval base, yet had to admit they didn't *know* where they were. *The crew might be preparing to hand us over to the enemy.*

She glanced at Tyler, then forced herself to relax. There was no reason to *believe* that they were in danger, even if she *couldn't* see outside. A human starship wouldn't allow a guest unrestricted access to a computer network either. And yet, she couldn't help feeling nervous as the freighter powered its way towards the gravity point - what she *hoped* was a gravity point. Too much could go wrong even if they weren't about to be betrayed.

Picking up the datapad, she forced herself to read through the latest set of interstellar bulletins once again. There were hundreds of stories about ships being stopped and carefully searched - and about its devastating effects on interstellar trade - but no one seemed to know what was actually going on. A private intelligence service on Kami, of all places, had published an analysis suggesting that the Harmonies intended to tighten their grip on the cluster before building an empire of her own. Levi couldn't help thinking, as she read her way through it, that it was far too close to some of the analysis reports she'd read on *Odyssey*, before the shit hit the fan.

No mention of us, she thought. *And only vague third-hand reports of something unpleasant happening at Harmony.*

Shaking her head, she put the report aside. It was unlikely she'd find any new insights, let alone anything that would actually help her over the next few days. None of the Galactics seemed inclined to do more than protest loudly, although she rather doubted they'd be announcing anything more serious until they'd completed their mobilisation. If, of course, they *were* mobilising. If the Harmonies were working with the Tokomak to snatch a human starship, it was quite possible that the other Galactics were in on it too.

And you're going stir crazy, she told herself, firmly. *You're trapped in a tiny cabin. You don't know what's happening outside the hull.*

She pushed the thought aside, briefly contemplating waking Tyler for another round of sex before standing and dropping into a set of basic exercises. It hadn't been *that* long since she'd left *Odyssey*, but she still felt alarmingly flabby. She *knew* it was an illusion, she *knew* she was still in excellent shape, yet her mind refused to believe it. Major Rhodan would probably have a number of sarcastic remarks to make, when he saw her again. She refused to contemplate the prospect of never seeing him again.

There was a sharp rap on the hatch. Levi checked her weapons, automatically, as she came up from her crouch and paced towards the entrance. Resistance would probably be futile, if the ship had been boarded, but she was damned if she was going quietly. Tyler shifted, clearly on the verge of waking up. She nudged him to speed up the process and then keyed the hatch to open. Perhaps, she thought as the hatch unlocked, it was a good thing that the visitor had knocked. A hard-entry team would have made its entrance with shaped charges and noisemakers.

"Captain," she said, relaxing slightly as she saw the alien. "What can I do for you?"

The alien captain - his name was beyond her ability to pronounce without a voder - seemed oddly put out by her nakedness. *That* was a surprise. The captain and his crew were all members of the same race, a hobbit-sized race of humanoid mice. Levi had even thought - and then buried it carefully at the back of her mind - that they'd hate to meet a race of humanoid cats! Indeed, they had always struck her as skittish. But the files made it clear that the little aliens were vicious bastards if pushed into a corner and forced to fight. Their teeth and claw-like hands weren't purely cosmetic.

"Human," the captain said. He hadn't bothered to ask for her name, even the fake name and background she'd prepared. She guessed she was paying him enough to keep from asking inconvenient questions. "Dress quickly, spacesuits and robes. This ship is going to be boarded."

Levi cursed, then spun around and poked Tyler, hard. The younger man jumped up, one hand reaching for the gun he'd concealed at the head of the makeshift bed. Levi caught his arm before he could do anything stupid, then helped him up. Tyler looked shocked at how effortlessly she lifted him.

"Get dressed," she hissed, reaching for her underwear. Thankfully, the marines had taught her how to dress quickly. "Run a wakefulness program, if necessary. We're about to be boarded."

"Their shuttle is already inbound," the alien captain said. "You have to be hidden on the hull."

Tyler stared at the alien. "They're searching the whole ship?"

"So we have been told," the alien captain said. His furry nose twitched. Levi's implants told her that that was an alien smile. "The other freighters in the system are complaining loudly."

"Shit," Tyler said. He looked at Levi. "Where *are* we?"

"Paean," the alien captain said. "One transit from Daladier and the Harmonies Chain."

Levi didn't need to consult her implants, as she donned her shipsuit and checked her helmet, to know where they were. Paean linked directly to Daladier, which was - in itself - one transit from Hudson. They were nearly there...assuming, of course, they didn't get detected by the enemy. She had no idea if the Harmonies were searching ships passing through Daladier itself - there was no way Hudson Base could avoid noticing that *something* was happening - but they were definitely in position to search ships at Paean.

"If you're on the hull, you can remain undetected," the alien captain informed them. He turned and led them out of the cabin as soon as they were dressed. A couple of other crewmen stepped past them into the cabin, carrying spray bottles and storage bags. "But you have to stay out of direct line-of-sight."

"Understood," Levi said. She looked at the captain's back as he hurried down towards the nearest airlock. "Can I have access to your computer network?"

The alien seemed to flinch. "For the duration of the search, using direct contact nodes," he said, reluctantly. "But not elsewhere."

"Very well," Levi said. "Thank you."

She tried to make contact again and succeeded. The alien network was cruder than she'd expected, once she was allowed through the firewall, but it was advanced enough to pick out the shuttlecraft approaching from the local defences. Two gunboats escorted it, their active sensors sweeping space for potential targets. The crudeness of the intimidation surprised her, but the mice-like aliens weren't considered great powers. No doubt the Harmonies thought they could push them around at will.

Potential allies, then, she thought. The aliens might not be a great power, but they *were* known for their engineering skills. Given freedom to innovate and unlimited resources, who *knew* what they'd devise? *But we have to survive the coming search first.*

She forced herself to think as the captain opened the airlock, motioning for them to enter the tiny compartment. If the Harmonies merely checked their paperwork and then allowed the ship to proceed...that was one thing. But a more careful search might just turn up evidence of human occupation. A sniffer drone might even pick up traces of human DNA. She smiled, remembering the clean-up crew. The evidence there were humans on the ship would be buried long before the searchers started making their way through the ship.

"Stay close to the hull," she reminded Tyler. She clamped a line to his suit as the outer hatch opened, revealing unblinking stars burning in the inky darkness of interplanetary space. If there were any alien ships in visual range, neither her naked eyes nor her implants could pick them out against the stars. "Don't speak unless you're using a linked cable. One stray transmission and we're dead."

She glanced down at her suit - coloured to match the hull - and then led the way out of the airlock. Hopefully, any wandering eyes would miss them as long as they stayed still, crouched next to the communications array. She'd used enough camouflage netting during exercises to know it was very effective, as long as the wearer stayed still. The human eye was attracted towards motion.

And so are most alien eyes, she mused. *But not all of them.*

It was a sobering thought. She'd heard a story, years ago, of how a camouflage scheme had failed because it had been configured to defeat human eyes. To the aliens, the marines might as well have been dressed in clown costumes and blowing trumpets as they tried to sneak up on their enemies. It hadn't been much consolation to the survivors to know that the aliens had had the same problem...

An alert flashed up in front of her eyes. An alien gunboat was coming in for a visual inspection of the hull. She clutched Tyler's hand, warning him to remain very still as the craft glided into view, a dark shape only visible as it occluded the stars. It was small, compared to the freighter, but she had no doubt it could cripple the ship if its crew decided to open fire. She stared at it, wondering what would happen if they *were* spotted...would the aliens send troops to snatch them or merely open fire?

The gunboat drifted away, moving with deceptive slowness. Levi watched it go, then cursed under her breath as the alien shuttle appeared, gliding down towards the airlock. *That* was unexpected. Most inspectors would enter through the forward hatch, the closest to the bridge...she silently willed Tyler to stay still as the aliens docked, their inspectors flooding into the freighter. Perhaps they thought the crew were hiding something...or perhaps they were just trying to be annoying. She found it hard to care.

She forced herself to monitor their progress through the ship's sensors. One party went to the bridge, where they inspected the ship's crew and their papers; the other started to search the ship, prowling through each and every cabin with a thoroughness she couldn't recall seeing from the Solar Union's customs officers. But then, very little was actually *banned* within the Solar Union. She was fairly sure there were people who would want something illicit, just because it was banned, but they would probably prefer to leave the Solar Union and make the transfer somewhere in interstellar space. Here...

They're going through all the shipping crates, she thought, grimly. *They must have realised how we escaped Kami.*

She felt her body start to ache, even though she could move a little within the suit without calling attention to herself. The Harmonies were being *very* careful...she couldn't help wondering, if they were dedicating so much attention to a single freighter, just how badly they'd slowed down traffic through the gravity point. They didn't have any *reason* to think the freighter was smuggling humans or they would have brought more troops, just to make sure the ship didn't have a hope of escaping. And while she knew they were assholes, they weren't foolish enough to waste time being assholes when they had a job to do.

Pity, that, she thought. *Forcing them to waste time might be useful.*

She glanced at the stream of messages pouring into the ship's communications array. Some of them were encrypted, but enough were in clear to prove that the Harmonies were searching *every* ship. Passage through the gravity point had slowed to a trickle...a constant barrage of complaints was being passed around the system, to no avail. She didn't have access to the gravimetric sensors, but she was fairly sure dozens of freighters were choosing to slip back into FTL and go the long way around, just to avoid the searchers. She couldn't blame them.

An alert flashed in front of her eyes. The enemy searchers were coming onto the hull! Cold ice ran down her spine as she looked towards the rear airlock, spotting three aliens in spacesuits stepping onto the hull. She glanced at Tyler, then turned her attention back to the aliens. They'd be discovered if they tried to move away from the communications array...

She pressed her hand into Tyler's. "Stay still," she muttered. "And keep your mouth shut."

Sweat prickled down her back as the aliens advanced, looking from side to side as they walked up towards their shuttle. There was nowhere to run...she briefly contemplated trying to crawl backwards until they had the mass of the freighter between them and the hunters, but she knew they'd be far too exposed. All she could do was remain still and pray they weren't spotted.

Their eyes aren't noticeably better than ours, she told herself. *But they could have augmented them too.*

The aliens marched closer, pausing just long enough to look at the communications array, then strode past, heading back to their shuttle. Levi let out a breath, feeling a surge of utterly overpowering relief. She'd concealed herself close to enemy camps before, close enough that she'd watched in horror as guards relieved themselves far too close to her, but this was different. She could have stabbed two of the aliens, perhaps three, before they overwhelmed and killed her. And even if she did manage to kill the entire squad, their friends would just slam a missile into the freighter and kill them all.

She tracked the aliens as they boarded their shuttle and disconnected, gliding slowly away into the darkness. Her entire body was drenched in sweat, but they were alive! They hadn't been caught! The freighter's drives hummed to life a second later, taking them deeper into the system. They'd be passing through the gravity point in less than an hour.

"Come on," she said, leading Tyler back to the airlock. Their air supplies wouldn't hold out indefinitely. "We'd better find out what happened."

The captain met them as they removed their helmets. "They checked everything," he said, shortly. Levi couldn't help thinking that he looked like a mouse that had been dropped in water and was still dripping on the carpet. "And insisted on scanning all our papers before allowing us to proceed."

Tyler glanced at him. "But we can proceed into Daladier?"

"Yes," the captain said. His nose lowered itself, seeming to lengthen as he bowed his furry head. "But what we'll find there..."

"We'll find out when we get there," Levi said. "Until then..."

She grinned at Tyler. "We're nearly home," she added. Hudson Base wasn't *home*, she had to admit, but it was the closest place *to* home for thousands of light years. Humans...and a naval squadron that might be able to help *Odyssey*. Humanity would know what had happened to her. "And then we can pass on our message."

"I hope so," Tyler said. He leaned against the bulkhead, looking wretched. "What happens if they search the ship again?"

"We hide again," Levi said. "And we do a better job of it this time."

THIRTY-THREE

We trust them because it is in their interests to support us, just as it is in our interests to support them.

Aliens are not stupid. Nor, save for the really old races, are they so ossified that the thought of talking to a young race like us is unthinkable. They are more than capable of recognising that we are the key to victory, to freedom...even to simple survival. Let us work with them to build a force that will be small, but powerful enough to give even the Tokomak pause!

-Solar Datanet, Political Forum (Grand Alliance Thoughts)

"The good news," Jayne said, "is that I found the classified datacore. It was concealed within the captain's cabin, disguised as a rather dubious piece of alien artwork. The bad news is that there's almost nothing of *value* within the datacore."

Elton leaned forward. "Are you sure?"

"There's nothing of value to us, at the moment," Jayne clarified. "I can download and decrypt a great many files on everything from ship movements to access codes and routine fleet updates, Captain, but there are no political briefs or anything that might help us to understand what is actually going on."

Rebecca frowned. "Are you sure? I mean...have you probed every last section of the datacore?"

"Not completely," Jayne said. "The RIs are dissecting the remaining sections now, Madam Ambassador, but if there's anything outside confidential ship and fleet management files it's very well hidden. We do understand this sort of system very well. Any files that were routinely accessed, regardless of their classification, would be located very easily. I don't believe we've missed any files that were accessed in the last year."

Elton studied the display for a long moment. "Do you think there were other datacores that were never attached to the ship's datanet?"

"It's a possibility," Jayne said. "But if it was never attached to the system, there wouldn't be any record of it. I've got the RI's vacuuming *King Hakim XIII's* datanet for signs there was a datacore that was hooked up once or twice before being disconnected again, but..."

She gave an expressive shrug. "So far, *zilch*," she said. "I did have the marines tear the captain's cabin apart, looking for a private datacore, but they found nothing."

"It would be *very* well concealed," Elton mused. Keeping a private datacore was not - technically - forbidden in the Solar Navy, as long as it didn't contain classified data, but it was frowned upon. The Galactics, by contrast, banned the whole practice. Given how little privacy the average citizen *had* on Harmony, he would be surprised if *anyone* dared to obtain their own datacore. "And probably non-existent."

He looked down at his hands. "We'll need to get answers from the ship's captain, if we can," he said. "There's no other solution."

"Yes, sir," Jayne said.

Rebecca coughed. "When you say we need to get answers," she said, "what exactly do you mean?"

"I don't know, yet," Elton admitted. "It depends on how willing he is to cooperate."

He keyed his wristcom. "Major Rhodan, please have the alien captain moved to an interrogation chamber and secured," he ordered. "We'll be down in a minute."

"Aye, Captain."

Rebecca looked appalled. "Captain, he *surrendered*!"

"I know," Elton said. "And I know we have an obligation to treat prisoners well, within reason. But the safety of this ship and crew comes first."

He rose. "Shall we go find out what he has to say?"

— —

REBECCA SILENTLY REVIEWED the rules on handling prisoners of war as she followed Captain Yasser down to the interrogation chamber, trying to determine what was and what wasn't legal. It wasn't something she'd had occasion to look up, in the past. The Solar Union's regulations, she discovered, were a little vague. POWs were meant to be treated well, as long as they behaved, but a great deal depended on how their country - or interstellar power - treated prisoners. She didn't think she liked that, even though she understood the chilling logic. Repaying an atrocity in kind, according to the files, helped prevent further atrocities.

And the Harmonies would have killed us all, just to keep their secrets, she thought. *What reason do we have, then, to be nice to our captives?*

She shook her head as she stepped into the observation compartment. The idea of *forcing* an alien to talk was horrific. Everything from direct neural access to simple torture struck her as horrific. And yet, the secrets concealed within the alien's head might make the difference between life and death. Should her principles stand in the way of extracting useful data?

It's a lot easier to make such a choice, she told herself morbidly, *when nearly a thousand lives don't hang on the decision.*

The alien was seated at a table, his hands and feet cuffed to the chair. It looked uncomfortable - it *had* to be uncomfortable. And yet, the alien seemed perfectly at ease, his dark eyes boring into the bulkhead as if he knew they were on the other side of it. Perhaps he did, she told herself. Interrogation chambers looked very similar right across the galaxy, even for races that were anything but humanoid.

She watched as Captain Yasser stepped into the chamber and took the seat on the other side of the table, leaning forward to meet the alien's eyes. The alien stared back at him evenly, even though he'd been stripped of his silver robe. Rebecca had a feeling that the Harmonies *hated* being underdressed. Even the rioters who'd nearly killed her had been covered from head to toe.

"We don't have a proper baseline for his species," Jayne said. Rebecca jumped. She'd been so focused on the alien that she hadn't noticed Jayne entering the observation chamber. "It won't be easy to tell if he's lying for a while."

Rebecca glanced at her. "I thought that lie detectors were perfect."

"They are, for *humans*," Jayne said. "We know how human bodies and minds work, Madam Ambassador. We know how they react when someone tells a lie. But here...we don't know enough about the Harmonies to pick out a lie. Not yet. Give us a few weeks and we might just have a working baseline."

"We don't have a few weeks," Rebecca snapped.

"I know," Jayne said.

"Your government lured us to Harmony," the captain said, addressing the alien. "Why?"

"This treatment is in contravention of Galactic Law," the alien droned. It recited a long string of provisions from memory. "I am not required to answer questions."

"Galactic Law demands that those who claim the protections of the conventions have to uphold them," the captain countered. "Your race attempted to capture or destroy a ship flying a diplomatic flag. You have put yourself outside the conventions."

The alien showed no visible reaction. "Your race does not have the authority to override the conventions," the alien stated. "You should take any complaints to the courts."

"Interesting," Jayne said. "No visible reaction, but a *lot* of agitation in the alien's brain."

Rebecca frowned. "Are you monitoring his thoughts?"

"His reactions," Jayne said. "We don't know enough to configure a mind-ripper to read his thoughts."

"The courts do not have to rule," the captain stated. "You put yourselves outside the protections by firing on our ship."

He leaned forward. "I have a number of questions that need answered," he said. "If you answer them, you will either be dropped off on a neutral world or granted asylum in the Solar Union, if you don't want to go back home. If you refuse to answer, we will take whatever steps are necessary to get answers out of you."

"This is an abuse of the conventions," the alien protested. He jerked his cuffed hands, rattling the chains. "Your race will pay!"

"Our race is already under attack," the captain said. "Now tell me... just what is going on?"

The alien made an odd face. "And if I refuse?"

"We'll calibrate a mind-ripper, probably by experimenting on one of your crewmen, then turn it on you and your officers," the captain said. "You will talk, whatever you do."

Rebecca felt sick. Mind-rippers had been banned, with good reason, ever since the technology had been discovered in captured alien databases. They might extract information from their victim - they were very effective, when properly calibrated - but they tended to leave the subject a drooling wreck afterwards. Torture would be kinder. The idea of using one...technically, it was a war crime.

But they can be used in extremis, she thought, checking the regulations. *And if it gets the ship home...*

The alien seemed to grow more agitated. "I don't know everything!"

"Then tell me what you do know," the captain said. "And we will listen."

There was a long pause. Rebecca silently prayed the alien would talk. The thought of using a mind-ripper...

Slowly, the alien began to talk.

"Well," Elton said, three hours later. "Do we have confirmation?"

"We *have* been monitoring the captives and using them for a baseline," Jayne said, as she keyed her console. "Overall, Captain, I'm ninety percent certain we would spot a lie, particularly if we went over it several times. The captive has not, I believe, tried to lie to us directly, but I think he did evade a number of questions. Luckily, we can rotate interrogators and keep asking questions."

Elton nodded. Once the alien had started to talk, he'd turned the interrogation over to the marines. He'd only wanted to start the ball rolling because *he, Odyssey's* commander, bore final responsibility for his ship and crew. If someone had to give the order to use a mind-ripper, that person had to be him. He'd take the blame if the post-mission court-martial decided he'd exceeded his authority and made an example of him.

Of course, when we get home, they're going to have some trouble deciding which offense needs to be put on the docket, he thought, wryly. There *would* be an inquest when they returned home, if not a full court-martial. *And which one they're going to hang me for, if they find me guilty.*

"Very good," he said. "What do we have?"

"There never was a coup, as we surmised," Jayne said. "Instead, the Kingdom of Harmonious Order is collaborating with its long-term allies, the Tokomak. The first objective was to capture *Odyssey*, which failed; the secondary objective is to re-secure Hudson and gain control of the gravity point chains leading towards Sol. In the long term, they intend to crush the Solar Union and scatter the Grand Alliance before it can become a real threat."

Elton felt cold. "So they know about the Grand Alliance?"

"Yes, Captain," Jayne said. "The captain didn't know *many* details, but apparently his superiors know more. They see it as an upstart alliance of younger races that don't know how to shut up, sit down and wait their turn."

"Which will never come," Rebecca said.

Jayne acknowledged her point with a nod. "I believe that the Harmonies have largely given up on capturing *Odyssey*," she said. "That explains the lack of pursuit after our *last* daring escape. They think that they can keep us from reaching Hudson until it is far too late for us to do anything. Right now, they're massing their forces for a drive on Hudson, with the overall goal of capturing or destroying Hudson Base."

"Commodore Longlegs would never surrender," Biscoe said. "And her squadron isn't the only armed force at Hudson."

"The Harmonies believe they have enough firepower to overawe the others, particularly when they are clearly allied to the Tokomak," Jayne said. "And they might well be right."

Elton closed his eyes for a long moment. "And so we have to reach Hudson Base before it's too late," he said. "And we don't even know when it *will* be too late."

Rebecca coughed. "We have messengers going there, don't we?"

"There's no guarantee they will actually make it," Elton warned. "Besides, they don't know the Harmonies intend to attack the base itself. All they have are our speculations..."

He leaned forward. "Right now," he added, "the survival of this ship is a secondary priority. Getting to Hudson before the enemy is our goal."

Marie cleared her throat. "Captain," she said. "I understand your point, but...how are we to get to Hudson Base? The shortest route from here to Daladier, let alone Hudson, involves passing through a pair of gravity points that are *sure* to be heavily guarded."

"We could take the captured cruiser," Major Rhodan suggested. "They'd let *her* through without a search, wouldn't they?"

"One would hope so," Elton said.

"I don't think we could fit *Odyssey* inside her hull, like we did earlier," Wolf put in. "She may be bigger than us, but she doesn't have the room for anything bigger than a light cruiser."

"She *does* have their command and authorisation codes," Elton said.

He leaned forward. "Right now, they're massing their fleet in the Parana System," he said, adjusting the starchart to focus on the Harmonies Chain. "You'll notice that it's one of the systems we passed through, one of the places they've been fortifying. Our friend out there" - he nodded towards the bulkhead - "had orders to return to Daladier and then link up with the fleet once they'd completed their mission."

"She's big enough to tow us," Wolf said.

"But not through a gravity point," Callaway countered. "Yeah, I suppose it could be done...but they'd see us. Wouldn't they?"

"They also have a cloaking device," Elton said. "Mr. Wolf. Can that cloaking device be transferred to *Odyssey*?"

Wolf nodded. "I believe so, Captain," he said. "It's not as advanced as our cloaks, but we can get it to work. We can even do a few modifications to improve it, once we have a solid look at their sensor tech."

"They've definitely improved their counter-missile programs," Callaway added. "We knew they'd made some improvements, Captain, but we underestimated just how far they'd managed to progress. They've not quite cracked our ECM, but they are well on the way."

"Then we definitely have to get to Hudson Base before them," Elton said. "Mr. Biscoe?"

"We also damaged the enemy ship," Biscoe pointed out, sharply. He jabbed a finger at the display. "Can we repair her well enough to pass muster?"

"Probably not," Wolf said. "But her hull is largely intact and her drive can be repaired...thankfully, the safeties blew before any irreparable damage was done. I think we can get her going again, Commander, and we *can* rig ECM to deceive anything short of a naked-eye inspection."

He shrugged. "Of course, if they *do* want to board *King...Whatever*... we're going to be screwed anyway."

"*King Hakim XIII*," Jayne said.

Elton held up a hand. "How long do you think you'll need?"

Wolf hesitated. "Ideally, three days," he said. He didn't *sound* confident. "We might be able to get it down to two, if we work double shifts. I'll have the cloak removed and installed here first, then try to get the battlecruiser back into working order."

He paused. "The one problem, Captain, is that we will need a crew on her bridge," he added. "We can run some of her systems remotely, but she's not set up for slave operations. I don't see any way to fix that in less than a few weeks."

"Understood," Elton said. He glanced at Biscoe. "You have a command."

Biscoe nodded. "Thank you, sir."

Elton concealed his tired amusement. Biscoe didn't seem too happy, but the appointment *was* something of a poisoned chalice. *King Hakim XIII* wasn't *that* badly damaged, yet...she would attract a great deal of trouble if the Harmonies realised she wasn't under friendly control. Biscoe's first true command might end badly.

"I'll continue the interrogations," Jayne said. "There may be command codes that we'll need to get through the defences."

"Good thinking," Elton said.

"Another question," Major Rhodan said. "What do we do with the prisoners?"

Elton hesitated. *Odyssey* didn't have the space for the POWs. And he didn't want to leave them on *King Hakim XIII* when the ship was going into action. A breakout at the wrong moment could be disastrous...

"Put the crew - not the officers - in life support balls," he said, finally. It wasn't ideal, but it was the best idea he could think of. "Make sure they have enough life support and supplies to last them a month. We'll tell the Harmonies where to pick them up when we slip through the gravity point."

"Aye, Captain," Rhodan said. "We're keeping the officers?"

"They might be useful," Elton said. "And besides, they're the ones most likely to cause trouble."

"If they know anything," Jayne said. "I'm starting to think that most of them don't know anything beyond the basics. I honestly don't know how the Harmonies managed to invent the wheel, let alone spacecraft. They're so...*conservative*."

"Keep trying," Elton said. "Some of them might be spying on their fellows."

"A spy would be better placed amongst the crew," Major Rhodan pointed out.

"Perhaps," Elton said. He could see the logic. "But a crewman wouldn't be invited to any tactical planning sessions."

He felt a flicker of sympathy for the alien crewmen. They'd gone from being treated like serfs to a set of life support bubbles that were, in effect, a prison. But he couldn't see any alternative. Killing them out of hand would be legal, but he was damned if he was committing mass slaughter because the POWs were *inconvenient*. The life support bubbles would keep them alive long enough to be rescued.

Or so we hope, he told himself. *We might not last long enough to tell the Harmonies where to look.*

Elton pushed the thought aside. "Well," he said. "Shall we begin? Dismissed."

THIRTY-FOUR

And yet, working with forces on Earth involves compromises and distasteful decisions - even when we were working with American or British troops. Let us not forget that most of the original Solarians came from America, Britain or the remainder of the Anglo-Saxon world - we had much in common with them, from a shared language to a largely shared outlook.

And yet, if we had problems with them, what might we have with aliens?

-Solar Datanet, Political Forum (Grand Alliance Thoughts)

"**T**hey're clearing us through the gravity point," the captain said. He opened his mouth, revealing sharp teeth. "Welcome to Daladier."

Levi nodded, curtly. The freighter's sensors were crappy, compared to the systems she was used to using, but it *was* clear that the Harmonies *hadn't* fortified the system. There were no fortresses orbiting any of the gravity points, although she knew - all too well - that there might well be an entire fleet lurking in cloak. And, given time, the Harmonies would probably be able to move modular fortresses down the Harmonies Chain to block any access from Hudson.

"There was more traffic, last time we were passing through," Tyler commented. "It's dropped, sharply."

"Ouch," Levi said. "Are you sure?"

"I modelled the local economy based on our readings here," Tyler told her. "There were nearly five times as many starships passing through the system. Now...the system is almost empty."

"I'll take your word for it," Levi said. There were hundreds of freighters heading to and from the gravity points, or moving out into interstellar space. It didn't *look* as though there had been any substantial drop. But then, she hadn't paid close attention to the system when *Odyssey* had made her way through the gravity points and up the Harmonies Chain. "How quickly can we get to Hudson?"

"Nineteen hours," the captain said. "Twenty-seven to actually dock at the transit port."

Levi groaned. Another twenty-seven hours? *Anything* could happen in twenty-seven hours! She told herself, firmly, to be patient. There was nothing to be gained by risking detection now, when they were so close. And besides, she needed a shower, a nap and a change of clothes. Her body was still sweaty as hell.

"We'll go back to the cabin," she said. "Inform us when we reach our destination."

"Of course," the captain said.

Levi hoped, silently, that the captain was being paid more than enough to keep him cooperative. Having his ship searched so thoroughly had to feel like a violation, particularly as he *knew* just how close they'd come to utter disaster. But he wouldn't want to surrender anyone to the Harmonies, she hoped. They'd have a few questions for anyone who hadn't betrayed his passengers at the first opportunity.

She led the way back to the cabin, showered and took a quick nap, trusting Tyler to keep watch. He woke her, seven hours later, to take a nap himself. She took her chair and waited, silently monitoring the ship's progress through the datanet. The captain had forgotten, deliberately or otherwise, to lock her out of the datanet once the search was over. She kept watching, closely, as the ship reached the gravity point and popped through into the Hudson System. They were nearly there.

It was tempting, very tempting, to send a signal directly to Hudson Base and request a pick up. But there were too many alien warships, including a number of starships from Harmony, in the system for her to take the risk. Better to reach Hudson and *then* call for teleport. She had no doubt Hudson Base could snatch them both up before it was too late.

"We made it," Tyler said, when he woke. "We're home!"

"Not quite," Levi said. "Start monitoring the local news channels. See what's going on."

She worked her way through a flood of data, ranging from sober news broadcasts to ranting posts that wouldn't have been out of place on the Solar Datanet. Everyone knew that *something* had happened, although they didn't know *what*. Rumours were flying everywhere, with hundreds of wild stories that she would have found unbelievable whatever the circumstances. About the only detail everyone agreed on, somehow, was that shipping up the Harmonies Chain was being blocked.

"They don't know what's going on," Tyler said. "Do they?"

"I doubt it," Levi agreed. "Anyone who does know is keeping their mouth firmly closed."

She expected trouble, all the way until the freighter entered orbit and docked at one of the orbital shipping facilities. Levi paid the bill without complaint, added a bonus and then led Tyler off the ship and deep into the station. It was designed to allow teleportation, according to the files, but she checked it carefully before calling for pick-up. There was a long pause, long enough to make her wonder if her contact codes were out of date, before the world went away in a haze of golden light...

...And they rematerialised in a prison cell.

"We're human," Levi said. She should have expected it. Beaming an unknown person into a prison cell was standard procedure, even though they'd had the correct codes. "We need to speak to Commodore Longlegs immediately."

There was a long pause. Her implants recorded a number of probes, ranging from standard ID checks to more careful scans of her authorisation codes and augments. It was a fairly standard procedure - duplicating her marine-specific implants would be tricky - but she couldn't help feeling they were wasting time. What was happening? They had to talk to the Commodore at once!

A hatch opened. A young dark-skinned girl, barely old enough to wear the uniform, stepped into the cell. "I'm sorry for the delay," she said. "We had to check your identities."

She motioned for them to follow her. "The commodore will see you shortly," she added, as they walked out of the cell. "Is there anything I can get for you while you wait?"

"Coffee," Tyler said. *"Please."*

"Of course," the girl said. "It would be my pleasure."

— —

CAPTAIN-COMMODORE JENNY LONGLEGS looked up as the two newcomers were escorted into her office, after a series of deep security scans that proved they were human and almost certainly trained in the Solar Union. One of them was a marine, with the heavyset appearance that seemed to be common among marines, male or female; the other was a young man, definitely a civilian from the way he held himself, who looked largely harmless. And they were both from *Odyssey*.

"All right," she said, as Sara brought three mugs of coffee. "What the hell is going on?"

"The Harmonies baited a trap," the marine said. "And we fell for it like idiots."

Jenny listened, feeling a growing sense of disbelief, as the entire story spilled out, piece by piece. The marine had clearly had plenty of time to compose her report. *Odyssey* had been attacked and forced to flee Harmony, then attacked again at Kami...after that, neither of the two travellers knew what had happened to the ship. They hadn't even managed to pick up a rumour that sounded believable. But then, neither had Jenny and her intelligence officers.

"We don't know where the ship is now," the marine finished. "But we do know she's going to be coming here."

"If she can get through the defences," Jenny muttered. She *had* heard that a number of gravity points were being fortified, although they were all at least two transits from Hudson Base. Most of the Galactics who provided security for the neutral world seemed unsure what, if anything, they wanted to do in response to such disregard for galactic norms. "We only have a single battle squadron here."

"You have to help them," the marine insisted. "Commodore..."

"We will," Jenny said. "But right now we don't know *how* to help them."

She tapped a switch, bringing up the starchart. "You last saw them at Kami," she said. "And you don't know where they went from there."

"No, Commodore," the marine said.

"Right," Jenny said. She carefully didn't point out that *Odyssey* and her entire crew could easily be dead by now. "They *have* to enter Daladier, unless they want to come home the long way. But we don't know *which* gravity point they'll try to force."

She contemplated a dozen possible routes for *Odyssey* to take, but she knew there was no way to be *sure*. Captain Yasser was known to be careful...perhaps he'd chosen to take the long road home. But that would take months, if not years...of course, he *had* managed to get a warning to Hudson Base.

"They might come after Hudson itself too," she mused, slowly. "There aren't many humans here, but we *do* have a base. They'll want the base intact, if possible."

"Or one of your ships," the marine said. "If the overall idea was to capture a human ship..."

"Not going to happen," Jenny said. "All right..."

She adjusted the starchart. "We'll inform the remaining races of just what happened to *Odyssey*, she said. "I dare say it won't be enough to convince them *all* to take a stand, let alone declare war, but it should galvanise them to live up to their treaties and defend Hudson Base. Just in case it won't, I'll order all non-essential personnel to evacuate Hudson Base and transfer to a freighter. If all hell breaks loose they can head straight back to Earth."

"Ouch," the marine said. "They'll be in cramped quarters for months."

"Better that than death," Jenny said. "In the meantime, we'll move the squadron to the gravity point and make transit into Daladier. Ideally, we'll remain near the gravity point and provide cover when *Odyssey* arrives."

The marine frowned. "Commodore...won't the Harmonies on station *know* you've moved to Daladier?"

"Probably," Jenny said. She lifted an eyebrow. "I didn't know you studied tactics."

"I've had several weeks to consider all the options," the marine said. She sounded more amused than embarrassed. It wasn't unknown for marines to move to the fleet and vice versa, but it was unusual. "Shouldn't we engage the Harmonies first?"

"I'd prefer not to make any overtly hostile moves," Jenny said. "Technically, any warring parties are supposed to remove themselves from Hudson. We're not *that* well liked in this sector. I don't want to give the Galactics any excuse to order us out. Things will be different, I assure you, if the Harmonies start the engagement."

She shook her head. "There are really too many unknowns," she admitted. "If we knew which gravity point they'd use, we'd be able to cover it directly. But we don't, so..."

"I understand," the marine said. "What now?"

"I'm going to dispatch a trio of courier boats back to Earth," Jenny said. "Your records will accompany them. Whatever happens next, Earth will *know* that *Odyssey* was treacherously attacked. As for you two...what do you *want* to do?"

"Stay with the squadron," the marine said, automatically. "I have to report back to *Odyssey*."

"As you wish," Jenny said. She hoped, for their sake as well as the Solar Union's, that *Odyssey* had survived. "And you?"

"I'd prefer to stay," the young man said.

Jenny frowned as she accessed her implants, scanning his file with a practiced eye. A young diplomat...not even a credentialed diplomat...but someone born and raised on an alien world. He might be useful, if he wanted to stay. And even if he wasn't, he'd earned the right to see the matter through. He wouldn't cause trouble.

And if he does, Jenny thought, *there's always the brig.*

"Very well," she said, briskly. She finished her coffee, then called for Sara. "I'll have you both teleported to *Schlieffen* and assigned quarters. My crew have already started preparations, so hopefully we'll be underway in less than an hour. It'll take longer to convince the other Galactics of just what happened at Harmony."

"We do have recordings," the marine said. "Can't those be used as proof?"

Jenny's lips thinned. "It depends on just what they show," she said. "We don't want to showcase our technology to potential enemies."

"Understood," the marine said.

Sara entered. "Yes, Commodore?"

"Take these two to *Schlieffen* and ask the XO to assign them quarters," Jenny ordered. "And then report back to me."

"Aye, Commodore."

Jenny watched them go, then looked up at the starchart. She'd known that *something* was wrong, but she hadn't had the slightest idea of *what*. The Harmonies had always been an unknown factor - it wasn't as if they deigned to talk to her - yet she'd had the impression they were sticklers for the rules. Why not? The rules were *designed* to keep the major powers on top. But now, the Harmonies had started a war...perhaps *several* wars. How many other major powers did they think they could fight at once?

They're well ahead of everyone else when it comes to fortifying their gravity points, she thought, numbly. *That frees up entire fleets to go on the offensive.*

She closed her eyes as she tried to think. The Harmonies had tried to capture *Odyssey*, first for dissection and then to cover up their crimes. But now the secret was out...how would they react? Abandon the chase, pay compensation and plot their next move...or go on the offensive? And who - or what - would be the target? If the Harmonies wanted human technology...well, *she* was sitting right on top of the largest collection of advanced technology in the sector.

The hatch opened. Sara returned, looking amused. "Commodore," she said. "They have been transported to *Schlieffen*."

"Good," Jenny said, shortly. "Do we have anything on the manifests that cannot be spared?"

Sara took a moment to think. "No, Commodore," she said. "Why?"

Jenny rose. "We're abandoning the station," she said. "Order the crew to prepare for transport to *Schlieffen* or one of the other cruisers. We'll rig the self-destruct to blow the station if she's boarded without the right command codes. Make sure the beacon warns anyone who tries to land."

"Aye, Commodore," Sara said. She frowned, suddenly. "There *will* be demands for compensation. We're providing long-term storage for several crates of goods."

"We'll pay, if necessary," Jenny said. She paced around the desk, thinking hard. "Right now, Sara, we're at war. And the first major battle may be fought here."

Sara nodded. "All of a sudden, the crates don't seem so important," she said. "I'll make it clear to the merchants, if they come back."

Jenny smiled. The merchants would probably take the losses in stride, if compensation was paid. If they didn't...well, they *were* at war. The freighters might well wind up being requisitioned for the fleet train. Hell, the merchant crews would probably volunteer for the Solar Navy. They *had* been working to produce a pool of talented spacers.

"See that you do," she said.

"We've assigned you two cabins," a harried-looking ensign said, pointing to a pair of hatches. "The captain will summon you when she needs you."

"Thank you," Levi said. She watched the ensign hurry off, then looked at Tyler. "Which one do you want?"

"The one with the shower and the human-sized bed," Tyler said. He opened the first hatch and smiled. "Paradise!"

Levi didn't bother to conceal her amusement. "It's smaller than your cabin on *Odyssey*."

"It's designed for humans," Tyler said. He waved a hand inside the hatch. "The shower is warm, the bed is cosy, the food is tasty, the terminal doesn't have to be reformatted to be usable..."

"You *do* gain more from the simple pleasures after you're without them for a few weeks," Levi agreed, dryly. She'd had the same experience at Boot Camp. "You'd be bitching and moaning about this cabin without the experience of sharing a cramped module..."

"Don't remind me," Tyler urged. He looked at her for a long moment. "Now what?"

Levi sighed, inwardly. She knew what he was thinking. "Now what, what?"

"About us," Tyler said. "Are we...are we together still?"

He looked awkward, torn between a desire to invite her into his cabin and an equally strong desire to keep it all for himself. And a little more, perhaps. Levi understood, better than she cared to admit. They'd been thrust together by circumstances and now...now they were no longer the only humans on the ship. Their relationship wasn't real...realistically, it had been nothing more than an extended one-night stand.

She sighed, again. "We were flung together," she said. "We started fucking" - she threw the crudity into the conversation to make him sit up and pay attention - "because we had very little else to do. And yes, I enjoyed it as much as you did. But now...now, we are no longer alone."

"I know," Tyler said.

Men, Levi thought. She'd been careful not to get emotionally involved when they'd been having sex. No matter how much she'd enjoyed it, she'd known it wouldn't last. Tyler had probably had the same thought, in the beginning. But he'd become involved with her despite himself. *He's still too young to understand.*

"If you want to ask me out, properly, when we return home," she said, "you may do so. And I will say *yes* or *no*, depending. But, for the moment, we both have other duties."

"We finished the mission," Tyler protested.

"That doesn't put an end to our work," Levi said. "And you and I both have to go back to the war."

She allowed her voice to soften. "If you want to leave this ship, there's still time," she added, quietly. "I'm sure you could get a seat on one of the courier boats."

"No, thank you," Tyler said. "I'll see it through."

"Very good," Levi said. She pointed at the hatch. "Get a shower, then some rest. You'll be needed soon enough."

Tyler nodded. "Yes, LT."

THIRTY-FIVE

Most of the problems we had when fighting on Earth did not come from the troops on the front line, many of whom later moved to the Solar Union, but from the politicians who did not take the engagements seriously. They cared little for the war on terror because they were not directly threatened by the terrorists.

This is obviously not true of the Grand Alliance. The Tokomak will not spare anyone who refuses to submit. The prospect of death, as the saying goes, concentrates the mind wonderfully.
-Solar Datanet, Political Forum (Grand Alliance Thoughts)

"I feel like a ninny," Biscoe said.

Elton looked up at him. Sitting on the alien throne, Biscoe looked like a child perched on his father's chair. The alien aesthetics honestly didn't make any sense to him. It wasn't as though the Harmonies were giants. The largest alien he'd seen had barely been a head taller than Elton himself. Their former commander had actually been smaller than him.

"I think you're meant to be keeping an eye on your subordinates," he said. He couldn't resist a smile. "Can you read the tactical console from up there?"

"Yes, but not too clearly," Biscoe said. He hopped off the throne and jumped down to the deck. "Their eyesight must be different from ours, sir."

"Or maybe they just want their subordinates to know they're being watched at all times," Elton said. He looked around the bridge. Being on a pedestal would have been good for a human commander's ego, he was sure, but bad for tactical awareness. "Is your first command ready to depart?"

"Yes, sir," Biscoe said. He waved a hand towards the helm. A pair of engineers had dismantled the original interface and replaced it with a spare console drawn from *Odyssey's* stocks. Thankfully, the Harmonies hadn't changed the underlying command and control systems they'd copied from the Tokomak. "We have drives, weapons and ECM."

"And no cloaking device," Elton said. He'd actually considered sending *King Whatever* - *King Hakim XIII* had been renamed - to Hudson Base alone, while *Odyssey* lurked in interstellar space, but he rather suspected they were running out of time. "Are your weapons at full readiness?"

"As best as we can," Biscoe said. "She *did* take a pounding, sir. We fixed the missile tubes and hung a few extra phaser arrays on the hull, but she's in no state for a real battle. The ECM won't protect us indefinitely."

"Probably not," Elton said. The Galactics had no reason, logically, to pay close attention to a starship that was too small to carry *Odyssey*, particularly one broadcasting the correct IFF codes. *King Whatever's* former commander *had* been ordered to link up with the rest of the fleet, after all. But he knew, all too well, that too much could go wrong. "Are you ready for an emergency evacuation?"

"We're all carrying teleporter transponders," Biscoe confirmed. "If *Odyssey* can't yank us up, we can beam to the shuttles and abandon ship."

Elton nodded, reluctantly. A shuttle in the midst of a battle would have the life expectancy of a snowflake in hell. Technically, shooting at unarmed shuttles and lifepods was illegal, but he doubted *that* would provide any protection. Biscoe and his crew would have a very slight chance of escape, nothing more. And yet, it *was* better than nothing. The Harmonies would do everything in their power to punish the humans for daring to capture their ship.

He looked around the bridge, trying to conceal his dismay. The Harmonies hadn't used anything like as much automation as *Odyssey*, let alone a human warship. Their AI technology was nowhere near as advanced as the Solar Union's - the Tokomak had flatly banned AI - yet their tech base *should* have allowed them to build more automation into their ships than they had. He had no idea if it was an alien jobs creation program or a tradition that had long since passed the point when it could be questioned, but it was a nuisance. He'd had to put over a hundred of his crewmen on *King Whatever* just to fly her. Getting them all off the captured ship, if the shit hit the fan, would be damn near impossible.

"Be careful," he said. "Do you have a proper communications set-up?"

"Yes, sir," Biscoe said. "We've got a talking head and, thanks to Fisher, a proper conversational overlay. We'll be screwed if they want to have a long chat or exchange recipes or something, but it should hold up long enough to get us through the gravity points and into Daladier."

"Let us hope so," Elton said.

He felt oddly morose as he checked the makeshift datanet. Sending Lieutenant Dennis and Mickey Tyler to Hudson Base had been bad enough, but this was worse. He wanted to keep his crew on his ship, where he could protect them...he knew it was a silly thought, yet it pervaded his mind. Cold logic told him that getting *Odyssey* home - or at least to Hudson Base - was more important than anything else, but his emotions insisted he should keep his crew on his ship.

"Make sure you keep a close eye on the drives," he warned. "You don't *want* to be stranded in interstellar space."

"We'll be towing you all the way," Biscoe said. "You'll be with us if we crash back down to realspace."

"How true," Elton said.

He concealed his amusement as he detected a flicker of impatience - quickly hidden - on Biscoe's face. It was always the same when a new commander took the chair - he wanted his superior officer to get off his ship as quickly as possible, just so he could bring the drives online and find out what his ship could *really* do. He didn't really blame Biscoe, either. It was far too likely he wouldn't have his new command for very long.

Although he'll probably receive a command if we return home, he told himself, as he took one final look around the bridge. *No one can say he hasn't earned it.*

"Good luck," he said. He drew himself up into a salute. "And congratulations, *Captain*."

"Thank you, sir," Biscoe said, returning the salute. He was, technically, entitled to be addressed as *captain*, now he was in command of a ship. Elton rather doubted he'd be able to claim captain's pay, but the Solar Navy would definitely give him a large share of the reward for capturing an alien ship. "We'll see you on the far side."

Elton keyed his wristcom. "Yasser to *Odyssey*," he said. "One for immediate teleport."

—

Rebecca barely noticed when *Odyssey* was yanked into FTL by *King Whatever*, even though the transit was rougher than usual. She was too busy reading the interrogation reports from the alien officers, then suggesting more and more questions for the marines to ask their captives. The result had been an influx of data that had alternatively fascinated or infuriated her. She'd already known they'd been conned, when the Harmonies had invited the Solar Union to send a representative, but now...now, she knew the Harmonies would *never* betray the Tokomak.

Which is the sort of detail that should have been included on the stolen databases, she thought, coldly. *But we took it for alien propaganda.*

She shook her head in annoyance. The Solar Datanet was immense - even if one discounted the considerable fraction devoted to porn - but it was tiny, barely noticeable, compared to the vast records the Galactics had amassed. There was so much data crammed into their files, even the relatively small databases they practically gave away for nothing, that analysing and fact-checking it all would be impossible. Even record-keeping librarian AIs couldn't hope to check and verify everything. The details concerning races on the other side of the known galaxy might as well be fiction, as far as she could tell.

We can verify the position of stars, I suppose, she thought. *But what about racial and political data?*

Years ago, someone had speculated that the Tokomak had ensured that certain details were permanently excluded from the galactic databases. It had prompted an interesting debate at the time, with some parties agreeing that it was possible and others discounting the idea that the bureaucratic-minded aliens would ever willingly leave something out of the records, let alone *lie*. But - now - Rebecca could see that they didn't *have* to do it deliberately. They had so much data flowing into their databases that *they* couldn't verify it either. A piece of misinformation could cause no end of trouble, simply because no one had the time or ability to check it.

We might be better off encouraging them to scrap the database and start again, she mused, absently. *But they won't do it...*

The buzzer rang. She looked up. "Open."

She turned as the hatch hissed open, revealing Captain Yasser. He looked tired, unsurprisingly. The crew had been working overtime for the last two days, trying to install a cloaking device in *Odyssey* and return *King Whatever* to something resembling flyable condition. Their captain had pushed himself as hard as anyone else.

"Elton," she said. "Are we on our way?"

"We'll enter the Ringer System in thirty-six hours, if the stardrive holds up," Yasser said. He sat down, facing her. "And then we'll know how good our talking head really is."

Rebecca nodded. She had faith in the captain and his crew - and besides, there was nothing she could do about it. Either *Odyssey* made it through the gravity points and reached Hudson or she was caught and destroyed. There were no other options. She just hoped the Harmonies didn't *know* they'd lost a ship.

"I've been helping with the interrogations," she said, changing the subject. She waved a hand at the terminal on the desk. "I think quite a few of the officers are going to want to defect when we reach home."

"I'm sure they'll be welcome," the captain said. "Did they tell you anything useful?"

"Their entire society is on the brink," Rebecca said. Even their *leadership* is breaking up into different factions. Some of them might actually want to help us."

"And they also told us that there had been a coup on their homeworld," Captain Yasser pointed out, dryly. "How can we be sure they're telling the truth?"

"The marines are sure they can spot a lie now," Rebecca said.

"And if they don't *know* they're lying," the captain countered, "the sensors aren't going to register it as a lie."

Rebecca made a face. "Point taken," she said. "But most of their stories do agree."

The captain shrugged. "Does it actually help us?"

"It might," Rebecca said. "They're a rigid culture - we figured that out, but we didn't realise just *how* rigid. Lots of ambitious officers thinking about a coup, even if they don't dare do more than grumble. The captives mentioned hundreds of officers who got their heads lopped off for daring to grumble *too* loudly."

"I suppose it must be a real problem," the captain said. "Ambition combined with a lack of social mobility..."

"Yeah," Rebecca agreed. "But if we could take down their surveillance network..."

The captain gave her a tired smile. "And how do you plan to do *that*?"

"It's a centralised system," Rebecca explained. "Couldn't it be taken out? Or hacked, perhaps. A *real* AI would make mincemeat of it."

"Assuming we could get an AI onto their homeworld," the captain mused. "They'd be very careful about allowing us anywhere near a central processor."

He shrugged. "This doesn't help us now, Rebecca," he said. "Sparking off an enemy civil war won't get us home."

Rebecca smiled, ruefully. "It isn't workable?"

"It might be workable, if we ever had a chance to get back to Harmony and land on the surface," the captain said. "But right now...there's no way we *can* get back to Harmony, let alone break through the defences. Taking down an entire empire by ourselves is the stuff of bad movies."

"Oh" Rebecca said. She'd had a boyfriend, once, who'd loved watching spy movies. "Are you telling me that *Jamie Bond* was unrealistic?"

The captain grinned. "Well...let's see," he said. "There's the bit when Jamie changes sex three times in two days. Then there's the bit when s/he manages to rewrite the teleporter with her bare hands to get into the white cat-stroking villain's lair. And *then* there's the bit where she somehow manages to convince a food processor to produce *antimatter* and *then* manages to teleport out a moment before the entire *planet* is destroyed..."

"You're spoiling my illusions here," Rebecca protested, mildly.

"I think the threesome sex scene was the most realistic part of the movie," the captain said, deadpan. "And *that* is saying something."

He leaned forward. "But what the producers missed was what happened *after* the movie," he added. "The story doesn't stop just because the end credits are rolling. What happens after Jamie kills the bad guy and blows up his planet?"

"Trouble, I imagine," Rebecca said.

"Yes," the captain agreed. "If you somehow crashed the surveillance system on Harmony, and you made sure the public knew it was crashed, you'd spark off a civil war. Millions, perhaps billions, of people would be killed. The other planets in their cluster would send starships and troops to put down the revolt - or, perhaps, to take out the homeworld and declare independence. Other powers would see a chance to take the

Harmonies down a peg or two and attack, sparking off a whole series of wars. Do you *want* that on your conscience?"

Rebecca considered it, sourly. The truthful answer was *no*, she *didn't* want it on her conscience. And yet, she felt *sorry* for the Harmonies. Not for their rulers, not for the aristocrats who were born into power…but for the commoners, the poor folk who had nothing, not even the hope of a better future. Knocking down the surveillance network might just give them a chance of a better life.

And it might also buy Earth some time, she thought. *The Tokomak would have to support their allies or lose them.*

She sighed as she dismissed the thought. The morality of the situation didn't matter. She couldn't *hope* to take down the enemy network, not while they were hundreds of light years from Harmony. And even if they did, the captain was right. The slaughter she'd unleash would be horrific. The nasty part of her mind insisted that it would benefit Earth - and that it wasn't her duty to worry about alien civilians - but she knew that was unconscionable.

"We may manage to free them, one day," the captain said. "Or they may free themselves."

Rebecca eyed him. "You know that isn't likely."

"Perhaps," the captain said. He smiled. "Their commanders haven't done such a good job so far, have they? They're out of practice. We blasted our way out of Harmony and escaped their fleet at Harmony because they didn't have any real experience to bolster their theoretical exercises. I dare say the coming war is going to cost their upper ranks terribly. They'll have to promote commoners into those vacant slots to give them a fighting chance."

"Maybe," Rebecca said.

"They won't have a choice," the captain insisted. "Military technology is improving - hell, even *they* managed to adapt a little. If they insist on putting pampered aristocrats in command, they're going to take heavy losses even if they don't lose the war. And allowing commoners to rise will up-end their entire social system. That might make them more dangerous, Rebecca, but it might also create a faction that wants to overthrow the current order."

"I hope you're right," Rebecca said. She keyed the console. "It just feels a little frustrating to be able to do nothing."

"We're on the way home," the captain assured her.

"Yeah," Rebecca said. She shook her head, feeling despondent. "And this is going to look *great* on my record."

"You won't be blamed for failing when you didn't have a hope of success," the captain told her. "And you didn't - they never intended to come to terms with us."

"That's not what my superiors will say," Rebecca said. "They'll spend the next few years trying to find a way to blame me for the disaster."

"Probably because they think there's no need for diplomats in a war," the captain said. "I dare say there will be *some* work for you. We won't be fighting the war alone."

"And some of our potential allies will back off if they think they can find an excuse to depart," Rebecca pointed out. No matter how many ships they'd lost, the Tokomak were still stronger than humanity and its allies. They could easily intimidate many of the younger races into submission. "Blaming us for *starting* the war will look like a *very* good excuse."

"We shall see," the captain said. "But until then...relax. Even if all goes well, Rebecca, we won't be back home for nearly a year."

"True," Rebecca agreed. It was time to put the whole affair out of her mind. She deactivated the terminal and rose. "Is the captain allowed to use the swimming pool?"

Captain Yasser smiled. "The captain's swimming prowess is not a government secret," he said. He rose, stretching. "Shall we go?"

Rebecca smiled back, despite her concern. The captain was right. It *would* be a long time before they returned to Earth. She wouldn't need a year to compose a report covering all the details *and* making it clear that they'd been lured into a trap. Her reputation would suffer, no matter how carefully she wrote the report, but it would survive.

And the Grand Alliance might survive too, she thought, taking his hand. *If, of course, we manage to parry the coming storm.*

THIRTY-SIX

And, as another old saying has it, the prospect of death concentrates the mind wonderfully...on the fact that it is housed in a body that is about to be hung. Or hanged - I can never tell the difference. Point is, anyone who joins our alliance does so at the risk of extermination, if the Tokomak join the war. Can we trust them to stick with us till the end?

The politicians you mention were protected from the war - and the costs it inflicted on their population. To a very large extent, they were also protected from their own people - kicking them out was hard and eventually impossible. Would this not be ALSO true of the galactic politicians? Collaboration with the Tokomak would bring vast rewards.

-Solar Datanet, Political Forum (Grand Alliance Thoughts)

"Captain," Marie said. She sounded annoyed. Helm control was currently slaved to *King Whatever*, rendering her redundant. "We are entering the Ringer System."

"Very good," Elton said. Whoever was on guard would have seen them coming, he knew, but they shouldn't have seen anything beyond a friendly battlecruiser heading for the gravity point. "Time to realspace?"

"Seventeen minutes," Marie said. A low shiver ran through the starship. "Captain, the battlecruiser's drive may not hold up that long."

"We'll just have to pray," Elton said. Dropping out of realspace and entering the gravity point without pausing to exchange messages wouldn't excite comment, he was sure, but crashing back into realspace *would*. If nothing else, the Harmonies guarding the gravity point would try to render aid to their injured comrade. "Mr. Callaway, is the cloaking device online?"

"Aye, Captain," Callaway said. "It *should* pass muster."

Elton made a face. They'd tested the stolen device extensively, but there had been limits. No cloaking device was *perfect*, not even the improved models coming out of Area 51. There was a small chance - but a very real one - that they would pass too close to an alien ship and be detected, even as they shadowed *King Whatever*. And if someone realised there *was* a cloaked ship at spitting distance, practically point-blank range, their immediate response would be to open fire. No one would question them.

"Let us hope so," he said. They *had* tested the cloak against *King Whatever's* sensors - and *they* were supposed to be the best the enemy had. "Make sure the field doesn't fluctuate when we drop out of FTL."

"Aye, Captain," Callaway said.

Only a madman would try something like this, Elton thought, as he leaned back in his chair and forced himself to relax. *A madman...or someone desperate.*

He'd told Rebecca that the plan had an excellent chance of success... but, in truth, it was the most dangerous stunt they'd tried. Someone - particularly someone as officious as the Harmonies - would ask questions if *King Whatever* returned to realspace too far from the gravity point. And they couldn't afford to *try* to answer those questions. They *had* to come out of FTL in the designated emergence zones, yet that would put them within weapons range of whatever was guarding the gravity point. *Odyssey* would be in *real* trouble if she was detected...

"Realspace in twenty seconds," Marie said.

"Cloaking device online," Callaway added.

Elton gritted his teeth. Their shields and weapons were down. There was no choice - the cloaking device couldn't hide their energy signatures - but it meant they were naked, if the enemy caught a glimpse of them and opened fire. He might be able to fire back, if the weapons were powered up in time, yet without shields...a lowly destroyer or frigate could cripple his ship. And then he would have no choice, but to take as many of them with him as he could.

Or trigger the self-destruct, he thought, morbidly. *They can't be allowed to capture this ship.*

"Returning to realspace...now," Marie said.

Another shudder ran through the ship. *King Whatever's* drives had held up remarkably well - the Tokomak had built them to last, even though they'd never anticipated an artificial gravity field - but it hadn't been a comfortable flight. Elton was all too aware that the shock of crashing back into realspace, almost uncushioned, would jar his ship badly. It was quite possible that the cloaking field would fluctuate, if only for a second. And the Harmonies, already paranoid, would *not* dismiss whatever they saw as a sensor glitch.

"Transit completed," Marie said.

Elton leaned forward as the display began to fill with icons. "Did they see us?"

"I don't think so," Callaway said, after a moment. "They're certainly not opening fire."

"Keep us in position," Elton said. "And hope that the talking head is convincing."

He felt his heart starting to pound as *Odyssey* shadowed *King Whatever* as she crawled towards the gravity point. The Ringer System had no less than seven gas giants and a massive asteroid field, making it invaluable real estate even though the sole rocky planet was too far from the star to be successfully terraformed. It *swarmed* with life. His sensors were picking up so many settled asteroids, industrial nodes and cloudscoops that they were threatening to lose count. It was a reminder, once again, of the terrifying industrial power of the Galactics...

...And just how great a challenge humanity faced, as it struggled to establish itself in the universe.

"They don't want anything bad to happen to this system," Callaway commented. "There's a *lot* of firepower here."

Elton nodded, stiffly. The gravity point to Chalmers was heavily defended, orbited by no less than seven fortresses and over fifty starships. His sensors picked up dozens of other starships and defensive emplacements within the system, even though galactic doctrine stated that defending independent asteroids was a waste of strength. They were too far from the other two gravity points to get a solid look at their defences, but he would have bet half his salary that they were just as heavily defended. Quite apart from the system's raw wealth and industrial base, it was a major transit node. The Harmonies were in an excellent position to dominate interstellar shipping for the foreseeable future.

Unless someone takes this system off them, he mused. *But then, they would have to take dozens of others too.*

"Captain," Callaway said. "The talking head is going to work."

"Stand by," Elton ordered.

He felt the tension rising as two giant freighters, each one easily large enough to conceal a battleship, emerged from the gravity point, escorted by a handful of destroyers. Normally, if he'd found himself so close to so much enemy firepower - and hidden under a cloak - he would have shut down the drives and pretended to be a hole in space. It would have maximised the chances of escaping detection. But that wasn't an option. He needed to keep going, remaining as close to *King Whatever* as possible. Any stray sensor readings might *just* be blamed on the battlecruiser.

"We have clearance to pass through the gravity point," Callaway said. "*And* a string of updates!"

He paused. "*King Whatever* is moving into position," he added.

"Move us after them," Elton ordered. "We have to jump *with* them."

And pray the cloaking field holds, he added, silently. *And that we don't get slammed together during the jump.*

"Aye, sir," Marie said. She sounded edgy. "Moving into position now."

Elton braced himself. A single mistake now would reveal their location. Escape would be impossible...

"Jumping in five seconds," Marie said. "Four...three...two..."

The universe dimmed, just for a second. Elton braced himself, even though he knew it was futile. If they'd been spotted, the enemy missiles would strike his ship before his sensors managed to reboot themselves. The urge to cower was almost overpowering. He half-expected the hull to explode inwards at any second...

"Transit complete," Marie said.

"They didn't see us," Callaway said. He shook his head in disbelief. "I'll be damned."

"Probably," Marie said.

Elton glanced from one to the other, wondering if they were up to something he ought to know about. Callaway outranked Marie, after all. But then, they'd *known* the odds of getting home were very low. He made a mental note to keep an eye on the situation - he could be wrong - and then leaned forward. They couldn't stay still for long.

"Move us out," he ordered. "Keep shadowing *King Whatever.*"

"Aye, Captain," Marie said.

He felt sweat trickling down his back. The Chalmers System was barren - no planets, no asteroids, nothing of great interest apart from a stray comet - but it *did* have five gravity points. Hundreds of starships were blinking into existence on the display, moving from one gravity point to another or altering course to head off into interstellar space. Unsurprisingly, the gravity points were heavily defended. There were two fortresses within easy missile range of their position.

But they missed us, he thought. *We made it through.*

"We'll be at the Daladier Point in fifteen hours, at current speed," Marie reported. "So far, her drive appears to be holding up."

"So far," Callaway muttered.

Elton frowned. If they could slip through the defences and into Daladier, they would be practically home free...unless the Harmonies had already invaded Hudson. The files they'd captured hadn't said when the invasion was going to take place, unsurprisingly. There was no way to know what was waiting for them. If the Harmonies wanted to make life difficult for him, and he assumed they did, all they'd have to do was take control of Daladier.

"Captain," Callaway said. "There's almost *no* traffic through the Daladier Point."

"Shit," Elton said.

He forced himself to think. A handful of freighters had come through the point, all heading into interstellar space instead of trying to reach the other gravity point. He had no way to be *sure* how many freighters passed through every day, normally, but the Daladier Point was strikingly quiet compared to the others. And, with Daladier only one transit from Hudson, he couldn't help thinking that that was an ominous sign. He was *sure* there was normally more traffic through the gravity point.

We don't know for sure, he reminded himself.

Wishful thinking, his own thoughts mocked. *The gravity point is too well located not to be used.*

He called up a starchart, but found no answers. The gravity point was starting to look like a trap, yet - if it was a trap - he saw no choice, but to spring it. If they altered course, if they headed to the next system, they'd add at least three weeks to their journey. It wouldn't have mattered so much, he knew, if they hadn't *known* Hudson Base was going to be attacked. They *had* to punch through the gravity point and make their way into Daladier...

"Keep us on course," he ordered. He glanced at the communications station. "Lieutenant Grave...is there any way we can query those freighters without revealing our identity?"

Grave hesitated, noticeably. "I don't think so, Captain," she said, finally. "Even if we left off the ID header, they'd be able to track the signal and pinpoint *King Whatever*. They might not answer or they might lie. We wouldn't know."

"Thank you," Elton said. Grave was *far* too inexperienced. She was normally part of the delta crew, but Williams had transferred to *King*

Whatever with two of his staff. "See if you can pick up any transmissions that might be informative."

"Aye, Captain," Grave said.

Elton allowed himself a stab of sympathy. Grave - and the other deltas - had been promoted shortly before being assigned to *Odyssey*. No doubt *someone* in the personnel department had thought the cruise would be boring, a chance to give the newly-minted officers some experience without risk. *Odyssey* hadn't been heading off to the Martina Sector, after all.

And what a cruise they've had, he thought, amused.

"Launch a stealth probe towards the gravity point," he ordered. "And inform me when it is in place to observe our target."

"Aye, sir," Calloway said.

Elton checked the live feed from *King Whatever* - so far, the giant battlecruiser was bearing up well - and ordered half the crew to get some rest. They'd need it. He haunted the bridge for three hours before putting Callaway in command and heading into his office to get some rest himself. There shouldn't be any danger, now they were well away from the fortress, but he still felt on edge. The enemy might realise what had happened at any moment.

But we can evade contact now, if we have to, he reassured himself. *If they wanted to stop us, they could just wait until we approach the gravity point and open fire.*

It wasn't a comforting thought, but he clung to it as he tried to get some rest. His sofa was comfortable, yet...sleep didn't come easy. He had to fight the temptation to use his implants, something he'd vowed never to do in combat. By the time he awoke and stumbled into the shower, he was feeling as if he hadn't slept at all.

"No contact, Captain," Callaway assured him, when he called the bridge. "We're proceeding on course."

"Very good," Elton said.

He washed himself hastily, then changed into a spare uniform. An update from the analysis deck was sitting in his terminal when he returned to the office, informing him that the Harmonies might well be moving their forces into Daladier. He snorted in annoyance as he scanned the update. The fortresses might have unwittingly told their quarry everything they knew, but it was unlikely they had the *latest* updates. Even the Harmonies had better things to do, right now, than making sure that every last outpost was kept up to date.

And we know they have to occupy Daladier before moving into Hudson, he thought, as he strode onto the bridge. *They don't have a choice.*

"They have made no attempt to contact us, Captain," Callaway informed him. "I believe there's no reason to think that they've seen through the deception."

Elton nodded, sourly. He'd seen talking heads used before, including a couple designed by aliens. The images themselves had been perfect - the Galactics outdid Hollywood when it came to strikingly realistic CGI - but the longer he'd watched and listened, the clearer it became that the designer didn't quite *get* humanity. It had been impossible to believe, after a while, that he was talking to a real person. There were just too many tiny flaws, too many things that a human designer would have included as a matter of course.

And we might have failed to spoof them, he thought. *For all we know, our talking head looks as though it came from the Uncanny Valley.*

"We'll proceed carefully," he said, as he took his seat. "Status report?"

"The cloaking device is holding, sir," Calloway said. "No power fluctuations that we can see. Engineering reports that the repairs to the drives are also holding, although Mr. Wolf would prefer to shut down the drive when we have a moment and carry out a full inspection."

"Which won't be possible until we reach Hudson Base," Elton said, shortly. Wolf had every reason to be concerned - he couldn't do more than patch up the drives without a shipyard or mobile repair unit - but *Odyssey* had to keep going. "And *King Whatever*?"

"Ah...Commander Biscoe reports no problems," Callaway said. "She's still leading us onwards."

"Very good," Elton said.

He watched, grimly, as *King Whatever* glided towards the gravity point. There were two fortresses on station, backed up by a small flotilla of destroyers and gunboats. It was a surprisingly small commitment, he thought, yet the Harmonies might be reluctant to advance their network of fortifications *too* close to Hudson. They might have uncontested control over Chalmers, but Daladier and Hudson itself were a different story. Putting up a defensive wall there would *definitely* annoy the other Galactics.

"Commander Biscoe is sending our ID codes to the enemy fortresses," Callaway said.

Elton nodded. No starships had popped through the gravity point in the last hour...something that *definitely* worried him. Word was spreading...but word of what? His imagination provided too many possibilities. The only thing that reassured him, oddly, was the lack of any major combat units blocking the gravity points. Fortresses were formidable, but they couldn't give chase. The destroyers and gunboats would be no match for *Odyssey* in a straight fight. He assumed the Harmonies knew it as well as he did.

Unless they have ships lurking on the far side, his imagination pointed out. A single destroyer could pop through the gravity point and tell the battleships to make transit, shifting the balance decisively in their favour. *How else could they coordinate an operation over interstellar distances?*

Grave looked up. "Captain," she said. "There's no response from the fortresses."

"Shit," Marie muttered.

"Don't panic," Elton ordered. He glanced down at his console. Flashwaking his weapons and shields would take time...too much time. They were dangerously vulnerable, if they'd been rumbled. "Hold us in position and *wait.*"

He hoped, silently, that Biscoe didn't do anything impetuous. Perhaps the enemy were just double-checking the ID code. Or perhaps, they were wondering why *King Whatever* had returned so quickly. It wasn't *easy* to keep interstellar travel on a planned schedule, but a paranoid mind might wonder if she was *suspiciously* early. Hell, for all he knew, the Harmonies suspected her commanding officer hadn't bothered to complete his mission.

"They're demanding an updated code," Grave said.

Red lights flashed on the display. "They're scanning us," Callaway said. "Sir...at this range, they'll penetrate the cloak!"

Elton took a breath. So close...

It isn't over yet, he told himself, sharply.

"Drop the cloak," he ordered. "Raise shields and charge weapons. Prepare to engage."

"Aye, Captain," Callaway said.

THIRTY-SEVEN

Perfection is an illusion.
Let us be honest about that, if nothing else. There is no such thing as true perfection. Everything we do is imperfect - everything we do has flaws that a nitpicker can point out, if he wishes. Even the best books, the best movies, the best military plans...they all have their flaws. The best planners know to plan for the unexpected because NOTHING is perfect.
Sure, the Grand Alliance will not be perfect either. But it is the only hope we have.
-Solar Datanet, Political Forum (Grand Alliance Thoughts)

"I think we surprised them," Callaway said, darkly.

Elton nodded in agreement. The Harmonies had known that *something* was wrong, but they hadn't known *what*. Perhaps they'd only intended to *scare* their fellow commander. And yet...it didn't matter. *Odyssey* had been exposed the moment the enemy had started to sweep space with active sensors. No cloak ever designed could stand up to *that*.

"Enemy gunboats moving into attack position," Callaway added. "The fortresses are locking weapons on us."

"Lock Hammers on them and return fire," Elton snapped. The fortresses might *just* give them a few seconds. *Odyssey* was right under their guns, after all. A *reasonable* commander might try to surrender. "Fire!"

"Missiles away," Callaway snapped. "Enemy fortresses opening fire!"

"Deploy ECM drones, stand by point defence," Elton ordered. "Fire at will!"

The gunboats zoomed in, ducking and diving around *King Whatever* as they closed on *Odyssey*. Biscoe opened fire a second later, his point defence scattering the gunboats and forcing them to evade his fire. Elton cursed as the fortresses unleashed a second salvo, targeting *King Whatever*. They might have hesitated to fire on a friendly ship - just as he would have been unsure about firing on a human ship - but their reluctance hadn't lasted. They *knew* that *King Whatever* was in enemy hands.

"Missiles entering point defence range," Callaway reported. "A quarter have been lured off-target."

They must not have got the latest targeting updates out here, Elton thought, as missiles started to vanish from the display. His point defence programs had been vastly improved too as his tactical staff learned from past encounters. *We might just have a chance.*

"Fortress One has been hit and destroyed," Callaway snapped. "Fortress Two has taken a glancing blow. She's badly damaged, but intact."

Elton hesitated. Fire another Hammer? They were down to five, without any hope of resupply. And yet, Fortress Two was still firing. The Tokomak had done a *very* good job of designing her.

"Withhold the remainder of the Hammers," he ordered. "And tell Mr. Biscoe to lead the way into the gravity point."

"Aye, Captain," Grave said.

"Enemy destroyers opening fire," Callaway said. "They're trying to brush past us!"

"Take them out," Elton ordered. If one of the destroyers got through the gravity point, whatever was waiting on the far side would have enough warning to get their weapons up and ready to fire before *Odyssey* arrived. "Helm, take us into the gravity point!"

Odyssey rocked, twice. "Two direct hits, starboard shield," Callaway reported. "Shields are holding..."

"Stay on course," Elton said. He cursed as one of the enemy destroyers jumped into FTL, curving a long arc through space before dropping back into realspace. It looked pointless, but any naval officer worth his salt would recognise it as a signal. The Harmonies guarding the other gravity points would know that *something* was wrong. "Time to gravity point?"

"Two minutes," Marie said. *Odyssey* shook, again. "We'll be following *King Whatever* within seconds."

"It can't be helped," Elton said. "Warn Mr. Biscoe to *move*."

"Aye, Captain," Marie said.

"Incoming fire," Callaway snapped. "Brace for impact!"

Elton gritted his teeth as more missiles slammed into the hull. Alarms started to sound a second later. "Damage report!"

"Shield Nine has been knocked out," Callaway said. He sounded frantic. "Shields Eight and Ten are working to compensate, but we have a weak spot!"

"Hold them in place," Elton ordered. Another enemy destroyer vanished from the display, but the remainder kept boring in for the kill. Worse, the gravimetric sensors reported a number of starships leaving the other gravity points. They'd be on top of him within minutes, at best. "Keep us going!"

"Aye, Captain," Callaway said.

⸻

COMMANDER RUPERT BISCOE would never have admitted it, but he was starting to get ever so slightly sick of *King Whatever*. She was a battlecruiser - and there was no way the Solar Navy would give him a battlecruiser as his first command - yet he couldn't help feeling as though she'd been designed by idiots. Or, perhaps, by people who'd wanted to hobble their crews as much as possible. *King Whatever* was tough, true, but she was also as slow and stupid as one of the pre-contact computers he'd seen in museums. Hell, he'd actually played a few pre-contact games - one of his boyfriends had loved refurbishing old machines - and *they'd* been quicker than *King Whatever*.

But she was still his first command.

"Take us into the gravity point," he ordered, sharply. The entire ship shook, repeatedly, as the nearest destroyer slammed blast after blast into his shields. He'd ordered her destroyed, but a lucky shot had knocked some of his missile tubes offline. The enemy commander had been smart - or lucky - enough to take up position in his blind spot and keep firing. "Move!"

"Aye, Captain," Williams said. "We're moving as quickly as we can!"

"Not quickly enough," Rupert snapped.

He cursed under his breath as another wave of missiles slammed into his shields. Five of his seven generators were on the verge of burning out, leaving his hull dangerously exposed to enemy fire. He keyed his console, launching a salvo of missiles back at the damaged fortress, hoping it would buy them some more time. A moment later, a spread of missiles from *Odyssey* smashed the pesky destroyer out of existence before she could roll over and make a run for it. Biscoe felt a moment of grim satisfaction, mingled with bitter relief. He wouldn't have to face that enemy commander again.

"Gravity point in ten seconds," Williams reported.

"Jump as soon as we're within the point," Rupert ordered. It wasn't going to be pleasant, even if they *were* practically crawling towards the point. "And prepare to engage whatever is on the far side."

Williams looked up. "Captain?"

"Do it," Rupert snapped. "They'll fire on us as soon as they get over the shock!"

He clenched his fists in rage. There was no way they could pretend to be innocent, not now. The hull was scorched and broken - one missile had come within bare metres of smashing his drive section to rubble - and his shields were failing. Another series of internal explosions underlined his thoughts. The enemy forces on the far side would take one look at them and *know* that something was badly wrong. Even if they didn't realise that *King Whatever* was no longer friendly, they'd want answers...

Williams cleared his throat. "Gravity point...*now*."

The shaking stopped. An instant later, Rupert doubled over. He'd expected it to be bad, but it was worse...far worse. He retched, uncontrollably. The pain struck him a second later...

"...Report," he managed. Williams seemed to be alive and well - damn him - but Lieutenant Valarie Richards was lying over her console, clearly out of it. "What happened?"

"Major damage, all decks," Williams managed. His voice sounded hoarse. "Captain...I'm picking up a single enemy fortress...no, make that *two* enemy fortresses...they're scanning us."

Rupert forced himself to stagger forwards and push Lieutenant Richards out of her seat. The helm console lit up at his touch, granting him control...it was almost pointless. *King Whatever* was so badly damaged that it was all her drives could do to push her off the gravity point before it was too late. The labouring sound echoing through her decks *couldn't* be healthy. He knew the engineering crew would do all they could, but they just didn't have the time.

"Two fortresses," he repeated. It was staggering...and infuriating. They'd come all this way, evading enemy fleets and tricking their way past enemy fortresses, only to be defeated at the final hurdle? "Do they have any ships escorting them?"

"Only gunboats, sir," Williams said. "But there are a *lot* of ships in-system. The scanners are too badly damaged to tell if they're friendly or not."

He broke off. "Sir, the fortresses are raising their shields," he added. "And they're hailing us, urgently. They want answers!"

"I'm sure they do," Rupert said. He ran his hands over the console. "Deploy drones for *Odyssey*, then divert all remaining power to drives and shields."

"Aye, sir," Williams said. A low hum echoed through the ship, rising for a long moment before falling again. "I do have some missiles..."

"Hold your fire," Rupert said. "Order all personnel to prepare to evacuate to the shuttles."

He felt an odd sense of calm come over him as he keyed in the final set of commands. Two fortresses...*Odyssey* wouldn't have a chance of breaking clear before they smashed her to atoms. But if one of the fortresses happened to be taken out first...his captain and crew might just have a chance to escape. He felt a rumble echoing through the ship as her drive fields strained against space, even though most of the drive nodes were on the verge of failure. They'd hold together long enough, he hoped, to slam *King Whatever* into the nearest fortress...

"They're repeating their hail," Williams reported. "Sir..."

"No response," Rupert ordered. Hopefully, *King Whatever's* shields would last long enough - once the fortresses started shooting - for her to reach her final destination. "Tell the crew to abandon ship, now! You too."

Williams blanched. "Sir..."

"Go," Rupert snapped. *Someone* had to remain on the bridge. The idiots who'd designed the command and control system had never considered the crew turning the ship into an oversized projectile. "That's an order, mister!"

"But..."

"Go," Rupert retreated. "And make sure *Odyssey* picks you up before it's too late."

He turned his attention back to the display, refusing to watch as the remaining bridge crew teleported to the shuttles. They might *just* have a chance to make it out, if *Odyssey* picked them up or they flew through the maelstrom towards the Hudson Point. A passing freighter might just save them...

But there's no hope for me, he thought, as the fortress grew closer. It sparkled with deadly light - the commander had overcome his reluctance to open fire - but it was too late. Oddly, the thought of certain death didn't bother him. *As long as the ship gets out...*

"Transit completed," Marie reported.

"I'm picking up a live feed from deployed drones," Grave added. "Sir...*my god*."

"Show me," Elton snapped.

The image appeared in front of him a second later, far too late. He watched, helplessly, as *King Whatever* glided towards the enemy fortress and slammed into her shields. The colossal explosion vaporised both the battlecruiser *and* the immense fortress. A second later, a whole string of red lights blinked up on the display: a second fortress, a small fleet of gunboats...and a set of shuttlecraft.

"The shuttles are hailing us," Grave said. "Captain, Commander Biscoe went down with the ship. A number of others were unable to evacuate."

"Understood," Elton snarled. He'd mourn later, if there *was* a later. The second fortress was already targeting *Odyssey*. "Deploy ECM drones, then bring the shuttles onboard."

"Aye, Captain," Callaway said.

Five Hammers left, Elton thought, as the fortress belched a lethal hail of red icons. The missiles would reach them bare seconds before the gunboats. *And no way to know what's waiting at the Hudson Point.*

"Helm, move us away from the gravity point as fast as possible," he ordered. "Tactical, prepare to engage with point defence."

"Aye, sir," Callaway said.

Elton forced himself to study the display, trying to think. He could expend one or more of his remaining Hammers on the fortress, but with so many gunboats between *Odyssey* and her target he was all-too-aware that the Hammer might be blasted out of space before it reached the fortress. And he *still* had no way to know what was waiting for him. The Harmonies might have moved a significant force into the system already...hell, they might have launched their invasion of Hudson by now. All he knew for *sure* was that traffic through the system had sunk to a tiny fraction of its former self.

And if they have taken Hudson Base, he asked himself, *what then?*

It was a bitter thought. *Odyssey* and her crew had been through hell. Commander Biscoe was dead, along with at least thirty others. God alone knew what had happened to Lieutenant Dennis and Mickey Tyler. The idea that it had all been for nothing, that *Odyssey* had already failed in her mission...it couldn't be faced. And yet, it *had* to be faced.

We could cut out of the system and find a place to make some proper repairs, if we knew, he thought. *But we don't know...*

"Incoming missiles," Callaway snapped. "Point defence engaging... *now*!"

Elton dragged his attention back to the engagement. The alien fortress clearly *did* have the latest set of updates. Only a handful of missiles were diverted by the drones, no matter how hard they tried to lure the seeker heads away from their targets. The remainder kept coming, followed by the gunboats. Hundreds were burned out of space, vanishing when the phaser blasts struck them, while the remainder...

"Brace for impact," he snapped. "All hands, brace for impact..."

The starship rang like a bell. Elton bit his lip, hard, as the gravity field flickered sharply, then nearly vanished altogether. A low rumble echoed through the ship, followed by a series of sharp retorts. He *knew* that was bad...

"Shields Eight, Nine and Ten have failed," Callaway reported. "Drive One is offline; Drive Two has taken significant damage and may fail at any moment..."

"Keep us moving as fast as you can," Elton snapped. He cursed under his breath. If they didn't risk using the Hammers now, it was unlikely they'd survive long enough to reach their *next* target. "Fire a Hammer, surrounded by conventional missiles and ECM drones."

"Aye, Captain," Callaway said. He broke off. "Sir, the gunboats are closing to attack range..."

"And there's a gaping hole in our shields to attract them," Elton finished. The fortress had fired a second salvo, but it would take them several minutes to reach attack range. "Divert point defence to taking out the gunboats."

"Aye, Captain," Callaway said. The ship shuddered, again. "Missiles away!"

Elton closed his eyes - just for a second - to say a silent prayer. The Hammer was far too noticeable, even surrounded by conventional missiles...the Harmonies might not know how to produce them for themselves, but they'd figure out the principles just by observing the weapons in action. A small black hole wasn't something that could be easily hidden. He opened his eyes again, just as the gunboats swooped down to attack. A dozen were picked off, easily, but the remainder lasted long enough to strafe the hull with phaser bolts...

"They can't get through the hull," Callaway reported.

"They *can* pick off our point defence," Elton said. The gunboats had sold their lives dearly, even if they didn't know it...he *knew* they knew it. They'd done more than enough damage to his point defence that the *next* volley of missiles might well do serious harm. "Retarget some of our own missiles to take out their salvo."

"Aye, Captain," Callaway said.

Elton allowed himself a moment, just a moment, of hope when the Hammer reached its target. The fortress fought desperately to save itself, but it was at precisely the *wrong* angle to take out a hammer. Dodging was the only solution and the fortress had nothing stronger than manoeuvring jets. Moments later, the Hammer plunged into the structure and vaporised it. The salvos of missiles cut off sharply...

...And then the first red icons emerged from the gravity point.

"Captain," Callaway said. "I'm picking up three...no, four...battleships. No...five..."

"Noted," Elton said. "Prepare to..."

"Incoming missiles," Callaway snapped. "Point defence is spinning around...ready to engage."

Elton swore. The fortress had been destroyed, but its crew might just have the last laugh. Their gunboats had weakened the point defence too badly and there was no time to make repairs...

"Spin us around," he ordered. It was a gamble, but they might just be able to interpose another shield between the hull and the incoming missiles. "And brace for impact..."

An alarm sounded. "Drive Two is down," Marie snapped. "I..."

The missiles slammed home. *Odyssey* bucked like a wild animal, the gravity failing completely. Elton took hold of his command chair as the lights flickered before slowly recovering, forcing himself to look at the status display. Entire compartments had greyed out, warning him that the internal datanet had failed. The damage was far worse than he'd dared fear. It was the beginning of the end.

"Drive Two is beyond repair," Callaway said. "Drive Three and Drive Four are still intact, but we've lost too many drive nodes to generate an FTL field."

Elton looked at the display. A steady stream of enemy starships were slowly emerging from the gravity point. Two had dropped into FTL and were racing towards the Parana Point, while the remainder were slowly heading towards *Odyssey*. They might not have a solid lock on her - and it might just be possible to reactivate the cloaking device - but it didn't matter.

"Activate the cloaking device, if possible," he ordered. "And then..."

He sucked in his breath. They were doomed. Cloaked or uncloaked, they didn't have a hope of evading detection indefinitely. The enemy already knew their rough location. And that meant...

Elton smiled, coldly. Maybe they were about to die. No, there was no doubt. They *were* about to die. But he was damned if he was selling his life cheaply...

We may die, he thought. *But at least the bastards will know they've been in a fight.*

THIRTY-EIGHT

I hope you're right.

But I am a pessimist and that forces me to doubt it. The Solar Union represents a very different mindset to either Earthers or our alien friends. To risk losing that, to risk surrendering all that makes us what we are, is beyond comprehension. If Solarians and Earthers are different, mentally if not biologically...what then are aliens?

Will we win one war only to lay the groundwork for another?
-Solar Datanet, Political Forum (Grand Alliance Thoughts)

"Captain," Lieutenant Pei said. "I'm picking up some unusual activity."

Captain-Commodore Jenny Longlegs looked up. "What *sort* of activity?"

"Ten minutes ago, two ships dropped into FTL - heading from the Chalmers Point to the Parana Point," Pei said. She was strikingly young for her post, but Jenny had never had any reason to doubt her competence. "Now, we have a number of starships - at least thirty - leaving the Parana Point and heading to Chalmers."

Jenny tapped her console, bringing up the live feed. It *was* odd - or at least against galactic regulations - for a ship to drop into FTL in the middle of a system. She'd never been sure *why*. But now...it was odd. And it was the first major fleet movement they'd seen since she'd moved the squadron into Daladier. The other Galactics back at Hudson were too busy arguing over what to do...

Pity, she thought, as she contemplated the situation. *We could have used some back-up - or even a strong neutral force sitting on top of the gravity point.*

"This could be them," Lieutenant Dennis said. "We have to go to their aid."

Jenny was inclined to agree, but there were other considerations. Her squadron was formidable - she knew she commanded the deadliest force in the sector - yet it was badly outnumbered. If the Harmonies were trying to lure them out of position - she assumed they knew she'd taken the squadron to Daladier - they might manage to block her retreat, forcing her to choose between a desperate engagement or a long trip back to base. Worse, there was no way to *know* what was *truly* going on. Any message from *Odyssey*, assuming there *was* a message from *Odyssey*, would take hours to reach them. By then, the affair might already be over...

She tapped her console. It was a gamble, but one she had to take. Besides, Hudson Base had already been shut down. Abandoning the system wouldn't look good on her resume - her lips twitched at the thought - but her superiors understood the tactical realities. If the Galactics wanted to chase her out of the system, they'd chase her out of the system. There was nothing to be gained by expending her squadron in a pointless engagement.

"Helm, take us towards the Chalmers Point," she ordered. "Best possible speed."

"Aye, Captain," Lieutenant Heinrich said.

Jenny leaned back in her chair as the drives powered up, preparing to hurl the squadron into FTL. She was blind and she hated that, but at least she was doing *something*. The last week had been more than a little frustrating. None of the Galactics, it seemed, were truly prepared for war. The Harmonies, damn them to hell, might get away with everything they'd done.

And galactic society plunges into chaos, she thought, morbidly. *Who knows what will happen then?*

"ENEMY SHIPS ARE falling into a search pattern," Callaway reported. "They're advancing out from the gravity point."

He paused. "They're also leaving two battleships to cover the gravity point itself."

"They probably expect us to try to double back," Elton said. It would have been reassuring, in a way, if he hadn't known the end could not be long delayed. Popping back through the gravity point would merely expose them to the enemy fortresses. "Can you calculate their search trajectories?"

"Yes, Captain," Callaway said.

Elton sucked in his breath as red cones of light appeared on the display. At least two enemy ships would pass within detection range...and the bastards *knew* they needed to investigate every random energy pulse within the area. It was possible, he supposed, that they could use ECM drones to force the enemy to waste time, but there was no way he could get *Odyssey* clean away before it was too late. The enemy would simply fire on every stray flicker of energy, confirming - to their own satisfaction - that it was nothing more than a drone before resuming the search.

"Deploy the remaining drones," he ordered. Maybe it was a waste of effort, but he could at least *try* to spite them. "Program them to pose as cloaked ships."

"Aye, Captain," Callaway said.

"And adjust our vector," Elton added. "Cut across the search cone rather than trying to outrun it."

"Aye, Captain," Marie said.

Elton made a face as *Odyssey* slowly altered course. She'd never been the most nimble of starships, but now...she handled worse than a wallowing bulk freighter. The damage control teams were struggling to get the

FTL drive back online, yet...Elton didn't need Wolf's grim updates to know that they just didn't have the time. The drive nodes would have to be completely replaced before *Odyssey* slipped back into FTL.

"Captain, we received an update from the drones," Callaway said. "Nine more ships just popped through the gravity point. They're joining the search party."

Shit, Elton thought. The new projections made it clear that they were trapped. Maybe - just maybe - they could have evaded the original hunters, but the newcomers expanded the search cones to trap *Odyssey*. They'd probably already projected just how far the human starship could move before it was too late. Hell, they'd probably overestimated it. They couldn't know *just* how badly *Odyssey* had been damaged.

He closed his eyes for a long moment. Forty-seven enemy ships, eight of them battleships...they were doomed. Even if they smashed the first enemy ship that found them, the remainder would blast *Odyssey* into space dust. The only consolation was that the Harmonies had no reasonable excuse for sending so many ships into the system. Who knew? Maybe the other Galactics would make them pay.

Sure, he thought, sardonically. *And perhaps the horse will learn to sing.*

"They're angling four destroyers towards us," Callaway said. "They'll pass within detection range in nine minutes."

Unless we're leaking, Elton thought. The cloaking device hadn't been *designed* for a human ship, let alone built to human specifications. *Odyssey* might well be radiating an energy signature *despite* the cloak. His sensors were so badly battered that he had no way to find out. *They might already know where we are.*

"Keep us angled away from them," he ordered, grimly. "And prepare to engage."

"Aye, Captain," Callaway said. "Standard missiles only?"

"Yes," Elton said. Four destroyers...even bruised and battered, they could handle four destroyers. It was their bigger brothers he was worried about. "Reserve the Hammers for the battleships."

Another red icon flashed up on the display. Gravimetric sensors had gone offline. Elton reached for the console to order Wolf to focus on repairing them, then dismissed the thought in some irritation. It didn't matter any longer. The Harmonies had more than enough ships within engagement range to finish the job.

"Picking up a wide-band signal," Grave reported. "They're inviting us to surrender."

"No response," Elton ordered, sharply. They'd either die quickly or die slowly - they'd still be dead. He had no reason to believe the Harmonies would treat them as POWs. "Tactical?"

"They're starting to close in," Callaway said. "They'll definitely have us in seven minutes."

And they may pick us up before then, Elton thought. Ideally, the enemy ships would move closer - much closer - before detecting *Odyssey*. If he fired from such short range, there would be a very good chance of blowing all four destroyers away before they managed to return fire. But he knew he couldn't count on it. *They'll be watching for us.*

"Lock missiles on their hulls," he ordered. There was no point in trying to be clever, not now. Disabling an enemy ship was pointless when there were nearly fifty others in the vicinity. "Prepare to engage."

He braced himself as the red icons glided closer. It was obvious the Harmonies didn't know *precisely* where they were - unless they were trying to lull him into a false sense of security - but they definitely had a rough idea. Their search pattern was crude and over-complex, yet it would work. No doubt they'd practiced the technique extensively. Hunting down a cloaked ship, particularly one that had sneaked too close to one's defences, was an important military skill.

Just like hunting submarines, he thought. One of his ancestors had been on HMS *Conqueror* when she'd become the first nuclear-powered submarine to fire her torpedoes at an enemy ship. He wondered, absently, if his long-dead ancestor would have approved of his conduct under fire. *And if they manage to get a solid lock on us before we raise our shields, we're dead.*

"Three minutes to certain detection," Callaway said. "Missiles locked..."

"Fire at thirty seconds from detection," Elton ordered. It was a gamble - the enemy *might* be kind enough to come closer - but it balanced the opportunity to inflict major damage with the increasing certainty of eventual detection. "Don't wait for orders, just fire."

"Aye, Captain," Callaway said.

Elton allowed himself a moment to look around the bridge. His crew had been largely untried, when they'd left Earth, but they'd acquitted themselves well. He was more proud of them than he could say. But... none of them were going to survive the coming battle. He knew that as surely as he knew his name. The Solar Union would never know what had happened to them. They wouldn't even be sure that *Odyssey* had been the first casualty in a renewed war.

I'm sorry, he thought.

"Two minutes," Callaway said. He paused. "They're slowing...they may have us."

Elton didn't hesitate. "Fire!"

Odyssey jerked as she flushed her missile tubes. They weren't at optimum firing range, but they were still close enough to give the enemy a nasty fright. The destroyers rotated, as if their commanders were torn between firing back and trying to get out of range before it was too late... their shields snapped into position, a handful of seconds before the missiles struck their targets. It wasn't enough to save them. Three destroyers were blown out of space and a fourth lost power, her hull bleeding plasma and air as she drifted out of position...

"Target Three is apparently powerless," Callaway reported. "Should I finish her?"

"No," Elton said, after a moment. "Hold fire."

He studied the enemy ship on the display, thinking fast. Could he *afford* to leave the damaged ship intact? Perhaps it was a trick, although he doubted any human or alien crew could shut everything down so quickly, let alone start venting on cue. No, the destroyer was out of commission for the foreseeable future. The Harmonies would probably scrap her, even though there was a universal shortage of ships. Building a replacement destroyer would be cheaper than repairing her.

"Captain," Callaway said. "The enemy battleships are moving onto an attack vector."

Elton nodded. "Helm, keep us moving," he ordered. A stern chase would normally be a long one, but *Odyssey's* drives were too badly damaged to keep them going for long. "And prepare to bring us about on my command."

He forced himself to watch as the assorted vectors shook out into a brutally simple equation with only one answer. The enemy ships, moving faster than *Odyssey*, would catch up with her in less than ten minutes. Perhaps sooner, if they risked sending some of their battleships ahead in FTL. Navigation would be a pain, but it wasn't as if there was any real chance of losing their quarry. And once they *were* in firing range, they'd open fire and pound *Odyssey* to scrap. Hell, if they knew how badly *Odyssey's* point defence had been weakened, they'd close the range as much as possible.

"Widen the sensors as much as possible," he ordered. "Configure two shuttles as makeshift drones, then launch them ahead of us."

"Aye, Captain," Callaway said. He hesitated. "Sir, that will take at least ten minutes..."

Under ideal conditions, Elton thought.

He kicked himself, mentally. He should have thought of it...why hadn't he thought of redeploying the shuttles earlier? Because the beancounters would have thrown a fit if they'd learned he'd casually launched two shuttles into a maelstrom rather than using a - relatively - cheaper drone. Not that it mattered, part of his mind insisted. *Odyssey* was more expensive than all of her shuttles and drones put together and *she* was about to be blown out of space.

"Get the crews working on it," he ordered. "And deploy them as soon as possible."

"Aye, Captain," Callaway said.

Elton nodded. It was a pity the shuttles weren't heavily armed or he would have deployed them as point defence platforms. Even the *marine* shuttles weren't configured for shooting down incoming missiles. He made a mental note to raise the issue with the procurement board, then dismissed the thought. There was no hope of getting home, let alone convincing the navy to reconfigure its entire fleet of shuttles.

New red icons flashed into existence. "Sir," Callaway said. "The drones picked up a new wave of ships dropping out of FTL. Arrival vectors suggest that they came directly from the Parana Point."

"Ah," Elton said. Oddly, he felt like laughing. The odds had been insurmountable *before* the enemy reinforcements had arrived. "Ship count?"

"Thirty-seven battleships, nineteen battlecruisers, seventy smaller ships," Callaway said. He looked up. "They can't get away now."

"It *will* be harder to miss," Elton agreed. A low chuckle ran around the bridge. "And if they want to waste time bunching up, let them."

He sobered as the display kept updating. The enemy reinforcements were already altering course, coming about to give chase. There was no doubt, now, that the Harmonies were *pissed*. They'd sent enough firepower to give *Sol* a very bad day after a single badly-damaged starship. He wondered, absently, if there was anyone watching the engagement from a safe distance. The Harmonies might not recover from the damage to their reputation, after the entire galaxy had watched them crush *Odyssey* with overwhelming force.

It might not matter, he thought. *They're still one of the biggest kids on the block.*

"They're not bunching up," Callaway reported. "Force One will be within engagement range in five minutes. Force Two will be within engagement range in twelve minutes."

"Understood," Elton said. Time had run out. There were no more clever tricks...nothing, but certain death. "Helm, bring us about. Take us right down their throats."

"Aye, sir," Marie said.

Elton felt his ship trembling as she - slowly, very slowly - came about. Her hull was creaking alarmingly, suggesting that she'd taken structural damage. Humanity had learnt a great deal about building starships over the past fifty years, but...there were limits. *Odyssey* needed months, perhaps years, in the yards before she could return to active service. She might even be scrapped, if she somehow got back home...

"Firing range in three minutes, Captain," Callaway said. "They're reducing speed."

"Probably wondering what trick we have up our sleeve *this* time," Elton said. "Prepare to open fire."

He paused. "Target our remaining Hammers on their battleships," he added. "And fire a salvo of standard missiles too."

"Aye, Captain," Callaway said. His fingers danced over the console. "Missiles ready..."

"Fire as soon as we enter firing range," Elton ordered.

He gritted his teeth as the enemy ships came closer. Their formation was different, somehow...they'd spread out their destroyers and frigates, even though that made them vulnerable to his fire. He puzzled over it for a long moment, then realised that it was their first true attempt at an anti-Hammer formation. The Hammers wouldn't be wasted on the smaller ships, allowing them a chance to engage the missiles from behind.

And they could trade a hundred destroyers for us and still come out ahead, he thought.

"Firing," Callaway said.

The enemy fired at the same moment, belching hundreds - thousands - of missiles towards *Odyssey*. It was overkill, *massive* overkill...it was, he supposed, a compliment of sorts, a droll admission that *Odyssey* had run rings around them. Elton looked at the display and saw death, advancing steadily towards them. Even the prospect of killing three - perhaps four - battleships failed to please him. If *Odyssey* survived the first salvo, the surviving battleships would finish the job.

"Point defence online," Callaway said. "ECM active..."

Elton nodded, shortly. It didn't matter. There was no way they could stop enough of the missiles to save themselves. And even if they did, there were plenty more missiles just waiting to be fired at them.

"Fire at will," he ordered.

The first Hammer vanished, picked off by one of the enemy destroyers; the remaining Hammers plunged into their targets, vaporising them with contemptuous ease. But the Harmonies kept coming...either they knew *Odyssey* had shot herself dry or they no longer cared. Their missiles were closing in...

"It's been a honour," Elton said, quietly.

Callaway started. *"Captain!"*

The display flared with new icons, *behind* them. Elton stared...new enemy ships? It wasn't just overkill...it was *more* than overkill. *Odyssey* was doomed. He fought down an insane urge to giggle as the sensors struggled to cope with the sudden influx of data. The Harmonies had brought over a hundred ships to crush a lone starship...

"Picking up IFF transmissions," Grave said. "Captain, they're *friendly!"*

Elton spun around. "What?"

"They're the Hudson Squadron," Grave said. On the display, the newcomers had already begun to engage the missile storm. "We're saved!"

THIRTY-NINE

That is an absurd argument.

Every war in human history can be said - reasonably - to lay the groundwork for the next war. The First World War laid the groundwork for the Second World War; the Gulf War laid the groundwork for the Iraq War; the American Civil War laid the groundwork for the Second American Civil War. Yet should those wars not have been fought?

And even if they were fought, they were not the sole cause of the next war. Their successors could have been avoided.

Yes, we may wind up fighting our former allies. But right now we are fighting the Tokomak!

-Solar Datanet, Political Forum (Grand Alliance Thoughts)

"Decloak," Jenny snapped. *Odyssey* was doomed unless she acted quickly. "Point defence, engage at will!"

"Aye, Captain," Lieutenant Pei said.

Jenny gritted her teeth. It had been sheer luck that they'd dropped out of FTL close enough to detect *Odyssey*, then manoeuvre into position to save the stricken ship. The Harmonies were trying to overwhelm her before help arrived...she cursed as her sensors picked up a second wave of enemy ships advancing towards *Odyssey*. Enough firepower, perhaps, to give her and her squadron a major headache.

"Tactical, engage the enemy ships," Jenny ordered. Her display updated. *Odyssey* was badly damaged, although she clearly still had *some* drives left. But no stardrive...Captain Yasser would have jumped into FTL if he could, given how many ships were chasing him down. "Communications, raise Captain Yasser!"

"Aye, Captain."

Jenny leaned forward as her first salvo roared towards the enemy battleships. They seemed to flinch, as if their commanders were unsure what to do. She silently blessed their hesitation as her missiles entered attack range and threw themselves on their targets, blasting through their shields and smashing the battleships to atoms. They'd been picking on *Odyssey*, a deep-space exploration and diplomatic starship rather than a pure warship. They were about to learn what a squadron of *genuine* warships could do.

"Enemy battleships destroyed," Lieutenant Pei reported. "The smaller enemy ships are retreating to join Force Two."

"Understood," Jenny said.

Captain Yasser's face appeared in front of her. "Commodore Longlegs," he said. He looked haggard, but he was grinning broadly. "It's *very* good to see you."

"Your messengers made it through," Jenny said, briskly. "What's your status?"

"Poor," Yasser said. He glanced at something off-screen. "Shields are practically gone; stardrive is offline; sublight drives are at barely thirty percent power; weapons and tactical ECM are pretty much gone too."

"But you made it," Jenny said. "I look forward to hearing your story once we get out of here."

"I'll send you a complete copy of the logs," Yasser said. "Something will get out of here, even if we don't."

"You will," Jenny assured him.

She thought, quickly. The simplest solution would be to take *Odyssey* in tow and drag her through FTL, but the Harmonies were unlikely to give them enough time to set it up. Their second force was *still* advancing, while more ships were racing to join them. Others might be heading straight for the Hudson Point, cutting her off. And that meant...she might just be at a considerable disadvantage.

"Set course for the Hudson Point," she ordered, shortly. "My squadron will cover you."

"Understood," Yasser said.

His image vanished. Jenny ran her hand through her hair, trying to find another option. She might *just* have enough time to evacuate *Odyssey* and escape into FTL before the Harmonies caught up with them, but she knew Captain Yasser would be reluctant to abandon his ship, let alone blow her up to save her from falling into enemy hands. Jenny couldn't even *blame* him for wanting to preserve his command. *Odyssey* had been through a hell of a lot in the last few weeks. And yet, a running battle might just work in the enemy's favour...

I could inflict horrendous damage and yet lose, she thought. Her ships carried enough Hammers to smash *most* of the enemy battleships, but the remainder would pound hell out of her. Worse, she wouldn't even be able to use her speed for best advantage. Her squadron would be tied to *Odyssey* as long as she remained intact. *And they know it.*

"Move us to cover *Odyssey*," she ordered, grimly. "Tactical, prepare to engage the enemy when they enter range."

She silently calculated the vectors, trying to find another set of options. But she could think of none. Assuming *Odyssey* was unable to pick up speed - and the status download made it clear that she was rather more likely to lose her drives altogether - they'd need at least fifty hours to reach the Hudson Point. By then, the Harmonies could have overwhelmed her squadron or - at the very least - blown *Odyssey* into space dust. If she abandoned *Odyssey*, she could break contact easily...

"Damn it," she muttered. She didn't *want* to tell Captain Yasser to abandon his ship. He'd been through too much already. But she couldn't think of anything else. Unless...a thought struck her. It wasn't something she would have considered, normally, but they were desperate.

"Engineering, could we extend the FTL field around *Odyssey* without a physical link?"

There was a pause. Her engineers would be hastily running simulations, she knew, trying to determine if it was actually possible. It *might* be possible. She'd heard of a couple of experiments in launching missiles through FTL without actually giving them a working stardrive, although none of the experiments had actually worked. Another science-fiction concept that hadn't quite proved usable in the real world...

"Our field isn't configured for such expansion, Captain," the engineer said, finally. "We're too small and *Odyssey* is too large. Even *with* a towline, Captain, she's not in good state. I don't think she would survive the trip."

Jenny cursed under her breath. "What if we mated hulls?"

"We'd still have the same problem," the engineer said. "I'd honestly recommend leaving *Odyssey* in sublight until we have a chance to carry out some proper repairs."

"Understood," Jenny said.

Odyssey would have to be abandoned, then. The thought gnawed at her. She'd hate herself for stripping Captain Yasser of his command after he'd done so much to keep *Odyssey* out of enemy hands. But there was no choice...

And then another thought struck her.

"Tactical," she said. "How many drones do we have left?"

"Thirty-two," Lieutenant Pei said.

"Good," Jenny said. "I've just had an idea."

She sucked in her breath. One last roll of the dice, then. Who knew? It might just work.

"THE DRIVE CANNOT be repaired, Captain," Wolf said. "Not without shutting everything down and dismantling the wrecked superstructure."

Elton nodded, grimly. He'd thought they were going to die. Now... now, he knew that *Odyssey* was going to die, even if her crew had a chance to survive. He hated to even *think* of abandoning his ship, but he couldn't see any alternative. There were too many enemy ships steadily closing to engagement range, too many ships that couldn't be avoided if Commodore Longlegs had to stay close to *Odyssey*. His ship had to die so that the remainder of the squadron could live.

"Order all non-essential crew to prepare for evacuation," Elton ordered, finally. He hoped - prayed - that the enemy wouldn't realise what they were doing and try to stop them. A salvo of antimatter-tipped missiles would cause enough distortion to make teleporting impossible, even if they missed their targets. "Activate teleporter transponders, then transmit complete copies of our logs to the squadron."

"Aye, sir," Grave said.

Elton looked around his bridge, feeling cold. It was a joke, a cosmic joke. His ship had survived so much, yet now she had to be abandoned... there wouldn't even be a chance to ram her into an alien battleship. He wanted to stay on the bridge, but he knew it would be pointless. *Odyssey* had kept her crew alive long enough for them to reach safety, at least...

"Message from Commodore Longlegs, Captain," Grave said. "She's ordering us to hold off the evacuation."

"*What?*"

"She's ordering us to wait, Captain," Graves said. "She didn't say why."

Elton blinked in shock. Commodore Longlegs was an experienced naval officer. She'd *know* just how hopeless the situation was, if she tried to escort *Odyssey* to the Hudson Point. The only hope of preserving the crew - and her ships - was to evacuate and abandon *Odyssey*, then make a run for the gravity point. She *had* to know it.

"The enemy ships will enter missile range in two minutes," Callaway added.

"I hope she knows what she's doing," Elton snarled. It wasn't the sort of thing he would have said out loud - normally - but this was different. What *was* the commodore *doing*? "Can you muster any more point defence?"

"No, Captain," Callaway said. "We don't even have a working uplink to the squadron datanet."

Elton gritted his teeth. The damage was *far* worse than he'd dared fear. Solarian starships were *designed* to slot into command datanets, even ones pulled together on the fly. The communications nodes were deliberately hardened, just to ensure the datanet stayed together as long as possible. Losing the datalink meant that *Odyssey* would be on her own, rather than fighting as part of a team. She'd be wasting a great deal of effort trying to shoot down missiles that had been already targeted by her escorts. Worse, there was a very real possibility she'd actually start shooting at a *friendly* ship.

"Engage any missile that threatens our hull," he ordered. They'd just have to hope that Commodore Longlegs knew what she was doing. "Fire at will."

"Aye, sir," Callaway said.

On the display, the enemy ships belched yet another wave of missiles.

"The enemy ships have opened fire," Lieutenant Pei reported.

"Return fire," Jenny ordered.

She watched, grimly, as the enemy missile salvo was steadily picked apart by her sensors, each missile assigned an ID tag and a place in the firing queue. A third of the missiles seemed to have been targeted on *Odyssey*, the remainder aimed at her ships...she puzzled over the odd pattern for a moment before deciding the Harmonies probably wanted to smash *Odyssey* even though they'd already lost. Perhaps it was the only way they thought they could regain some face after the series of disasters they'd suffered.

And they're going to pay for it, she thought, as her own missiles lanced into the teeth of enemy point defence. *They know they're going to pay for it.*

She smiled, coldly. The Harmonies were luckier than they knew. *They* might prefer lumbering battlewagons, but *humanity* had designed a fleet of fast and deadly cruisers that packed a considerable punch and were *extremely* hard to hit. If she had had complete freedom to manoeuvre, she could have picked their formation apart. But she didn't...as long as she wanted to protect *Odyssey*. They knew it as well as she did.

We'll give them one hell of a shock when the real war starts, she thought, as a stream of missiles blasted into the enemy ships. A dozen died, but there were dozens more to take their place. *Yet if we're trading one of our ships for ten of theirs...they're still going to come out ahead.*

"Enemy missiles entering point defence range," Lieutenant Pei reported. "Engaging...now."

Jenny nodded. "And the drones?"

"Still moving into position," Lieutenant Pei said.

"Good," Jenny said.

She leaned forward, watching as the enemy missiles started to vanish from the display. They were doing better than she'd expected - she assumed they'd learnt a great deal from facing *Odyssey* - but they *really* weren't prepared to face genuine warships. *Her* crews had trained on the assumption that their enemies would have superior missile technology. Theirs...she didn't know for sure, but she had a sneaking suspicion their combat exercises were carefully scripted to ensure that there were no surprises. It might look good, to the untrained eye, yet only chaos could teach spacers how to react to the unexpected.

"*Jellicoe* took four hits," Lieutenant Pei reported. "*Raeder* took two. No significant damage reported."

"Continue firing," Jenny ordered. Any *sane* enemy would have backed off by now, if only to lick their wounds and prepare for the next encounter, but the Harmonies were still pressing forward. And they might just win too. "The drones?"

"In position," Lieutenant Pei said. "Deploy?"

"Deploy," Jenny said.

On the display, the enemy ships belched yet another wave of missiles.

"Captain, the enemy ships are closing in," Callaway reported.

"I can't push the drives any harder," Marie added. "Drive Four is on the verge of complete failure."

"Hold her steady," Elton ordered. The constant series of shudders running through the hull was not a good sign. *Odyssey's* drive field was fluctuating so badly that it was slapping constantly against the hull. Sooner or later, something vitally important would fail because of the battering. "Tactical..."

"Captain," Callaway interrupted. "New contacts!"

Elton looked up at the display. New icons were flickering into existence, far too close to the fleeing squadron for comfort. The Harmonies... no, *other* alien starships. A dozen races, he thought. Most of them were Great Powers...

"Picking up a wide-band signal," Grave reported. "Captain, they're ordering the Harmonies to back off and return to their territory."

"Good," Elton said, stunned. He hadn't expected the Galactics to get their act together in less than a year, if they bothered to do anything. Given that the Tokomak were backing the Harmonies, he rather doubted they'd lift a finger to help the human race. "Are they going?"

"I don't know," Callaway said. "They're stopped firing, but..."

He broke off. "Captain, they're altering course," he added. "They're retreating!"

"Good," Elton said, again. Was it good? Had they moved from the frying pan into the fire? Or...he looked again at the newcomers. There was something odd about their formation. "I wonder..."

"Commodore Longlegs is ordering us to continue our course towards the gravity point," Grave reported. "And she wants to know if we think we can be towed."

"Check with the engineer," Elton ordered. He leaned back in his chair, feeling weak. They'd made it back to Hudson Base, intact. It was over. "And stand down from red alert."

"Aye, Captain," Callaway said.

— —

"It was a trick," Elton said, an hour later.

"Yes," Commodore Longlegs said. "We used drones to convince them that the other Galactics were on the verge of intervening."

Elton shook his head in amused disbelief. "And they bought it?"

"Any watchers would have seen you, then us, give them a pasting," Commodore Longlegs pointed out. "Their reputation would have gone straight into a black hole."

She smiled. "I've taken the opportunity to review your logs," she added. "You've been through hell."

"We made it," Elton said.

He looked down at his terminal. "My chief engineer estimates that we can repair the stardrive within the week, if you provide men and equipment," he added. "Is that doable?"

Commodore Longlegs frowned. "Hudson Base has been abandoned," she said. "The base is untenable now. Either the Harmonies will get over their shock and mount a renewed offensive or we'll be ordered to leave, after the others realise what we did. They won't be too pleased if we accidentally spark off a full-scale war.

"But we can find a patch of space somewhere between the stars to carry out repairs," she added, after a moment. "I assume you intend to head straight home?"

Elton nodded. *Odyssey* had been battered beyond belief, but she was still largely intact. Her designers had done a *very* good job. A week of intensive repairs would be enough to get her back to Earth, assuming they didn't run into any further trouble along the way. There was no point in sticking around. Commodore Longlegs and her squadron *might* be able to influence events in humanity's favour, but *Odyssey* was in no state to lend her weight to any future engagements.

"We should be able to get home shortly after the first courier boats," he said. "And after that...we'll see what happens."

"War," Commodore Longlegs said, flatly. "If your prisoner interrogations are accurate, Elton, this was all a Tokomak plot. The cold war is about to turn hot - again."

Elton made a face. Rebecca had been right. *Odyssey* might have escaped one trap - and then several more - but the overall mission had failed. The Harmonies had not become humanity's allies, while the other regional powers remained uncommitted. And while his ship had fought well, they'd shown the enemy too much for his peace of mind. How long would it be, he asked himself, before the Tokomak started producing Hammers of their own?

"They learned a great deal about us," he said. The Tokomak probably considered the Harmonies expendable. Hell, from their point of view, knocking the Harmonies down a peg or two was greatly to be desired. They *had* once been competitors for galactic power, after all. "But we also learnt a great deal about them."

"Let us hope it's enough," Commodore Longlegs said. She smiled. "We'll get back through the gravity point, then find a place to do some repairs."

"Understood," Elton said.

"And well done," she added. "Your ship and crew performed magnificently."

Elton smiled as her face vanished. She was right. *Odyssey* had performed well. Thrown into a maelstrom she'd never been designed to face, she'd survived. She'd been outnumbered and outgunned, but she'd survived. He had good reason to be proud of his ship and her crew.

And yet, some of them had given everything to help the ship escape...

But we'll have to mourn the dead later, he thought, as he rose. *And thank them for their service.*

He keyed his terminal. "Mr. Callaway, keep us on course towards the gravity point," he ordered. "We're going home."

FORTY

This discussion has passed the point of usefulness and is hereby locked. Please reread the 'Guidelines for Political Discussions, Debates and Flame Wars' (updated 2080) and conduct yourselves accordingly. Posters who are unable to consistently follow the guidelines will be banned. There will be no further warnings.
-Solar Datanet, Political Forum (Grand Alliance Thoughts)

"It could have gone a little better," Rebecca said, as they waited outside Admiral Stuart's office. "There were a *lot* of repetitive questions."

She rubbed her forehead. She'd seriously considered remaining behind with Commodore Longlegs, rather than travelling back to Earth. Now, she rather wished she *had*. The diplomatic service might have concluded - reluctantly - that Rebecca had been given an impossible task, but the post mortem had only just begun. *No one* wanted to risk sending *another* starship into a trap.

"I had the same experience," Captain Yasser said. He looked as tired as she felt. "The Board of Inquiry had a lot of repetitive questions too."

Rebecca snorted. "They couldn't get everything from your logs?"

"They want to know what I was thinking, every time I made a decision," Captain Yasser said, dryly. "And then they want to know what I *didn't* put in the logbook."

The hatch opened. "Ambassador Motherwell, Captain Yasser," Admiral Stuart's secretary said. "Please, come in."

Rebecca rose, feeling oddly as though she was going to see the principal. She was in her sixties, but Mongo Stuart was easily forty years older than her. *And* he was living history, a man who'd been on the spot when the Solar Union was founded. She was part of history too now, she supposed, yet it was really nothing more than a footnote. Mongo Stuart's name would be mentioned for centuries to come.

Assuming we survive, she thought, numbly.

"Captain, Ambassador," Admiral Stuart said. He waved a hand at a pair of comfortable chairs. "Please, be seated."

Rebecca sat, crossing her legs. She'd resisted the urge to wear a formal diplomatic outfit to the inquest, even though that might have been a mistake. The long dress she wore might as well belong to a middle-aged woman who was restarting her career after raising a handful of children. But she hadn't felt as though she truly belonged in the diplomatic service any longer. There was no way to avoid the simple fact that she'd failed, that - in the end - she'd been about as useful as a steam engine on a starship. Captain Yasser sat next to her, his face expressionless. It occurred to Rebecca, as she gathered herself, that he might be as concerned about this meeting as herself.

"There has been a great deal of debate over your misadventures," Admiral Stuart said, without preamble. "Fortunately, the early discussions in both the navy and the diplomatic service agree that neither of you are to blame for the disaster. The Harmonies baited a trap - at the behest of the Tokomak - and we fell for it."

"Yes, sir," Captain Yasser said.

Stuart looked at Rebecca. "You'll hear a more formal response from your superiors in the next few days," he added, "but it has been generally agreed that you did everything in your power to open lines of communication. The Harmonies never intended to negotiate in good faith and so you cannot be held accountable. Your career will not suffer."

"Maybe," Rebecca said. She shook her head. "I need a holiday."

"That would be a good idea," Stuart said.

He switched his attention to Captain Yasser. "I have to tell you that there was some debate concerning your role in the affair," he added. "A number of officers felt - arguing with the benefit of hindsight, mind you - that you took *Odyssey* far too close to Harmony without ensuring your own safety. Others countered by pointing out that there was no reason to expect the Harmonies to discard over a thousand years of tradition just to bait a trap. They in *turn* have been countered by remarks about the fortresses...and how they should have tipped you off."

Rebecca glanced at Captain Yasser. His face was utterly unreadable, but she knew him well enough to detect the tension in his body. He could lose his command over the affair - or, perhaps, his chance at *another* command. There was nothing she could do, she knew, to make up for *that*.

"Once you *did* realise there was a problem, your conduct was magnificent," Stuart continued, after a long moment. "You escaped Harmony, you ensured that a message was sent back to Commodore Longlegs, you managed to keep inching towards Hudson until you made it to Daladier. At that point, you finally ran out of luck...but you managed to keep your ship intact until Commodore Longlegs arrived to pull your ass out of the fire. Correct?"

"Yes, sir," Captain Yasser said.

"It is generally agreed that you did very well," Stuart said. "Losing the freighters was a blow, although a small one; we can and we will pay compensation to the surviving crews and their families. About the only matter of concern, Captain, is that you should have sent *King Whatever*" - his lips quirked into a brief smile - "directly to Hudson. However...it was your call to make and it all worked out in the end."

"Commander Biscoe died on that ship," Captain Yasser said, tonelessly.

"Yes," Stuart agreed. "And he died a hero."

He shrugged. "You too will receive a formal notification," he added. "You'll retain your command - under the circumstances, public opinion will probably not allow us to scrap *Odyssey*. She will be repaired. I imagine there will be other missions soon, too. If you wish to take up a new command, several are available..."

"I'd like to stay with *Odyssey*, sir," Captain Yasser said.

"Very well," Stuart agreed.

He rose. "I'm afraid there will be more inquests over the coming weeks," he warned. "You will have to justify all the medals you requested... although I don't think there will be many problems in getting most of them confirmed. And you will have to assist us in preparing for the coming war. But, for the moment, just know that you - both of you - did well."

"Thank you, sir," Captain Yasser said.

Rebecca nodded. "There will be war, then?"

"I don't see how we can avoid it," Stuart said. "The galaxy just isn't big enough for both of us."

ELTON WAS TORN between relief and an odd despondency as they made their way out of the admiral's office and walked down to the park. It was almost deserted. There were few children on Sparta - the asteroid was not a permanent posting - and most of the asteroid's inhabitants would be at work. Their lives had always been busy, but Elton had a feeling they'd grown busier since the first courier boat had reached Earth.

Nine months, he thought, morbidly. He sat down on the grass. *Who knows what's happening back at Hudson?*

"They could have thrown the book at us," Rebecca said. She sat next to him, looking both young and old in the bright light. "You kept your command."

"Once she's repaired," Elton said. "Mr. Wolf believes it will take at least six months to repair *everything*."

"But she's still intact," Rebecca said. "And so is your career."

Elton raised his eyebrows. "And yours."

"I may not get any further postings," Rebecca said, ruefully. "The Galactics may have heard of me."

"Ouch," Elton said. "So...what will you do?"

"I'm not sure," Rebecca said. "It's very rare for an ambassador to be given another posting within five years. We might go native, you see. I may spend the next few months at clown college..."

Elton looked up. "Clown college?"

"Diplomatic school," Rebecca said. She flushed. "That's what we call it, just to remind ourselves not to take it too seriously. Or I might go on a long vacation. Or write a book."

"I'll be sure to buy a copy," Elton said.

He shook his head slowly. They'd made it home...and now he felt as though he was at a loose end. He'd been the captain of a starship, her sole master...now, he was just another man on an asteroid. He would return to the command chair - he knew that, on a level that could not be denied - but it wouldn't be quite the same. Their adventure was over...

But the war is just beginning, he thought. He felt a shiver running down his back. *The peace here, so far from Harmony, is about to shatter.*

"Thank you," he said, quietly. "For everything."

"You too," Rebecca said. "For saving my life, amongst other things."

She rose. "I have to report back to the office," she said. "I'll see you tonight?"

Elton smiled. "Sure," he said. "Why not?"

He watched her walk away, then lay back in the grass. For once, he had nothing to do. His ship was in the hands of the engineers, his crew were already on shore leave...he didn't even have to report back to the admiralty. He was at a loose end...

...But he was home.

And that, he told himself firmly, was all that mattered.

"I DIDN'T EXPECT *that* from him," Mongo Stuart said.

Steve Stuart looked up from the datapad. "Hoshiko, bless her, is a fighter first and foremost," he said. "My granddaughter wants to fight - she won't let anything stop her from fighting if she feels she must. Captain Yasser is more restrained, more inclined to be cautious, but he can still fight."

Mongo shook his head. "More inclined to be cautious," he repeated. "Did you *read* the report? Half the stunts he pulled would get someone kicked out of the academy."

"We chose him because we thought he could be relied upon to be diplomatic," Steve said, dryly. "But we also knew he could fight, if necessary."

He shrugged. He - and Mongo - had always had an affinity for fighters, for men and women willing to risk their lives in defence of their country. They were heirs to a family tradition of service that stretched all the way back to Robert the Bruce and the Scottish Wars of Independence. Steve had fought for the United States of America, following the tradition set by his father, grandfather and countless other ancestors; Hoshiko had fought for the Solar Union and humanity itself. But the universe needed more than *just* fighters. It needed explorers and diplomats and...

"There will be war, of course," he said. Maybe they didn't need explorers and diplomats right now. "The Tokomak will be coming back."

"Of course," Mongo agreed, coolly. "We're not ready."

"Then we'd better *get* ready," Steve said. "Last time, we gave them a thrashing because they didn't expect us to have developed our own weapons and defences. This time...it will be different. They know too much about us."

"They may even have advanced on their own," Mongo said.

Steve nodded. "We need to proceed with the Grand Alliance vote," he said. "If nothing else, the *Odyssey* Affair should focus a few minds. We need allies and...there's nowhere else to get them."

"It will also divert attention from Earth," Mongo warned. "*That* will upset *some* of the factions."

"Including too many of our relatives," Steve said. He was the single most famous man in the Solar Union. He'd even done *most* of what people *said* he'd done. But he knew his word alone wouldn't be enough to convince everyone. It was a nuisance, but he wouldn't have it any other way. "Earth...may not be beyond salvation, yet we don't have the time to intervene."

It was a bitter thought. He'd loved America. He'd grown up believing in the American Dream. But the dream had been dying even before he'd captured an alien ship. He wondered, sometimes, if he'd actually *killed* the dream. He'd given the people America needed - the talented, the innovative, the fighters - a place to go. And, in their wake, the country had slowly started to collapse into chaos. Would it have been different if he'd never founded the Solar Union?

In truth, he knew he'd never know.

"We can't sit here and wait to be hit," he added, shortly. "We need to take the fight to them."

"I know," Mongo said. "And I believe that your esteemed granddaughter has some ideas along those lines."

EPILOGUE

All in all, Supreme Ruler Neola told herself, it hadn't been a *complete* failure.

Sure, the human ship had managed to escape an inescapable trap. And sure, the display of human weaponry had shocked all the observers. And, worst of all, the Harmonies had been humiliated in front of the other Galactics. She freely admitted that it was annoying - and frustrating - but it hadn't been a complete disaster.

She sat in her comfortable chair, studying the reports from her analysts. The human weapons were advanced, true, but there was nothing genuinely *new*. Using a gravity field generator to produce a pinpoint black hole was not something the Tokomak had ever considered, but it was hardly beyond their ability to duplicate. She had a thousand teams already working on duplicating and mass-producing the human weapons. And while their gravity field generators were not powerful enough to produce a gravity well powerful enough to yank a ship out of FTL, that too would change.

And, best of all, she knew enough about the human weapons to counter them.

It would be costly, she admitted to herself. But she could afford those losses, while the humans - and their allies - could not. Speed was not something that came naturally to her people, but even *they* could put a major fleet together and deploy it before the humans built their own and took the war back to the core. Even if she was wrong about that, her forces were already moving to secure the gravity points necessary to move ships to Sol. The humans would have to bleed themselves white just to break through a *single* gravity point.

And the Harmonies are now more tightly tied to me than ever, she thought. *And they know to listen to me now.*

She looked up at the starchart, silently calculating the odds. It wouldn't take *that* long to switch to mass production, as well as bringing the immense reserves they'd built up over the centuries online. And then, Sol would be crushed. She had no compunctions about sending a hundred thousand ships to do the job. Maybe it would be massive overkill, but she didn't care. A fleet twice the size of the one she'd led to Earth, years ago, would have won the battle.

And then...

We will win, she promised herself. *And humanity will be exterminated.*

The End

AFTERWORD

Roper: *So now you'd give the Devil benefit of law!*
More: *Yes. What would you do? Cut a great road through the law to get after the Devil?*
Roper: *I'd cut down every law in England to do that!*
More: *Oh? And when the last law was down, and the Devil turned round on you—where would you hide, Roper, the laws all being flat? This country's planted thick with laws from coast to coast - man's laws, not God's -and if you cut them down - and you're just the man to do it - d'you really think you could stand upright in the winds that would blow then? Yes, I'd give the Devil benefit of law, for my own safety's sake.*
-A Man for All Seasons.

I talked about diplomacy in the *To The Shores* afterword, which you can also download from my site. I'd like to talk about something a little different here.

Shortly after it became clear that Donald Trump had won the 2016 election, a campaign started in an attempt to convince the Electoral College to declare Hillary Clinton the President instead...on the grounds that Hillary Clinton had won the popular vote. This attempt failed and rightly so - the victory condition for a US Presidential election is not winning the most individual votes, but winning the majority of the *states*. The President must command a broad swath of support from all over the country, not just the highly-populated states. Like him or hate him, Trump won by the rules.

Indeed, if the rules were different - if an election *could* be won by individual votes - both candidates would have campaigned differently. Neither of them *did* because they both knew the rules.

This was neatly summed up by a cartoon in which a chess player, having been checkmated by his opponent, insisted that he should be the winner because he had more pieces left than his opponent. No chess player ever born would consider that a valid argument. In order to win a game of chess, you have to checkmate your opponent. It doesn't matter which player has the most pieces when the game ends. A player can lose a game without losing any pieces - I've seen it happen - or win with only a handful of pieces remaining. And a player can seem to have an advantage...right up to the moment his defence slips and his opponent manages to turn the tables. I've seen that happen too.

(Yes, I love chess. Sue me.)

The point here is that the people involved - the political candidates as well as chess players and everything else in-between - *must* have a shared understanding of the rules. If you go into a game of chess *without* that agreement, you're likely to run into arguments about legal moves or sensible tactics. Is your opponent being an idiot or do they have a different idea about how the rules actually work? And if he *does* have a different idea...what happens when your view and his collide?

In chess, the rules exist to allow two players to share a game without disputes; in politics, electoral rules exist to determine who actually wins and why. They impose order on a chaotic system. Breaking the rules - either by sweeping the pieces off the board or by trying to redefine the victory condition when you're losing - should be punished. Why? Because if one side shows no respect for the rules, and if there is no punishment, why should the *other* side follow the rules? And if neither side is willing to follow the rules, we have chaos.

This is problematic. Breaking the rules is sometimes seen as a good thing - Captain Kirk, for example. You can certainly put forward an argument that the rules need to be broken, that the rules are weighted against one side - and if you *can* put forward a coherent argument, you can convince people to discard some (all?) of the rules. But constantly breaking the rules - and doing so for tactical advantage, such as Obama changing his tune on accepting the election results after Trump won - only weakens them. And the weaker the rules, the less respect anyone has for them.

I was taught to debate in school. We would often be told to attack or defend a particular position, *without* regard to how we actually felt about it. There were rules, which we were expected to follow. We liked winning - and we knew that victory went to the person who convinced most of the audience to agree with him, not the one who shouted the loudest or broke the rules. And the debate helped us to understand other points of view.

The problem today is that the rules are being broken, smashed to rubble, by people on both sides. People are gaining tactical victories at the expense of long-term victory (and even stability.) Everything is permissible as long as it is in a good cause! Liberals might cheer when conservative speakers are chased from campuses by angry mobs, for example, but the long-term effect is a growing upswing of demand for more repression. Those who do not choose to follow the rules cannot complain when their opponents do the same.

This is potentially disastrous.

On the micro scale, I've seen internet forums and discussion boards implode because the moderators either make the rules worthless by selective enforcement or simply not having any rules. This sort of process inevitably turns once-promising internet forums into wretched hives of scum and villainy. But on the macro scale, this rips apart social trust and throws us back into our human tribes. Greater principles - the nation, for example - are forgotten when tribalism is the only key to survival.

Among the many absurdities proclaimed over the last few years is the concept of 'punching up/punching down.' Put simply, stripped of the gibberish, it asserts that the difference between a good act and a bad one is defined by the perpetrator. A poor man who stabs a rich man is punching up, while a rich man who stabs a poor man is punching down. Though some mumbo-jumbo, this somehow translates into the poor stabber being excused for his crimes while the rich stabber is a murderer.

Such an argument makes no sense. A murderer is a murderer, regardless of any other details. Yet people will try to argue that the murderer can be excused because his victim was higher up the social scale (or lower down the victimhood scale) than himself. This is, in many ways, merely a continuation of the kind of thinking that pervaded Nazi Germany and Apartheid South Africa. If the victim is lower class, who cares?

I do. And so should you.

If the rules can be twisted until justice is forgotten, if the rules are abused until people no longer respect them, if the rules can be bent until they are broken, then we don't have a society. We have anarchy.

And in an anarchic state, the strong rule.

Many years ago, I wrote a short story for one of the *Ring of Fire* compilations. It didn't get picked up, probably because it was more of an insight piece than anything else. It really presented a small exchange between John Simpson and Rebecca Stearns, back during the first political campaign in *1632*. John Simpson was campaigning on a platform that called for restricting the franchise, while Mike Stearns (Rebecca's husband) was arguing for opening up the franchise as much as possible. (It's a little more complex than that, but I think that's the basic idea.)

Simpson comes across as a jerk in the first book - with reason. (He gets a lot better in *1633* onwards, kudos to Flint and Weber.) And yet, he has a point.

The American mindset - held by every one of the time-displaced Americans - is that the election will determine the winner. None of them, including Simpson, will resort to violence to change the outcome. (Indeed, Simpson serves with honour in the later books.) But the same cannot be said of the natives, the Germans of 1632. They *don't* have the mindset to accept the results. What happens when there *is* a major political disagreement?

We see Simpson as being wrong, mainly for promoting an unpopular (and un-American) view. Rebecca is sweet reason, and she's presented as being in the right, but she's also sheltered and naive. The extremism shown by Gretchen (certainly by local standards) is horrifically dangerous, if it goes sour. Simpson is right to be concerned.

What happens when people decide the rules are no longer working for them?

What happens when people decide that the time has come to smash the board?

Our world is not perfect. And sometimes the rules do need to be changed. But it is something that has to be done slowly and carefully... *not* out of disappointment, spite or simple ambition.

Christopher G. Nuttall
Edinburgh, 2017

And now, check out…

LEGION

by Leo Champion

The desperate. The underfunded. The completely expendable.
The United States Foreign Legion was created as a disposable force to deal with America's colonial conflicts. Paul Mullins was an American citizen with a successful career in advertising. Until one drunken night when a barroom acquaintance convinced him that you could back out of a Legion enlistment.

He's going to spend his next five years alongside a bunch of opportunists, felons, lunatics and screwups, in the dirtiest parts of America's interstellar empire. The other military branches despise the Legion. The government considers them expendable. Secessionists, aliens and Earth's other powers loathe them. The colonial business community grudgingly appreciates them, but that isn't worth much.

Mullins has a cheap uniform and sixty pounds of lowest-bidder equipment. He has an obsolete twentieth-century rifle and a vindictive enemy who outranks him. He's about to find strength in himself that he never knew existed.

And to survive one thousand, eight hundred and twenty-six days in the Legion, he's going to need every bit of it.

ELEVEN

"**L**ieutenant!" came the shout as F Company was boarding the train. Croft turned. A furious-looking Army major, accompanied by a captain and four MPs, was striding towards them.

"Yessir?" he asked. Worried.

Sergeant Alonzo was up to something last night. It may or may not have anything to do with the alarms. I hope it had nothing to do with this.

"Hold that train!" the senior MP, a first lieutenant, shouted. He gestured two of his men, a sergeant and a private, towards the engine.

"What the hell's going on?" demanded a civilian passenger, leaning out the window. "Terrorist attack?"

"Worse," the major said.

"What is it, sir?" Croft asked. He drew himself to attention and saluted.

The F Company men ignored the officers and MPs, aside from a few curious glances. They continued boarding the train, getting into the three third-class carriages that'd been added for them.

"Lieutenant, you spent the night in the terminal with these men, right?" the major asked.

"Yessir."

"Did you happen to see any *Marines* anywhere? Looking around, maybe checking out security?"

Oh, thank God.

Croft shook his head.

"No sir."

"Because somebody pilfered over four million dollars worth of Army property from a transhipment point last night," the major snapped. "Not to mention *repeatedly* shocked two of *my* men, and almost ran down a third as they got away."

"Sir, was that the alert?"

"Yes."

"It might not have necessarily been Marines," said the MP captain. He gave Croft what might have been a cynical squint. "*Anyone* can shout 'semper fi', and anyone with a computer can put USMC insignia on a clipboard."

"Are you implying something, sir?"

"Yes," said the captain, "I am. Your company stayed overnight in the terminal. Can you account for the whereabouts of all *your* men, Lieutenant, during that time?"

Croft gulped. Hoped his nerves weren't showing.

When Alonzo and that working party came back, some of them had very *self-satisfied looks on their faces. I've never seen* anyone *looking self-satisfied because they did a good job unloading a shuttle.*

On the other hand, he was Legion. If the orientation training on Chauncy had taught him *anything*, it was that the USFL's *unofficial* motto was something to the effect of 'We take care of our own because nobody else gives a damn.'

Alonzo could not *possibly have taken those men, somehow gotten into a highly-secure Army depot, and stolen* – how much?

"*Well*, Lieutenant?" the MP captain demanded.

"Sir," said Croft, heart in his throat. "I can absolutely vouch for the whereabouts of all of these men. When they were not under my immediate supervision, they were under the care of trusted NCOs."

"Sir, their First Div and its First Brigade're both HQed in this town," one of the MPs reminded the lieutenant.

The MP lieutenant nodded. He and the major exchanged glances.

"If these men stole the equipment," the major pointed out, "then it's probably on this train somewhere."

In addition to six passenger cars, the train – pulled by a heavy steam locomotive – had a cargo element as well. Behind the sixth passenger car were four closed boxcars, three unloaded flatcars, and several empty gondola cars, which were essentially open steel shoeboxes on wheels.

"It'd be in one of the boxcars," said the captain. "Lieutenant, I want your men to search them."

Oh shit, thought Croft.

"The hell you're delaying my train any further," snapped a middle-aged man in a white dress uniform. The slightly frayed seams of his coat were trimmed with gold, and there was a single silver eagle on each side of his high collar. His brown riding boots had smears of dirt on them.

"Who the hell are you?" the major demanded, turning. "Colonel. Sir."

"I'm the commander of security and operations at this goddamn rail-yard, is who I am," said the – obviously Colonial Guard – colonel. "This train is already fifteen minutes past schedule, thanks in part to your goddamned shenanigans, and I'll be damned if you'll make it half an hour. We've *already* had to delay a freight today."

"Sir, we have reason to believe that stolen military property may be aboard this train," said the MP officer. "In one of these boxcars."

"*My* men," snapped the colonel, "loaded those boxcars. I can assure you that they would have noticed a tank – or was it perhaps an artillery piece?"

"No, sir," said the major. "Crates. Of– "

"Do these men *look* like Marines to you?" the colonel demanded. "The guard lieutenant at my barracks *clearly* reported a shout of 'Semper fi' as the perpetrators left. My barracks is right next door to your facility, Major."

"Sir, there's no evidence of any Marines within three hundred miles," said the major desperately. "Whereas these men–"

"I think this lieutenant knows something, sir," said the MP lieutenant. "He *looks* like he's hiding something."

Oh, shit, fuck, shit, thought Croft. He wanted to close his eyes and pray, or fall to his knees and beg. *Cashiered on my very first day of active duty. How proud would Father be of me for* that.

"He looks," the Colonial Guard colonel said, "like *any* poor young lieutenant would look if he was being accused of larceny by three superior officers – *from outside his chain of command.* And speaking of chains, this man has a *train* to catch."

The CG colonel glared at each of the three officers in turn.

Out of the corner of his eye, Croft noticed Gonzalez get out of the front passenger car.

"Major, Captain, Lieutenant, I strongly suggest – in fact, I *order* you – to get the hell out of my depot. And stop delaying my train. You are *not* going to search it and if you have a problem, you are more than free to appeal to Governor Harris."

"Sir–"

"Write an email to Richmond, major! And get the hell out of my damn depot."

The major, the captain and the MPs turned around.

The colonel turned to Croft and Gonzalez with a smirk on his face.

"Army motherfuckers," he said. "I hate them almost as much as you Legion boys do, Lieutenant."

He nodded at Gonzalez.

"Sergeant, too."

Gonzalez belatedly saluted.

What do I say to that? Croft thought.

"Seems to me that someone might owe *someone* a favor," the colonel said. Winking broadly.

Yes. I do owe you, Croft reluctantly agreed.

"Sir, if there's anything I can do for you–" Croft began.

The colonel extended his right hand slightly, unobtrusively, and ran his thumb across the palm.

What? I'm mistaking this gesture. This man cannot seriously be asking me for money.

It has *to be some colonial idiosyncrasy.*

I'm not *being asked for a bribe. Not by a full colonel. An O-6. I* must *be misreading this.*

Gonzalez coughed loudly.

"Sir, it looks as though your boots could use a shining," the sergeant said to the colonel.

"Shoe-shines aren't cheap in this town," the colonel pointed out.

"No, sir. I don't think they are. And – it's the tenth, isn't it? Almost a month until payday. Perhaps, sir, you'd accept a small cash loan from my lieutenant here, sir."

Oh my God, he was asking for a bribe, Gonzalez knows it – and he expects me to give him one?

That had to contravene so many regulations that it wasn't funny.

As though hiding the obviously stolen military property in whichever boxcar it's in, isn't contravening regulations?

He was in it up to his neck already. Reluctantly he took out his wallet.

"Sergeant," he asked, "about how much would a quality shoe-shine cost around here?"

"Can't get one for less than five hundred," said the colonel. "Although" – he eyed Croft's watch – "sometimes they take goods of comparable value."

Croft took out five hundred-dollar bills and folded them over a couple of times, planning to palm them and transfer the money through a handshake. Then a brainwave struck.

He gave the money to Gonzalez.

"Sergeant, I assume you know where a good shoe-shine boy can be found, and the procedures for hiring them. Colonel, with your permission?"

He gestured with his head towards the train. Then saluted.

"Of course, Lieutenant. Dismissed."

Croft got into the first passenger car, and was joined a moment later by Gonzalez. There was the hiss as air-brakes were released, and the train slowly began to move forwards.

Jesus, thought Croft, collapsing into the nearest seat. Gonzalez sat down next to him.

"Where the hell *is* Alonzo, anyway?" Croft demanded.

Gonzalez shrugged.

"Probably expediting something, sir. Don't worry – he'll get back to Roanoke on time."

"I can't believe what that man did, sergeant. Is that *normal* around here?"

"Yessir. With the CGs, yeah. I'm just surprised he didn't ask you for more. Given that he's a colonel."

"*Why?*"

"Well, sir, he probably didn't think you had five hundred cash on you. He wanted that watch of yours," said Gonzalez. "By the way, sir, so you know for the future, you could have bargained him down to half that."

"No, I mean – why is it – oh, God. Never mind."

— —

"Mr. Calhoun," said the boy. He wore the navy-and-white livery of a railroad messenger, and he didn't even look at Skorzy.

"Yes?"

"Got a message from" – the boy *eyed* Skorzy this time – "an officer at the railway depot. You know, the one with de-lu-sions at being a poker champ. Says this time you owe him *big.*"

"Go on," said Calhoun.

"Know how everyone thinks it was jarheads stole that shit from the Army base last night?"

Skorzy raised an eyebrow.

"Yeah?" Calhoun said.

"Wasn't 'em. Those Legion fucks that landed last night? Some of *them* did it, I guess."

"How's he know that?" asked Calhoun.

"Guy says he talked with some of the stevodores. Legion sergeant comes along, lines up an extra boxcar and has the night shift load it with crates. Sonsabitch crates had military marks on 'em, officer says they told him. And pretty damn heavy, a few."

A broad grin spread across Skorzy's face.

That train was scheduled to have left twenty minutes ago. Even with the incompetent way the Earthie oppressors managed railroads, it'd be hard for them to screw up the timing of a mostly-passenger train by more than an hour.

"What sort of protection does that train have?" he asked.

The boy looked at Calhoun. Calhoun nodded.

Fucking urban assholes with their goddamned internal politics, Skorzy thought. It would be good to get back to the south, where people worked together and didn't play stupid counterproductive power games. Where Cee-Free-En-Vee had *forced* people to work together at gunpoint, if necessary.

Hell, this kid can't be older than fifteen and he's *getting into those games.*

"Don't think it has shit," the boy said – to Calhoun. "It's an express run to Roanoke, limited passenger stops in between. About three-fifty miles. Due to arrive there at six p.m."

"Guards," said Calhoun. "Not timetables."

"Ah, yeah. Don't think Colonel Buxford bothered to put shit on it. Two hundred Legion men aboard, after all."

Two hundred green Legion fish, thought Skorzy.

"When's it leave?" Calhoun asked.

"Six thirty," the boy said. "Delayed a bit. Actually got moving at quarter to."

Calhoun glanced at his watch. Skorzy didn't need to – he knew it was ten to seven.

"We can't do shit," Calhoun growled. "Why didn't you get this to us earlier?"

"Had work to do."

"For the oppressors?"

The boy seemed to shrink for a moment under Calhoun's furious glare.

"Hey, Mr. Calhoun, I gotta earn a living," he replied. Towards the end his voice became a defensive mutter.

Skorzy smiled again.

"Get me to a safe telephone," he said. "*I* can do something."

I CAN'T BELIEVE we got away with it last night, Mullins thought.

He'd managed four hours of sleep, too – about when his body said he *should* be sleeping, given the ship's time that after ten days he'd become semi-accustomed to. Four hours in the terminal, then – well, the ETA for this train was six o'clock local. Eleven hours from now.

Eleven hours to go three hundred and fifty miles on a damn railway, he thought. *That's – about thirty miles per hour, thirty-two or so.*

I suppose that's what you get with a steam train.

They used steam locomotives on New Virginia, according to a book in the Yetzl library, primarily for economic as opposed to technological reasons. The planet did have oil, and lots of it, but refined hydrochemicals were worth the costs of shipping back to Earth. Coal wasn't.

Also, the local secessionists had a bad habit of interfering with oil production, mainly by shelling the planet's refineries. Orbital ones had been considered, but dismissed as cost-impractical. It was cheaper to live with the secessionist shelling than invest a ten-figure sum in building something that the secessionists would probably find some way to catastrophically sabotage anyway.

He glanced out the window, in the hope that the view might have changed. It hadn't. Sloping ground off the immediate right of way, a forest of stubby trees, kudzu everywhere.

I'm going to get some sleep, he thought. Rifle across his lap, he lay back on his duffel bag and closed his eyes. *Four hours isn't much.*

JOHNNY CALDWELL SMILED and kicked the dead Legion corporal again. His thirty-four men were pilfering the corpses for whatever they had.

We should have bopped them anyway, Caldwell thought. In fact, he'd been strongly tempted to – some of his men had been itching to, and he'd never been all that good at keeping guys like Rogers, Mitchum and Johnson under control.

One easy hit-and-run, and the occupation government was down two Goldnecks, eight Legion regulars and fifty Black Gangers. The only effective fighters, the eight regulars, had been taken down with multiple bullets each in the first volley. The Goldneck gang-chiefs hadn't had a damn chance either. Killing the cowering, unarmed, surrendering Black Gangers had been simple target practice.

"Get those bodies gone," Caldwell said. He gave the dead corporal another kick for good measure. "We've got about an hour."

"Yeah?" asked Rogers. "We could rig this in fifteen minutes."

"Think this train's the *only* one on the line? Another one could come at any time."

"We should fuck with 'em all," Rogers insisted. "Shut this line *down*."

"Up to me," said Caldwell, "we would. You know how the bossmen've been lately. Bitching at us to pussy out and keep our heads down."

"Why this exception, anyhow?" asked Mitchum.

"Because," Caldwell said. Now they were in the field, there was no harm talking. "We got word from Godfrey. One of the bossmen said a company of Legion fish came in yesterday. So'd a big Army shipment. Legion boys figured they'd lift the best goodies from the Army and make it so jarheads got the blame. We're talking something like four million in goodies."

There were a few impressed wolf-whistles. Also a couple of growls.

My boys know that that shit's a lot more dangerous to everyone if the Legion has it, than if the Army'd kept it.

"So those Legion boys," Caldwell went on, "grab it. And we're gonna rob *them*. Y'all clear on why we want this par-tic-u-lar train? And why they let us fuckin' *do* something for the first time in nearly a year?"

There was a chorus of 'yeah's, 'ayup's, and 'uh-huh's.

"Not to mention," Caldwell said, "if we play this one right, we get to wipe out two hundred of those USFL fucks while they're still green fish."

The train's stopped, filtered through Mullins' sleep. *For more than a few seconds.*

Slowly his brain began the slow process of returning to consciousness.

Bang. Bang. Crash.

This was *not* one of the Juarez shooting ranges.

He opened his eyes, already reaching for the M-16 on his lap.

A man from First Platoon was lying in the aisle, screaming. Blood everywhere. The others in the carriage were looking around, ducking. Someone from First had a medical kit in hand and was crouch-walking over to the wounded guy.

"Load your magazines! God damn it! Load your magazines!" somebody shouted.

"What the hell?" someone else shouted.

Sergeant Gonzalez appeared in the doorway.

"Single shots only! If I hear a man firing burst or full-auto, I'll have him flogged!" he yelled over the confusion.

Oh, shit. Oh, fuck. Oh, shit.

Mechanically he opened the pouch that held his one magazine. Shoved it into the receiver, drew back the bolt. Thumbed the fire-select off safety and onto single-shot.

A bullet smashed through the reinforced-glass window less than a foot away, driving itself into his seat.

He looked through what was left of the window, which wasn't broken – just spiderwebbed hard with thick white lines around the bullet-hole. On the other side of that, they seemed to be in a narrow cut. Where Mullins crouched, the hill was at about eye-level; further ahead, it got higher. On the other side were rocks, kudzu and stubby little brown trees.

More gunfire came in. A window smashed, disintegrating into glass fragments. Someone else screamed.

"Shoot back, god damn you!" Janja yelled. He lay on his chest on a seat, looking through the sights of his rifle.

Good idea, thought Mullins. Janja had been in at least one war that he knew of, and as an officer. He imitated the Rajput's position, looking down his rifle.

If it moves out there, I'm going to blow it away.

A long burst of automatic fire came along the length of the carriage.

A dull *whump* of an explosion from somewhere, maybe towards the back of the train.

Movement – a running man. Mullins blazed three shots at him. Missed.

"Shoot back! Take cover and return fire!" Janja yelled.

Reuter took up the shout.

"Return fire! Don't fuck around – return fire, guys!"

Mullins' window disintegrated; shards of glass flew everywhere. He buried his face onto the padded brown seat to protect his eyes. Sharp pricking on his back, one piece big and heavy enough to cause a pretty damn painful cut.

Gunfire and screaming. *Lots* of screaming. A fair amount of panicked shouting, too.

With his left hand, Mullins reached around to his back and carefully brushed the glass off. He felt warm, wet blood around the particularly painful cut.

No time to worry about that now. If that's all that happens to you today you'll be damned lucky.

With the muzzle of his M-16, he pushed the remaining fragments of glass out of the window frame. With the dull, scratched glass gone, his view was a lot better. Sharper. He resisted the temptation to lean out.

BENT DOUBLE WITH his pistol raised, Croft ran down the aisle of the third civilian passenger car. They were taking less fire, presumably because nobody was firing from them.

What do I do if I meet a bad guy?

I shoot him, of course.

Can I do that?

Bullets scored through the glass near him, shattering windows.

He wanted to hide like the passengers were doing – get under the nearest seat. That wasn't a possibility.

When he reached the far door – the next bit would be the engine – he braced himself.

They managed to stop the train. They might well be on board the engine.

If they're on board the engine, I have to shoot them.

That had to be firm. He'd read about too many guys hesitating on the trigger the first time they came face-to-face with an enemy. Too many of those accounts had been second-hand, because the guys who'd hesitated hadn't lived.

What if I hesitate anyway?

You're not going to hesitate, James. You're hesitating right now, and that's fine. You're not going to hesitate when you get out there. Any figure who isn't the engineer or the fireman, you shoot.

What if the engineer or the fireman were secessionists themselves?

If you see either one of them pointing a gun at you, you assume they are and you shoot them.

Clear? *Is that clear, James?*

Yes, said the other part of his mind. It was clear.

He wrenched the door open – and saw the coal tender between him and the engine. It might have been twelve or fifteen feet long, and from where he crouched he couldn't see anybody.

The shooting was louder, though.

A narrow, two-foot-wide gantry ran alongside the left side of the tender. A single railing was on the outside of it.

I am going to be completely exposed the moment I get out there.

There was no other option.

Pistol raised high in his right hand, he bolted out, scurried along the catwalk.

"There's one!"

Bullets clanged into the side of the tender around him. He bolted *forwards* – six feet, four feet, two feet, and something nicked his shoulder, and then he threw himself forwards into the covered safety of the cab. There was a loud hissing, but it didn't seem to be coming from inside the cab.

The driver lay sprawled on his back near his controls. The fireman was desperately holding a cloth around the man's neck. Blood everywhere.

"Radio," Croft snapped. *"Now."*

The fireman didn't look up. He shook his head.

Croft looked around the cab. Most of the equipment was indecipherable to him. There was a single digital screen – *Yes! A GPS!* – and a headset with a dial. Set into the control panel next to dials that presumably monitored boiler pressure and the like.

Head low, he pulled the handset out and turned the dial to one of the frequencies he'd memorized.

"Mayday! Mayday!" he yelled into the radio. "This is – F Company – between Godfrey's Landing and Roanoke. We are under attack by a sizeable secessionist force! Mayday! Request urgent air support! Repeat! Mayday! Over!"

"F Company," came a calm voice on the other end, "I hear you. Where are you boys, and we'll get help out to you right away. Over."

Croft read off the co-ordinates from the GPS.

"Roger that, F Company. You CGs, Army, what?"

"Legion! We're en route to Fourth Brigade, First Division in Roanoke. Repeat, *Mayday!*"

"We'll get to you boys," the calm voice said. "Air support is on the way. Hold tight, you understand? Just hold on. You got flares or smoke to mark Buddy's positions? Over."

"Not that I know of, over."

"You're on a railway line. Keep your boys *on* the line. Preferably hold tight. Understand? Over."

"Yessir," said Croft.

"Hold tight, soldier. Over and out."

Time to get back to my men.

For the first time, the fireman looked up.

"Help Mike," he said.

The engineer's booted left foot was thrumming faintly. The man was bleeding to death.

If I had my first aid kit – if I were ready for combat...

I'm not.

"Sorry," Croft said.

"You bastard," the fireman said without real malice. "Kill those fuckers, then. Kill *all* of them."

Pistol in hand, Croft ran back along the tender. The door to the passenger car was still open.

Inside, a man with an assault rifle – it had a short barrel and a banana clip, and something in Croft's mind placed it as an AK variant – was walking slowly down the aisle, covering the seats.

"Throw yer goodies down in the aisle," he said. "Toss 'em down on the floor and nobody gets hurt, y'all hear?"

Wallets, cash, watches and jewelry were already on the floor.

You secessionist bastards are nothing but common thugs, Croft thought with a sudden surge of hatred.

That surge was enough to overrule everything. He lined the sights of his .45 up on the man's back and fired. Twice.

The man doubled over and collapsed on his face.

Croft ran, bent double himself, down the carriage. Ready for more of these bastards, should they come through the other door. He was a couple of paces past the dead secessionist when he thought of the man's gun.

I don't know how to use it.

Gonzalez probably does. I'll take his M-16.

The secessionist, a tanned man in a white wife-beater, jeans, boots and a bush hat, had collapsed on top of his weapon. Gingerly but quickly – *I don't have time, and more could appear through either door at any moment* – Croft rolled the corpse over.

Only to find that the man wasn't – quite – dead. Blinking green eyes stared up from a bushy-bearded face.

"Gimme your gun," Croft said to the secessionist. He took the weapon out of the man's hand. Several banana-clip magazines were in his belt; he gathered those up too. Considered a coup de grace with his pistol. Shook his head a moment later – he couldn't kill a guy in cold blood.

He stuck the magazines into his own belt and ran.

— —

AN ALARM RANG in the alert lounge of the Army air base at Godfrey's Landing. It was a plain room with tables and a dartboard. The ready crew, sixteen men – the pilots and gunners of eight DH-22 attack helicopters – sat around reading newspapers and books. One of them was listening to a portable digital music player; three were engaged in a desultory quarter-ante poker game. Now, the men jerked to their feet, whirled instinctively towards the door.

"There is a USFL unit under attack," came over the loudspeakers in the room. "Repeat, a USFL unit is under secessionist attack on the Godfrey-Roanoke railway line. Co-ordinates..."

"Legion?" demanded the lieutenant-colonel in charge, sitting down again. He raised a white mug with the squadron's logo on it.

"*Fuck* the Legion," he said. "They can go to hell. I'm finishing my coffee first."

— —

MULLINS SNAPPED OFF another shot at a running figure. Missed. The figure hurled something onto the roof of the carriage; it landed with a *kathump* and a *whoosh*.

Another man, barely visible and then only for a moment, hurled a similar object through the window of the carriage.

It exploded. Flames went everywhere. Men screamed. One man clasped at his eyes and tumbled back.

Oh shit, Mullins thought. Legion counterinsurgency training had involved these things. He'd seen Molotov cocktails before.

Another Molotov came through a window towards the front of the carriage, on the other side to Mullins. Exploded.

The seats began to burn. Fire crept up the sides of the carriage, which was becoming an inferno.

Johnny Montague tumbled back, weaponless. His flat hands were beating his face; the front of his shirt and trousers were on fire.

Oh God, oh shit, we're all going to die.

No. He had to stay the hell calm.

First, he had to help Johnny. His bag was still on the seat – he'd been lying on it, using it as a rest. He picked it up and pressed it to Montague's chest, pushing him back against the nearest seat. Rolled it over and over on his shirt, then down the legs of his pants. Smothering the flames.

Another window shattered. Screaming and shouting.

"Hold tight, damn it!" Janja yelled. "Fucking *hold* and shoot the fuckers when they pop their heads up! Mullins, good idea with the bag. Get started on the other flames – use other bags."

The hell with that, Mullins thought. *I want to shoot back.*

No. The blazing Molotovs would kill everyone if nobody did anything about the fire.

Montague lay on his back, breathing hard. His shirt and trousers had been burned through. Underneath were ugly crimson burns. His hands were still pressed to his face.

Mullins got up, threw his duffel bag at the edge of the nearest flames, began rolling it over and over. Hopefully too fast for any part of the solid, heavy *bag* to catch on fire. The flames began to dissipate, slightly.

More bullets came in. Somebody who'd been kneeling, doubled back and collapsed. There was a messy grey spatter on the wall behind him.

Oh, God, thought Mullins, and tried to focus on keeping his head down and dealing with the flames.

GONZALEZ GRATEFULLY TOOK the short-barreled AK-type gun.

"You call for help, sir?"

"Yes. From the engine."

"Future reference, sir, no need. Automatic distress signal from the GPS when the train stops for more than thirty seconds in an unexpected place. Other hand, can't hurt."

Croft gave a curt nod.

"And you killed one of the fuckers. Good job, sir."

"When d'you think help's gonna arrive, Sergeant?"

Gonzalez shook his head.

"Air support? Don't hold your breath, sir. Army doesn't give a shit about us."

"Oh, *shit*," Croft murmured. A thought struck him. He hadn't *discussed* that extra boxcar with Gonzalez – in fact, he'd been very careful not to, because there were things he simply did not want to know.

It occurred to him now.

"Sergeant, do you realize how *bad* an idea it would be if Sergeant Alonzo's goodies got into the hands of these guys?"

Gonzalez smiled.

"I wouldn't worry, sir."

"What the hell do you *mean* you wouldn't worry, Sergeant? This train is loaded with four million dollars' worth of stolen black-market illicit Army stuff and you're *not worried*? I say we do something. We've *got* to protect that boxcar and keep that stuff out of secessionist hands!"

"Sir, I *really* wouldn't worry about that," Gonzalez repeated.

Are you some kind of goddamned traitor *or something?*

"Sergeant, you hold on. I'm going to take a party down the length of the train. We're securing those goddamned boxcars and that's an order! Which one is it, d'you know?"

Gonzalez took Croft by the shoulders.

"Sir. I *would not worry*, sir. It's the third boxcar, but we *don't care*."

Something's going on, thought Croft, *that I don't understand.*

Was some of the stolen gear sabotaged or something? Grenades rigged to explode the moment the pin was removed, that kind of thing?

Another layer of gunfire suddenly began. Sharp cracks. M-16s.

From *outside* the train. Both sides.

What the hell *is going on?*

Suddenly, the incoming fire started to slacken. Within twenty seconds, it had completely stopped – there was nothing but sporadic outgoing shots and occasional bursts.

WHAT THE FUCK *is going on?* Mullins thought. The outgoing fire *couldn't* have been enough to drive the bad guys away.

That was only partially his concern. What was more his concern was that the fires were getting out of control. Duffel bags could only do so much, and they burned easily enough themselves. He'd lost half a dozen and put only a negligible dent into the fire. The carriage was becoming an inferno as the fires spread. Soon they'd join with each other.

"Get the hell out of the train!" Janja shouted.

"They'll murder us without cover!" Reuter shouted back.

"They're *gone*! I don't know why, but they've bugged out!"

"And we're gonna die if we stick around in *this* thing for long," Gartlan yelled. He placed his foot on a window ledge, ducked out and dropped out of sight.

Others followed.

Shit, thought Mullins, looking at Montague. There were a bunch of corpses, but there were also a few wounded guys. They'd burn alive.

He bodily picked Montague up. Thank God that after eighteen weeks of Legion training, he was still a little scrawny guy. More muscular than he had been, but he couldn't weigh more than a hundred forty.

"Hey, Gartlan! Belzer!"

Those two, who were crouching just below, looked up.

"Wounded man. There's more."

He dropped Montague into the waiting arms.

"*Good* idea," said Pratap with an approving nod. He picked up another wounded guy.

There were perhaps twenty wounded men who showed signs of life. Mullins, Dashratha, Pratap, Janja and three guys who he didn't know so well waded through the increasing flames, taking them and passing them through the windows.

Then he jumped out himself.

"You're burning, man," said someone. A moment later, that guy crash-tackled Mullins into the gravel and started beating at his shirt and trousers. Two others joined him.

What happened to the incoming fire? Why aren't they taking advantage of it?

"Hey, you boys!" came a voice from above.

Four hard-looking men in camouflage shades of green and yellow were on the top of the cutting. They wore helmets and carried M-16s.

Those aren't bad guys, Mullins thought.

It didn't matter if they were. He'd left his rifle in the carriage, which was now – alongside the other two that had held Legion men – *thoroughly* ablaze.

"Yeah?" asked Janja. Realizing. "Medic! Get us your nearest medics!"

"Sir," said Croft, saluting the lieutenant-colonel. The man wore combat dress like his men, and was followed by three staffers. Two held M-16s; the other wore a backpack radio.

"*Damn*, sir, am I glad to see you."

The lieutenant-colonel grinned.

"Figured you would be, Lieutenant. Joe, how many'd we bag?"

"Twenty-eight and counting," said the man with the radio.

"Short one train," said a man with an M-16 and sergeant-major's insignia.

"Sir, Colonel Rodriguez says he's on the way in. Landing up ahead."

"Let's go meet the man," the lieutenant-colonel said to Croft.

— —

COLONEL RODRIGUEZ WAS a surprisingly small man with shoulder-length black hair in two long braids. Instead of a helmet, he wore a black cavalry hat with gold crossed-rifles on the crown. He was accompanied by a radio man, a command sergeant-major – three stripes, three rockers and a crossed-rifles insignia between them – and a pair of bodyguards.

Behind him, a light helicopter was taking off. Its blades and the engines drowned out speech for a little while.

Croft drew himself up and saluted his brigade commander.

"Are you *asking* to get us both sniped, Lieutenant?" Colonel Rodriguez snapped.

The lieutenant-colonel's radio man spoke into his headset.

"Got four prisoners, sir," he reported to his boss.

Rodriguez snapped something to his radio man. The guy took out his headset and spoke into it.

"It was an ambush, sir," said Croft. Realizing.

"Yes, Lieutenant. They got you good and hard, and I'm sorry about your casualties."

"No, sir. I mean, you knew they were going to attack. You knew they knew about the goodies, and you were ready for them to do something."

Rodriguez raised an eyebrow.

"Yes. As it happened we *were* tipped off that this train was almost certain to be attacked. What goodies are you talking about?"

The colonel paused for a moment, then went on.

"Come to think of it, I do think I might have heard something about some Army property disappearing from the Godfrey port area. Care to show me what you might be talking about?"

Oh, shit.

"I think it's in one of the boxcars, sir," said Croft. A bit nervously.

I might be court-martialled anyway. A full colonel and his staff now officially know we've stolen military goods.

"Well, show me which," Rodriguez said. "Let's see it."

He started walking towards the train. His staff, the lieutenant-colonel and the lieutenant-colonel's staff followed.

Under the direction of a Legion platoon, the civilian passengers had gathered in front of the engine. The tracks, Croft saw, had been torn away. That was obviously why the train had stopped – the moment the engineer had seen it, he'd hit the brakes. With just enough time to avoid a derailment.

Battalion and brigade medics were working on the wounded F Company men as they passed. Other F Company men leaned against the side of the cutting, breathing hard or just drinking from canteens. Croft thought he saw a bottle of something stronger being passed around – but if the senior officers weren't going to notice that, he wouldn't.

The burning passenger cars had mostly burned themselves out. They were skeletal, charred wrecks. A few flames flickered here and there.

Sergeant Gonzalez came walking up. Saluted.

"Lieutenant Croft, a moment, sir?"

"Sergeant Gonzalez. Just the man I wanted to see. Two questions, Sergeant. Did you take a roll call?"

"Yessir. Of one hundred and ninety-one men, we have eleven dead, forty-one wounded, and four missing presumed dead."

Shit, thought Croft.

Eleven of his men had been *killed*. In his first combat.

Oh, *fuck*.

He slumped. *Oh, God. Eleven guys, who I was responsible for, are dead.*

No. Not eleven. *Fifteen.*

"Jesus," he exhaled.

Fifteen men dead. Fifteen individuals. I didn't know them and I wasn't formally in command of them, but I was responsible for them.

Why the hell *did I take up this career?*

Someone clapped him on the shoulder.

"Lieutenant. We don't have all the information yet, but you seem to have done a good job," said Colonel Rodriguez. "These men had limited ammunition, no chain of command, no communications. You were taken by complete surprise and you still managed to bag at least a dozen of the sons of bitches."

"I lost *more than that*, sir," Croft groaned.

"And you'll lose still more before your career's up," said Rodriguez. "It's always hard the first time."

"Sir, you had a second question?" asked Gonzalez.

"Yes," said Croft. "Which boxcar was the one Sergeant Alonzo organized?"

"Second one after the passenger cars, sir. Bastards opened it, for what little good it did them."

"Take us to it, Sergeant. Sergeant-Major Jackson, stay with Lieutenant Croft for a moment. You know what to do."

Jackson was a big blond man. When the command party had gone, walking slowly down the line, he took out a small silver flask.

"Here, sir. This'll help."

Croft numbly took the flask and raised it. Brandy, and *good* brandy.

"Take at least three swigs, sir. You need it."

"Fifteen of my men," Croft muttered.

"Not your men, sir. Men you just happened to be traveling with. Like the colonel said, sir, they weren't organized, armed properly, equipped for combat. You didn't fuck up – those asshole CGs did. *They're* the ones who're supposed to secure this fucking railway line, sir, if you'll excuse my German."

That was two veterans who said he hadn't fucked up. That and the brandy – he took a third swig – made him feel a bit better.

"How d'you mean, Sergeant-Major?"

"Sir, procedure on this stretch of line is that they *should* have had half a company, an advance group and an armored car, anytime they're taking a train of importance. Worthless fucking bastards probably black-marketed the gas, the ammo, and the spare parts they need to run their damn cars."

"I haven't been impressed with the CGs so far," Croft admitted. "One of their colonels pretty damn blatantly asked me for a bribe."

"How much you give him?"

"Five hundred."

Jackson let out a low whistle.

"Damn, sir, you really *are* a fish, aren't you? You could have bargained him down to three hundred, easy. What'd the son of a bitch want?"

"Relates to the boxcar," said Croft.

"Speaking of which, sir, you feeling good enough to get moving?"

Croft nodded.

"Colonel's walking slowly for our sake. Let's not delay him any further, shall we, sir?"

"No," said Croft.

The boxcar lay open, well outside the cut. An area of about three feet on either side of the tracks was smooth and flat. On Croft's side, the ground beyond that fell away in a gentle, lightly-wooded slope.

On the slope, amidst thick green weeds, two secessionists lay messily dead amidst splintered bits of wood. Three crates with US military markings had been stacked nearby. Another secessionist, one who'd clearly been shot, lay by them.

Gonzalez inspected the three stacked crates, nodded. Using them as a step, he climbed up into the boxcar. He was followed by Rodriguez, the lieutenant-colonel, then Sergeant-Major Jackson and Croft.

The boxcar's open doors gave plenty of light to see by. Crates with military markings were stacked everywhere, some almost to the ceiling.

Rodriguez tapped one of the crates.

"What's in this one?" he asked Gonzalez. "Give me that crowbar."

Gonzalez shook his head.

"Sir, you *really* don't want to open that one."

"What's in it, Sergeant?"

"Grenade, sir. Same thing as killed those two out there. How about I open the next one for you?"

Rodriguez, the lieutenant-colonel, Sergeant-Major Jackson and Croft crowded around as Gonzalez, grinning, levered the stencilled top off the crate.

Inside was a cinder block.

Rodriguez looked at Croft, then at Gonzalez.

Gonzalez opened another crate. It contained half a dozen old bricks.

"I thought this car was full of midnight-requisitioned Army stuff," said Rodriguez.

Gonzalez smiled.

"Sir," he said, "I have no idea what you're talking about. Do you really think *Legion* people would steal Army property – and then have colonial stevodores load it onto an unguarded train?"

"No," said Colonel Rodriguez slowly. "I would not."

— —

Senior Sergeant Alonzo nodded his head in time to a jazzy Beat Brothers song as he drove his truck down the tarmac road to Roanoke. Behind, when he glanced at his rear-view mirror, he could see the other three trucks, tarpaulins over their loads. They were being driven by the corporal and the two lances who'd been called in to help look after F Company in his absence. Their seventy-two hour passes had been an easy trade for ten percent of the crates, chosen randomly.

And if we're lucky, he thought, *we even whacked some Buddies out of this whole deal.*

— —

Printed in Great Britain
by Amazon